fool·me twice

OTHER BOOKS AND AUDIO BOOKS
BY STEPHANIE BLACK:

The Believer

fool·me twice

a novel

STEPHANIE BLACK

Covenant Communications, Inc.

Cover image © Kati Neudert/iStock Photo

Published by Covenant Communications, Inc.
American Fork, Utah

Printed in the United States of America
First Printing: March 2008

14 13 12 11 10 09 08 10 9 8 7 6 5 4 3 2

ISBN-13: 978-1-59811-527-7
ISBN-10: 1-59811-527-8

Acknowledgments

For helping me with this book in so many ways, thank you to David and Bonnie Overly, Marshall and Sue McConkie, Amy Black, Suzanne Lucas, Dianna Hall, Amy McConkie, Shauna Black, and Melanie Goldmund.

Thanks also to Kerry Blair, Robison Wells, the marvelous "Goosies," and the bloggers and readers at Six LDS Writers and a Frog.

My gratitude also goes to editors Kirk Shaw and Angela Eschler, and to all the wonderfully talented and supportive people at Covenant.

As always, thank you to my husband, Brian, for everything he does to strengthen and encourage me.

Prologue

Bryce Ludlum parked beyond the curve in the road in case any of the Seavers' neighbors happened to be awake at 2 AM. That old vet with the buzz cut who lived next door probably noticed everything and had 911 on speed dial.

Bryce mopped his watering eyes on his sleeve, the craving inside him growing more vicious. He'd sworn to himself that he'd never sink to burglary, but the money from his landscaping job evaporated the instant he got it, and his mother wouldn't cough up a cent. She was already livid over his misuse of her prescription pads.

Besides, it was almost like old Mrs. Seaver *wanted* him to take the money. She'd hung around while he'd trimmed her azaleas, blabbing about her fear of banks and how her husband said she was senile to keep so much cash under the mattress. And when she'd paid him for the month's work—peeling the bills off a fat wad of cash—she'd offered him an extra fifty bucks if he'd stop by this weekend and pick up her mail and newspapers while she and her husband drove to Vermont to visit her sister.

And she'd given him a key so he could water her houseplants.

He didn't *want* to take the money. He'd pay it back later. But right now, the vision of stacks of crisp green bills made Bryce's heart race. From the way Evelyn Seaver talked, it sounded like she had enough squirreled away to keep him comfortable for a good long while, plus enough to get him away from Britteridge so he could escape the cops. Mrs. Seaver was a twittery old fool to have confided her weird financial habits to her landscaper, but she wasn't brain-dead. Once the money turned up missing, she'd point the cops toward Bryce. He'd better leave the state. New York sounded good.

A tremor shot through Bryce's hands as he shifted his empty backpack, tightening the straps. Sweat crawled down his sides and snaked along the sides of his face. The July night was miserably warm, cursed with one of Massachusetts' summer heat waves.

All the Seavers' neighbors, including the nosy twosome next door, had turned off their lights. Fighting nausea, Bryce hurried to the door of the Seavers' tidy white Cape Cod house. He shoved the key into the lock and eased the door open.

Under the mattress. The master bedroom was upstairs; he remembered that from when Mrs. Seaver had taken him around the house to show him her spider plants and philodendrons. Just a few more minutes and he'd be out of here, his backpack stuffed with the funds that would bring blissful relief.

Bryce switched on his flashlight and hurried up the stairs, his footsteps muffled on the stair runner. The Seavers wouldn't be back until Sunday night, so he'd have at least two days to get out of town before they discovered the theft and set the cops on the hunt. And chances were, the police wouldn't look for him very hard. It wasn't like he was an ax murderer or a terrorist.

At the top of the stairs, he flashed the light into the room on the right and saw a carved headboard looming above a bed. This was it.

He walked into the room and froze. Under the ruffled comforter was the distinctive lump of a human being. *What the—*

Bryce's heart bumped around in his chest, and sweat stung his eyes. Mrs. Seaver had said they'd be gone. And *she* was gone—the beam of the flashlight showed only William Seaver in the bed. Had Bryce misunderstood their plans? No. Mrs. Seaver wouldn't have needed Bryce to pick up the paper and mail if Mr. Seaver were staying behind. He must have changed his mind at the last minute. Maybe he wasn't feeling up to the drive—his health *was* lousy.

Bryce retreated and stood trembling on the threshold. He didn't want a confrontation. But the thought of slinking out of here with his empty backpack flapping against his ribs made his stomach churn.

Mr. Seaver must sleep like a rock or he'd already be awake from Bryce's intrusion. And the money was probably on Mrs. Seaver's side of the bed, since she was the one who hid it.

Bryce crept into the room, his ears filled with the whistling sound of William Seaver's snoring. Stripping off his gloves so he could feel the money more easily, Bryce knelt at the unoccupied side of the bed. Delicately, he lifted the comforter and slipped his hand between the mattress and box springs.

Nothing. Bryce pushed his arm farther beneath the mattress and groped.

Seaver grunted and rolled over. Bryce yanked his arm out and curled in a tight ball on the floor.

When Seaver's snoring resumed, Bryce tried again, searching from the head of the mattress to the foot, shoving his arm in up to the shoulder.

Nothing.

The money must be on Mr. Seaver's side of the bed.

Bryce crawled around the foot of the bed to the side where Seaver snored. He lifted the edge of the comforter and inserted his fingers between the mattress and box springs, hoping that near the edge he'd feel a big envelope, or whatever Mrs. Seaver used to hold the money.

Breathing faster, Bryce slipped his whole hand into the crevice, then his arm as far as it could go before Seaver's weight sealed off the opening. *Where was the money?*

Mr. Seaver wasn't snoring anymore.

Panic erupted inside Bryce. Without stopping to think, he yanked his hand from under the mattress and shoved Seaver to the side.

"Who's here?" Seaver hollered.

Bryce grabbed the edge of the mattress and yanked upward with all his strength. Seaver slid off the bed with a thud. Bryce pushed the mattress to the floor and pawed the box springs.

No money. Nothing.

The light clicked on. Seaver was standing by the bed, his cane held aloft like a baseball bat. "*Ludlum.* What are you doing here?"

"Where's the money?" Bryce cried.

"What money, you drunken idiot?" Seaver swished the cane. "You think you can rob me?"

Everything was lost now anyway. Bryce would have to run, and he couldn't do it without the cash. "The money. The money your wife keeps in the house. Give it to me, or I'll break your stinking neck."

"Try it, punk." Seaver slashed the air with his cane. "We don't keep money in the house."

"Liar!"

Seaver advanced, waving the cane. "Get your sorry tail out of my house."

Bryce backed away from the cane. "The money—just give it to me and I won't—"

"You're stoned. Or high. Or whatever you kids call it these days." Seaver waved his cane wildly, forcing Bryce into the hall. Seaver swatted the light switch, illuminating the hallway and stairs. "Get out!"

Bryce grabbed for the cane but got a savage whack across the forearm that made him yell in pain. This guy was nuts. Bryce had to get out of here. But there *was* cash in the house. Even if Mrs. Seaver had made up the story about the hoard under the mattress, Bryce had seen the stack of bills when she'd paid him. There was at least a thousand bucks there.

The kitchen. She'd paid him in the kitchen. Maybe she'd left the money there. Bryce turned toward the stairs.

"Punk thief. Go on—run!" Seaver's cane crashed against Bryce's shoulder. Furious, Bryce turned and grabbed for the cane. This time he managed to snag it.

He fought to yank it away from Seaver. The old man stumbled, his wrinkled hands still gripping the curved handle. Bryce swung the cane to the side in an attempt to break his attacker's grip, and Seaver staggered, his knees buckling. Bryce yanked again, ripping the cane from his grasp.

Off balance, Seaver flailed crazily to catch himself, but failed. He tumbled down the stairs, legs flying up, his striped pajamas flapping around skinny ankles.

At the bottom of the stairs he lay still.

Bryce gaped at Seaver; the old guy was lying in a heap with bony limbs bent. Still clutching the cane, Bryce rushed down the stairs and leaned over him.

Blood. A lot of blood.

He'd killed Seaver. Murdered him.

Bryce dropped the cane and leapt back from Seaver's body. Light burst inside his skull, accompanied by sharp pain.

Bryce fell to his knees. Warmth trickled down the back of his neck. Dazed, he looked up and saw a heavy wooden curio shelf affixed to the wall. He must have cracked his head on the edge of the shelf. Now his blood was on the shelf. More evidence.

Bryce swore and wrenched open the front door. Dizzily, he stumbled down the steps.

* * *

Evelyn Seaver shivered as she stepped through the doorway. After the suffocating warmth of the garage, the house felt particularly chilly. William was always excessive in his use of air conditioning.

She walked carefully through the darkened family room and along the hallway, heading for the stairs. The stair light was on, illuminating part of the living room. Evelyn clucked her tongue. So wasteful, to leave a light blazing in the middle of the night.

A crumpled figure in striped pajamas was sprawled at the bottom of the stairs. Evelyn froze, her hand pressed to her heart. William's cane lay next to him, along with a small wooden carving of a horse and a copper vase that had spilled its bouquet of dried flowers.

Resisting the impulse to return the knick-knacks to the curio shelf, Evelyn moved to William's side and leaned over him. He groaned. There was blood on his face from a split lip and, most likely, a broken nose. A large bump pushed through his thinning hair.

Evelyn stared at him, her heart pounding uncomfortably fast.

Chapter 1

"Megan, I need it *now*. Doug won't even order the parts without it."

Tension cramped the muscles in Megan O'Connor's neck. "Mom, we had an agreement. I'd cover car payments and insurance, but you'd take care of maintenance and repairs."

"I don't think this qualifies as *repairs*. It's more like a catastrophe."

Curtains stirred at the kitchen window, and the late September breeze chilled Megan's skin. She walked to the window and took her time sliding it shut.

"Megan—"

"Insurance will cover most of it. You'll only have to pay the deductible."

"Only! Five hundred dollars? You know I don't have that kind of cash on hand."

Megan focused on the curtains, arranging the fabric so the gathers were even.

"My dear, I can't talk to your back."

Slowly, Megan crossed the few feet of ceramic tile that separated her from the table where her mother waited.

"A loan, honey." Pamela O'Connor caressed her coffee mug with a hand so smooth it looked polished. "I'll pay you back."

She wouldn't. She never did. Megan had paid to repair the burst pipe last winter. She'd paid for the roof repairs. She'd replaced her mother's contact lenses. "I just can't afford to pay for every—"

"This is a crisis, honey. One of those nasty, unfair things that always happens to us. I can't believe you don't understand that by now."

"I understand that—"

"Probably a group of drunk teenagers." Pamela shook her head mournfully. "The windshield, the headlights, the tail lights—hundreds of cars available, but they choose *ours* . . ."

Megan waited for Pamela to launch into her "fate hates us" lament, topped off with tears for Megan's late father, his long-ago failed business, and the mounds of money that had evaporated before Kristen and Megan had started kindergarten. But Pamela just sat, her slim arms resting limply on the table.

"I try to help out," Megan said. "But you know I'm saving money—"

"Oh, honey, you're too old for school now."

"I'm twenty-four," Megan said curtly. "That's hardly granny status."

"I thought you were taking some kind of literature class online."

"I am. But what I want—"

"What good would school do you anyway? Before the layoffs you were making good money at that pharmaceutical company, even without a degree."

"It was a decent job, but I really don't like being an admin. I've always wanted—"

"Just look at me. A master's degree in sociology and I'm working for pennies selling flowers to rich people."

Megan looked away to hide the disgust in her eyes. Pamela always described her job at the florist's as if she were Eliza Doolittle from *My Fair Lady*—peddling blossoms in a desperate struggle to keep food on the table. *Eliza Doolittle doesn't get pricey dye jobs to keep her hair sun-streaked blond.*

"You could pick up some extra hours," Megan said firmly. "In a couple of months—"

"And how am I supposed to get to work in the meantime?"

"You could walk. It's only about a mile."

Pamela's frosted eyelids drooped. "You know what kind of people are out there, even in a little town like this. It could have been *me* they attacked, not the car! Did you think of that? Plus there's the weather. It will snow soon, and after that bout of pneumonia last winter, I don't want to take chances."

"You had bronchitis, not pneumonia. And it's not even October yet. Besides, *I* walk almost everywhere I go."

"You're odd that way. Like your father. But at least he didn't expect *me* to do all that walking. What would he think if he knew his daughter has a bank account full of money, but she'd make me hike all over town rather than help me?"

Stung, Megan said, "I don't have a bank account full of money."

"You're always at work. You must have something to show for it."

"Even with both jobs combined, I'm not making as much as I did at Hardisen. You can't expect me to—"

"If you'd taken out better insurance coverage on the car, we wouldn't be in this pickle."

Anger and guilt tangled inside Megan, but she forced herself to speak calmly. "Mom, we had an agreement. Car repairs are—"

Pamela's voice went satin soft. "Darling, don't you think I know what's really eating at you? This is about Luke Wagner. You're on the rebound. That's why you're suddenly so set on going away to school. Most girls grab the first new man they see—you grabbed a university catalog."

Humiliation scorched Megan's cheeks. "This has nothing to do with Luke. That . . . that was over months ago. And I've always planned on college."

"I didn't hear you talking about college while you thought you were going to become Mrs. Wagner."

"We were never engaged," Megan said icily.

"I know you talked about it. And Luke *is* quite a catch. A doctor!" Pamela laid a graceful hand on Megan's arm and leaned toward her, eyes bright. "He's still smitten with you. I can tell. You're so beautiful—how could he not be smitten? Your lovely, long strawberry-blond hair and fair skin . . . Don't you ever think of patching things up with him?"

Megan drew her arm away. "We're not talking about Luke. We're talking about the car. You agreed to pay for repairs."

"Oh, honey, you know I don't have that kind of money right now. I begged Doug to let me pay our portion in installments, but he said he can't order the parts without money up front."

Megan knew that Doug at the garage had no problems ordering parts. He'd just dealt with Pamela before and knew he'd have to fight her for the money unless he got it before the work was done.

"If you're worried about earning money for school, you could drop your volunteer work at the library," Pamela suggested. "That would give you more time to do paid work."

Megan fought the urge to snap at her mother. Running the library's tutoring program she'd founded in high school was the only thing that kept her sane. "I'm only there a couple of hours a week as it is. I hardly have time to breathe. I *can't* pick up more hours at my jobs. Why can't you switch to full time?"

"None of this talk is going to help us right now. We need to get the car fixed. I don't have the money. I'm so sorry to have to ask you for help, but I'm desperate."

"You could get a cash advance on one of your credit cards," Megan began, but Pamela dismissed the words with a flick of her manicured nails. Her credit cards were probably maxed out; they often were. Likely she was already behind on the payments.

"Glass everywhere—all over the ground, on the seats." Pamela's voice trembled. "And the police won't do anything. 'Just random. So sorry, Mrs. O'Connor.'"

Megan bit her lip. "I know it must have been terrible for you, Mom, but we had a deal. I wish I . . . right now I just can't afford—" Megan glanced at the clock. "I need to get to work."

"I'd expect this kind of selfishness from Kristen." Tears glistened in Pamela's eyes. "I never expected it from you."

Kristen, who had abandoned Pamela and Megan when Pamela was only two months a widow. Kristen, who had strutted away from Morris Glen and never looked back . . .

Megan's hand shook violently as she wrote the check, her signature jerking above and below the line. Five hundred dollars of her school savings gone.

Pamela tucked the check in her pocket and presented Megan with a quavery smile. Megan rushed out of the kitchen before Pamela could say how much she loved her, how Megan was the joy of her life, the only child who cared.

Megan yanked off her supermarket smock and donned the gingham dress and apron she wore for her evening job.

Halfway to Trina's House of Barbecue, the tears started, scalding her eyes. As soon as she saved more money, there would be another expense and another, and she'd be stuck in Morris Glen, Pennsylvania, forever, hawking the blue-plate special and running into Luke Wagner everywhere she turned.

Megan walked faster, wanting to flee the anger that tore at her whenever she thought of the tears glittering on her mother's cheeks.

Tears and a helpless, well-practiced smile.

If Megan didn't get out of here soon, she was going to lose her mind.

* * *

Kristen O'Connor plunked into a chair and smiled smugly at her white-haired great-aunt sitting on the couch opposite her.

"Done," Kristen said. "All done, and no problems at all. Three cheers for me."

"Your shoes are a bit soiled, dear. If you don't mind—?"

Impatiently, Kristen tugged off her shoes, noting the offending blades of grass that had adhered to the soles when she'd cut across Aunt Evelyn's dewy lawn. "As I was *saying*, the final straw just broke the camel's back. She'll be absolutely desperate to make a break when I approach her."

"I hope you returned the crowbar to the garage. To the correct hook."

"I'll put it back. Don't worry."

"Do it before you leave, dear."

"Sure, okay." Evelyn Seaver's fussy ways got on Kristen's nerves, but she knew she'd better keep Evelyn happy if she didn't want to get cut off from the best opportunity of her life. She still found it hard to believe that a finicky crone like Evelyn would concoct a scheme like this. At Evelyn's age, why bother?

Kristen rubbed a fingertip over the smooth skin of her face. She wasn't going to wait until she was a wrinkly old walnut to get her hands on some money.

"Do realize, dear, that to make your story credible, you'll have to convince Megan that *you* are the one who sought *me* out," Evelyn said. "If you tell her I contacted you first, she'll never believe I'm so ignorant of your family that I didn't know she existed."

"Yeah, I know. I'll do that. Don't worry—I'll make the story good. I know how to push Megan's buttons, and the timing couldn't be better, what with the whole Luke thing. You just make sure the stage is set when she arrives." Kristen surveyed the hardwood floor gleaming in the morning sunlight, the vivid scarlet and caramel-brown area rug, the matching wing chairs, the polished colonial-style pewter pieces arranged on the mantel.

"This place looks like an Ethan Allen showroom," Kristen complained. "It's too fresh. Too nice. Close the windows. Close the blinds. Turn on the heat—make it about eighty-five degrees in here. Get one of those icky air fresheners that make the place smell like fake flowers. We want grim and stuffy."

Evelyn's perfectly lipsticked mouth curved in a small smile. "Excellent suggestions. You have quite a knack for planning. I'm fortunate to have your help."

Kristen was pleased at the compliment but hid her pleasure behind a shrug. "It's not hard for me to manipulate Megan. Miss A-plus would buy the Brooklyn Bridge if I were the one selling it."

Evelyn nodded, prim and pink in her linen dress. "Common sense *is* such a necessary quality. I'm glad you're able to combine a sharp intellect with practicality."

"I can take care of myself."

"I imagine Megan must idolize you. You have such vibrancy. Such determination."

Kristen couldn't help smiling. "So," she said, pulling out her PDA. "What's next?"

* * *

Seated at her desk, Evelyn Seaver labeled the newest tape and tucked it into the envelope where it would stay until she was ready to take it to her safe-deposit box. She opened her leather-bound notebook, took out her pen, and wrote a summary of her conversation with Kristen.

She hummed a Strauss waltz as she filled the page with flowing lines of writing. Really, the tapes were enough, but recording the events with pen and paper allowed her to analyze them and feel Judith's approval. How delightful it would be to read these records in years to come! And when she was too old and feeble to do much else, she could listen to the tapes as she dozed in her rocking chair, her aged body warmed by the knowledge of her triumph.

It was all working out so beautifully.

Chapter 2

"I'm sorry, Mrs. Hanover, but it's the Pepsi that's on sale, not the Coke." Megan held up the bottle of soda. "I can have Cliff swap this for the Pepsi."

Ginny Hanover squinted at the readout on the register, the papery skin around her eyes crinkling in deep folds. "The sign said ninety-nine cents for the two-liter bottle. You charged me $1.79."

"The *Pepsi* two-liter is on sale, ma'am. The Coke is at regular price. Cliff can swap the—"

"My husband doesn't like Pepsi. He's particular about his colas. That sign was *right next* to the Coke display. Ninety-nine cents, in big red letters."

Another customer joined the two people already in line behind Mrs. Hanover. A toddler swung an open bag of M&M's, scattering candies over the floor.

"Ma'am, the sign said Pepsi," Megan said, doggedly pleasant. "I'm sorry it confused you. Do you want a different bottle of soda or will you take this one?"

"I *want* this store to stand behind their ads. Have you even seen the sign, Miss O'Connor?"

"Yes, ma'am." A few cracks threaded through the politeness in Megan's voice. The sign was blue with a giant Pepsi logo.

The man behind Mrs. Hanover glared at his watch. Cliff the bagger rattled a grocery sack and yawned.

"Would you like to speak to the manager?" Megan asked.

Mrs. Hanover sniffed. "Aren't you smart enough to deal with this yourself? You charged me $1.79. The price should be ninety-nine cents. You need to deduct eighty cents from my total."

The man behind Ginny Hanover stepped forward and slapped two dollars on the counter. "The Coke's on me. Now can we move this along?"

Mrs. Hanover gasped and clutched her purse like the two dollars were meant to buy her honor. "No, thank you," she said frostily.

"Your total comes to $32.95 without the soda, ma'am," Megan said. "Or I can have Cliff bring you a bottle of Pepsi—"

"I already told you we don't like Pepsi." She dug into her purse. "Are you stupid as well as dishonest? No wonder Hardisen fired you."

Aflame with embarrassment, Megan accepted Mrs. Hanover's money. "The layoffs were company-wide. They had nothing to do—"

"You've certainly fallen far, haven't you? The high-falutin' scholarship girl, now too stupid to run a cash register." She snatched her change from Megan's hand. "This store is a disgrace, and the bag boys—" She shifted her harangue toward Cliff. "Idiotic, incompetent teenagers, never there when you need help—"

Cliff's eyes were glassy with boredom, and it was obvious he wasn't hearing a word of her rant. He pushed her cart toward the exit, and she followed him with angry, toddling steps.

Megan wished she could tune out like Cliff.

"Done daydreaming?" The voice of the two-dollar guy jolted Megan to attention. She rang up his groceries without speaking.

Next, a toddler wrinkled the wrapper of her M&M's and drooled onto the counter while her mother purchased what must have been a two-year supply of Cheerios. Then two hand-holding teenagers paid for their ice cream bars with a couple of dollars the boy fished out of his shoe.

When Megan had a break in the line, she grabbed glass cleaner and paper towels to wipe up the toddler's rainbow slobber.

"I squashed her bread," Cliff said out of the side of his mouth.

"You what?"

"Mrs. Hanover. Her bread. Under the laundry soap. Flat as a pancake, and it will taste like Tide." He grinned and raked his fingers through his spiked hair.

"Cliff, you didn't!" Megan stifled a smile.

"Hey, why not? Every time she comes in here, she treats us like garbage. Let her complain to Carruthers if she wants. I don't care.

This little store is a joke anyway. Ten bucks says it gets bought out within a year."

She had to admit that Cliff had a point. As he walked off to assist the customer at the next checkstand, Megan stowed the glass cleaner and snuck a glance at her watch.

A customer approached and Megan turned automatically, her "work" smile fixed in place.

Her heart jumped.

"Hi, Meg." Luke Wagner set a deli sandwich and a bottle of water on the counter. "How are you?"

"Hi, Luke." She tried to sound indifferent, but she was blushing and knew Luke would notice. She rang up the sandwich and reached for the water.

No one was in line behind Luke, so he leaned over the counter and whispered, "I've missed you."

Megan drew the water bottle across the scanner. "This isn't a good time to talk."

"Then when is?" He leaned a little closer and Megan's heart started doing gymnastics. "You're never home anymore. You don't return my calls."

She looked up at him and wished she hadn't—those sweet hazel eyes, endearingly vulnerable. There was a hint of pleading in them now, accompanied by the smile that could melt Antarctica. He swiped his debit card through the reader and reached to pick up his sandwich and water. His hand brushed her arm.

"You're working at Trina's tonight?" he asked.

Megan nodded.

"I'll come by at closing. We need to talk."

"Don't come by, Luke." She lowered her voice to a whisper as another customer stepped into line. "We've already talked."

"But you haven't listened. I'll see you tonight." He smiled at her and walked away.

The rush of customers continued until Megan finally made a hasty exit, forty-five minutes after her shift was supposed to end. She sprinted home in the rain and burst through the front door with pants soaked to the knee from puddles she'd been in too much of a hurry to avoid.

Megan tossed her smock aside, donned her gingham dress and apron, and swept her hair into a ponytail. She snatched her paperback of *The Brothers Karamazov* to read on her break, wondering when she was ever going to have time to finish it. She might as well drop that online class. She grabbed a banana and a handful of saltine crackers to ward off starvation, then sped out the door, barely remembering to grab her purse and raincoat on the way.

"I've missed you. We need to talk."

Why couldn't Luke leave her alone? And what was this crazy part of her that hoped he *would* stop by Trina's House of Barbecue tonight?

Stay away from him. He'll make you miserable. She'd chanted those words to herself for the past three months, and they were back now as she hurried through the rain.

Near the end of the block, a car pulled over to the curb just ahead of her. She glanced at it, irritated at the way she'd hoped, just for an instant, that she'd see Luke's VW. She didn't recognize the car, a silver Corolla, but the voice that came from the open window sent the tingling heat of adrenaline through her body.

"Hop in."

Megan hesitated for only an instant before opening the door and settling into the seat.

Kristen floored the gas pedal like she wanted to get out of the neighborhood as quickly as possible.

"What are you doing here?" Megan asked.

"Why? Have I been banned?"

"I was just curious." Megan tried to sound casual. It didn't work.

Kristen grinned at her. "Good grief, Meg. Are they doing another remake of *The Beverly Hillbillies*?"

"What?"

"You look like Elly May."

Heat spread over Megan's face. "It's a uniform." She pulled her raincoat closed to cover her skirt and was doubly embarrassed to realize she was still clutching a banana, some crackers, and Dostoevsky. "I work at Trina's and I'm almost late. Can you drop me there?"

"You're not going in tonight. You called in sick."

"I did?"

"You're coming down with the stomach flu. You felt sick at Gardner's all day, and now you've started throwing up. Yuck. Who wants a waitress with the pukes?"

"You called my manager and told her I was sick?"

"I told her *I* was sick. I told her I was you. We're going to dinner in Philly."

Megan stared at Kristen. Why was she acting like this? Since Kristen had gone off to college the week after their father's funeral, she'd only come back a handful of times. When she did visit, she avoided her sister as if she had leprosy and spent all her time with old high school friends.

"I can't go to dinner dressed like Elly May," Megan began.

"I brought some clothes for you."

"How did you know where I work now?" Megan made her voice bland, pretending she didn't care that Kristen had gone to the trouble of finding out about her. "Did you talk to Mom?"

"Talk to sweet young thing Pamela, you mean?"

Megan tried not to grin, but her lips curved upward anyway. "So you've finally started calling her that?"

"No. I'm not in the business of supporting her delusions. Do you call her that? She's not that much older than us, you know."

Megan laughed, thinking of their mother's speech, given on their sixteenth birthday, about how she was really too young for such a matronly title as "Mom" or "Mother," and now that her daughters were practically the same age as she was—Kristen had snickered for weeks over that lapse in logic—wouldn't it be nice if they addressed her as "Pamela"?

"It's funny," Megan said. "I can think of her as Pamela, but when I try to call her that, I remember the look on Dad's face . . ."

"Yeah, he wasn't thrilled with the idea. But you know, Meg, you don't have to live to please him anymore. Call her whatever you want."

Megan's momentary amusement evaporated, and tension and uncertainty returned. "So did you talk to Mom tonight?"

"Please! So she could pin me to the wall and torture me with lectures on how heartless I am and why am I not like darling Megan who doesn't mind having Mommy's apron strings knotted around her neck?"

"What do you know about it?" Megan asked coldly.

"Do you still think you're saving money for school?"

"I *am* saving money for school."

"Uh-huh. As if Medusa will let you do that. Car repairs this time, wasn't it?"

A saltine crunched in Megan's fist. "Who told you that?"

"You know Morris Glen. Gossip, gossip. You think it isn't common knowledge that *Pamela* sucks you dry?"

"She doesn't—"

Kristen laughed and tossed her red-gold hair back from her face. She'd grown it out. This was the longest Megan had seen it since they were teenagers—since Kristen, sick of people mixing her up with her twin, had come home from the salon with a haircut so short that their mother had thrown a fit. *"Why would you cut off that gorgeous hair? If you're trying to make yourself ugly, you succeeded. You've always had such strange taste. Do you think you're being chic?"* Kristen had rolled her eyes at this tirade, but later that night Megan had glimpsed her crying.

Now Kristen's hair was shoulder-length, parted on the side, and artfully layered so it framed her face and settled in curves on her shoulders. Megan touched the damp ponytail dangling down her back. *Elly May Clampett.*

"Why do you defend Mom?" Kristen merged onto the freeway. "She's drinking your blood."

"She needs me."

"For how long? 'Oh darling, just for a year until I get used to being a lonely little widow. I'm sure Cornell will hold your scholarship.'" Kristen's voice dropped to its normal pitch. "I hate to tell you this, Miss Math Whiz, but seventy-two months equals six years. Not one year."

Megan watched the windshield wipers sweeping rain off the glass and said nothing. It bothered her how Kristen could speak so flippantly of their father's death, minimizing the shock and pain that had derailed Megan's plans and made her academic aspirations seem pointless. At the time, Megan hadn't been able to comprehend how Kristen could go charging off to school like nothing at home had changed.

But maybe Kristen had been right.

"Do you want to stay in Morris Glen until you're an old lady?" Kristen asked. "You know Mom will never let you go. I'll bet she smashed up her car herself just so she could make you pay."

"Kris!"

"She got scared thinking you might actually earn enough money to spring yourself from her jail, so she did something about it."

"That's absurd."

"She's a nut. You deserve a better life."

The rest of the crackers crumbled in Megan's hand. Kristen had *never* talked to her like this.

"Where have you been?" Megan rolled down the window so she could get rid of the saltine crumbs. "Are you still in New York?"

"Nope."

Megan waited for Kristen to elaborate, but she didn't, so Megan didn't press her. She didn't want to get rebuffed for prying.

Kristen pulled over at a gas station so Megan could change out of her uniform. When Kristen had said she'd brought clothes, Megan had assumed she'd taken clothes from Megan's closet, but this outfit was new. Jeans, a sleek, perfect fit. A sweater in a shade of pink that Megan knew would flatter her. A hairbrush, a makeup case. Even a delicate, rose gold necklace and matching earrings. Megan slid the elastic band off her ponytail and brushed out her hair.

"Much better," Kristen said when Megan returned to the car.

"Are these your clothes?" Megan asked.

"They're yours. Happy birthday, a little late."

"Thanks." Delighted, Megan turned to toss her uniform into the backseat. As she got a better look at Kristen, her smile faded. Kristen had put on a long brown wig and glasses.

"Kris, for crying out loud—"

Kristen held up a hand. "Don't go all sensitive. This is nothing personal. But you know what will happen if we walk into the restaurant doing the clone routine. 'Oh, you're *twins*! That's so *cute*. Do people get you mixed up all time? Can your mother tell you apart? Do you ever pretend to be each other?'"

"I don't think *I'm* the one being sensitive. And when's the last time anyone called us 'cute'? We're not three years old."

"Just humor me, okay? If it helps me enjoy dinner, what's the big deal?"

"Fine, whatever." Megan kept her voice neutral. "But if you feel that strongly about it, dye your hair in pink-and-green stripes and get your eyebrows pierced. No one will mix us up then."

Kristen laughed. "Touché," she said.

The restaurant Kristen had chosen was a small Italian place. Flames danced in a stone fireplace, and the air was delicious with the smell of roasted garlic and fresh tomato sauce. Megan wondered if she'd slipped into a dream. She was supposed to be at Trina's making root beer floats and balancing slabs of ribs on platters while barbecue sauce dripped on her apron and customers demanded five-star service for a three-dollar tip. Instead, she was sitting companionably with the sister she hadn't seen in over a year, nibbling bruschetta and watching Kristen's every flicker of expression as she tried to figure out why her twin had come.

Even with the ridiculous wig and glasses, Megan loved watching Kristen. It was almost like looking in a mirror, but a mirror that showed her as she wanted to be, not as she was. Light blue eyes sparked with keen intelligence; confidence emanated from the curve of a smile. A natural peach-colored blush along the cheekbones made Kristen look healthy and energetic. On Megan, the same coloring looked fragile, childish.

Over mussels in cream sauce, Kristen asked Megan about her work and listened attentively to tales of life in Morris Glen, laughing at her sister's anecdotes like Megan was the wittiest woman alive. Megan found herself laughing too, able to see the humor even in her run-in with Mrs. Hanover. Kristen had never shown this kind of interest in her life.

Why now?

Kristen dipped a fragment of bread in a golden drizzle of olive oil. "I heard you broke up with Luke Wagner."

Megan's mood soured instantly. "Can't we talk about something else?"

"Sorry." Kristen gave a crooked smile. "I just thought you might want to vent. Congrats on dumping the jerk."

Warmed by Kristen's approval, Megan managed a smile in return. "You heard the whole story?"

"I heard he was lying through his teeth to you. I heard he had a girlfriend here in Philly."

"*Girlfriends,* plural. He was seeing at least two other women—while showering me with lies about how I was his one and only. I thought I'd be getting an engagement ring for my birthday. Instead, I got approached by an embarrassed friend who'd seen him with his sweetie-pie and thought I should know."

"Ouch." Kristen mimed driving a knife into her heart. "Did he deny it?"

"He said the woman was just a friend from med school who was passing through town, so they met for dinner. As for the public display of affection, he claimed my informant misinterpreted what she saw. Sure, he put his arm around her and maybe kissed her on the cheek, but it was just a brotherly thing and it was ridiculous for me to be jealous. I almost bought it until sweetie #1, who already knew that Luke had a sweetie #2—me—found out there was a sweetie #3, got furious, and decided all Luke's women should know what a creep he is. She called me. That's when I broke it off. That was three months ago, but Luke's still calling me and stopping by the store and sending flowers, insisting he's changed and that these other women never meant anything to him, and I'm the only one he loves. And I . . ." Megan let her voice trail off, embarrassed at how much she was confiding in Kristen. The more she confessed, the more ammunition Kristen would have to zing her with later.

"You're afraid you might fall for him again?" Kristen asked.

"No," Megan said sharply. "I'm not that stupid."

"You're still in love with him, aren't you?"

Megan nearly denied it, but the sympathy in Kristen's eyes coaxed the truth to the surface. "I don't know *how* I feel. I just know it hurts to be around him." She shook her head and reached for her water glass. "I just wish I didn't have to see him around town. I wish people—Mom included—would quit acting like it was the biggest mistake of my life to dump Dr. Charming. I wish . . . I wish I'd quit complaining and just eat my dinner."

Kristen laughed. "He's a weasel, babe. Stay away from him."

"I know, I know. I can't figure out what he sees in me anyway. I think he just doesn't like to lose."

Kristen rolled her eyes. "Give yourself a little credit, oh queen of False Modesty. You're pretty. You're smart. You're sweet and reliable and patient and hardworking and loyal and trusting and all that perfect doctor-wife stuff."

Megan said nothing. No one else had Kristen's skill at turning compliments into insults with only a slight twist in tone.

"Hey, I really mean all that," Kristen said, reading Megan's expression. "You're terrific wife material and he knows it, no matter how much he messes around. He'll never do better than you. No wonder he's groveling at your feet. But let's talk about something more interesting—like dessert. The chocolate cake here is to die for. You saved room, I hope."

Glad for this change of subject, Megan reached for the dessert menu.

When they finished, Kristen paid for the dinner in cash and left a generous tip for the waitress. "Don't want to get you mad at me," she teased. When they got to the car, Megan expected her to drive straight home, but she didn't head for the freeway.

"Kris, I really need to get back," Megan protested reluctantly. There was nothing she wanted to do less than go home.

Kristen snickered at her half-hearted objection. "Forget it. I've got a hotel room booked for us. We're staying the night. There are some things we need to talk about."

Megan's nerves buzzed. "Like what?"

"Like how to get you out of Morris Glen. Permanently."

Chapter 3

"What would it take?" Kristen lounged on the bed, shoes off, cream silk blouse untucked, wig and glasses abandoned on the nightstand.

"Money." Megan toyed with a pen stamped with the Doubletree logo. "What else? I'd leave tomorrow if I could afford it."

"Once you go home, you'll never leave, and you know it. You cross that threshold and you'll end up married to Luke—at least until he runs away with the next floozy he sees—or you'll end up chained to Mom's kitchen chair, writing checks until you die."

"Are you offering to put me through school? Because unless you are, this conversation is a waste of time."

"I'm offering you the chance to put yourself through school. Come with me, and soon you'll have half a million dollars."

The pen fell out of Megan's hand. "You're joking."

"Am I laughing?"

"What are you offering me? A job running drugs?"

Kristen giggled. "You know I'd never get involved with that kind of crud."

"Then how can I make that much money?" She paused. "It's not like I've got any high-priced skills," she added before Kristen could say it for her.

"I need your help," Kristen said. "Just for a short while."

"*My* help?" Megan sat rigid, afraid if she so much as blinked that this whole conversation would disappear into dreamland.

Kristen was still lounging on the bed, but her eyes had a hard, clear look like blue topaz, and Megan knew Kristen was closely gauging her reaction.

"I've been living in Britteridge, Massachusetts," Kristen said. "Do you know where that is?"

"Um . . . let's see. Massachusetts. I think that's one of the fifty states. Is it near Wyoming?"

"Ooh, funny. Did you learn that joke in the geography bee? What I meant—"

"I know what you meant. Britteridge is a town north of Boston. There's a new hotshot college there."

"Yeah, its one claim to fame. We have a great-aunt who lives there."

"I didn't know that."

Kristen shrugged. "How could you know? Mom didn't even talk to Grandma—why would she stay in touch with some geezer aunt? Besides, our old auntie and Mom had a falling out years ago. Aunt Evelyn didn't even know Mom had kids."

"What happened?"

"How would I know? Evelyn didn't explain. She just said she used to live near Mom's family when Mom was young, but she hasn't had anything to do with her for decades and likes it that way. Really, can you blame her?"

"Will you quit being so rude about Mom?"

"Give me a break. Just because you're her perfect angel child doesn't mean *I* have to pretend she's a saint."

"I never said—" Megan stopped; she didn't want to get drawn into that argument. "How did you find Aunt Evelyn?" she asked instead.

"Research." Kristen's eyes gleamed with mischief. "I got this urge to explore my family roots. Feel the ties of love and blood that transcend generations—"

"You thought maybe you could find a relative and hit her up for cash?"

"Megan." Kristen leaned forward. "Not to sound cliché, but I struck gold. The hag has over a million bucks—that's a million bucks *after* all the taxes and junk—and that's not counting the value of her house, which will add at least another half mil. And no kids. Her only daughter died years ago."

"You think—" Megan cut the words off. Kristen was dangling bait in her face so she could laugh when Megan leapt at it like a fool.

Megan purged the excitement from her voice before continuing. "You think she might leave her money to us? Grandnieces she didn't know existed until you knocked at her door with dollar signs in your eyes?"

"Well, she still doesn't know *you* exist."

"What a surprise." Why did it sting so badly to know that Kristen hadn't bothered to mention her to their aunt? Ever since they were teenagers, Kristen had made a practice of pretending Megan didn't exist. Even tonight, with that ridiculous disguise—like there was no humiliation greater than having the world see that she had a twin.

"Don't look so sulky, Megan. I'm here because I need you."

"Need me for what?"

"Our dear old auntie—her name is Evelyn Seaver—is dying of cancer. Doc says it's hopeless, so Evelyn decided no treatment—she'd just kick it whenever nature gave the word."

"That's really sad."

"How sweet of you to boo-hoo about an old woman you've never met."

Megan flushed. "How cold of you not to boo-hoo about an old woman that you *have*."

Kristen grinned. "The point is we've got a real shot at her money. I've been working her for a couple of months. I moved to Britteridge so I can help her out whenever she needs it. The compassionate niece."

"What excuse did you give for showing up on her doorstep? Unless she's an idiot, she must know exactly what you're after."

"Well, she was suspicious at first. But I told her I was feeling adrift, that I wanted to make some family connections. Aunt Evelyn is a lonely woman and not so clear in the head. And I'm doing a brilliant job playing the family card. I've got some friends who are Mormons. You know how they're big into genealogy and stuff?"

Megan shrugged. She didn't know much about Mormons at all.

"There's a girl in my apartment complex who's a Mormon. Rachel Drake. I've been sucking up to her, giving her the impression that I'm interested in her church. She's helping me research my family. Rachel and I kept visiting Evelyn to interview her about her ancient relatives. Evelyn's paranoid about strangers, but after a few visits, she was yakking my ear off. What lonely old lady could resist my charms, especially when I'm willing to listen to her blab endlessly about Uncle Loser and Great-Great-Grandma Nincompoop?"

"Let me get this straight," Megan said. "You're pretending to be interested in the Mormon church, so you can pretend to be interested in genealogy, so you can pretend to be interested in Aunt Evelyn, so you can quickly build a relationship with her and get her to leave you all her money when she dies?"

"More or less."

Megan dug her sock-covered toes into the carpet. "How complicated can you get? Why don't you just forget the whole Mormon thing? You don't have to be Mormon to want to learn about your family."

"Yeah, but it's fun having a bunch of Mormons treat me like the queen of England. You wouldn't believe what they'll do for you if they think they can catch you in their net. Besides, this way I don't actually have to *learn* anything about genealogy. I've got Rachel doing all the work. And there are advantages to hanging around with Rachel. She's loaded, and she's always throwing money around."

"Rachel Drake," Megan said. "Is she Michael Drake's daughter?"

Kristen's perfectly tweezed eyebrows shot upward. "You know about him?"

"He used to own some computer company, but he got tired of the rat race and sold it off. I can't remember the name of the company, but I think it was here in Pennsylvania. He used part of his fortune to found Britteridge College. They have a strong emphasis on moral values along with high-quality—"

"Sheesh, give it a rest. I forgot you used to memorize all those college brochures. But listen, Megan, I've got a real shot at this. Like I said, Aunt Evelyn has no kids and no connection with any of her other relatives. She was widowed this past summer and she's sick and lonely. I'm charming and devoted. Why shouldn't she leave her money to me instead of to some charity?"

Megan's heart pounded so rapidly that she felt light-headed. Kristen was serious. *A million dollars. Maybe a million and a half. But—* "I don't understand why you'd bring me into this."

"Don't you think I want to share my good fortune?"

Megan looked at Kristen in silence.

Kristen threw her hands into the air and laughed. "Ow! Look who's gotten all cynical! Okay, here's the scoop. Evelyn's probably got another couple of months before the Grim Reaper does his thing, and I'm going nuts. She's on too much heavy-duty pain medication to drive, so I'm running all her errands. She's too tired and sick to take care of her house, so I'm doing all her cleaning. And *now* she wants me to move in with her and be her nurse. I'll do it if I have to, but I thought, why not cut you in on the deal? You show up in Britteridge pretending to be me. Be Evelyn's slave for a couple of months until she dies. She leaves her money to me. I cut you your share. Five hundred thousand. And before you start griping about how I'm getting twice as much as you, remember that this whole thing was my idea. I found Evelyn, I buttered her up. You're just showing up now that I've got everything set. Half a mil is more than fair—more than enough to get you that college education you've been dreaming about."

"I never said I thought it was unfair." Megan's skin tingled like ants were crawling over her body. *Half a million . . .* "But what do you mean 'pretending to be you'? Why would I masquerade as you?"

"Meg-*an.* Get a clue. I'm the one she loves and trusts. You're a stranger, and there's no time for you to worm your way into her wrinkled little heart."

"Why can't you introduce me? If she's so lonely, wouldn't she snap me up just like you?"

"Didn't you listen to what I told you? She didn't 'snap me up.' I had to gain her confidence one step at a time. She's not desperate for someone just to *be* with her or take care of her. She could hire a live-in nurse if that's what she wanted. She's desperate for someone to *love* her, and she thinks I do. She thinks we've got this bond, and if all of a sudden *you* show up and I say, 'Here's the Stepford Wife version of me, who'll take care of you, and I'm leaving—"

"You could give her a little time to get to know me before you leave."

"The woman is dying. She doesn't *have* time. Can't you trust me on this? I know Aunt Evelyn. You don't. If I shove a sister in her face and run out on her, she's going to feel betrayed—and she'll start suspecting I was just in this for the money all along. If that happens, bye-bye inheritance."

"This is stupid." Megan folded her arms and glared at Kristen, excitement, skepticism, and guilt battling inside her. "You've been watching too much TV. The elderly lady with no heirs and a couple million dollars that she'll bequeath to the first person who shows her a little affection—"

"*Bequeath*? Do real people even use words like that? Tell me, Megan, do you still read the dictionary for fun?"

"Yes, I just finished it," Megan said coolly. "Want me to tell you how it ends?"

Kristen laughed. "Okay, okay. But listen, people believe what they want to believe, and Evelyn wants to believe in me. I've made a big deal about how my dad is dead and I don't get along with my mother, how I never really knew my grandparents and I've always envied people with strong family ties, how lucky I am to have found her at last—all the stuff that makes Evelyn feel like she's the best thing that ever happened to me." Kristen ran her fingers through her wig-flattened hair so it settled in feathery curves on her neck. "Two weeks ago, she changed her will. Her money goes to me, provided I live in her house and care for her until she dies. See why it's vital that she thinks you're me?"

Megan stared at Kristen. "She's already changed her will?"

"Yep. I'm good, sweetie. I'm very good. And I'm giving you the chance to help me. You move to Britteridge and be me. I leave for a while to regain my sanity. When Evelyn dies, you'll have more than enough money to put yourself through school and to get far away from Mom the Vampire and Dr. Weasel. See how easy this is?"

Megan blinked, still half convinced she was dreaming. *Too easy*, she wanted to say. *It can't be this easy.*

"Meggie, I really need you," Kristen said pleadingly. "You know I've never had much patience, and caring for Evelyn takes patience by the truckload. I'm afraid I'm going to lose my cool one of these days and offend her—and offend myself right out of a million bucks. But you—heck, if you could handle Mom all these years, I know you can handle Evelyn for a few months. You're a lot better caretaker than I am. Help me, will you?"

Kristen needed her.

Kristen was begging for her help.

Trying not to show how much Kristen's plea had affected her, Megan asked, "How can I be sure you won't stiff me once you get the money?"

Kristen applauded. "Good girl. Glad to see you watching out for yourself. Look, if I don't cut you your share, all you have to do is go to Evelyn's lawyer and tell him how you took my place for those last few weeks. Remember, in order to get the money, I have to live in her house until she dies. If you told the law firm of Scrooge, Tightwad, and Skinflint I wasn't there, I wouldn't get a cent. We're in this together. Got it?"

Megan nodded, averting her gaze from Kristen's gemstone-blue eyes. "I just . . . feel funny about pretending to be you. It's . . . well, it's fraud, isn't it?"

"Fraud?" Kristen's voice strained as though she were trying to keep from shouting. "Who are we hurting?"

"Well . . . no one, I guess. But—"

"Evelyn *wants* to give me her money. We had a long talk about this the day she showed me the will. She *wants* to keep her money in the family, but before I came, she didn't think she had any relatives who cared about her, so she was going to leave her money to charity. But now she loves me and thinks I love her. Together, you and I will give her exactly what she wants—tender care from a loving, devoted niece. She'll die happy. How can you possibly feel guilty about that?"

"I'm . . . just not sure that . . ."

"You don't have your head on straight, because you're still reeling over what Luke did to you. This isn't like that at all, Megan. We're not being dishonest. We're being practical. Luke was using people and hurting them in the process. We're *helping* Evelyn. Big difference."

They *were* helping Evelyn, Megan conceded. And why shouldn't Evelyn's money go to family when she died? If their mother had gotten along with Evelyn, she would have left her money to Kristen and Megan in the first place.

"If you don't want to help me, then don't. I can always take you home." Kristen pulled a mocking smile. "Paper or plastic, Mrs. Hanover? Do you want creamer with your coffee, Mr. Peterson?"

"Ouch." Megan rolled the Doubletree pen beneath her fingers. "I never said I didn't want to help."

"Then come with me. What's left for you in Morris Glen? Your dream guy turned out to be a toad. You lost your job at Hardisen—a job I know you didn't like anyway—and now you're scrambling around working night and day for cheapskate bosses who wouldn't know a living wage if it bit them on the seat of their polyester golf pants. Every time you make some extra cash, Mom swipes it. Is this what you call a life? It's time to bail out. Let's help each other, and we can both get what we want."

Megan felt like she was squinting at something glittering so brightly that she couldn't make out any of the details, but the pressure to decide now . . . the chance to earn half a million dollars in just a few months. The chance to get away from Luke Wagner and start over.

School. The dreams she'd repressed for years.

Who are we hurting?

Masquerading as Kristen was a harmless charade. If Evelyn would be happier thinking Megan was Kristen, why not let her think that? Evelyn would still get the same loving care. They weren't cheating her out of anything.

Half a million dollars.

"I'm in," Megan said.

"Smart girl." Victory sparkled in Kristen's eyes. "We'll stay here at the hotel for a couple of days while we start the process of changing you into me." She bounded to her feet. "I've got the information you need in order to act like—"

"Wait a minute. You mean we're starting immediately?"

"When did you think we were starting? After Evelyn's funeral? You're on the payroll as of tonight."

"But . . . Mom. My jobs. I can't just up and move to Massachusetts. I've got to make arrangements."

"No offense, darling sister, but you're too nice. If you start talking to people at home, you'll feel so guilty about leaving that you might slip up and give something away. Can you imagine what Mom would do if she knew about this? She'd demand ninety percent of the money or she'd call Evelyn and tell her we're crooks out to strangle her in her sleep."

"Kris, I can't just disappear. People are going to think I got kidnapped."

Kristen laughed like the idea was far funnier than Megan had meant it to be. "I'll call your bosses and pretend I'm you. I'll say I've got a great job opportunity in Phoenix and I'm moving immediately."

"You can't do that for me. And what about the library? I'm in charge of—"

"You're still running that tutoring program? Good grief, you've been doing that since you were fifteen. Hand it over to someone else. It's not like you need it to dress up your scholarship applications anymore."

"I do it because I enjoy it," Megan said.

"More than you'd enjoy going to school yourself?"

Megan didn't answer. She *could* hand the tutoring program over to Jessie. Jessie practically ran it for her anyway, now that she was so busy.

"As for your job in Phoenix, let's invent something that's right up your alley. How about we say you've been hired as an officer manager by a new educational software company. You're hoping to eventually work with the designers to create software programs to assist struggling students."

"And . . . somehow I forgot to mention to anyone that I'd applied for this job?"

"You didn't mention it, because you didn't think it was going to happen. You found the company on an Internet job listing. You interviewed by phone. You were worried they wouldn't want you because you don't have a college degree. But they made you an offer, so you're leaving immediately. And you didn't want to make a big round of good-byes, because it's so hard to leave your beloved hometown you thought it would be easier to just slip away."

Megan gripped the upholstered arms of the chair. "I can't quit my jobs without warning. I need to give two weeks' notice."

Kristen started laughing so hard that when she tried to walk, she stumbled over her shoes where she'd left them on the carpet. She didn't try to regain her balance but collapsed on the floor, tears of mirth overflowing her eyes.

Megan gritted her teeth, resisting the urge to kick Kristen in the ribs. Kristen always got giddy when she was feeling triumphant, but did she have to be so obnoxious about it?

"See what I'm saying?" Kristen panted, looking up from where she lay near Megan's feet. "You're too nice. Two weeks' notice? Sheesh. Put Hicksville behind you and let's go make some real money."

Megan doodled a dollar sign on the hotel stationery. "I owe these people some consideration."

"You *owe* them? Minimum wage doesn't buy much gratitude, sis." Kristen started laughing again. This time Megan did try to kick her, but Kristen twisted out of reach.

"I wasn't making minimum wage," Megan said.

"If you want the inheritance, you'll come with me now. The window of opportunity is about to slam shut." Kristen sat up and wiped her face. "You don't have to stress yourself out calling people back home. I'll talk to your bosses and make things sound so good that they'll agree only an idiot wouldn't have jumped at this new job."

Her bosses. She didn't mind so much about Mr. Carruthers. But Nicky at Trina's had given her a lot of support, adjusting Megan's hours so she could keep the job at Gardner's Foods, covering for her when Carruthers's demands made her late for Trina's.

"I *have* to give notice," Megan said. "You can stay with Aunt Evelyn for a couple of extra weeks—"

"*Megan.* Let's get one thing straight. If you're in, you're in on my terms."

Megan wanted to protest, but the flinty look in Kristen's eyes stilled her tongue. What if Kristen decided she didn't need Megan after all? Megan pictured an angry Kristen dropping her at home and speeding away to collect her inheritance, leaving Megan to slog along for the rest of her life, working two jobs, avoiding—and yearning for—Luke Wagner, and writing checks for Pamela.

"Why don't you go take a hot shower." Kristen's expression softened. "I'll take care of all the yucky stuff."

"What about Mom?"

"She's the last person you want to talk to. I'll tell her I'm you and I'm staying with friends right now and that I'll call as soon as I get settled in sunny Arizona."

"When will that be?"

"Never, if you have any brains. She's poison."

"Kris, she's our mother. I can't cut her out of my life."

"You won't be cutting her out. I've already set up an e-mail account under your name. I'll send her regular e-mails telling her about 'my' exciting new job and gushing about how much I love and miss her. Sound good?"

Megan frowned. "You're planning to write e-mails using my name?"

"Safer that way. Safer for your sanity and my peace of mind. C'mon—you'd hate lying to her. Admit it. And you'd hate reading her guilt-trippy replies. Let me handle her for a while. If you want to go back home when we're done with Evelyn, be my guest. Mom will run through your money in a week."

"Her finances—how is she going to get by without me to—"

"Gosh, Megan. You mean she might have to take care of herself for once? Maybe she could start by getting a real job and working full-time. Or if she's too lazy for that, she could always sell her pearls. She could live for months on one of her necklaces."

Megan rubbed her forehead, suddenly so drained that she lacked even the energy to look up at Kristen.

"Easy does it, babe." Kristen switched to her melted-chocolate voice. She stepped behind Megan and massaged her shoulders. "You've had a long day, and I've thrown a lot at you. Even too much good news can be exhausting. C'mon—take a shower and relax. I'll call your bosses and the library and Mom and whoever else you need me to talk to."

"You can't call the library," Megan murmured. "It's closed now."

"I know. I'll do that one tomorrow."

Megan roused herself. "I'll do the calls."

Kristen's hands tightened painfully on her shoulders. "Sorry, but I don't trust you—not in a situation where you've got to stand up for your own needs at the price of disappointing someone else. If you were good at that, you wouldn't have let one year of helping Mom cope with Dad's death turn into six years of being her servant. Have I made my point?"

Megan tried to come up with a rebuttal. She didn't have one.

Kristen's hands were gentle now, massaging Megan's scalp. "I can read your mind. You don't *want* to make the calls. You hate doing stuff like that. You just think you have to do it to be the responsible good girl. Know what? You're off the hook this time. I'll take care of it." She leaned close to Megan's ear. "Can I call Luke too? I'd love to give him an earful."

Despite herself, Megan smiled at the mischief in Kristen's voice. "Don't you dare."

"Don't worry. I wouldn't. But boy is it tempting . . . Now, go take that shower, and let me get to work springing you from jail."

Megan lingered in the shower for a long time, the steaming water hammering down with a din that blocked out the sound of Kristen's voice from the bedroom. She hated to admit it, but Kristen was right—she shrank from the thought of making those calls, disappointing the people who relied on her. And Mom . . . she'd be devastated.

A wave of guilt swamped Megan. She couldn't run out on Mom like this.

She nearly stepped out of the shower to stop Kristen, but the memory of that five-hundred-dollar check made her draw the shower curtain closed again. Pamela had sworn to take responsibility for her part of the finances. She'd sworn to curtail her spending, sworn that Megan wouldn't have to carry so much of the load. And then with the first expense that arose, she'd come running to Megan, like always.

"You cross that threshold and you'll end up chained to Mom's kitchen chair, writing checks until you die."

Kristen was probably right about that too.

Megan turned her face to the spray, letting it pound against her closed eyelids. She stayed in the shower until she was certain Kristen had had time to complete all three calls. When she emerged from the bathroom in a billow of steam, the cool air of the bedroom was a relief. Kristen was sitting cross-legged on her bed, her PDA in her hand and a small, satisfied smile on her lips.

On the other bed lay Megan's suitcase. Kristen must have gone into the house and packed for her. Megan opened the case and pulled out her nightgown. She expected Kristen to give her a report of the calls, but Kristen said nothing, and Megan didn't feel like asking. Megan combed out her hair in silence, then for lack of anything better to do, switched on the late news. Out of the corner of her eye, she studied Kristen, complacently arched over her PDA, her neck a graceful curve above a mint-green nightshirt.

By the time this adventure was over, Kristen would respect her in a way she never had before. If Megan played a vital role in putting a million dollars in Kristen's pocket, Kristen would *have* to respect her.

Kristen finally set the PDA aside. "I'm going to be gone all day tomorrow. I told Evelyn I was going to New York this week to spend some time with my boyfriend. I'll drive to New York tomorrow and do some sightseeing so I'll have a stack of pictures to show Evelyn."

"Why go to so much trouble to create an excuse for being out of town?" Megan asked in surprise. "Can't you just tell Evelyn you were in New York but didn't take any pictures?"

"Sheesh, Meg. Taking pictures of the Empire State Building for Evelyn isn't the *only* reason I want to go to New York. I want to see Alex. While I'm gone tomorrow, you'll be studying the information here—" Kristen held up her PDA "—and learning how to be me. You'll also get a haircut."

Megan ran her fingers through her damp hair. As much as she admired Kristen's stylish haircut, the thought of hacking off eighteen inches of the strawberry-blond waves that flooded down her back made her queasy. She'd *never* worn her hair short.

"Don't look so green," Kristen said. "It'll grow back. And you might find you like it shorter."

"Maybe so." Megan tried to sound like she didn't care one way or the other, but she was picturing the quiet evenings when she would sit at Pamela's feet and Pamela would brush out Megan's long hair while they watched classic movies. Those evenings had become rare with Megan's hectic work schedule, but Megan still treasured them.

"Toss me my purse," Kristen said. "It's by the TV."

Megan retrieved it, and Kristen opened the purse and pulled out an envelope.

"Here's what you'll need. These are pictures of my hair—front, back, and both sides. Tell the stylist these are computer-generated pictures of you with the haircut you want. The address of the salon and the time of the appointment are written on the envelope." She handed it to Megan. "Oh, and I made the appointment under the name 'Nancy Lurp.'"

"Kris! You nut. Why did you do that?"

Kristen flopped back on her pillow and giggled. "I don't know. I guess I was feeling cloak-and-daggerish, what with all these secret plans to sneak you into Evelyn's house. Remember good old Nancy?"

Megan laughed. 'Nancy Lurp'—the imaginary villain who'd been their nemesis when Kristen and she had played detectives in the field behind their house. They'd spent countless summer days inventing mysteries and searching for clues to thwart the diabolical schemes of Nancy Lurp.

"Remember—remember—" Kristen was laughing so hard she had trouble talking. "Remember when we found that . . . weird green rock . . . and decided it was a nuclear death ball—"

"—and we were yelling about it, and that old guy out for a walk heard us and called the police—" Megan collapsed onto her bed and laughed until tears ran down her face.

Nancy Lurp. Was Kristen's use of the name from childhood just random, or was she deliberately reaching back to a time when Megan and she had been close? A time before Kristen had decided being an identical twin was a freakish embarrassment?

Kristen wiped her eyes. "I wish I could see you try to keep a straight face when you tell the salon people your 'name.'"

"I can keep a straight face, no problem," Megan said. "I've got to stay in character, and Nancy never did have much of a sense of humor."

Chapter 4

Kristen wasn't worried about leaving Megan alone in Philadelphia for the day. Megan had swallowed the bait, and the hook was embedded in her throat. She'd be the good student while Kristen was gone, following every instruction to the letter and panting for more orders so she could prove her genius.

Kristen bit her lip. She'd need to be more careful of her moods. She *had* been a little too edgy this morning when Megan refused to surrender the information about her tutoring program so Kristen could call the library. Megan had insisted she'd tell the library that she was leaving; there were things she needed to discuss with the librarian who helped run the program, and it would be difficult for Kristen to learn enough about the issues to pass herself off as Megan. Trust Megan to jump into the old I'm-smarter-than-you routine. Megan was confident she could swiftly learn enough about Kristen to take over her entire life, but she didn't think Kristen could learn enough about her to make a phone call.

Kristen had considered bullying Megan into cooperating by again threatening to cut her out of the deal, but she sensed this would be a risky time to push too hard. This tutoring program was Megan's pet, and if Kristen refused to let her deal with it personally, Megan would be angry and puzzled—and might start wondering if there were hidden reasons why Kristen didn't want her talking to anyone back home. So Kristen had shrugged it off and pretended to concentrate on doing her hair and makeup while Megan made the call. Megan had done fine, holding to the story of the job in Phoenix and avoiding any mention of Kristen.

Kristen fiddled with the radio of her rental car. Unable to find a good station, she impatiently switched it off. Maybe she *was* being paranoid about Megan's contacting people at home, but the more Megan talked, the more chance she'd blow it somehow. After Megan had talked to the librarian, Kristen had jokingly apologized for being such a control freak. She explained that she was just terrified Pamela would mess this up for them. She begged Megan to promise she wouldn't talk to anyone else in Morris Glen without checking with Kristen first. Megan had rolled her eyes, but she'd promised so readily that it was obvious she didn't *want* to talk to anyone. No doubt she had a killer case of the guilts over leaving so abruptly, plus she wouldn't like repeating that phony job story over and over.

So far so good. Kristen had manipulated Megan with just the right touch. Not too heavy, not too light.

Normally, Kristen got grouchy after being stuck in the car for more than an hour, but the thrill of facing new challenges and conquering them brilliantly kept her spirits high throughout the three-hour drive. The dishwater-blond wig made her scalp itch, and the round glasses and frumpy knit dress made her look like her eighth-grade history teacher, but being in disguise added to the fun.

She wished her father were alive so she'd someday have the chance to zip over for a visit in her Jaguar, drenched in money with Alex at her side. Dad wouldn't even know how to talk to her if he couldn't give her one of his lectures on how she'd never get anywhere if she didn't apply herself, and did she see how hard goody-goody Megan worked, and why couldn't Kristen be more like her?

Yeah, sure. More like Megan, wallowing helplessly in Hicksville. Until I grabbed her by the collar and pulled her out. Who's the successful twin? Who has the skills and guts and brains to succeed?

When Kristen arrived at her hotel in Virginia, she checked in under the false name stamped on the credit card Alex had given her, the same card she'd used to make her reservation. After a few moments in front of the bathroom mirror to confirm that her disguise was perfect, she headed out again, following the directions she'd printed off a computer at the library. She wanted to make sure she knew exactly how to get to the Cherry Blossom Mansion before nightfall. This whole trip would be a huge waste of time if she didn't catch Gail Ludlum coming out of the wedding reception tonight. She didn't know where Gail was staying—in a hotel or with a friend?—so it was either meet her at the reception or miss her in Virginia and end up talking to her in Britteridge. And Evelyn had been adamant that it was a bad idea to meet with Gail at home, not just because someone might see them talking, but also because she wanted Gail to have time to calm down before she returned home. If Gail looked rattled before things started happening, someone might get suspicious.

Personally, Kristen thought it was absurd to drive all the way to Virginia to meet with someone who lived a couple of miles from Evelyn, but if Evelyn wanted to do this the hard way, Kristen would play along.

Kristen found the Cherry Blossom Mansion easily, drove past it, and headed back to her hotel. Room service sounded good right now.

Sitting in her room and munching a Caesar salad, Kristen reviewed the DVD of Bryce Ludlum that she planned to show Gail tonight.

Mama Gail was going to have a rotten evening.

* * *

The first few snips of the scissors had Megan chewing her lip and digging her nails into the arms of the chair, but anxiety gave way to bewilderment as she watched the transformation. The stylist was as skilled at her work as the salon's high prices implied, and when Megan walked out of there—feeling strangely like gravity had weakened—her hairstyle was identical to Kristen's. She glanced curiously at herself in every shop window she passed, and soon she was smiling at her reflection. Why had she agonized over getting her hair cut? She looked classy. Confident.

It took several blocks before she realized she was walking with Kristen's slight, graceful swagger, her chin high. And people were looking at her. Not staring, but darting brief, admiring glances in her direction. Kristen had always attracted admiration. As for Megan, she'd been the reflection, only half visible. If Kristen had still been living in Morris Glen, Luke Wagner would never have looked twice at Megan.

Strange how that thought stung. Why should she care now?

Megan shoved Luke out of her mind. She was finished with him, and thanks to the money Kristen was offering her, she'd never have to see him again.

The sun warmed her shoulders, and the sky was the clear blue of Kristen's eyes. *Of my eyes.* Megan brushed her hair back from her face with a flip of newly manicured nails and smiled a brief Kristen-smile at a young man with a stubbly beard. He grinned back.

Megan wished she could stroll through the door of her house to see Pamela's reaction. Her own mother wouldn't recognize her without the doormat demeanor and the Elly May ponytail.

Mom. Megan's cheerful spirits darkened. She could imagine what Pamela had said to Kristen last night, accusing Megan of cruelty and abandonment.

It *had* been cruel to leave without warning. Why had Kristen insisted on rushing things? Megan should have demanded a few days to prepare Pamela for her departure. Maybe she should call now and try to comfort her . . . but she'd promised Kristen she wouldn't call home. And Megan already knew how the conversation would go. Pamela would weep, berate, and beg. Megan would begin to buckle under a mountain of guilt, the same way she'd buckled on her vow to hold Pamela to their agreement regarding car expenses.

Pamela was perfectly able to take care of herself. Let her do it. And it wouldn't have helped to forewarn her, because Pamela wouldn't change. If Megan gave her a day, she'd spend that day haranguing Megan, trying to get her to change her mind. Same with two days, a week, a month, or a decade.

Pamela would be fine. But to help her over the transition period, Megan would temporarily leave the household bills on automatic withdrawal from Megan's bank account. It made Megan wince to imagine how deeply she'd have to dig into her savings to cover the bills while she had no income, but it wasn't fair to expect Pamela to immediately assume responsibility for all expenses. She'd need time to adjust her lifestyle.

What she really needed to do was sell the house. She didn't need the space. She hated caring for the yard.

She'll be fine, Megan repeated to herself. *Quit obsessing.* She quickened her pace. She needed to get to the hotel and resume studying the information Kristen had given her. By the time Kristen returned from New York, Megan wanted to be so well versed in Kristen's life that Kristen couldn't help but be impressed.

Back in her hotel room, Megan settled in the chair she had occupied all morning, but instead of reaching for Kristen's PDA, she opened her purse. From the inside pocket, she withdrew the flannel bag that protected the hinged, gold-tone picture frame Kristen had given her for Christmas when they were seniors in high school—the last time Kristen had given her a gift until the clothes and jewelry yesterday.

Megan fingered the gold chain around her neck. She had checked the tiny tag on the chain. No metallic paint this time; the chain was 14-karat gold.

Megan opened the hinged frame and studied the picture of her father and herself posing arm-in-arm on the Appalachian Trail, their backpacks propped against a tree nearby. Would her father have condemned her for running out on Pamela without at least attempting to prepare her?

Yes.

But he also would have reprimanded her for lingering at home for years instead of having the guts to pick up the dreams she'd let crash to the ground when he died. He'd been so proud of her achievements, so excited that she was headed to Cornell. The night before his heart attack they'd sat at the kitchen table, planning the drive to Ithaca and deciding where they wanted to stop along the way.

Megan closed her eyes for a moment, pulling her emotions under control before looking at the second photo.

In this childhood snapshot of her and Kristen, they were dressed in matching green sweaters and sitting on a bale of hay. Megan remembered that day clearly—the way they had pretended they were detectives, searching for clues as they followed their parents through the corn maze; the way they'd giggled over the 'clue' they'd found—a 7-Up bottle they'd decided contained poison.

And now, for the first time since they were kids tracking Nancy Lurp, Kristen had come to her, needing her.

Megan ran her fingers through her hair, the strands sliding silkily between her fingers. She didn't like the idea of pretending to be

Kristen, but she understood Kristen's reasons, and she wasn't going to gripe about it.

She didn't want to risk shattering this fragile bridge Kristen had finally built between them.

* * *

Gail Ludlum walked out of the Cherry Blossom Mansion and along the brick sidewalk that led to the parking area. She paused near a wrought-iron lamppost and squinted at the rows of cars, trying to remember where she'd parked.

"Must be getting senile," she muttered, slipping one foot out of its shoe and flexing her sore toes. She was definitely senile, or she wouldn't have worn these shoes, she decided. Any pudgy, fifty-five-year-old woman who crammed her feet into pointy-toed, high-heeled pumps deserved what she got.

There was her car, a blue Honda Accord parked at the far end of the lot. Gail tucked her foot into her shoe and hobbled toward it.

She'd debated whether or not to attend Larry and Tara's wedding, but Bryce had asked her to go and personally deliver his congratulations. Larry had been like a brother to him during that one disastrous year at George Mason University—until Bryce's drug problem had made school impossible.

Gail clopped up to her car, cursing her shoes and cursing the rhinestone bobby pins stabbing her scalp.

The passenger door of the car to the left of Gail's vehicle swung open, and Gail hung back, not wanting to get in the way.

A young woman with long, blond hair stepped out of the car. Gail expected the girl to walk past her, but she stopped at Gail's side.

"I have some information about your son," she whispered.

Disconcerted, Gail stared at the girl. There was something familiar about her, but Gail couldn't think of her name. "Do I know you?"

"We've met. Get in your car and follow me to the Hampton Inn. Here's the address, in case you get lost, and my room number." The girl thrust a slip of paper at Gail. "Once we arrive, wait ten minutes, then head up to my room. We'll talk there. Believe me, you don't want anyone to overhear this conversation."

Gail's heart started a jerky throbbing in her chest. "Listen, missy, I'm not following you anywhere. How dumb do you think I am?"

"Fine," the girl said casually. "I'll take my information to the police."

"What—information?"

"It concerns an incident last July."

"July?" Gail's mouth went Death Valley dry. "I don't know what you're talking about." Despite the protest, her thoughts flashed to that sweltering night when she'd gotten the call that Bryce was in the emergency room, suffering from narcotic withdrawal, a laceration to the back of the scalp and a host of bruises from an airbag that had deployed when he drove over the curb and hit a fire hydrant. The paramedics had said the laceration was not from the auto accident, but Bryce had been too incoherent to explain how he got it.

Gail had never found out exactly what happened that night.

The girl smiled. She was wearing round glasses that were the wrong shape for her face, and a frumpy knit dress that bunched around her slim figure.

"Follow me to my hotel, or I've got a pile of evidence I'll be turning over to the Britteridge police," she repeated.

"Fine," Gail snapped.

Perspiration beaded beneath Gail's velvet jacket as she drove. Maybe this girl was a vengeful ex-girlfriend out to get Bryce belatedly arrested on charges of drug possession. Or did she think she had something even more incriminating?

What *had* occurred that July night? For several weeks after Bryce's accident, Gail had had the sense he was waiting, terrified, for something to happen. Nothing ever did, at least nothing Gail witnessed, beyond the expected penalties for driving while impaired. And to Gail's intense relief, Bryce had agreed to go into a treatment center. Now he was doing so well.

But what if Bryce *had* done something terrible?

What did this girl want? Money? What else could she possibly be after?

At the hotel, Gail sat in her car and watched the girl walk into the hotel, her body moving with snakelike grace. After the requisite ten minutes, Gail plodded after her.

The girl's hotel room door swung open the instant Gail's knuckles touched it. Gail stepped into the room, and the girl swiftly shut the door behind her.

"Glad you could make it." Her cocky little smile knocked Gail's misaligned memories into place, and Gail gawked at her.

"You're Rachel Drake's friend," Gail said. "You were at the Drakes' Labor Day picnic. Kristen, isn't it?"

"Good call, doc. Glad to see your Alzheimer's isn't too advanced yet. Have a seat."

"Your hair—"

"A wig. Tonight I'm working incognito. I would have gone for a hairdo like yours, but the party store was out of fright wigs. Sit down."

Stiffly, Gail sat at the table.

Kristen dropped a manila envelope in front of her. "Brace yourself. Your son was up to some bad stuff last summer."

Gail blinked at the envelope, her throat constricting. "If you think you can blackmail him over his drug problem, that's old news. He's clean now."

"Glad to hear it." Kristen sat in the other chair. "Off doing good works down south, I hear. Building houses for poor people. How noble."

"Listen, sweetie, I don't know what your problem is—"

"You remember hearing last summer about William Seaver, the old guy who tripped on his cane and fell down the stairs? Died of a compressed skull fracture."

"Yes, I—of course I saw that in the local paper. Sad accident. But what does—"

"Want to know what really happened?"

Gail clenched her shaking hands together in her lap. "I don't know what you mean."

Kristen opened the envelope she'd placed in front of Gail and removed a DVD. The label was blank except for a date: July 11.

"William Seaver was a paranoid old coot," Kristen said. "He was my great-uncle, if you're interested."

"Your uncle!"

"A couple of years back, he got this bee in his bonnet that Aunt Evelyn was having an affair while he was off playing golf. The guy was nuts, obviously. Evelyn was too old and *way* too prim and proper for any hanky-panky, but he thought she was carrying on with their next-door neighbor. He rigged a few cameras in the house—one by the front door, one by the garage door, one at the top of the stairs. He was an electronics nerd, so this was tons of fun for him."

Kristen opened a laptop computer. "He and Evelyn patched things up before he died—maybe he got back on his meds or something—but the cameras remained. And on July eleventh, they got some interesting footage. Want to see?"

"What do you want from me?" Gail whispered.

Kristen popped the DVD into the slot on the computer. "Shall I make popcorn?"

Chapter 5

Stir-crazy and with the muscles in her forehead crocheted into knots from staring at Kristen's PDA screen too long, Megan left the hotel at nine o'clock in the morning and went for a walk. When she returned an hour later, Kristen was there, furiously pacing the room.

"Where have you been?" Kristen snapped.

Startled at the anger in her voice, Megan held up a bakery bag. "I went for some breakfast. And to stretch my legs."

"Didn't I tell you to stay in the hotel once you'd finished getting yourself fixed up?"

"No, *Mother*, you didn't. You told me to memorize the info you gave me, and I did. What's wrong with you, anyway?"

"Did you talk to anyone while you were out? Introduce yourself?"

"I said, 'Two chocolate croissants, please' to the bakery guy. We didn't get friendly enough to exchange names. Oh, I also ran into Mom and told her all our plans."

"Cute," Kristen said acidly.

"Kris, relax. All I did was go to the bakery. One of these croissants is for you if you want it." Megan set the bag on the table.

Kristen snatched the bag and took out a pastry. Megan studied her. Maybe she was just in a bad mood from the drive. Megan could sympathize with that; she always felt cranky and claustrophobic after too much time in the car.

"How was New York?" Megan asked tentatively.

Kristen sprawled on the bed. "Fun." She sounded irritable, but most of the anger in her voice had faded. "Turn around. Let me see the back of your hair."

Megan pivoted slowly.

"Not bad," Kristen said. "All right. Quiz time. Let's see if you really did learn anything."

"Quiz away." Megan took the other croissant.

"What's Evelyn's house number?"

"24."

"Does Evelyn prefer tea or coffee?"

"Tea. She hates coffee."

"Where does she keep her pain medication?"

"In an antique silver pillbox on the table near her recliner in the family room. And she doesn't like you to take out a pill and hand it to her. Just give her the box."

"Describe Rachel Drake."

Megan had expected more questions about Evelyn first, but she quickly pictured the photo of Kristen's friend Rachel. Rachel had been eating a bowl of cereal when Kristen snapped the picture, and she was brandishing a spoon at the camera and laughing. Curly, brown hair cut in a casual bob, rounded cheeks, eyes the color of maple syrup. Deftly, Megan described her.

"What does Rachel want to do when she graduates?" Kristen asked.

"Be a wedding consultant."

"Rachel's brother," Kristen said. "What's his name?"

"She has three brothers. Evan, Trevor, and Joshua. Evan is married and lives in Kentucky. Trevor is twenty-five and lives in Britteridge. Josh is sixteen and lives with his parents in Andover, about twenty-five minutes away from Britteridge. Josh is a junior in high school. Trevor works at Britteridge College in the admissions office." She pictured the photo of Trevor. Sandy hair, trimmed short and neat. Brown eyes like his sister's, and broad, muscular shoulders. He looked like the kind of guy who would stop to help you change a flat tire, and if you didn't have a spare, he'd heave the car over his head and carry it to the nearest garage for you.

"Who is Tricia Mortimer?"

"Lives in the apartment next door to you, number 32. Short, black hair, New England Patriots fanatic, elementary ed major. From New Hampshire."

"Tom Hoffman."

"Apartment manager. Looks like a sickly Clint Eastwood."

"Larissa Mullins?"

"Rachel Drake's friend. Platinum blond hair, thin face, doesn't like makeup. Working on a master's degree in art."

"What's Evelyn's phone number?"

Megan recited it.

"What's my cell phone number—I mean the cell phone registered to me that you'll be using?"

Megan recited it.

"What's the phone number you'll use to get in touch with me?"

Megan recited it.

"Tell me how to get from Evelyn's house to the post office."

Megan pulled the pad of hotel stationery toward her and sketched a map. She labeled the streets and drew a square for the post office. "Here's the grocery store." She added another square then sketched another road and labeled it. "If you turn left here, then bear right, you'll find the shopping center that has the dry cleaners Evelyn prefers—"

"Quit showing off," Kristen said, but she was smiling. She shot a few more questions at Megan, then jumped to her feet.

"Here's the plan. Today we drive to Britteridge, but not together. You'll drive in my car. I'll drive a rental. You'll stay in my apartment tonight. You don't have to be out of the apartment and settled at Evelyn's until Thursday the sixteenth, so you've got a week and a half to get used to Britteridge before you're onstage full time."

Apprehension surged through Megan. She hadn't expected Kristen to hand everything over to her so quickly.

"Don't worry," Kristen said. "I'll be in a hotel half an hour or so away. Whenever I go out, I'll be in disguise so there aren't two Kristens running around, but I *will* stick around for a couple of weeks until you're feeling secure."

"Good thing," Megan said. "I'm out of practice pretending to be you. We haven't tried this game since the time you paid me to swap shirts with you and stay home to clean your room so you could sneak out with your friends. We figured Dad wouldn't look up from his newspaper long enough to notice the switch."

"Why would he have noticed? He thought he had only one daughter anyway." There was an edge of bitterness to Kristen's voice and Megan instantly dropped her joking smile.

"Kris, you know that's not—"

Kristen made an impatient gesture. "Tomorrow, you'll visit Evelyn and show her my pictures of New York. I'll go over them with you before we leave this morning so you can tell her all about 'your' trip."

Megan nodded.

"We'll meet after your trial run with Evelyn so we can discuss how things went," Kristen added. "Sound good?"

"Yes. Where will you go after I'm settled?"

A gleeful smile curved Kristen's lips. "Paris."

"Paris!"

"Alex is taking me to Paris. He's going on a business trip, and he invited me to come with him. We'll stay for ten days after he finishes his work."

"No wonder you were so anxious to get free of Evelyn," Megan said dryly.

"You got that right. Paris—or nursemaiding a whiny old lady? Wow, tough choice."

"You'd better bring me a nice souvenir, or I'll rat on you to Evelyn's lawyer." Megan regretted the teasing remark even as she said it. Considering Kristen's mercurial moods this morning, there was no telling how she'd react.

"Blackmail!" Kristen clutched her heart. "Fine. I'll bring you a shirt that says, 'My Evil Twin Went to Paris and All I Got Was this Lousy T-Shirt.'"

They both laughed.

"Get packed up," Kristen said. "I'll take your suitcase, and you'll take mine. We'll switch purses too, so you'll have my ID. I'll leave my credit cards in the purse, but don't use them. Evelyn gave me an ATM/Visa card for her account, and she likes me to use that for everything I buy, even personal stuff."

"Evelyn gave you access to her bank account?" Megan asked in astonishment.

"Just the one checking account. She doesn't keep more than a couple thousand dollars in there at any given time. But yes, she wants to support me. She doesn't want me going out and taking a job that would cut into my ability to care for her. Just be reasonable in what you buy, and Evelyn will be fine with it. Don't buy a diamond necklace, but if you want some new shoes, buy them on Evelyn's tab. I know it feels weird, but she'll expect you to do it, and she'll be offended if she thinks you're paying for things on your own."

"Sounds good and bad."

"I know. It's like being a kid again, but really, use the card. It makes Evelyn feel good, and that's our goal, right?"

"Hey, if it makes her feel good to have me spend her money, I'll spend away."

"That's the spirit. And I'll take your purse in case I need a driver's license or what all. I'll keep my passport, of course, since I'm going to—" she grinned widely "—need it. Besides, you don't have one I could steal, do you?"

"Unfortunately, no."

"We'll fix that once we've got some real money. Where would you like to go? Name our destination. London? Australia? The Great Wall of China?"

Unable to repress a smile at the way Kristen had teamed them up with all the "we" ideas, Megan asked, "How will you pay for the hotel you'll stay at before you leave? Are you going to use my credit card?"

"Don't get twitchy worrying about your bill. I'll use one of my cards. I already took it out of my purse. Now, I'm going to go soak in a hot bath. My back is in knots."

As soon as Kristen closed the bathroom door, Megan took her own purse and dumped it on the bed. If Kristen was going to take her purse, Megan wanted it to be neat. She chucked a granola bar wrapper, a dozen receipts from Gardner's, and an expired coupon for laundry soap. Kristen probably didn't want her lipstick either. And the picture—Megan tucked the flannel bag more smoothly around the frame and hid it in the pocket of her jacket.

"Name our destination."

If Kristen's friendship was part of the package, Megan didn't care where they went.

Chapter 6

Kristen found Alex in the living room, his lean body stretched out on a recliner and a newspaper in his hands. Behind him, a sliding door led out to a wooden deck. Trees aflame with gold, copper, and crimson covered the slope that led down to Britteridge Pond. How much did a house in a location like this cost? A familiar anger twisted Kristen's stomach, but this time it was edged with anticipation.

Soon she'd have the money she deserved. Well, some of it anyway. This was just the beginning.

Alex didn't look up from his newspaper. Kristen knew he was pretending not to care that she'd returned in order to annoy her, but she found it funny. Alex was so transparent. Mr. Cool, Mr. I-can-take-you-or-leave-you. *As if.* Besides, she didn't mind a few uninterrupted seconds to study Alex's flawless, tanned face; his cropped, sun-bleached hair; his sinewy arms. Alex wasn't a big man, but he was all muscle.

He finally lowered his newspaper, allowing Kristen a look at a muscled torso sheathed in a tight black T-shirt. She gave an appreciative grin.

Alex folded his newspaper and dropped it by the side of the chair. "Well?"

"Does that mean 'welcome back, I missed you'?"

"It *means* are we set? Did everything go all right?"

"Of course we're set. Did you know you look like a cop? I'm surprised your friends trust you."

Alex surveyed her with eyes the cool green of honeydew melon. "And you look ridiculous in that black wig."

"You don't like it?" Kristen ran her fingers through her ebony hair.

"You look like the Addams Family."

"Fine." Kristen removed the wig and dropped it on the couch. "But I wore my brown one in Pennsylvania and my blond one in Virginia, so in Britteridge, I'm Morticia." She took a picture from her pocket and held it out. "Take a look. It's Megan. Not bad, huh?"

Alex rose smoothly to his feet and came to take the picture. "Yeah, she looks like you. But are you sure she can handle it?"

"She'll handle it all right. She wants the cash. Bad. But more than that, she wants to impress me."

"But under pressure—"

"I know how Megan thinks, Alex. Once she's hooked, she's hooked. You could pull out her fingernails, and she still wouldn't risk ruining things with me by blowing our 'inheritance.'"

"I guess it's not hard to play Kristen O'Connor." Alex ran his index fingers along Kristen's cheekbones. "A cynical smile and a triple helping of arrogance covers ninety-five percent of it."

Before he could kiss her, Kristen stepped back and was gratified by the frustration in his eyes.

"The work's all finished," he said curtly. "Want a look?"

"Good, yes." Kristen followed him out of the living room and up a staircase. "Nice place," she commented. "Our guest will be comfortable."

Alex stopped in front of a door at the end of the hall. "Solid wood, nice and heavy." He tapped the door with his knuckles. "And I added this lock, just to be safe."

Kristen eyed the shiny dead bolt, strangely out of place on an interior door. "I hope the owner doesn't mind," she joked.

"He'll never know. I'll fix it up before we leave so he won't be able to tell anything was done."

"Not that he'll be here anytime soon," Kristen said. "Evelyn told me he hasn't been here in years. Why he wants to keep paying taxes on the place is beyond me."

Alex stepped into the bedroom and flipped the light switch. All the furniture was gone, except for a bed Alex had pushed close to the door of the adjoining bathroom. Cardboard was taped over the window.

"We'll keep her blindfolded," Alex said. "But it's still safer if we have as little contact with her as possible." With his toe, he nudged a steel cable coiled on the hardwood floor next to the bed. One end of the cable was connected to a metal plate bolted to the floor. At the other end was a hinged metal band.

"This is her leash." Alex picked up the shackle. "It'll be fastened around her ankle."

Kristen took the shackle and tested its weight. It was heavier than she expected.

"Take a tour of the room and see what her boundaries are," Alex suggested.

Holding the shackle, Kristen walked into the bathroom, the cable uncoiling behind her. She circled the bedroom and found she couldn't reach the door to the hallway. Same with the window.

"Clever," she said.

"We'll put a stash of food in the room—non-perishable stuff like crackers and dried fruit. A cup for water. We'll peek in a couple of times a day to check on her, but other than that, we don't need to have contact with her."

"How can we be sure she'll stay blindfolded? Won't she rip it off first chance she gets?"

"She can't take it off. We'll glue it to her skin with an adhesive that will rip holes in her face if she tried to remove it. You need a solvent. We'll take it off her while she's drugged, right before we release her. By the way, did you get the dope?"

"I'll pick it up from our doctor friend this afternoon."

"Good. Make sure to get enough, because whenever we leave her unguarded, we'll need to drug her. We can't take the chance that some stray nature nut will wander by and hear her yelling. Let's keep this nice and easy."

Kristen snapped the shackle closed to test the locking mechanism. "Nice and easy," she echoed.

* * *

Megan had just inserted the key into the lock on Kristen's apartment when a "Boo!" from behind made her jump. She whirled to see a smiling face, lively brown eyes, and dark curls ruffling in the breeze.

Rachel Drake.

Stage fright smacked Megan with a second wave of adrenaline. *Stay calm,* she berated herself. *It's not that hard.*

"Sheesh, Rach, you scared me," Megan said.

Rachel laughed. "That was the idea." She was taller than Megan had realized, nearly matching Megan's five-eight. She was dressed in a cranberry-red sweater, chunky beaded jewelry, and a floral skirt, and Megan's first impulse was to ask why she was so dressed up. Just in time, she held the question back, realizing she should already know the answer. It was Sunday, and Rachel was a regular churchgoer. Kristen had mentioned that Mormons usually got dressy for their services.

"I saw your car pull in and thought I'd come welcome you back," Rachel said. "How was New York?"

"Who cares how New York was?" Megan swung Kristen's apartment door open. "Try asking me about *Alex*."

Rachel giggled. "How was *Alex*?"

"Oh, babe, words don't do him justice. You'll have to keep wondering."

"Brat."

Megan's heartbeat raced as she imagined Rachel saying, *Where is Kristen and who are you?* but there wasn't even a hint of suspicion in Rachel's eyes.

"You're just in time," Rachel said. "A bunch of us are getting together at my place for dinner. Want to join us?"

Quickly, Megan debated the offer. Would Kristen accept? Probably not. After hours in the car, Kristen would be tired and cranky.

"Thanks, but I'm so exhausted that I think I'll stick a cup of soup in the microwave and go to bed early." Megan was glad to have an excuse to decline. She didn't want to spend the evening under scrutiny.

"If you change your mind, you know where to find us. Or wait—forget the cup of soup. The lasagna's already out of the oven. I'll run grab you a piece. That way you don't have to worry about dinner and can just relax."

"Oh no, don't go to any trouble," Megan protested. "I can just—"

"Don't even try to resist. I know your weakness for Italian food, and this is my grandmother's recipe. Four kinds of cheese, plum tomatoes, fresh basil, Italian sausage—my apartment smelled so good while it was cooking that I was ready to eat the walls."

Megan smiled, realizing she was famished. She'd been so nervous on the drive up here that she hadn't stopped for lunch, so all she'd had to eat today was that chocolate croissant. Knowing Kristen, she wouldn't have any good food on hand, so a decent meal would mean going to a grocery store or a restaurant. Megan didn't feel like going out. And Rachel looked so eager to be helpful. "If you're going to force it on me . . ."

"Be right back." Rachel breezed off.

Megan stepped inside Kristen's apartment and looked around. *Bland* was the best word for the place, everything beige and brown and sturdy. Though Kristen hadn't mentioned it, it was obvious the apartment had come furnished. This décor didn't reflect Kristen's taste at all.

Megan drew a deep breath to loosen the tension in her shoulders. She'd had her first test with one of Kristen's friends and she'd passed. Rachel seemed nice—*too* nice, hyper-nice in a way that would get on Kristen's nerves. It surprised Megan that Kristen was willing to put up with her, no matter the advantages of having a rich friend who threw money around. Megan supposed it was because Rachel did all the genealogy research Kristen had used to soften up Evelyn, but still . . .

She walked into Kristen's bedroom. The carpet had been recently vacuumed, but some of the books had fallen over on the shelves, and the dresser top was cluttered with stray earrings, drinking glasses, and magazines. Kristen wasn't a slob, but she tended to clean the center of a room and forget about the edges.

Megan opened all Kristen's drawers, then fingered through the clothes hanging in her closet. Kristen preferred solid colors in shades of blue and green. Megan held an aqua-blue, V-neck sweater up to her chin and looked in the mirror above the dresser.

Not bad.

Megan returned the sweater to the closet and pulled out a mint-green sheath dress. It was going to be fun wearing Kristen's clothes.

She hung up the dress and went to examine Kristen's books. In addition to the books haphazardly arranged on the shelves, several piles of books were pushed up against the wall. The surfeit of reading material made Megan smile. Megan could never fit all her books on the shelves at home either.

Interspersed with a bunch of novels were business textbooks from Kristen's brief stint at SUNY Stony Brook on Long Island. Odd that Kristen would keep them. She'd dropped out of the program, dismissing it as useless. Maybe she kept the books so she'd look more academic in a college town?

Megan slid the textbooks off the shelf one by one. She'd driven past Britteridge College on her way here and had admired the beautifully landscaped grounds and the classic look of the buildings. Soon . . . when she had her share of Evelyn's money . . .

She couldn't go to Britteridge College, of course. Even after Evelyn's death, Kristen and she couldn't remain in the same community without raising eyebrows. But there would be plenty of possibilities once Megan had the money to pay her way.

She imagined the astonishment that would appear on Pamela's face when Megan showed up with a college diploma *and* an excellent job offer in hand. Pamela had always told Megan education was overrated and success was mainly a matter of luck.

Megan would love to prove her wrong.

She absently straightened Kristen's bookshelf. A green, leather case that looked like a cross between a purse and a small briefcase sat on the end of the shelf. Megan unzipped the case and found two books bound in green leather. The thicker of the two was a Bible. The thinner—Megan read the print on the spine—Book of Mormon, Doctrine and Covenants, Pearl of Great Price. Kristen's name was embossed on the covers of the books in gold italic script.

These books must be a gift from Rachel. Kristen had mentioned that she occasionally attended Rachel's religious study class. Megan had asked her what they discussed, but Kristen's answer had been less than informative. *"Oh, some guy named Leffy or Lefty who goes around preaching at people. I don't really pay attention. If anyone asks me about it, I just say, 'It gave me such a good feeling.' They love that."*

Megan flipped through the volume that contained the Book of Mormon. The gold foil on the edges of the new pages stuck together in several spots, and Megan carefully worked the pages apart with her fingertips. Apparently, Kristen hadn't bothered to do much reading.

The doorbell rang. Megan hurried to answer it.

Rachel held out a foil-covered plate. The aroma of garlic, tomato, and basil made Megan's mouth water.

"Dinner is served. Trev made the bread, and it looks awesome."

"Your brother made the bread?" Megan took the plate. The Drakes weren't at all what she'd expected.

"His best focaccia yet. How is your aunt doing, by the way? Okay, dumb question. You haven't had a chance to talk to her since you got back."

"I talked to her last night." Actually, Kristen had talked to her, but close enough. "She's hanging in there, but she'll be glad when I move in."

"You're so sweet to help her out, but I'll miss having you here at the Tacky Arms." Rachel licked a fleck of tomato sauce off her thumb. "I love old people, the more eccentric the better. My Grandma Katrina—the one who just passed away—had purple hair. I mean *really* purple hair, like grape popsicles. She also had a collection of about forty lava lamps and a big, ugly cat named Louis XVI. She made him a velvet pillow embroidered with a picture of a guillotine. I think it was a warning, but it didn't work. He still scratched the furniture."

Megan laughed. "I can't imagine Aunt Evelyn allowing *any* kind of animal into her house. Or a lava lamp, for that matter." She held up the plate. "Thanks again for the dinner. And thank Trevor too."

"Our pleasure. Oh, I wanted to remind you about the service project this Friday. I can't remember if I gave you the time."

Service project? Was that the "singles' party" at Rachel's church that Kristen had told her to attend?

"Seven?" Megan asked.

"Yep. Guess I did tell you."

"What are you going to wear?" Megan hoped the question didn't sound awkward. She'd never been to a church gathering like this and didn't know if she should come in a dress or cutoffs.

"Just jeans, a sweater, something casual. We'll be decorating pumpkins and sorting donated Halloween costumes. Then donuts and cider."

"Isn't it early to carve pumpkins? They'll be black mush by Halloween."

"We're not carving them. We're painting them and donating them to a homeless shelter and a women's shelter. For the kids, you know. So bring your artistic skills."

"You want to loan me some?"

"Sorry. I can't even do stick figures."

"I'm sitting by you, then, so I won't look so bad."

"Deal. And . . . are you interested in coming to institute on Tuesday?"

The religion class. Kristen had told her to attend that as well, though Megan couldn't fathom why it mattered. "Sure."

Rachel waved and headed back toward her apartment. "You look fantastic, by the way," she called over her shoulder. "New York did you good. Oh, sorry. I mean *Alex* did you good."

Laughing, Megan closed the door.

From Megan the shadow to Kristen the vivid. Why had she ever been reluctant to play Kristen? This wouldn't be hard.

It might well be the best time of her life.

Chapter 7

The white wooden shingles and dark blue shutters looked freshly painted, the grass was trimmed, and the dried buds had been picked from the pots of chrysanthemums, but somehow, Evelyn Seaver's house still had a lonely, deserted look. Maybe it was the closed blinds, Megan thought.

Or maybe her apprehension was warping her view of the house.

The home of a dying, elderly woman.

Taking more time than she needed, Megan located the correct key on Kristen's key ring and unlocked Evelyn's front door. Despite the key, she felt as though she were breaking and entering.

She stepped inside and paused to orient herself, Kristen's slapdash sketch of the floor plan fresh in her mind. Directly in front of her was a staircase with a carved handrail and a red-and-blue stair runner. The bedrooms were upstairs. To her right was the living room, dimly lit due to the closed blinds. A hall led off from the living room; if she turned right, she'd find a study and a bathroom, to the left a dining room, kitchen, and family room. Beyond the family room was the garage.

Steeling herself, Megan proceeded toward the family room, where Kristen had said Evelyn spent most of her daylight hours. The hallway was lined with dozens of framed photographs. Megan glanced at them as she walked past and saw several pictures of a dark-haired girl.

"Kristen?" A tremulous voice came from the family room.

"Yes." Megan hurried her step.

In a recliner across from a TV waited a skinny, white-haired woman in a pink bathrobe. Megan's first impression was that despite the white hair, Evelyn didn't look as old as she had anticipated.

"Welcome back, dear!" Evelyn tapped the remote to switch the television off.

Megan moved forward to hug Evelyn. Evelyn's body was surprisingly firm beneath Megan's embrace.

"How are you feeling?" Megan asked.

"A little better. Aurora was here yesterday, and she said I'm looking spry." Evelyn gave a dainty laugh. "She's certainly a glass-half-full girl, isn't she?"

Aurora Capra. The home nurse who stopped in periodically to check on Evelyn.

"You're certainly looking good this morning," Megan said, not sure if this were true. Evelyn looked colorless and tired, but how else could she look?

"How was your trip, dear? New York is such an exciting city. Did you go to the top of the Empire State Building?"

"Yes, we did. I took a bunch of pictures. Would you like to see them now, or would you like some tea first?"

Evelyn rubbed her hands together. "I do love pictures. Bring a chair next to me and let's see them."

Megan pushed an ottoman next to Evelyn's recliner, sat down, and drew the packet of Kristen's pictures from her purse.

"You're flushed, dear," Evelyn said. "It can't be *that* warm outside, can it?"

"The—room's a little stuffy," Megan said, appalled that her nervousness was visible. *Calm down. Rachel thought you were Kristen. Evelyn will too.* "Do you mind if I open a window? It's a beautiful morning."

"Please do."

Megan moved to the window with alacrity. The room *was* warm, stiflingly so, and it reeked of roses. Megan spotted the offending air freshener plugged into an outlet.

She returned to the ottoman and opened the envelope of pictures. Evelyn rested her hand on Megan's arm and spent an interminable length of time studying each photo, oohing and ahhing over everything from the Statue of Liberty to the tie-dyed T-shirt a newspaper seller was wearing. By the time Evelyn was halfway through the stack, Megan had no doubts whatsoever about why Kristen had been willing to give her a cut of the money in exchange for some freedom. If this was an example of the tedium involved in caring for Evelyn, it was amazing Kristen hadn't already gone nuts.

"So exciting." Evelyn sighed as she finished her examination of the final picture. Quickly, Megan slid the pictures into the envelope lest Evelyn start through the stack again. "Your gentleman friend and you are such a handsome couple. Dear, could you fetch me a glass of water and hand me my pills? I'm overdue, and the pain . . ."

Megan brought the water and handed Evelyn the round silver pillbox from the table near her chair.

"That breeze is lovely." Evelyn gestured at the rippling curtains. "But it does give me a small chill."

"Should I close the window?"

"Oh no. Just hand me that afghan, would you, please?"

Megan took the folded blanket off the back of the couch. Hanging above the couch was an oil painting of the same girl whose photos Megan had glimpsed in the hallway. She was a pretty girl with long, dark hair parted in the middle, a shy smile, and pale blue eyes like Evelyn's. This must be Evelyn's daughter. Megan had asked Kristen how she'd died, but Kristen didn't know.

Megan draped the afghan over Evelyn's legs. "Is that better?"

"Much. I missed you, dear. It was a long week."

"I missed you too. Would you like something to eat along with your tea?"

"No, thank you. You know my stomach can't handle much these days."

"How about some toast?"

"No, no. Just the tea will be fine."

"I'll bring it right away." Glad to escape, Megan headed for the kitchen. Remembering Kristen's instructions, she opened the door to the pantry and fetched a bottle of water. Evelyn didn't mind taking her medication with tap water, Kristen had said, but she insisted on bottled water for tea.

Megan poured water into the flowered teapot on the stove. While the water heated, she quietly familiarized herself with the kitchen. Baking sheets were in the drawer under the stove. Silverware to the right of the dishwasher. Copper pots hung from a wall-mounted rack, each pot polished so brightly that Megan couldn't imagine using any of them for cooking. She opened the cupboards, taking inventory. Everything was precisely arranged, with nary a crumb in sight. Kristen had warned her Evelyn was a neat freak, and Megan made a mental note to put everything back exactly where she found it.

She opened the fridge. It was well stocked; Kristen had filled it for Evelyn before she left, though she hadn't expected Evelyn to eat much. Most of the food was simple and bland: applesauce, yogurt, sliced turkey, apples.

Megan closed the fridge and finished making Evelyn's tea. English Breakfast tea in the mornings, Kristen had said, with just a taste of sugar.

Carrying the tea, Megan headed back to the family room, her throat already clogging with the cloying smell of roses.

"What would you like me to do this morning?" Megan set the cup and saucer on the table next to Evelyn.

"The bathrooms need a good cleaning, dear, if you wouldn't mind."

"I'll start right away. Call if you need me."

As Megan walked along the hallway, the photographs again drew her attention. Curious, she stopped and switched on the light so she could see the pictures more clearly. It surprised her that someone so lacking in family connections would have a wall of pictures rivaling the busiest grandmother's photo gallery.

A baby in a ruffled yellow dress. The same girl, now a toddler, pushing a teddy bear in a stroller. A first-grader with a dimple in her cheek and missing front teeth. A radiant young woman in a cap and gown, accepting a diploma. Megan skimmed all the pictures. There were at least a hundred photographs here, and every one of them was of the same girl. Evelyn's daughter.

How old had she been when she died? Megan studied what looked like the most recent of the pictures. Her early twenties, maybe? She was wearing a rose-pink pantsuit and a blouse with a white bow at the neck. Her hair was styled in big, fluffy curls.

The proportions of the picture were odd. It was tall and narrow, looking as though part of the picture had been trimmed away to remove an unwanted element. The photo was matted on pink cardstock to fill up the extra space in the frame.

"She's lovely, isn't she?"

Megan whirled to see Evelyn standing at the end of the hall.

"You startled me." Megan forced a laugh.

"I'm sorry, dear. It's these slippers. They turn me into a veritable cat burglar."

Megan manufactured another laugh. What a fool she was to stand here gawking at photographs Kristen would have seen dozens of times already.

"I'd better get started on the bathrooms," she began, but Evelyn shuffled to her side and took her by the arm.

"This is my last picture of Judith." She touched the frame of the picture Megan had been studying. "Her twenty-first birthday."

"She's beautiful," Megan said, relieved Evelyn didn't seem suspicious of "Kristen's" sudden interest in the pictures. In fact, Evelyn looked pleased. There was pink in her cheeks and a dreamy smile on her lips.

"She died that night," Evelyn said softly.

Megan was shocked. "I'm so sorry." To die on her birthday—and she was only twenty-one. "How . . . did she die?"

"She was riding her bicycle home, very late. She loved to bicycle. If it wasn't snowing or raining, she was on her bicycle. Do you enjoy bicycling, dear?"

"I haven't done much of it. But I do a lot of walking and hiking." Too late, she realized she'd answered more for herself than for Kristen.

"Oh yes, oh yes. A healthy girl." Evelyn stroked Megan's arm. "Judith was hit by a car. She died almost instantly."

"I'm so sorry."

"I know, dear." Evelyn's fingers tightened on Megan's arm. "You never forget, you know. Time doesn't heal. I've carried that night in my heart for twenty-six years. I remember every detail."

Megan laid her hand over Evelyn's, not knowing what to say.

"You remind me of Judith. So sweet and kind." Evelyn smiled at Megan. "It feels right to have you here. I know Judith would approve."

* * *

"Well?" Kristen tilted horn-rimmed glasses down and looked at Megan over the top of the lenses. "How'd you do?"

"Fine," Megan said. Along with the eyeglasses, Kristen was wearing a black wig and a billowy, purple blouse that was far from her usual sleek style. Megan had to admit just those few changes made a decent disguise; Megan had glanced at the woman behind the wheel of the white Saturn and had nearly driven past her, ready to continue searching the North Shore Mall parking lot for another car matching the description of Kristen's rental.

"Go on," Kristen said. "Who have you talked to? Are you remembering all the stuff I told you, or do you need to ask me anything?"

"I'm remembering things fine. Except for things you neglected to tell me in the first place. I searched for fifteen minutes this morning before I found the toilet brush."

Kristen threw back her head and laughed. "Sorry about that. Yeah, she keeps all the bathroom brushes and cleaning rags in that cupboard in the garage. Weird, I know. She thinks they're icky or something and doesn't want to store them in her pristine house. So did you run into anyone besides Evelyn?"

"Just Rachel Drake." Megan toyed with Kristen's purse, repeatedly unzipping and zipping it. "She invited me to dinner last night, but I told her I was too tired." Megan decided not to mention Rachel's bringing dinner over. Either Kristen would make fun of Rachel for offering or Megan for accepting.

Kristen eyed the Gucci handbag in Megan's lap. "Easy on the purse, all right? You know how much that thing cost?"

Megan zipped the purse and set it on the floor of the car. "I know it's ridiculous to fork over that kind of money for a purse—or to use Evelyn's money on it."

"It was a birthday present from Rachel. Told you there were benefits to being friends with Princess Bubble Brain."

"Some friend you are. Rachel goes out of her way to be nice to you and you insult her behind her back."

"Don't get preachy. Rachel will never know, so why can't I say what I think? Rachel's fun, but she's an airhead."

"She didn't strike me as an airhead."

"All right, you convinced me. She's Einstein's clone. Now, besides the toilet scrubber debacle, did everything go all right with Evelyn?"

"Yes. We looked at your New York pictures. I made her tea. I cleaned the bathrooms. She watched a couple of game shows. No problems." Megan debated mentioning what Evelyn had said about her daughter's tragic death, but decided against it. Kristen would tear Megan apart if she knew Megan had been gawking at those photographs of Judith like she'd never seen them before.

"Oh, Rachel mentioned her religion class on Tuesday and the church project on Friday," Megan said.

"You told her you still wanted to come, I hope."

"Yes, but I don't see why it matters. Your kissing up to the Mormons is silly. If you're really interested, fine, but why fake it?"

"Frosting on the cake, babe. Evelyn likes it when I go to churchy stuff. She thinks religion makes young people—and I quote—'more proper.'"

"Is she religious herself?"

"I think she's Catholic, but she never goes. But she likes Mormons. Strict moral code and all that." Kristen twisted the key in the ignition. "You should have an easy week, but don't drop your guard no matter where you are. Britteridge is a small community, and word spreads fast. If you blow your identity with Rachel or any of her friends, I guarantee Evelyn will know about it within the hour. Got it?"

"I've got it," Megan said irritably. "How many times do we have to go through this? I'm you. No matter what happens, I'm you. If a policeman pulls me over and asks my name, I'm you. If Michael Drake—"

Kristen tuned the radio to a jazz station and spun the volume up loud.

Chapter 8

After a tedious few days spent cleaning Evelyn's already immaculate house, running errands, and packing up Kristen's belongings to ferry them to Evelyn's basement, Megan was glad when Friday night arrived. As edgy as she was about attending Rachel's church party, at least it would be a diversion—the first one all week. Rachel's religion class had been canceled on Tuesday when the teacher had been called away at the last minute for a family emergency, a fact that had annoyed Kristen when Megan told her. Why was she so set on Megan's getting cozy with Rachel Drake and her friends? She must really believe that a show of religious involvement would make her look even better to Evelyn. Either that or she just didn't want her supply of Gucci purses to dry up.

Rachel drove Megan to the church in her red Lexus, chattering happily about upcoming midterm exams, the opening of a new pizza place two blocks from their apartment complex, the glories of the crisp October evening, and an embarrassing childhood trick-or-treating incident involving a caramel sucker and a fake beard. Megan laughed in all the right places and encouraged Rachel's chatter; it kept her from having to come up with anything to say herself. Kristen must be nursing jaw injuries from holding back the sarcasm she used to flatten people as bubbly as Rachel.

As a steeple came into view, Megan felt a twinge of curiosity. She hadn't set foot in a church since she was five or six. She had vague memories of going to Sunday School as a child—she didn't even know which church they'd attended—but after her father's business had collapsed, Pamela hadn't bothered to attend anymore. Pamela figured if God wanted worship, He should have kept them rich.

Rachel's redbrick church was large, angular, and somewhat plain in appearance, with no stained glass or crosses. A granite sign on the lawn proclaimed it *The Church of Jesus Christ of Latter-day Saints* and added *Visitors Welcome.*

Rachel pulled into the parking lot and tossed Megan a happy smile. Too happy. Strained-worried happy. Megan stiffened. Had Rachel at last sensed something wrong about her, something fake?

"I'm glad you could come," Rachel said. "Decorating pumpkins . . . it's a little goofy. But it's for a good cause. I hope you have fun."

"Pumpkins and paintbrushes and good-looking guys? How can I not have fun?"

Rachel laughed, and Megan relaxed. Rachel wasn't nervous because she was suspicious. She was nervous because she wanted tonight to make a good impression on Kristen.

"Hey, Rach." A slender blond girl strolled up as Rachel and Megan stepped out of the car. "Hi, Kristen."

Larissa Mullins. "Hi, Larissa," Megan said.

"How was New York?"

"Loved it."

"But don't ask her about the scenery," Rachel said. "The only scenery she noticed had a mysterious smile and a perfect tan."

Larissa laughed. "And how's your aunt doing?" she asked, but Megan didn't have to answer, because a brunette was approaching, calling out hellos.

"Kristen, great to see you. You look terrific. Did you get your hair cut?"

You have no idea. "Just trimmed." This girl hadn't been on Kristen's list, but Megan wasn't surprised there were more people who knew Kristen than she had bothered to document.

"You have such gorgeous coloring," the brunette sighed. "Peaches and cream. I could sell my soul to Oil of Olay and I still wouldn't have skin like that."

Megan gave her a half smile. Inside, she squirmed at not thanking the girl or handing back a compliment in return, but Kristen always accepted compliments like the giver was just stating the obvious.

Rachel swung open the door to the church, and they trooped inside. Megan was careful not to look around like a newcomer, but she took in what she could. They were in a foyer with wall-to-wall, industrial carpeting; a flowered couch; and a couple of chairs. Religious paintings adorned the walls.

Rachel led the way to a set of double doors that opened onto a large hall. Lines for a basketball court were painted on the wood floor, and there was a curtained stage on one side of the hall. Basketball in the church? And what was the stage for? Megan imagined a crowd of clean-cut Mormons sitting attentively on folding chairs and watching *Hamlet.*

Eight rectangular tables covered with butcher paper and set with jars of paint and brushes were arranged in the center of the room. Pumpkins were heaped near one wall. *Painting pumpkins.* Megan hadn't held a paintbrush since sixth grade. No women's shelter would want a pumpkin she'd painted, unless they wanted to decorate their dumpster.

A big man with sandy blond hair walked into the room, his powerful arms wrapped around a box loaded with still more pumpkins. *Trevor Drake.* He lowered the box to the floor next to the pile of pumpkins.

"More?" The brunette grinned at him. "We're going to be here all night."

"Hey, if the farmers' market wants to donate more pumpkins, I say bring 'em on. Jenna Elliot will paint them."

"Oh, thanks," the girl—obviously Jenna—said. She, Trevor, and Rachel started pulling pumpkins out of the box and adding them to the spread that already looked like several acres' worth. Megan hung back. Kristen wouldn't bother to help. She'd stand and watch, coolly amused and superior.

Megan didn't remain a spectator for long. Person after person rushed up to greet her like her being there was the highlight of the evening. A few of the faces Megan recognized from Kristen's list, but most of them she didn't know. The girls showered her with compliments; the boys grinned and joked and shook her hand, and one shy young man blushed a shade of red that must have ruptured his capillaries. An older woman with a gray pageboy haircut and a polished agate pendant the size of Megan's palm greeted her like a long-lost daughter.

So this was what it felt like to be the center of attention.

Trevor Drake, carrying the empty pumpkin box, strode past Megan on his way out the door. He nodded a greeting.

"Hey, Trev," Megan said.

"Kristen." His greeting was as brief as his smile. Kristen had warned Megan that Trevor was stuffy—some kind of leader in their church, too busy planning his next sermon to notice when Kristen tried to flirt with him. *Preacher Boy* was her nickname for him.

"All right, gang, let's get to work." The older woman clapped her hands. "Brandon will give us an opening prayer. Brushes and paints are on the tables. And remember, these are for kids, so no dripping blood or dangling eyeballs, please. Think cute."

"Model 'cute' for us, Valerie," one of the boys called, and a girl with dimples and curly hair hid her face in her hands.

"When you get tired of painting, there are several bags of donated Halloween costumes on the stage. We need to sort them, put them in individual bags, and label the bags with the type and size of the costume. If there's no label, just make your best guess on the size. For example—Darth Vader, size 6-8; or cowboy, toddler size."

"Did you donate the cowboy costume, Trev?" Jenna teased. Trevor tipped an imaginary hat at her.

"It warn't a costume, ma'am," he drawled. "It's my regular clothes."

Jenna laughed. "How a cowboy like you ever ended up in Boston, I'll never know. They should have stopped you at the border."

Rachel leaned toward Megan. "Trevor served his mission in Texas," she explained. "He's never recovered."

"That's just an excuse," Jenna said. "He's always been a cowboy at heart. The truck proves it."

"Brandon." The older woman gestured to a boy sitting on one of the tables. He walked to the front of the room, folded his arms, and bowed his head. Everyone around Megan did the same, and she hastily copied them. She hadn't expected a prayer at a party. Did these people think God would notice a round of pumpkin painting?

After a resounding "amen," everyone swarmed the pumpkin pile. Megan grabbed the smallest pumpkin she could find—less room to make mistakes that way—and joined Rachel at a table. Larissa Mullins sat next to Rachel.

A guy wearing an MIT sweatshirt stopped behind Larissa and squeezed her shoulders. His skin and eyes were so dark that he made platinum-blond Larissa look ghostly pale. "How's it going, Picasso?" he asked.

"Oh . . . I'll give it a seven out of ten," Larissa said with a grin. "You?"

He held up an imaginary scorecard. "Eight-point-one. Would be a nine, but I had a test this afternoon that just about killed me."

"Hey, at least it's over," Larissa said.

"Yeah, and let's hope my academic career isn't over along with it." He walked to the other side of the table and sat down opposite Larissa.

Trevor Drake brought his pumpkin over and thudded it onto the table next to the MIT guy.

Larissa held her pumpkin at arm's length, plainly pondering how to make the best use of its ridged orange surface. *Wonderful,* Megan thought. She'd be bumbling around with a paintbrush under the eye of an art major.

"I'm no good at this," Rachel groaned, pulling brushes out of the cup in the middle of the table and examining them one by one.

"Don't sweat it." Trevor snagged the first brush his fingers touched. "They're kids. They won't care."

"Yeah, sure." Rachel selected a brush, rejected it, and chose another. "Anything I could paint would give little kids nightmares."

"No gruesome stuff," chided the MIT guy.

"I'm not talking gruesome," Rachel said. "Just dumb."

Megan knew she ought to say something. Kristen didn't like being at the periphery of a conversation. "Kids specialize in dumb."

"Then I'll be a hit."

Jenna Elliot sat down next to Megan and set a tall, thin pumpkin on the table. "Check this out. Weird, huh?"

"It looks like a mutant zucchini," Trevor said.

Megan glanced at Trevor. *Mutant zucchini?* Not exactly a stuffy remark. So far he'd been friendly with everyone. Trevor wasn't nearly as cold as Kristen had described him. Just because he hadn't fallen for Kristen's flirting . . .

Megan reluctantly took a paintbrush. She wanted to see what the others at the table would come up with before she started on her own pumpkin, but that was distinctly un-Kristen. Megan opened a jar of green paint and dunked her brush.

"Triangle eyes are *way* 1980s, Trev," the MIT guy said.

"Classics never go out of style, Mark." Trevor completed a second triangle eye and swung the pumpkin around for inspection. Rachel applauded.

Megan painted two green circles for eyes. They resembled patches of mold. She added red dots in the center of the eyes. *Yuck*. Glowing zombie mold. Could you erase paint?

Jenna swirled her brush along the sides of her pumpkin, creating golden curls. "Goldilocks."

Rachel, her pumpkin still blank, turned toward Megan while Megan was painting black rings around the green eyes.

"That's cute," Rachel said.

"Cute like roadkill, maybe," Megan replied.

"Quit obsessing, Rachel." Trevor dipped his brush into the jar of black paint. "You're not in a contest. Get creative."

Rachel sighed and reached for the blue paint.

"If you're going to plan weddings for a living, you'd better get over your fear of decorations," Mark teased.

"I don't have a problem with decorations." Rachel daubed paint on her pumpkin and frowned at it. "I can tell you what looks good, and I can hire someone to make it look good. I just can't paint. Or draw. Besides, I don't think painted pumpkins are a hot item for weddings these days, though they'd be less tacky than some trends I've read about."

"How did you enjoy institute last week, Kristen?" Trevor asked, jolting Megan to wary alertness.

Rachel rolled her eyes. "Hello, Trev. It got canceled."

"*Last* week, I said. Not this week."

Megan tried to think of anything Kristen had said that would make a good response, but nothing came to mind. She opted for a generic, "It was good. I enjoyed it."

"What did you like about it?" Trevor asked.

Megan swished her paintbrush in a jar of water and wiped it on a paper towel. "It was all very interesting."

"What specifically did you find interesting?"

Megan imitated the casually flirtatious smile that was one of Kristen's specialties. "When you winked at me, Trev."

Jenna, Mark, and Larissa all laughed, but Trevor studied her with solemn intensity. Out of the corner of her eye, Megan saw Rachel smiling widely in an effort to disguise the *get off her case* glare she was firing at her brother.

"I love the story of Nephi," Jenna said. "The things he went through . . . but he was always so faithful. So forgiving."

Nephi. He must be the "Leffy or Lefty" Kristen mentioned.

"Don't count on such quick forgiveness if you leave *me* in the desert to get eaten by wild beasts," Rachel said to Trevor. More laughter. Trevor cracked a smile this time, but he was still studying Megan.

"What did you like about the story of Nephi, Kristen?" he asked.

Megan felt her face reddening under Trevor's scrutiny. "His faith." She copied the word from Jenna. "He was always so strong." Trying to head off further questions, she pulled out Kristen's trump card. "I just felt really good about what we studied, you know?"

Jenna, Larissa, and Mark all nodded, looking pleased, but Trevor's expression didn't flicker.

"In what ways did Nephi's faith impress you?" he asked.

Megan wanted to strangle Kristen. Why had she shrugged off Megan's questions about what she'd learned in Rachel's religion class?

"I just wished I could be more like him," Megan said, which seemed like a safe answer.

"Amen to that," Mark said.

"What experiences—" Trevor began, but Rachel shifted in her seat, and Trevor jumped slightly and shut his mouth.

"Pass the purple paint, Mark," Rachel said. "Larissa, that cat is awesome."

Larissa held up her pumpkin to display the expert beginnings of a black cat. Everyone exclaimed over Larissa's talent, and Trevor Drake, apparently the victim of a kick under the table from Rachel, resumed painting his pumpkin in silence.

Megan dipped her brush in whatever color of paint was nearest and noticed with dismay that her hand was shaking. Trevor Drake hadn't been making friendly conversation. He'd been testing her. He didn't care what she thought about Nephi. He suspected she didn't know anything at all.

Dismay made Megan's palms sticky with sweat. Did Trevor realize she wasn't Kristen—that she'd never attended Rachel's religion class?

Trevor was focusing on the pumpkin in front of him, but his eyes, the same autumn brown as Rachel's, had a grim look.

Afraid another interrogation was forthcoming, Megan faked an airhead attack and lifted her paintbrush from the jar without wiping the bristles; when she raised the brush toward her pumpkin, paint dripped onto her sleeve.

"Oops!" Megan examined the drop of paint on her pale green sleeve.

"If you wash that out right away, it shouldn't stain," Larissa advised.

"I'll do that." Megan headed for the doors, squelching the urge to run in order to escape Trevor Drake.

The corridor was deserted, to her relief. She found the restroom, removed the blouse she'd layered over a cap-sleeve T-shirt, and shoved the paint-stained sleeve under a rush of cold water. In the mirror, her face looked flushed and tense.

Kristen never looked like this. She was failing, failing, failing.

What mistakes had Megan made? Everyone else had accepted her. Rachel hadn't shown the tiniest bit of doubt. But Trevor . . . she thought of the way he'd greeted her. Brief. Cool. Cool from the beginning, even before he'd started nailing her with questions.

Cool from the beginning. Before she'd said a word to him. Before he'd given her more than a glance.

He hadn't stared at her. He hadn't looked puzzled or startled. If he'd realized that a phony had taken Kristen's place, wouldn't he at least have managed to look surprised? Or was he used to people swapping places with their identical twins?

Megan smiled sheepishly, embarrassed at how quickly she'd panicked. Trevor didn't doubt she was Kristen. He just didn't like Kristen.

Megan squirted soap onto her palm and rubbed it into the blotch of paint on Kristen's sleeve. Apparently, Trevor was perceptive enough to sense Kristen's lack of genuine interest in his religion. But why would that get him baring his teeth? Was he offended someone would treat his religion so lightly? That made sense. Preacher Boy wouldn't like it if someone were napping through Nephi.

The last traces of black paint swirled down the drain. Megan wrung out her sleeve, draped the damp blouse over her arm, and straightened her T-shirt. She couldn't hide in the restroom too long or someone would probably come to see if she needed help. She headed back toward the gym.

The rest of the evening was uneventful. Conversation remained light and friendly, Megan's third pumpkin turned out borderline cute, and a guy so handsome he made Luke Wagner look like the toad he was flirted with her during donuts and apple cider. Trevor Drake didn't do any more digging, but a sober expression remained on his face whenever he looked at her. Tree-trunk for a spine and a Book of Mormon for a brain. What a winner. He probably thought Kristen was just here for the men, which was a motive Megan could relate to. There were several guys she wouldn't have minded getting to know, and another handful that weren't bad as runners-up.

Still, it unnerved her that Trevor had seen through Kristen's feigned interest in religion. He'd be just the one to alert Evelyn to the greed that underlay Kristen's familial devotion. Had he said anything about Kristen to Rachel?

On the ride home, Megan took advantage of Rachel's chatter about the pumpkin painting to insert a comment about Trevor.

"I'm not sure your brother is big on painting vegetables. He didn't look like he was enjoying himself—at least not when he was around me."

Rachel's laugh weakened into a sigh, and for an astonishing five seconds, she was silent. "Kristen . . . I'm sorry about Trevor. He's not usually . . . I mean, he's really a lot of fun. But I know he's been kind of . . ." she trailed off.

"No worries," Megan said. "I just get the feeling he doesn't like me much."

"It's not that." Rachel's voice tightened. "He's just overprotective."

"What does he think he's protecting you from?"

"From auditioning for Twit of the Year." Rachel smiled, but it looked faked. "Sorry. I shouldn't vent like this. But sometimes he bugs the heck out of me."

"What twit-like things does he think you're up to?"

"Spending money. Shocking, huh, that money might be good for something other than sitting in a bank account?"

"I can think of two or three other things money is good for." Did this have anything to do with Kristen, or was Rachel going off on a tangent?

Rachel eased up on the accelerator. They were on a narrow, pitch-dark road, walled in by trees. Megan guessed that in daylight this back-road shortcut must be a dazzling stretch of autumn colors, but in darkness, she found the deserted road creepy.

"The point is, it's *my* money." Rachel spoke quietly, but her irritation was obvious. "From my grandmother. It's none of Trevor's business how I use it. And I'm not a fool, though you'd never know it from the way Trevor hovers. I planned this carefully. I decided how much to set aside and how much I'm free to spend. I *am* thinking about the future, thanks, and I know how much I'll need to set up my consulting business. But Trev thinks he's got to be Dad Jr., worried if I spend more than five bucks at a time."

Realizing she'd touched a nerve, Megan tried for the light approach. "I think your family could run through a lot of five-dollar expenditures before they needed to start worrying."

"Tell it to my dad. My parents were always so paranoid we'd grow up spoiled that getting five bucks out of them was like pulling teeth." Rachel sighed. "Okay, I really sound whiny now. Forget I said all this and we'll pretend this conversation was about the weather."

Megan laughed, but she wasn't ready to let the subject go until she connected up the threads Rachel had left hanging—why Trevor's overprotective attitude about Rachel's spending habits had anything to do with Kristen. "So . . . Trevor doesn't like me because he thinks I'm hanging around to hit you up for cash?"

"Oh, no," Rachel said quickly. "He's just always worrying I'm going to get sucked into something dumb."

"What has he said about me?"

"Nothing, really. He's just always nagging me to be careful."

Rachel was a clumsy liar. "Hey, I'm not offended. I understand why he's cautious. But he doesn't need to worry. It's not your wallet I'm after. It's his."

Rachel gave her a startled glance, then got the joke and grinned. "You're planning to marry him for his money, right?"

"Do you think it will work?"

"What about Alex?"

"Alex who?"

Rachel giggled. "Well, since Trev will only marry an LDS girl, you'll have to join the Church. Do you want to start meeting with the missionaries?"

Megan laughed and veered the conversation into a discussion about two of Rachel's Mormon friends who had recently gotten engaged. While Rachel talked about their wedding plans, Megan fired angry thoughts at Kristen.

What had Kristen done in the early days of her interaction with the Drakes to get Trevor so hostile? And why hadn't she been smart enough to *learn* about Rachel's church instead of zoning out during religion class?

Megan would have to tell Kristen that Trevor Drake had already nailed her as a phony who was only after money—despite Rachel's attempts to pretend otherwise. If Trevor started broadcasting his suspicions about Kristen's character, word would get back to Evelyn. If that happened, so much for their inheritance.

Chapter 9

Concealed behind the curtains, Evelyn stood at her bedroom window and watched Megan alight from Kristen's Corolla and walk toward the house. Megan moved with a natural grace that appealed to Evelyn more than Kristen's liquid-smooth swagger. From the way Kristen walked, it was apparent she wanted and expected the attention of every man she passed, but Megan moved like she simply enjoyed the rhythm of walking and was unaware of how appealing she was.

Such a lovely, modest girl. So few young women these days deserved the title of *lady*. Judith had always been so classy, just as Evelyn had taught her. Evelyn sensed Megan was the same way. Pamela must love Megan very much.

Pamela will miss Megan very much.

Evelyn turned away from the window and checked her appearance in the mirror. A touch more white powder, perhaps. She was looking entirely too robust this morning. The knowledge that things were moving forward in perfect order energized her and made it difficult to maintain the mien of an ailing old woman. Sometimes the charade got tiresome, but Kristen had insisted it was the best way to hook Megan, and Evelyn had to concede she was right. Besides, Evelyn rather enjoyed Megan's tender ministrations. Not since Edward's death had anyone coddled her, and it was a pleasant diversion.

Ironically for Kristen, the charade was also the best way to hook *her*. Creating this so-called alibi allowed Kristen to maintain the illusion that she could walk away when this was over.

"It won't work that way, dear," Evelyn murmured, glancing at her closet where she'd placed the envelope containing the most recent of the tapes and written records.

She stowed her powder in the drawer of her vanity table and shuffled out of her room to greet Megan.

* * *

Kristen sagged into a chair and flung a limp hand toward Megan. "Water," she gasped. "I'm going to faint."

"Will you quit clowning around?" Megan sat stiffly on the edge of Kristen's hotel bed. "This is important."

"Good grief, it's not exactly the secret of the century that Rachel's brother doesn't like me. I told you the guy was a preachy stuffed shirt."

"The problem isn't that he doesn't *like* you. Plenty of people don't like you. The problem is he sees through you. He knows you care more about Rachel's money than you do about Rachel. And if he thinks you're that mercenary, it's not much of a stretch to think he'll figure out you don't care about Evelyn either."

"I *do* like Rachel. I can't help it. She admires me so much it's fun to be around her." Kristen picked up her black wig and put it on backward so the hair covered her face. "Believe me, if Trevor knew I was feigning devotion to my ancient auntie just to get my mitts on her money, he'd already have gone marching over there in a suit and tie to warn her." Kristen parted the hair with her fingers and peered out at Megan. "He'd consider it his religious duty."

"Will you take off that wig? I feel like I'm talking to Chewbacca's sister."

Kristen laughed and flung the wig onto the table.

"What's up with you today?" Megan asked. "Are you all twitterpated over your Parisian getaway? Because if you don't pay attention to what's going on here and now, you may come home to find that Evelyn has willed her money to charity."

"So I'll change my name. Get it? Change my name to *Charity*?"

Megan slid her arms out of Kristen's cream-colored leather jacket and laid it on the bed. The hotel room had seemed chilly when she first walked in, but now she was sweating. "I'm not saying Trevor knows you're manipulating Evelyn per se. But he can see the dollar signs in your eyes."

"What does *per se* mean anyway? Is that like per person? Per diem? Persnickety? Persimmon?"

"*Fine.*" Megan stood. "*You're* the one who made a big deal about how we'll only get Evelyn's money if she keeps believing you really love her. *You're* the one who wants me to masquerade as you so we don't give Evelyn any reason to doubt your devotion. *You're* the one who keeps lecturing me about how if I blow it with anyone in Britteridge, Evelyn will find out immediately. Now I'm telling *you* that Trevor Drake is questioning your character, and you don't think it matters. Fine. If you want to be stupid, be stupid. You've got a lot more to lose than I do."

Kristen's gaze went cool. "Here's what's going on, if you can't figure it out for yourself. Trevor Drake doesn't know how to deal with a pretty girl who isn't part of the Mormon sheep congregation. He thinks I'm hot, and he doesn't know what to do with those feelings, since he's not supposed to notice a heathen like me. No wonder he doesn't like having me around."

Megan raised her eyebrows in disbelief. "Could you possibly get any more vain?"

"I'm just stating facts. Besides, he probably wouldn't trust *any* non-Mormon friend of Rachel's. Preacher Boy probably thinks all the unconverted are con artists in waiting. It's nothing to do with me personally."

"Your little ploy of acting interested in Rachel's church might have been more effective if you'd actually learned something about it."

"I did learn something. They do family research. And they have a *lot* of meetings."

"Gee, you're ready to write a book on them."

"You're such a chicken. You start squawking just because you found out Trevor knows his sister is a bubble-brain who needs babysitting. Wow, that's a shocker. If you're done whimpering about Trevor, do you have anything else to report before you stomp out of here in a huff?"

Heat rose in Megan's face. "No. Everything was fine. Rachel and her friends all thought I was you. I didn't mix up any names. We painted pumpkins. That's it."

"Good. Because soon I'll be climbing the Eiffel Tower, and tending the home front will be all up to you."

"Why don't you leave now?" Megan asked coldly. "You can hang out in New York until it's time for France. It's not as though you're any help to me here."

Kristen leapt to her feet and started clapping. "Bravo! Look who's ready to take on the world single-handed! Acting like me has been good for you. You're starting to sound like a grown-up. Ready for round two?"

"Round two?"

"Rachel's religion class is Tuesday night, if the teacher can manage to show up this time."

"I'm not going. I told Rachel I'd be too busy moving my things over to Evelyn's that night."

Anger flared in Kristen's eyes, then disappeared like she'd clapped a lid over it. "Wrong answer. Go to the class."

Megan frowned. *Go to the class and spend the evening getting glared at by Trevor Drake? No thanks.* "You're pushing this Mormon thing way too far."

"I want to get you completely established before I leave. You've got to be comfortable with all parts of my life, including my circle of hymn-singing friends."

"Kris! This is a waste of time."

Kristen strolled toward Megan. "Oh, honey." She tousled Megan's hair. "Haven't we already settled the question of who's in charge here?"

Megan slapped her hands away.

"Go to the class," Kristen said. "Go get religion."

"This is absurd."

"Play it my way or you're out of here. I'll move in with Evelyn myself. I'll get the money and you'll never see a penny of it. You can go back to your measly dead-end life and marry Lukie-pooh. Good luck."

Kristen's blue eyes were so cold that Megan shuddered. Kristen looked like she could drive a knife into Megan's heart and walk away without even bothering to watch her fall. "All right . . . for goodness sake, if you think it's that important . . ."

Kristen's face relaxed. "That's the right attitude."

"I suppose you also want me to go to church on Sunday, join the choir, and volunteer to vacuum the pews?" Megan channeled her discomfort into sarcasm.

"Nah, I'm not that cruel. It's a fine line, see. I want them to think I'm interested, but I can't look *so* interested that they wonder why I haven't joined up yet. Evelyn will be impressed enough that you're going to the Tuesday class. You don't need to do Sunday, too."

Kristen picked up a shopping bag. "If anyone asks you where you were this afternoon, you were at the mall. This is what you bought." She tossed the bag to Megan.

Megan opened it and found a baby-blue cashmere turtleneck and a silk scarf patterned in green and blue.

"I know some of my clothes aren't your style, so I thought you might want something new," Kristen said.

Caught off guard, Megan fingered the delicate scarf. "You—didn't need to do this."

"Hey, you're saving my sanity. I owe you. Sorry I've been kind of wound up today. I guess I'm more excited for Paris than I realized. Listen, Meg, you're doing a fantastic job. I'm amazed at how fast you memorize stuff and how quickly you're getting settled in. You're going to pull this off, no problem."

Surprised anew at this praise, Megan closed the bag and looked warily at Kristen.

"I shouldn't have hassled you about overreacting to Trevor," Kristen conceded. "It *would* be smart to warm him up. Turn on that sweet charm of yours and watch the ice melt." She wiggled her eyebrows. "And if charm doesn't work, try quoting Lefty at him."

"Nephi." Megan smiled tentatively. "I'll do what I can."

"Good girl. I'll check in with you next week to see how things are going. And by the way, I'm moving to a different hotel, so don't try to contact me here. Just use the cell phone."

Megan walked out to her car, her thoughts spinning. Maybe it *was* a good idea to attend Rachel's religion class. Megan could do damage control and allay some of Trevor Drake's suspicions. She'd call Rachel to find out what they were studying on Tuesday. Then she'd read like a fiend until she could answer any question Trevor chucked at her.

Kristen had been foolish not to make her phony interest in Rachel's church thicker than tissue paper, but the problem was not beyond fixing. Megan could take care of it.

The bright October sunshine streamed through the windows of the car as Megan drove back to Britteridge, but beneath the glow of the sun and the memory of Kristen's compliments, she still shivered when she thought of the fury that, just for a moment, had flashed in Kristen's eyes.

* * *

Dr. Gail Ludlum's throat was so constricted that the grilled salmon and roasted red potatoes had nearly choked her. Now she sat at the Drakes' dining room table, poking at a slice of chocolate mousse pie and keeping a smile nailed to her face. Even when she'd been at her most worried about Bryce, she'd never felt this miserable.

"You're a sweetheart to help me with these costumes." Sandra slid her empty pie plate aside. "I didn't realize how far in over my head I'd gotten."

"You *like* being in over your head, dearie," Gail said. "You must have gills. You don't even have a child in the play this time, but you're still underwater."

Sandra laughed. "I tried to get Josh to audition, but he looked at me like I was from Mars. If it doesn't involve shooting baskets, he's not interested. Truly, though, when I volunteered, I thought I'd be fine. I didn't realize how many changes of costume Mr. Torelli would want for the lead. And these skirts are huge! I can barely lift the fabric, let alone sew it."

"Torelli never does anything small-scale. I spent weeks sewing that wretched Horace Vandergelder suit for Bryce. I've never liked *Hello, Dolly* since. Can't the man just rent costumes? Or do a modern interpretation with everyone wearing jeans?"

"How's Bryce doing?"

A bite of pie stuck in Gail's throat. She picked up her water glass and gulped hard.

"Very well." She set the glass down. "He sounds so upbeat in his e-mails."

"Oh, Gail, that's such good news."

"Helping people who have so little compared to him has really affected him. He feels he's doing something important at last, and that's going a long way toward helping him stay clean."

"Was it hard for him to miss Larry's wedding?"

Gail's stomach tightened so painfully that she feared she was going to vomit all over Sandra's linen tablecloth. She'd dreaded keeping her weekly lunch date with Sandra and had dreaded sticking around to help her sew hoopskirts for the high school's production of *The King and I.* But she needed that key, and today was her best chance to get it. Kristen O'Connor's voice still rang in her ears. *"If you screw up, Mommy, Bryce pays. Got it?"*

"He would have liked to go to the wedding, of course, but we both agreed it was better if he stayed in Georgia," Gail said. "He's at too fragile a stage right now. Larry's a nice kid, but he's a party boy, and there's no telling what went on at the bachelor bash. Better to keep Bryce away from that."

"Definitely. You must be very proud of him."

"I am," Gail said fiercely. "It's taken a lot of guts for him to overcome what he has. He's a good kid. He's talking about going back to school next year."

"You know Michael would always welcome him at Britt."

"I know, and I appreciate that. We'll see what he wants to do." Gail couldn't even look at Sandra. Sandra was her dearest friend, closer to Gail than her own sister. And now—

Everything will be all right. It will all be over soon and things will be back to normal. Everything will be fine.

And what else could she do? Wouldn't Charlie want her to protect their son? Gail thought yearningly of her late husband and wished she could feel his support. *Charlie, you understand, don't you? What else can I do?*

"You don't look like you're enjoying that pie," Sandra remarked.

Gail surrendered and pushed her pie aside. "I love it, but something's wrong with my stomach today. I'm afraid I don't have much of an appetite."

"I hope you didn't pick up a bug from one of your patients."

"Oh no, I'm sure this isn't anything contagious. I just feel a little off. Why don't we get to work on those hoopskirts?"

"Are you sure you're up to it?"

No, she wasn't up to it. She wanted to go home and hide. "Sure I am. Let's get to work."

Sandra lifted her eyeglasses from where they rested on top of her short, chocolate-brown curls. "To the sewing room, then," she said, settling the glasses on her nose.

Gail rose to her feet, a plastic smile on her face. "I'm going to make a pit stop. I'll catch up with you."

Sandra nodded and headed out of the dining room.

Feeling as though something inside her were being ripped to pieces, Gail hurried toward the utility room and the pegboard where the Drakes kept copies of all their keys.

Chapter 10

Triumph surged through Megan when Rachel shot Trevor a *told you so* smile as he approached them after class on Tuesday night. Megan had prepared well and had learned enough to follow the discussion and make a couple of comments. By the time class ended, Rachel was beaming like someone had lit a thousand-watt bulb inside her.

"Hope you don't mind waiting a few minutes," Trevor said. "I need to run a couple of things by the bishop."

"No problem," Rachel said. "Is that okay, Kristen?"

"It's fine," Megan said, wondering who "the bishop" was and picturing the pope. At first, Megan had been dismayed when she learned Rachel and Trevor always carpooled to institute, but now she was glad. The ride home would give her a chance to see if she could detect any softening in Trevor's attitude.

Trevor disappeared down a hallway, and Rachel led Megan to a couch in the foyer. They sat beneath a picture Megan was pleased to recognize. It was a depiction of the boy prophet Joseph Smith being visited by God and Jesus Christ. She'd read about his vision in a history section at the back of one of the leather-bound volumes Rachel had given Kristen.

"It's going to be *so* nice when the expansion on the campus institute building is finished," Rachel said. "I was walking past it today, and it's going to be more than twice as big as before. Dad's thrilled that there's such a demand for the classes."

"So you'll be meeting there instead of here at the church?" Megan hoped this wasn't a dumb question to which Kristen would have already known the answer.

Rachel nodded. "Most of the classes are meeting in rooms around campus right now, but the evening classes are here. Once the building is done, we'll all meet there. It's gorgeous. Lots of marble."

"Sounds nice."

Rachel picked up her purse then set it down, smoothed a wrinkle out of the sleeve of her blouse, and bent to rub a dirt smudge off the toe of her shoe. "So . . . did you enjoy class tonight?"

Megan opened her mouth to give a glib response about how it was great, but something in Rachel's fidgety nervousness brought her up short and made her consider the question.

This mattered to Rachel.

Suddenly Megan felt guilty for going along with Kristen's idea of feigning interest in Rachel's religion as a way to manipulate both Rachel and Evelyn. She didn't feel it was right to trifle with someone's sacred beliefs.

"Speechless, huh?" Rachel's cheeks turned pink. "Sorry for putting you on the spot. I understand if—"

"I did enjoy the class." Megan was surprised to realize she was telling the truth. She'd been so focused on impressing Trevor that she hadn't looked beneath that goal to realize she *was* interested in what they were discussing. And she'd enjoyed preparing for class over the past couple of days—in fact, she was eager to jump back into the Book of Mormon and see what else it said. It was like nothing she'd ever read before.

Was it fun just because it was intellectually stimulating?

"What specifically impressed you?" Trevor's question from the pumpkin-painting party sprang into her thoughts.

"I'm glad you weren't bored," Rachel teased, still looking uncomfortable. "Kris . . . are you okay?"

Megan realized she was staring into space. "I did enjoy it," she repeated. "There are just—so many things I've never thought about before that I guess I feel . . . overwhelmed. Does that make sense?"

"Sure. It's a lot to take in."

Megan was glad Trevor wasn't here. It gave her a chance to speak her mind without the need to impress him getting into the mix of her feelings and words.

"You know what amazes me most?" Megan said. "It's the way God . . . this will sound silly to you . . . but it's the way He pays attention. All those times in Nephi's life when God helped him or warned him or strengthened him—God was always aware of him. And Joseph Smith. He was just a kid, but when he prayed—" Megan gestured at the picture above them.

"What do you . . . believe about God?" Rachel asked.

"I don't know. I always sort of believed He was there. I just never thought about Him much. And I guess I assumed He didn't think much about us either—that maybe we were His creations, like some kind of artwork, but now He'd moved on to other things."

"He loves each of us," Rachel said. "There's a scripture that says something like—oh heck, I'm bad at quoting stuff. Trevor's the memorizing machine. I'll ask him. But the Lord says something like 'Can a mother forget her nursing baby?' She *could* forget—and you know how unlikely *that* would be, for a mother to forget her own child—but the Lord will never forget us. He says it's like we're 'engraved on the palms of His hands.' Does that make sense?"

"So He's saying His love and concern for us is even greater than a mother's love for her child."

Rachel's smile glowed. "Exactly! And when He talks about us being graven on His hands, that's referring to the nail prints in His hands when He sacrificed His life for us. Talk about love!"

Megan thought of her father's love, her hand absently touching Kristen's purse, where she'd put the flannel-wrapped picture. "It interested me that when God visited Joseph Smith, He knew his name."

"Somebody who loves you *that* much is bound to know your name," Rachel said with a small laugh. "God's love isn't some kind of, you know, vague affection for a bunch of people He's never met. He loves *you.* He knows you. Personally."

Personally? It was difficult to imagine God being aware of Megan O'Connor. And if He *was* aware of her, what did He think about her sitting inside a church, lying about who she was?

You're not hurting anyone, Megan reminded herself. *What does it matter?* She spoke lightly, not wanting to reveal the discomfort she was feeling. "Somehow, I think God has better things to think about than me."

"He knows *you,* Kristen. And He loves you." Rachel's eyes filled with tears.

Megan smiled awkwardly, both embarrassed and touched by how much Rachel seemed to care about Kristen.

"Don't mind me," Rachel said, digging a tissue out of her purse. "I'm always getting weepy."

Trevor strode into the foyer. "Ready, ladies?"

"That was quick." Rachel rose to her feet.

Megan avoided looking at Trevor as they walked out of the church. Tears seemed strangely close to the surface for her now, and she was afraid if she tried to speak, her voice would crack. What was the matter with her? Was Rachel's weepiness contagious?

She drew a deep breath. The night air was pleasantly crisp, and Megan didn't bother to put on Kristen's leather jacket. The long sleeves of the silken blouse she'd taken from Kristen's closet were warm enough for the brief walk from the building to the car.

"Nice night," Trevor remarked, squeezing into the backseat of Rachel's car. "Good trick-or-treating weather."

"Oooh, yes." While Rachel drove, she talked about the work she was doing with Larissa Mullins for Britteridge's upcoming town Halloween party. Megan was grateful for this diversion; detailed descriptions of pumpkin-shaped sugar cookies, toddler Halloween games, and the six-foot-tall ghost Larissa had created out of cheesecloth gave Megan time to collect her emotions without anyone aiming a question at her.

"Slow down, Rach," Trevor warned as Rachel cruised along the narrow road that formed the shortcut to the west side of Britteridge.

"I'm going the speed limit." Rachel let up on the accelerator. "Well, now I am."

"This road is totally Halloween-esque." Megan finally trusted her voice enough to speak. "You ought to turn it into a haunted lane and take the older kids on a spooky hayride."

"Terrific idea," Rachel said. "Only problem is, it's too far away from the elementary school where the party . . ." She leaned forward and squinted at the road. "What's that? Oh, it's just leaves."

Megan looked at the debris. A few small branches and a multitude of colored leaves were scattered across the road.

"Slow *down*," Trevor said.

"Will you stop nagging me? It's only some—"

There was a bang, and the car jerked. Rachel screamed and yanked the wheel. The car jounced off the road and came to a stop with the front bumper only inches from a tree.

"What was that?" Rachel gasped. "The tires—I think I blew a tire—"

Megan clung to the edge of her seat, her heart hammering.

"Stay in the car," Trevor said. "Let me have a look."

"I thought it was just a small branch," Rachel said shakily as Trevor stepped out of the car. "I thought it was just some leaves."

"It looked that way to me," Megan agreed.

Rachel switched the engine off, but left the headlights on so Trevor could see what he was doing. "I think I blew a tire."

"I think so too." Megan wondered if it would be too tactless to suggest that next time Rachel let Trevor drive.

"I thought it was just a little branch," Rachel repeated as they watched Trevor lean over the left front tire. "I thought—"

Motion at the edge of the trees a few yards ahead of them caught Megan's eye. Two dark figures rushed toward the car. Megan gasped.

"*What*—" Rachel began.

There was a pop, and Trevor staggered, yelling in pain. He collided with the car and fell, disappearing out of Megan's line of vision.

"Trevor!" Rachel screamed.

Megan wrenched open the flap of her purse and snatched Kristen's cell phone. "Lock the doors!" she yelled, but even as Rachel fumbled for the button, Rachel's door flew open and a gloved hand shoved a gun in her face.

"Don't move." The man's voice was raspy. "And you, girl, give me that phone."

Terrified, Megan thrust the phone at him.

"What did you do to my brother?" Rachel cried.

"All set." The second attacker spoke from outside the car. The first man stepped aside, and a second, bigger man reached into the car and started to drag Rachel out.

"Kristen!" Rachel shrieked. "Help me!"

Not stopping to think about what she was doing, Megan threw her arms around Rachel's waist and clung with all her might. The man yanked Rachel's arm, and Megan's ribs scraped along the steering wheel as she fought to hold on to Rachel. Rachel ended up half in and half out of the car.

Megan sucked in a huge breath of air and screamed as loudly as she could. The man dropped Rachel's arm. His fist flashed forward and slammed into the side of Megan's face. Fireworks erupted in her head, and for a stunned instant she didn't know where she was or what was happening. A tremendous yank nearly ripped her shoulders out of joint, and Rachel was gone.

"Rach—Rachel—" Megan's head spun. She tried to step out of the car to follow, but ended up on her hands and knees in the dirt. A hand clamped around her arm and pulled her to her feet.

The smaller gunman's masked face slid in and out of focus. Megan tried to speak. "What do you—want with—"

He shoved her toward the trees. "That way. Go."

Megan fell again and landed hard, twigs and rocks scraping her palms. The cold jab of a gun against her ribs impelled her to stagger to her feet.

She stumbled toward the trees, her steps illuminated by a flashlight held high by the gunman. She was going to die. Out of sight of the road, the gunman would shoot her.

"Stop here," the gunman rasped. "Kneel down and put your arms all the way around that tree."

"Please—"

The gun barrel dug into the back of her neck. "You've got two seconds or I'll shoot. Cooperate and you'll walk away from this. This isn't about you. We just need you out of the way for a while."

Megan sank to her knees and wrapped her arms around the tree. *Isn't about you* . . . it was about Rachel . . . they'd taken Rachel . . . what had they done to Trevor?

"Cross your wrists."

Megan had to press her body against the tree and stretch her arms as far as they would go in order to comply.

The gunman circled to the other side of the tree and stopped. Megan heard a tearing sound and felt tape being wound around her wrists. Bark scraped her face. The smell of pine filled her lungs.

Footsteps rustled on dry pine needles. The gunman was behind her again. He grabbed her hair, jerked her head backward, and pressed a strip of tape over her mouth.

His footsteps receded, heading toward the road.

Chapter 11

Trevor Drake rolled over and tried to sit up. The effort brought a sickening wave of dizziness. He sank back against the dampness of the ground and lay still, eyes closed.

When the ground stopped moving beneath him, he opened his eyes and stared at the dark branches rustling overhead. His hands were tied behind him, his ankles were bound together, and tape covered his mouth.

What happened?

He blinked at the speckling of stars in the sky and breathed deeply of cold air that smelled of dirt and leaves. He remembered bending over the tire. A burst of pain that knocked him to the ground. Struggling to move and finding himself paralyzed. A shadowy shape bending over him and the icy barrel of a gun against his neck. Rachel screaming. Then nothing.

The tires—the assailants must have planted a spike strip across the road to puncture the tires—retractable so they wouldn't disable any cars that passed before Rachel's. They must have known the Drakes were at the church tonight and that they always took this isolated shortcut home.

Where was Rachel now?

Trevor tensed his abdominal muscles and pulled himself to a sitting position. Moonlight slipped through the trees. Branches rattled and a leaf drifted to settle on his shoulder.

A square of white caught his eye. An envelope was stuck to the front of his sweatshirt with a strip of duct tape.

A ransom demand. They'd taken Rachel.

And what about Kristen O'Connor? Worth nothing to the kidnappers, Kristen was probably dead.

How long had he been unconscious? From the stiffness of his muscles and the cold that permeated his body, he'd been lying here for a while, he realized.

He was probably near the road. He doubted the kidnappers would have taken the trouble to drag him far. If he could get to the road, there was a chance he could flag down a passing car—

He groaned, the sound muffled by the tape over his mouth. If it was late, the chance that someone would pass along this road was slim. He needed to free himself and go for help. He twisted his body, trying to feel if his cell phone was still in his pocket.

It wasn't.

He contorted his arms, pulling savagely at the tape binding him. Several minutes of struggling left him feeling like he'd torn apart the muscles in his shoulders, but the tape held. He needed to find a rock or a broken branch, something he could rub the tape against to weaken it.

Trevor dug his heels into the leaf-covered dirt and dragged himself forward, praying for calm, for Rachel, and for swift, painful contact with the useful edges of a rock.

* * *

The wind that had seemed pleasantly cool when she left the church had now chilled Megan to the point of violent shivering. She tried repeatedly to break the tape by rubbing it against the bark of the tree, but her wrists were bound so tightly that she couldn't get her hands at an angle that would allow her to attack the tape without shredding the flesh on her hands and arms.

She tried to keep circulation in her legs by alternating between standing and kneeling, but whenever she changed position, her arms scraped along the bark of the tree. The thin fabric of her blouse offered almost no protection, and soon her skin was so raw that moving her arms hurt as if she'd dragged them across a heated barbecue grate.

No one was going to find her, not tonight. It already felt like she'd been here for hours, and she'd heard only one car drive past. It might be morning before someone noticed the disabled Lexus. And even if they noticed it, why would they think to search the woods? They'd assume the owner had walked into town. Dimly, Megan envisioned herself dying of hypothermia and dehydration while cars drove past, oblivious.

No one would notice when she didn't come home tonight. Evelyn wouldn't miss her until morning, when Megan didn't show up to make her tea. Evelyn would call Kristen's home number and cell phone and get no answer. Would she be worried enough to follow up, or would she assume Megan had just gotten delayed?

Was anyone waiting for Rachel or Trevor Drake tonight? Rachel didn't have any roommates. Megan didn't know if Trevor had roommates or not; she just knew he lived in a condo near Britteridge College.

Would *anyone* alert the police before tomorrow afternoon?

Megan's legs were partly numb and partly seized with pain that zapped her muscles like electrical shocks. She had to stretch. Gritting her teeth against the burning in her arms, she struggled to rise to her feet. Halfway up, her knees buckled and her right cheekbone banged against the tree.

She tried again. This time her legs wouldn't lift her at all.

Through the pain came the unexpected thought of Nephi, the man she'd read about that week. Attacked by his own brothers, tied up and almost left to get torn apart by animals in the desert—attacked again and tied up for four days on a storm-racked ship . . .

Four days. How had he survived four days of this without losing his mind?

God had saved Nephi's life multiple times. Would He save hers? Why would He bother?

But Rachel said He knew and loved Megan.

Did He? She didn't even know how to pray.

She tried to remember the way the girl had prayed at the beginning of Rachel's religion class, but she couldn't think past the spasmodic shivering that pulled her muscles into knots. *So cold . . .*

* * *

Trevor tore the last of the tape from his ankles and staggered to his feet. Shoving branches out of the way, he headed toward the metallic glint he'd spotted through the trees.

The sight of Rachel's abandoned Lexus hit Trevor with a rage so overwhelming that he had to stop and close his eyes, waiting until his fury dimmed enough to allow for rational thought. Fantasizing about ripping the kidnappers apart wouldn't help Rachel. It would only cloud his mind with hate.

He tried the door on the driver's side. It swung open.

He moved the seat back as far as it would go and collapsed against the leather upholstery. In the illumination from the dome light, he read the note the kidnappers had taped to his shirt.

We have Rachel. Call Daddy and Mommy to come pick you up and get the car towed—discreetly. Don't let word get out that you've got a problem. If the police get wind of this, Rachel dies. And don't forget your girlfriend. She's waiting for you out there in the trees. Your cell phone is under the driver's seat.

So Kristen was alive, thank heavens. They must have tied her up and left her like they had him.

He reached under the seat and retrieved the phone. They'd left it so he could call for help without drawing attention to the situation. If he'd stumbled into a gas station, filthy and bloody and searching for a pay phone, news of Rachel's kidnapping would have been all over town in a heartbeat.

Rachel's keys were on the passenger seat. Trevor unlocked the trunk, opened the survival kit his father insisted Rachel carry, and took out a flashlight.

Steeling himself against the knowledge of the pain he was about to inflict on his parents, he dialed their number.

* * *

Was it footsteps or was she imagining it? Megan tried to look behind her, but she couldn't control her muscles. Her head tilted sharply to the side, and when she tried to lift it, she knocked her temple into the tree. A flashlight blinded her. She squeezed her eyes shut.

A hand curved around the back of her head, steadying her.

"Kristen, it's Trevor." His fingers scraped lightly against her jaw, catching the edge of the tape that covered her mouth.

"This might hurt. I'm sorry." He tore the tape loose. It did hurt, but Megan didn't care.

"Hang on and I'll cut you loose." Trevor moved to the other side of the tree.

Tears of relief spilled down Megan's face. "Are you all right?" she croaked.

"Yes. Hold as still as you can. I'm using a pocketknife and I don't want to cut you."

"I can't—I can't stop shivering—I'm sorry—"

"Kristen, it's all right. I'll have you free in a moment."

She felt a tug on her arms and a sensation of pressure on her wrists, but she couldn't feel the warmth of Trevor's hands. "Rachel. Is Rachel all right?"

"They took her."

"What do they—what are the—" Her brain was as numb as her hands, and her chattering teeth diced up the few words she did manage to speak. "The—the—demands—"

"I don't know yet. They left a note saying we'd get instructions later. My parents are on their way to pick us up."

"The police—have to call—"

"I can't call the police yet. Not until I've talked to my parents. The note said if we call the police or let word of this get out, Rachel dies."

Rachel dies. How could Rachel die?

This wasn't happening. None of it was happening. Rachel and her maple-syrup eyes and her giggle and the way she cried when they sat beneath the picture of Joseph Smith. And the leaves in the road, just some leaves . . . *Just some leaves.*

Rachel's scream. *"Kristen, help me!"*

Trevor spoke. "Can you hear me? Kristen, can you hear me?" She was moving. Trevor was carrying her. Her arms were free, but she couldn't lift them.

"Hang on," he said. "Just hang on."

She was crying. Why was she crying now that she was safe?

Trevor settled her in the cushioned front seat of the Lexus and turned the key in the ignition.

"Here." He offered her what looked like a flat, rectangular mat. She tried to take it, but her hands were too clumsy.

"It's a heat pack." He draped it over her lap. Warmth radiated into her skin.

Trevor pushed the button to turn on the car's interior lights. "The car will be warm in a minute, but until then—" He unfolded a foil blanket and tucked it around her. "We're stuck for the moment. All four tires are blown. But my parents will be here soon."

She couldn't even nod. Her teeth were chattering, her body shaking, her shoulders heaving with sobs.

"Kristen." Trevor rested his hand on her shoulder. "Can you talk to me? What did they do to you? How badly are you hurt?"

"I'm . . . not . . . hurt." Pain like countless red-hot needles stabbed her hands; her legs ached like they'd been tied in knots, her head throbbed, and her arms burned. But she knew Trevor was asking if the kidnappers had beaten her or worse.

With a light touch on her chin, he turned her face toward him. "What happened here?" His fingertip brushed her cheekbone.

"I—they—one of the kidnappers was trying to . . . drag Rachel out of the car. I grabbed Rachel . . . tried to hold on. He hit me . . . I'm—I'm sorry. I tried to stop them—"

"There's nothing you could have done. You risked your life to try." Trevor's voice was gentle, and Megan felt threads of calm weaving through her hysteria, tugging her emotions under control. She closed her eyes and leaned against the headrest. The warmth of the heat pack was beginning to penetrate her chilled muscles, but the shivering continued.

"How did you find me?" she asked.

"The note said where you were. It looks like they just wanted to keep us out of commission long enough for them to get Rachel away."

She opened her eyes. Trevor's face was ghostly white and smeared with dirt. "What did they do to you?" she asked, her voice gradually steadying.

"They zapped me with something. Must have been a Taser. It knocked me flat for a few seconds. It hurt like crazy and I couldn't move. Next thing I know, there's a gun against my neck and someone tells me if I move, I'm dead. After that, I don't know. I remember

Rachel screaming, but that's it. They must have drugged me. They tied me up and left me over there." He waved in the direction of the trees, and Megan saw that his hand was badly scraped and the sleeve of his sweatshirt stained with blood. He must have fought like a madman to free himself.

"Can you tell me everything you saw?" Trevor's voice was *too* calm, a smooth shield over what must be a conflagration of emotions. "How many of them were there?"

"Two. At least two that I saw." Megan tried to bring her memories into focus, but her mind raced, refusing to settle on details. All she could remember was blurry darkness, masked figures, and her own terror.

And Rachel's scream.

"Two men," she said again. "They were wearing ski masks. But then again . . . I can't be sure that . . ."

"That what?"

"I assumed they were men, but I don't know that for certain. The one who dragged Rachel out of the car—" She closed her eyes and concentrated, remembering the deepness of the kidnapper's voice, the size of his gloved hands, and the way his dark jacket fit close to his body.

"The bigger one was a man. But the one who took me—I'm not sure about him. Or her. That one spoke in a weird, raspy voice, like he was trying to disguise it. He was wearing a bulky jacket. And he wasn't all that big. It could have been a woman." She cringed at the thought of how Kristen would react to that report. "*Great job, Megan. You've established that your attacker was definitely a man or a woman. The police sketch artists will love you.*"

"I'm sorry," she said. "I'm so sorry. I should be able to tell you more. It happened so fast—"

"Just tell me what you remember and don't worry about what you can't. What happened after I went down?"

Megan described what little she could, despising how useless she was. Any detail might be vital to catching the kidnappers, and she couldn't offer anything remotely helpful. "I'm sorry," she said again.

"Kristen." Trevor's hand settled back on her shoulder. "Don't be so hard on yourself. Nobody thinks clearly under those circumstances."

Kristen would think clearly, Megan thought. Kristen would have kicked the gun out of the kidnapper's hand and ripped off his ski mask. And rescued Rachel.

"Are you getting warmer? Push that blanket off so you can get some heat from the car." Trevor angled one of the vents so the heat blasted Megan more directly. She pushed the blanket down, so grateful for the heat pouring from the vents that she wanted to embrace the dashboard.

"Will you be all right for a minute?" Trevor asked. "I want to look around."

Megan nodded.

Trevor walked around the car, taking miniscule steps and shining the flashlight over every inch of ground. Megan wondered what he expected to find. A business card dropped by one of the thugs?

The growl of an engine and the crunch of leaves beneath tires were startlingly loud in the stillness. Megan turned to watch Trevor hurry toward an SUV as it pulled in behind the Lexus. A smaller car followed the SUV.

A few minutes later, Trevor walked back toward the Lexus, accompanied by a man who must be his father. The man stepped in front of Trevor and opened Megan's door.

Megan looked up into the face of Michael Drake. He wasn't as big as his son, but his strong, even features were similar to Trevor's. He had the same eyes—eyes that were now filled with anguish.

"Kristen. I'm sorry for what you've been through." He sounded genuinely concerned about her, but Megan figured the last thing he wanted to do was waste time comforting a stranger when his own daughter's life was in danger. She tried to think of a way to tell him not to bother with her, but she couldn't find words.

"I need your cooperation," Michael Drake said. "We're still determining what course of action will be best for Rachel. We have a dear friend with us, a doctor. She'll take you to our house and see to your injuries. Please stay with her and refrain from contacting anyone outside the household, including the police. Will you do that, please?"

Megan nodded. She couldn't imagine looking into the face of this terrified father and arguing with him.

"Is there anyone who will be worried about you?" Mr. Drake asked. "Anyone waiting for you to come home?"

Megan shook her head. "My aunt will expect me in the morning, but no one will miss me tonight."

"Very well. Please go with Dr. Ludlum." He strode toward the SUV.

Trevor leaned down to look in at Megan. "Let me help you to the car."

"I don't need a doctor. I'm fine. I don't want to cause anyone any trouble."

"Don't be ridiculous."

"I'm all right." Megan tried to step out of the car, but when her feet hit the ground, fire shot from her toes to her hips. She sat heavily down again.

"I'll carry you," Trevor said.

"No. I just need a minute. My legs are still half asleep."

A woman hustled toward the Lexus, her coat open and flapping in the wind. She elbowed Trevor aside and leaned over so she was eye-level with Megan. She had a plump, motherly face and wild, curly blond hair going gray at the roots. Megan remembered her from the information Kristen had compiled. Gail Ludlum. Rachel's mother's friend.

"Hi, doll," she said. "Remember me? We met at the picnic a few weeks back. I'm Gail Ludlum. And you look like you could use a little TLC. This knight in shining armor here is going to take you to my car, and we'll get you fixed up."

Humiliation clawed at Megan's raw emotions. The Drakes and their friends should be worried about Rachel now, not fretting about Megan's scrapes and bruises. She tried to summon some of Kristen's cool confidence.

"I'm fine," she said firmly, sliding out of the car and clinging to the top of the door to pull herself to her feet. "I just need to clean myself up. It's silly for—"

"Eh? Sorry, I'm a little deaf. Trev, carry the lady to my car. If she protests, ignore her—she's delirious."

Trevor bent and lifted Megan off her feet. In one corner of her mind she heard Kristen mocking her, but Gail Ludlum's motherly bullying and the solid strength of Trevor Drake's arms were so reassuring that she didn't have the will to object. Trevor deposited her in the front seat of Dr. Ludlum's car and went to join his father.

"Before we start off—" Gail Ludlum was already in medical mode, checking Megan's temperature, pulse, and blood pressure and quizzing her about what had happened. Apparently satisfied Megan wasn't going to die en route to the Drakes' house, she finally pulled out onto the road. Megan watched the gleam of the red Lexus until they rounded a curve and the car disappeared from sight.

What was happening to Rachel now?

Tears flooded Megan's eyes. Embarrassed, she turned her head away from Dr. Ludlum and swiped angrily at her wet eyes. Why was she crying again? She was alive. She was safe.

But all she could think of while Gail drove to the Drakes' home in Andover was Rachel's terrified scream.

Chapter 12

Evelyn Seaver sat in her rocking chair, watching the ornate metal dial of the pendulum wall clock William had given her on their first anniversary. The gift had been a nice thought, of course, and William's generous impulses were rare enough that it would have been foolish not to appreciate it. Not until the day after William's death had she disabled the chimes. She'd always found the noise irritating, much like William himself. Pompous, abrasive, bossy, suspicious—it was a wonder she'd put up with him for as long as she had. But he *had* served a useful function. Marrying a Britteridge native had allowed Evelyn to slip seamlessly into the life of the town, positioning herself for the moment when she would act.

She'd been a good wife to William over the course of their brief marriage. Certainly she'd tolerated him far longer than he'd deserved. Such a different man from Edward. Edward, who had given Judith her lovely, dark hair and the dimple in her left cheek.

Evelyn stroked the lid of the flowered cloisonné jewelry box she held in one palm. Her fingertips explored the satiny lacquer and the ridges of copper wire, moving ritually from one side of the lid to the other.

Judith.

She opened the jewelry box and lifted a delicate gold necklace. The pendant was shaped like half of a heart, with a jagged center edge like a puzzle piece. She held the necklace up so she could see the word engraved on the pendant.

Best.

The *Friends* half of the necklace had no doubt been thrown away long since, an unwanted token of guilt.

Such a ridiculous purchase. Judith had been fourteen and Pamela fifteen, both of them too old for schoolgirl bangles. But the necklace had caught Pamela's fancy, so naturally Judith had gone along with her. Judith had been so young in many ways. So soft, so eager for approval.

Like Megan.

Evelyn stroked the puzzle-piece edge of the heart and rocked. Tears trickled down her face, familiar tears that had worn into her heart like erosion.

Justice. After twenty-six years, justice.

* * *

Trevor paced the perimeter of the family room. He hurt like every muscle in his body had been sheared in half and stitched together crooked, but he had to keep moving. Sitting still for even a few minutes pushed apprehension and frustration to such an excruciating pitch that he feared he'd go insane.

His mother sat on the couch, staring at the phone. Her frantic tears had quieted to an expression of silent agony that slashed Trevor's soul every time he looked at her. His father stood facing the window, his body as stiff as wood. Sixteen-year-old Josh sat on the floor near the fireplace, his head bowed, his hands aimlessly ripping a newspaper to shreds.

None of them spoke. They'd already reviewed every detail of what had happened, ten times over. They'd speculated on who might be behind the kidnapping and had come up with a list so unfocused and useless that Michael had torn it up and thrown it in the fireplace. They'd prayed. Now, there was nothing left to do or say until they heard from the kidnappers.

Why was it taking so long? It was three o'clock in the morning, six hours since Rachel had been taken. Were the kidnappers in transit, taking her to some hideout far away? Or were they delaying contact just to break the Drakes down and make them more receptive to the demands when they finally came? Anything would be better than this agonizing silence.

Almost anything.

"We need to call the police," Josh mumbled without raising his head from his knees. No one responded; Josh had said the same thing at least five times already. Michael had already stated their decision. They would not involve the police, at least not until they heard from the kidnappers.

Michael did a credible job of presenting this as a calm, unified decision between Sandra and him, but Trevor knew he was torn. Trevor had overheard part of his parents' anguished discussion on the matter when he'd gone to ask them if he should wake Josh. Michael had wanted to call the police—negotiating with kidnappers was foolish, and immediate police involvement was the safest course of action. Sandra had fiercely opposed him—they couldn't do anything to anger the kidnappers, or Rachel would suffer the consequences.

Sandra had won. Trevor knew his father well enough to guess that Michael's capitulation didn't mean he'd come around to Sandra's point of view, but only that he wasn't willing to take the risk of going against her when Rachel's safety was not guaranteed either way. If Michael insisted on talking with the police against Sandra's wishes and Rachel died—

The guilt would kill Michael.

But if he *didn't* call the police and Rachel died—

Trevor paused in his pacing and looked at the plushy red chair that was Rachel's favorite spot for reading.

"This is my fault." He pushed the words out of his throat. "When the tires blew like that, I should have realized it was an ambush. If I'd been more alert—"

"Trevor, *don't*," Sandra said. "Don't blame yourself."

"This is not your fault." Michael turned, and Trevor saw the sheen of tears in his father's eyes. "You were caught by surprise and brutally assaulted. There's nothing you could have done."

"Am I intruding?" Gail Ludlum spoke hesitantly from the doorway.

"Come in, Gail." Sandra wiped her eyes and added the tissue to the pile next to her. "How is she?"

"Asleep, poor thing." Gail ran her hands through her wild hair and sighed. Her face was chalky and her eyes were as red as Sandra's.

"I can't believe she can sleep after—everything," Josh muttered.

"Hon, nobody stays awake when Dr. Gail wants them to sleep." Gail sat on the couch next to Sandra. "Speaking of which, Sandra, why don't you let me give you—"

"No," Sandra said flatly. "I'm not closing my eyes until we hear what those monsters want."

Gail didn't argue. "Trevor, if I can intrude a little further, I heard what you just said. And if you don't put those thoughts out of your mind, I'll slap you silly. Kristen told me what happened. You never had a chance. Two armed attackers? Your car completely disabled? If you'd managed to dodge the Taser, you wouldn't have dodged the bullets. You'd be dead and Rachel would still be gone. Remember that and stop beating yourself over the head."

"This Kristen O'Connor," Michael said abruptly. "She's Rachel's neighbor, the one who's interested in the Church?"

Trevor hesitated a beat before saying, "Yes . . . that's her."

"What's wrong?" Michael asked.

"I don't know. Nothing. Yes, Kristen is Rachel's friend. Yes, she's attended some Church meetings. Obviously, she was at institute with us tonight."

"Trevor doesn't like her." Josh added a new handful of newspaper confetti to the pile in front of him.

"I didn't say that, Josh."

"You did last week, more or less. Why can't you come right out and say what you think of someone? We're family. You don't always have to do the phony polite thing."

Trevor suppressed his annoyance. He should have known better than to vent his concerns to Josh when they'd gone hiking last week. Now Josh was blowing his comments out of proportion.

"I really don't know her very well," Trevor said in answer to the question in his father's eyes. "She's only lived here for a few months. She has an elderly aunt or great-aunt in Britteridge, and she moved here from New York to help her out. She's been living in the same apartment complex as Rachel, but Rachel said her aunt is doing worse and wants Kristen to move in with her."

"That's very kind of her to come here to help her aunt," Sandra said.

"Either that or she didn't have much to leave behind," Josh suggested. "Maybe she just got sacked at her job."

Trevor didn't say anything. He'd also suspected Kristen must not have had a very good situation in New York if she was willing to move to Massachusetts—or that her aunt was paying extravagantly for her assistance.

"I talked with her at the picnic," Sandra said. "She seemed like a delightful girl."

"The picnic?" Michael asked.

"Rachel invited her to our Labor Day picnic," Sandra explained. "You were out of town."

"Why don't you like her?" Michael asked, his gaze on Trevor.

Trevor shrugged uncomfortably. If he tried to dodge the question, it would inflate the matter to larger proportions.

"Sometimes she strikes me as . . . calculating," he admitted. "Rachel is convinced she's on the verge of being baptized, but she doesn't seem to know much about the Church or to care—or I *thought* she didn't, but tonight at institute, she made some very perceptive comments that showed she'd really been studying the Book of Mormon. I may have misjudged her."

"Why did you think she'd go to meetings and so on if she weren't interested?" Sandra asked.

Trevor shrugged again. "I wondered if she were cozying up to Rachel for the perks. You know how Rachel's been lately. Ever since she got her share of the money from Grandma, she can't keep her purse shut. She gives Kristen expensive gifts, and they've spent a couple of weekends on the Cape on Rachel's tab. And you know how Rachel is about Italian food. She and Kristen have been all over the North End trying out different restaurants, and I weaseled it out of Rachel that Kristen never pays. Lately I've heard them chatting about how they want to go tour the British Isles. Rachel was getting all dreamy about seeing castles."

Sandra sighed deeply. "Oh, Rachel."

"Listen, I'm being unfair." Trevor was ashamed of how petty his report on Kristen sounded. "Kristen has never done or said anything really wrong. Rachel insists she always pays for things because she's invited Kristen as her guest, which makes sense, I guess. It's not hard to imagine Rachel getting excited about sampling every pasta dish in Boston and dragging Kristen along with her." He smiled thinly. "The fact is, Rachel knows her much better than I do, and Rachel adores her."

"If Rachel doesn't learn to watch her spending, she's never going to get that wedding planning service of hers off the ground, no matter how talented she is," Michael said mechanically.

Sandra drooped back against the couch, the interest leaving her eyes. Trevor knew what she was thinking: who cared about Rachel's recent spending spree? All that mattered right now was getting Rachel home.

Trevor resumed pacing, feeling guilty for having attacked Kristen's character with no real justification.

Why *did* she bother him so much? She showered Rachel with charm and attention, but she had a way of slipping in subtly mocking gibes that good-natured Rachel didn't seem to notice. She'd gotten flirtatious with Trevor a couple of times, but the *I know you think I'm hot* tone to her flirting had annoyed him.

And when her face was in repose, there was something about her eyes that was just—cold.

Or maybe there's something about your brain that's just paranoid. Ever think of that, big guy?

He thought of the way Kristen had acted tonight—the anguish in her voice when she'd asked about Rachel, the vicious bruise that had left her cheek blossoming purple. It was difficult to reconcile his former impression of Kristen with the thought of her risking her life to try to save Rachel from the kidnappers.

"Better keep an eye on Kristen," Josh said grimly. "If she's so grabby with Rachel's money, maybe she'll sell this story to the paper for a hunk of cash. I'll bet some seedy tabloid would drop a bundle for an exclusive scoop on the kidnapping."

Sandra gave Josh a panicky look. Trevor opened his mouth to tell Josh he wasn't being fair, but Michael spoke first, his voice stony. "Kristen will not do that."

"She'd never want to." Gail Ludlum spoke gently. "Trev, how are you feeling? Why don't you let me—"

"Thank you, but I'm fine. I showered and cleaned myself up. I don't have anything worse than scrapes and bruises."

Gail rubbed her puffy eyelids. "It's an awful shame you Mormons don't drink coffee. I could use a cup."

"Hot chocolate?" Sandra said absently.

"No, dear. I don't want anything except to be here for you." Gail reached over and gripped Sandra's hand.

"Why don't they *call*?" Josh slashed his hand through his pile of shredded newspaper. Torn bits flew everywhere. "What are they waiting for?"

"For us to lose any control or perspective that we have," Michael said. "They have power right now and they're making sure we know it."

The phone rang. Michael and Sandra both lunged for it.

Sandra got there first. She snatched up the receiver. Trevor looked over her shoulder. The caller ID read *Anonymous.*

"This is Sandra Drake. Who is this?"

Trevor pressed the heel of his hand against his chest as if he could manually slow the crazy speeding of his heart.

"Hello? *Hello?* Who's there? Please don't hang up—*hello?"*

Michael took the phone, listened, and set it back in the base. "Did they say anything at all?"

Sandra shook her head, her eyes frantic with pain. "It had to be them. Who else would call at three in the morning? Why didn't they say anything?"

Trevor folded his arms tightly, straining to control his rage at the people who would taunt his mother like this. "They're toying with us," he said.

Chapter 13

Dressed in the clothes Dr. Ludlum had hung in the closet for her the night before—were they Rachel's?—Megan sat on the guest room bed, leaning against the pillows she had piled behind her and trying to think through the numbing effects of exhaustion. The sedative Dr. Ludlum had given her had worn off at about six in the morning, and Megan had been awake for the past two hours, fatigued to the point of immobility but unable to get back to sleep.

She wanted to go home.

Not home to Kristen's apartment or to Evelyn's house. Home to Morris Glen. Trina's Barbecue sounded like a haven right now. The worst thing that had ever happened at Trina's was a drunk man tripping over a chair, bumping into Megan and causing her to drop a pot of decaf.

Memories from last night kept rearing up, constricting her throat and bringing cold perspiration out on her skin. She wanted to scream at Kristen for getting her into this situation, though intellectually, she knew it wasn't Kristen's fault. When Kristen had badgered her to attend Rachel's religion class, how could she have anticipated that someone would kidnap Rachel on the way home?

She should call Kristen and tell her what had happened. Kristen's snarky remarks notwithstanding, she must be fond of Rachel, or she wouldn't have spent so much time with her, no matter how many Gucci purses or outings to Cape Cod were involved. But Megan didn't dare call Kristen from the Drakes', where someone might overhear her. Kristen would murder her if she got so flustered she blew her masquerade and their inheritance.

Megan's thoughts shifted back to the kidnapping and she shivered, feeling again the chill of the wind and the roughness of bark scraping her face and arms. Had the kidnappers contacted the Drakes with their ransom demand? How much money did they want?

Pull yourself together. No matter how much cash they ask for, it will be a drop in the bucket for the Drakes. Rachel's parents will pay, Rachel will come home, and everything will be fine.

Megan slid off the bed and stood up, grimacing at the stiffness in her legs. She should be at Evelyn's this morning, making tea and tidying up. She didn't belong at the Drakes'. She was a stranger whose presence would force them to keep their public faces in place at a time when their emotions were in turmoil.

It was already ten past eight. She'd told Evelyn she'd be there around eight. She'd better call. It would take her at least twenty minutes to drive to Britteridge.

Her car. She didn't have her car. It was at Kristen's apartment, and she couldn't possibly impose on the Drakes to take her home. After she talked to Evelyn, she'd call a taxi.

Kristen's purse was on the dresser. Megan opened it in search of Kristen's cell phone. She rooted through three pockets of the purse before she remembered the kidnapper had taken the phone. She must *really* be rattled if she'd forgotten that.

Calm down. They don't want to hurt Rachel. They just want money. They aren't killers or they would have shot you last night, not left a note telling Trevor where to find you.

She reached for the phone on the nightstand and drew her hand back. She should check with the Drakes before she told Evelyn what time she'd be in Britteridge. Michael Drake had asked her to stay here last night, but she didn't imagine he'd intended to take her on as a long-term guest.

There was a knock on the door. Relieved she didn't have to hunt for someone so she could deliver the message that she was leaving, Megan opened the door to see Trevor Drake. Only slight shadows under his eyes and a bruise near his temple gave any indication of what he'd been through the night before. "How are you feeling?"

"All right," Megan said. "How about you?"

He shrugged. "Come get some breakfast."

The thought of facing the Drakes grouped around a silent breakfast table made her cringe. "Thank you, but I told my aunt I'd be at her house around eight, and I'm already late. Have you—heard from the kidnappers?"

"Not yet. That's what I need to talk to you about. Until we have a better idea of what we're dealing with, my parents want to keep this completely quiet. They haven't even talked to the police."

"I understand. I won't say anything."

"Kristen. Have you looked in a mirror? When anyone sees you, you're going to get bombarded with questions about what happened. Do you have a good answer for that?"

Megan lifted her hands to her face. She *hadn't* looked in a mirror. She'd avoided it, not wanting to see how she looked after her ordeal.

She turned away from Trevor and walked into the bathroom.

The bruise where the kidnapper had struck her was a massive blotch of purple and black, swelling over her cheekbone and up into the hollow under her eye. There were smaller bruises on her forehead and left temple, scrapes on both cheeks, and red marks on her jaw where the tape had irritated her skin. If her injuries weren't enough to attract questions, she was so pale that her skin looked gray and her eyes had a trancelike glaze.

She was embarrassed to admit to Trevor that she hadn't even thought about how to answer the inevitable questions about her appearance. How stupid could she be? She wasn't thinking clearly. She wasn't thinking at all.

Reluctantly, she emerged from the bathroom. Trevor was still standing in the doorway.

"I'll cover up what I can with makeup," she said. "And if anyone asks questions, I'll say I . . ." She tried to think of an acceptable way she could have gotten so banged up, but nothing came to mind. "I'll cover it with makeup," she repeated.

"Kristen, listen," he said shortly. "I know this is inconvenient for you, but it would mean a lot to my family if you'd stay here at the house, at least until we hear from the kidnappers and decide what to do."

Megan frowned in confusion. Why would they want her underfoot at such a stressful time?

They *didn't* want her underfoot. The piercing way Trevor looked at her reminded Megan of what she'd forgotten in the stress of last night—Trevor didn't like or trust Kristen. Were the Drakes afraid that if she got out of their sight, she'd spread the news of the kidnapping all over town without regard to what her blabbing would do to Rachel?

Even though she knew the Drakes' mistrust was directed at Kristen, not her, it was still so humiliating that Megan felt she'd dissolve like the Wicked Witch of the West if Michael or Sandra Drake so much as glanced at her.

"I won't say anything to anyone about . . . what happened." Megan spoke softly but still ended up sounding as miserable as she felt. "I'd never do anything to endanger Rachel."

"I'm not saying you'll talk. I'm just saying if you walk out of here looking like someone beat you up—plus Rachel is gone—can we please try to keep questions from arising until we've decided what to do?"

Megan drew a deep breath, trying to steady both her emotions and her voice. "How are you planning to explain Rachel's absence? She's supposed to be at school today."

"If anyone asks, the story is that Rachel has come down with a bad case of the stomach flu and is staying with my parents while she recovers. Do you know if she had anything planned for today besides school? We checked her calendar and there was nothing listed."

Megan had to struggle just to remember what day of the week it was. "I . . . don't think she mentioned anything."

"All right. Now, regarding your aunt, I understand she needs care. Dr. Ludlum has volunteered to go over this morning and stay with her."

"That's kind of her. But my aunt wouldn't be comfortable with a stranger in her home." Visions of Evelyn becoming offended and the inheritance evaporating made Megan's mouth go dry. She felt incredibly petty worrying about money right now, but Kristen wouldn't accept any excuse if she blew it.

"You shouldn't be working at your aunt's this morning anyway," Trevor said. "After what you went through last night, you belong in a hospital, not making beds and washing dishes for someone else. Gail's a professional. She knows how to help sick and elderly patients. If she explains to your aunt that you're ill—"

"I feel fine," Megan insisted. "I'm just a little sore." A lot sore, shaky, weak, and with a queasy feeling in her stomach that made her doubt she could swallow anything besides water. How *was* she going to manage this morning? Evelyn had mentioned yesterday that the yard needed to be mowed and edged and the bushes trimmed. Her neighbor usually took care of yard work for her, but he was recovering from gallbladder surgery.

Megan would manage. She had to. "I'll be fine. I really have to go take care of her."

"We're just asking you to stay until we hear from the kidnappers and have a better idea of what we're dealing with. It shouldn't be long."

Megan wavered. How could she be callous enough to march out of here and add to the Drakes' worries? But Evelyn . . . Kristen would never forgive her.

"Can we compromise?" Megan asked. "If you want me to stay, I'll stay. But let me go take care of my aunt first. She wouldn't be comfortable with Dr. Ludlum. And she won't get suspicious about—" Megan gestured at her bruised face. "I'll think up some excuse and she'll believe it. I wasn't planning to be there the whole day. Just a couple of hours this morning, and then I was going to finish moving out of my apartment. But I can go straight to my aunt's and come straight back here. I don't want your parents worrying that—" Tears stung her eyes. Embarrassed, she straightened the pillows on the bed as an excuse to avert her face from Trevor.

"How did you plan to get to Britteridge?" he asked.

"Taxi." She picked up the copy of the Book of Mormon she'd left facedown on the quilt and returned it to the bookshelf where she'd found it this morning when she'd been desperately seeking something to divert her thoughts. "I'll have the taxi drop me at my apartment so I can get my car."

"You don't need a taxi. I'll drive you."

"You don't have to do that." Megan swiped the wetness from her cheeks before turning toward Trevor. "You want to be here with your family."

"I want to make sure you don't overexert yourself. You shouldn't be driving. If you're determined to go to your aunt's, I'll take you there. I'll help you do what you need to and I'll bring you back here."

"You're not in any better shape than I am," Megan protested.

"Want to bet?" He crooked an elbow and held up his hand. "We'll arm wrestle. Whoever wins is obviously in better shape and gets to drive."

Megan smiled. She admired Trevor for finding a flicker of humor in the situation. "Fine, I surrender." Just the few minutes she'd spent on her feet had her ready to keel over. If Trevor wanted to help her at Evelyn's, she'd be a fool to refuse him.

"Come have some breakfast," Trevor said. "I'll take you to Britteridge after you eat."

"Never mind breakfast. I couldn't eat anyway."

"You'll at least have some orange juice and toast, or Gail will skin me alive—assuming I'm still alive after she finds out I'm taking you to your aunt's."

"Is Dr. Ludlum here?"

"Yes, she came to stay with my mother. Dad had to go over to the college."

"To work! I can't believe—" Megan stopped in embarrassment. What business was it of hers how Michael Drake coped with his daughter's kidnapping?

"Believe me, he didn't want to go in. A businessman from England who's thinking of founding a school on a philosophy similar to Britt's flew over here to tour the college and talk to Dad. If Dad assigns someone else to meet with him, it will ruffle a lot of feathers. He *would* have backed out anyway rather than leave my mother on her own today, but she shoved him out the door. She doesn't want us to do anything that would stir up unnecessary questions."

"Are you going to work, then?"

"No. I can take the day off without making a stir. Dad asked me to help Mom with whatever she needs."

Yet Trevor had offered to take Megan to Britteridge, leaving his mother behind. Megan's imagination filled in the rest of the instructions Michael Drake had given his son. *"Your job is to keep an eye on Kristen. Make sure she doesn't do anything stupid."*

Kristen would be beyond furious at being treated this way, but Megan's anger flickered out almost before it ignited. Naturally the Drakes were terrified that the smallest slip could start a rumor that would make its way to either the kidnappers or the police. Was it any wonder Trevor's parents had asked him to keep tabs on the only other person—besides Gail Ludlum—who knew what had happened last night?

"Kristen . . . I hope you know how much we appreciate your cooperation." Trevor's voice was softer, warmer, and he looked a little puzzled, like Megan's responses hadn't been what he'd expected. "In asking you to keep quiet, we don't mean to be insensitive to what you've been through. If you'd like to confide in your parents, of course that would be—"

"*No.*" Megan was instantly abashed at how abrupt she sounded. "I mean, thank you. But my mother . . . she would *not* be good at keeping her mouth shut. I won't say anything to her until Rachel is home. And my father . . . he died a few years ago."

"I'm sorry." Trevor made the ritual words of sympathy sound sincere.

"Let's go have breakfast." Choking down food she didn't want sounded better than continuing this conversation about her family.

As Megan followed Trevor to the kitchen, one question filled her mind. How would her mother react if Megan were kidnapped? Would she be like the Drakes, desperately following the kidnappers' instructions to the letter in hopes of getting Megan back? And once the ransom demand came, would Pamela be willing to give up any possession, sacrifice any amount of money to—

Megan tried not to finish that thought.

* * *

A dozen times on the drive to Britteridge, Megan nearly said something to break the silence, but each time she swallowed the words and resumed staring out at the multicolored leaves fluttering on the trees. Any topic unrelated to Rachel was too trivial to mention, and any topic concerning Rachel was too painful.

Trevor stopped at Kristen's apartment so Megan could pack an overnight bag. Standing in front of the bathroom mirror, Megan did her best to camouflage her scrapes and bruises with makeup.

"Not bad," Trevor said when she returned to the living room.

"Not bad if you stand at a distance and squint." Megan gingerly touched the bruise on her cheek. "If anyone asks about it, I'll say I took a tumble on the stairs."

Trevor rose to his feet. "Ready?"

"Yes." Megan picked up Kristen's overnight case. "How are *you* planning to explain—" She indicated the bruise near Trevor's temple where his head had struck the ground when the kidnappers attacked him.

"I haven't thought much about it," he admitted.

Megan hid a bleak smile. Apparently she wasn't the only one rendered spacey by stress. Trevor had had enough presence of mind to remind her she needed to invent an excuse for her appearance, but he hadn't bothered to think one up for himself.

Trevor drove her to Evelyn's house. As she reached to open the door of his truck, she realized her hand was trembling. What was the matter with her? Evelyn wasn't going to doubt her story, but the thought of facing anyone outside the Drake family and pretending nothing was wrong made her want to curl into a ball and cry.

"Kristen! Help me!"

What was happening to Rachel now?

"Doing all right?" Trevor asked.

Megan forced herself to nod.

"Kristen, it's not too late to get Gail to—"

"No, it's not that. I'm okay physically. I just can't . . ."

"Can't what?" Trevor's voice was steady. Megan envied his calm and wondered how much of it was faked.

"I can't stop thinking about Rachel." She looked down and realized she was clutching Kristen's purse so hard that her fingernails were sinking into the leather. She loosened her grip and flexed her aching fingers. Her hands looked white and bony, and the scrapes where she'd grated them against the tree bark were blood red. "How do your parents stand it?"

"With a lot of faith."

Megan thought again of Nephi and the litany of miraculous rescues that had attended his life. But what of the man she'd read about this morning? He'd had tremendous faith as well. And he'd been killed.

"From what I've been reading, faith doesn't always mean protection." Megan knew this line of talk would hurt Trevor. If she had any sense she'd be quiet, but an aching need to know pushed her onward. She looked at him. "What about Abinadi?"

Trevor's eyes widened. "You've been doing a lot of reading."

"I woke up early this morning and couldn't get back to sleep. I'm sorry. I know you don't want to talk about this, but it's . . . bothering me."

Trevor looked away from her, his jaw muscles tight. "Faith equals spiritual protection," he said after a moment. "But it doesn't always equal physical protection. It depends on the will of God—whether He needs you around longer as a Nephi, or if your work on earth is finished, like an Abinadi. When I say my parents are relying on their faith, I don't mean they know for certain that Rachel will return safely—unless they've received some inspiration they haven't shared with me. But they know God will give them—and Rachel—the strength and comfort they need, no matter what. Does that make sense?"

"I think so. But it's not what I want to hear right now."

"I know." Trevor's voice went hoarse. He swallowed. "Kristen, Rachel will be fine. The kidnappers want money. They'll get it. They know if they return her unharmed, they've got a chance to escape and enjoy that money, but if they hurt her—I don't think they'll risk the consequences." He opened his door. "Let's go see what your aunt needs and take care of things here as quickly as possible."

Evelyn was sitting in her recliner in the family room, watching a cooking show. "Darling, I was starting to get anxious. I thought perhaps you'd been in an accident."

"I'm so sorry to make you worry."

"And my goodness, you've brought a friend along. I do wish you'd warn me before you do that."

Before Megan could apologize again, Trevor stepped forward and offered his hand to Evelyn. "Trevor Drake. I apologize for barging in unannounced. Kristen isn't feeling well this morning. That's why she's late. I came along to do the heavy lifting so she won't overexert herself."

"Oh, Mr. Drake. You're dear Rachel's brother." Evelyn gripped Trevor's strong hand with both of her fragile ones. "Dear me, you've hurt your head."

"It's nothing."

"I'll bring your tea." Megan retreated to the kitchen, leaving Trevor to chat with Evelyn.

When Megan returned with the steaming tea, Evelyn pursed her lips and looked worriedly at Megan as she set the cup on the table.

"Dear child, you do look ill. And whatever happened to your face? You're hurt, too!"

So much for the makeup. "Last night I tripped on the stairs outside my apartment and went head over heels."

"Oh my!" Evelyn pressed her hand to her heart. "What a fright!"

"I'm all right. Still in one piece, anyway." Too late Megan realized that Trevor and she should have come up with a joint story—like a car accident that explained both their injuries. Hastily, she changed the subject. "What would you like us to do this morning? I know you mentioned the yard."

"Yes, it needs to be mowed and edged. And the bushes around the front porch need to be trimmed."

"I'll get started on that." Trevor rose from the couch.

"That's good of you, Mr. Drake. The garage is through that door there. You'll find the tools you need. The lawn mower is filled with gas. Please be sure to put everything back exactly where you found it."

"Absolutely. My mother trained me well. Kristen, holler if you need me." He headed into the garage.

"Such a nice young man." Evelyn sipped her tea. "I take it he's sweet on you, dear?"

Fat chance, Megan thought. *I attract creeps like Luke Wagner.* "He's just a friend. How are you feeling this morning?"

"Not well at all. I slept poorly last night. The pain was much worse."

"I'm so sorry. Maybe we should talk to your doctor about adjusting—"

"No, no. My medication is adequate. It was just a bad night. Dear, if you're up to it, there's a picture I wanted you to rehang for me. But if it would be too difficult—"

"I'm fine, Aunt Evelyn. Where's the picture?"

"It's in the office, on the wall above the desk. It's a painting of the Annisquam Harbor Lighthouse. I've decided I want it here in the family room. I spend so little time in the office, and I've always loved that painting. There's something so reassuring about lighthouses, don't you think?"

"Yes, they're very charming," Megan said automatically.

"You'll find a hammer on the pegboard in the garage and picture hooks in the top left-hand drawer on the workbench."

Megan went to the garage to fetch the hammer and hooks. From outside, she heard the roar of the lawnmower. Thank goodness for Trevor Drake.

She spent the next hour trying to situate the picture in a location that pleased Evelyn. At Evelyn's direction, she hammered hook after hook into the wall and hung the painting, only to have Evelyn change her mind and request that the hook be removed and the hole immediately patched. Evelyn finally settled on the spot over the fireplace, which involved removing the oil painting of a farm that already hung there.

Megan's arms and back were aching so horribly by this point that she said, "I'll put this in the office for now," and, clutching the farm painting, rushed out of the room before Evelyn could start on an endless round of deciding where to hang the displaced painting.

"That's definitely the right location." Evelyn was gazing happily at the lighthouse painting when Megan returned. "See how the red in the painting coordinates so prettily with the bricks of the fireplace?"

"It looks perfect," Megan said with feeling.

"Tomorrow you can do the touch-up painting to finish repairing the nail holes."

"That sounds fine. Let me put the hammer away."

"While you're out there, dear, please go to the mailbox and bring in the mail. No one brought it in yesterday, and I was feeling too ill to go for it myself. It *does* bother me to miss the mail."

"I'm sorry." That was her third blunder in two days: she'd forgotten the mail, she'd been late this morning, and she'd brought Trevor unannounced. She could almost hear Kristen's voice. *"We've got over a million bucks on the line and you're acting like the punch line in a blond joke."*

Megan hurried to the mailbox and fetched the mail, hoping fervently she'd be able to leave soon. She wanted to get back to the Drakes' and collapse.

"Throw out the junk mail," Evelyn said peevishly as Megan offered her the stack of mail. "Just give me the important things. What's that magazine there?"

"A *Ladies Home Journal.* Would you like it now?"

"Put it in the magazine rack. Anything else?"

"A Bell Atlantic bill. And a letter."

"Who from, dear?"

Megan looked at the tall white envelope. A sticker on the envelope read "Luftpost" and another sticker, "Par Avion Prioritaire." Curious, she glanced at the stamps. *Deutschland.* She flipped the letter over and read the return address on the back.

"Troy Seaver," she said. *Seaver! A relative?* Evelyn had a relative in Germany who wrote to her?

"Put the bill in the top right-hand drawer in the desk and give me Troy's letter."

Megan gave her the letter. Kristen had said Evelyn had no contact with any other relatives. Kristen didn't know about Troy.

Cautiously, Megan posed a question, prepared to fake sudden remembrance if Evelyn was surprised by her ignorance. "You have a relative who lives in Germany, Aunt Evelyn?"

"A nephew by marriage, yes. He's lived there for many years but plans to come back to Britteridge someday, so he holds onto a house here. I look after it for him, or I did before my illness. Dear, this tea doesn't taste right." Evelyn pointed at the nearly full cup. "You must have used a heaping teaspoon of sugar. That's far too much."

"I'm sorry. Would you like a fresh cup?"

"No. Just a bit of dry toast. You seem distracted today." Evelyn handed her the cup. "Distraction makes for shoddy work."

Frustration surged through Megan, and she had to fight the urge to dash the cup to the floor and scream. What did any of this matter? Rachel's life was in danger. Who cared about lighthouses, tea, and junk mail?

Kristen would care. No matter how bad Kristen felt about Rachel, she would still consider Evelyn's money her top priority.

Focus, Megan chided herself. *College, remember? The reason you're here?*

Megan hurried into the kitchen. To her dismay, tears started flowing as she worked. She touched her palm to her swollen cheek and stood, eyes closed, struggling to force her emotions under control.

The soft friction of Evelyn's footsteps made Megan jump. She wiped her eyes with a napkin and snatched the toast from the toaster.

"I meant to tell you I wanted the whole-wheat toast," Evelyn said, coming to stand next to her.

Megan slid the plate of white toast aside. She didn't dare speak, knowing that the shakiness in her voice would make it obvious she was fighting tears. She took the whole-wheat loaf from the breadbox, hoping Evelyn would return to her chair in front of the television so Megan could have a moment alone to compose herself.

"Dear child." Evelyn stroked Megan's bruised cheek with one dry fingertip. "You're very shaken up, aren't you? That must have been a terrible fall. And here I am fussing about toast." Evelyn took the bread from Megan and set it aside.

"Go lie down, dear. As soon as Mr. Drake finishes in the yard, I'll have him take you home."

"I'm fine—" Megan began, but Evelyn patted her hand and interrupted softly, "You're so good to me. So good. I don't want you to suffer. Go rest. I'll be fine."

Chapter 14

Gail Ludlum's hands shook so badly that it took her four tries to dial the number she'd written on an index card. Once everything was settled, she'd tear up the card and send the pieces to the sewer.

She wished she could do the same to Kristen O'Connor.

Deep breath, honey, she counseled herself, glancing around to make sure she hadn't attracted any attention. *Start looking too sick here and some gallant trucker will call 911.*

The phone on the other end started to ring. Gail scanned her surroundings one more time, wishing someone would stray too near the pay phones so she would have an excuse to hang up and delay the call. Unfortunately, the parking lot of this truck stop was nearly empty. Through the windows of the café, she could see only two customers sitting at the counter.

"Yes?" Kristen's voice slithered into Gail's ear. Gail gripped the receiver and spoke words she hated.

"They're cooperating. No police, no publicity. If anyone asks about Rachel, they'll claim she's holed up in their house, sick with the stomach flu. Michael Drake went to work today. Joshua went to school. Trevor went to help your sister at Mrs. Seaver's."

Kristen snickered. "I know. How chivalrous of Trev. Sounds like Megan's worming her way into his heart."

"You swore no one would get hurt," Gail whispered furiously. "And right off the bat, you take your own sister and—"

"Whoa, Doc. That was her own fault. She tried to interfere, so my partner had to give her a little push."

"A *little* push? Half her face is purple. And she was hypothermic when—"

"She's fine, isn't she? Quit whining. How much time did you spend at the Drakes' today?"

"I was there from about eight in the morning until Michael came home around six. I canceled my appointments so I could stay, like you said."

"Tell me about Sandra. What's her attitude? Is she thinking of pulling any funny business on us?"

"Absolutely not." Gail spat the words into the phone. She'd never imagined she could regard another human being with the depth of revulsion she felt for Kristen O'Connor.

And for herself.

Everything will be fine. In a couple of days Rachel will be home and this will all be over.

"Is Sandra keeping mum or has she been weeping and wailing to friends?"

"She hasn't told a soul outside their immediate family, except for me. You said to keep it silent, and she'd die before she'd breathe a word. Why do you think Mike was at Britt today? Sandra talked him into going so his absence wouldn't draw attention. Why do you think Trevor's hovering around your sister? To make sure she doesn't spill anything. Evan—that's their oldest son—wants to fly in from Kentucky, but Sandra won't let him come, because she doesn't want anyone to wonder about this sudden visit. Convinced yet?"

"Michael?"

"Quietly furious. If you were dealing with him alone, you'd have the FBI breathing down your necks, but he won't go against Sandra and she's adamant that they follow your instructions precisely."

"I hope you're telling the truth, Doc. I'd hate to mess up that glowing future you've fantasized for little Bryce—"

"Just give them the demands, you snake, and finish this."

"They'll get word tonight. Make sure you visit Sandra tomorrow and find out how they're reacting. Call me tomorrow night at ten from a different phone. Got it?"

Gail gripped the phone, wishing she could smash it to smithereens. "Yes."

"You're a great help," Kristen said silkily. "Bryce is lucky to have such a loving mommy."

Gail slammed the phone onto the hook.

* * *

The phone rang at 9:30 that night, startling Megan into spilling her hot chocolate all over the Drakes' kitchen table—a foolish overreaction. The phone had rung several times that evening, and Megan had writhed in anguish as she watched the fear and hope that leapt into the Drakes' faces every time the bell trilled, followed by acute disappointment and strain as they plodded through dealing with whoever was on the other end of the line and pretended nothing was amiss.

But this time, the expression on Michael Drake's face was different. Megan froze, forgetting about the spreading puddle of cocoa.

"Yes," Michael said into the receiver. "This is Michael Drake."

Sandra stood motionless at the stove, clutching the spoon she'd used to stir the hot chocolate. Joshua, sitting across from Megan, gripped a mug heaped with melting marshmallows. Trevor stood next to his father.

"What do you want?" Michael asked. Megan had never imagined that such a quiet voice could carry such piercing rage.

There was a long pause. Megan had to gasp for air; she hadn't realized she'd been holding her breath.

Michael gripped Trevor's shoulder like he was steadying himself. "Rachel—*wait*—"

The spoon fell from Sandra's hand and hit the floor with a clang that made Megan jump.

"Yes," Michael said curtly. Another pause. "That's unnecessary. I'd prefer—" Pause. "Fine. But if you are assuming—hello?"

Sandra gave a choked whimper. Michael lowered the phone.

Megan could almost hear the heartbeats of everyone in the room, a pulsing pressure on her eardrums.

"What did they say?" Sandra rushed over to grasp her husband's arm. "Is Rachel all right?"

"Yes. They let her say a few words."

"What did she say?"

Michael put his arm around Sandra. "She said, 'Hi Dad, it's me. I'm all right.' Then they took the phone away."

"Did she *sound* all right?"

"She sounded scared, honey. How else would she sound?"

"What are the demands?" Trevor's arms were folded, the muscles in his shoulders taut against his shirt.

"I need to speak with your mother alone." Michael led Sandra out of the kitchen.

"How can he *do* that?" Josh's face reddened. "Doesn't he think we want to know what's happening?"

"It's up to Mom and him to decide what to do," Trevor said. "It's right that they should discuss it privately."

Megan rose unsteadily to her feet and fetched a dishcloth to wipe up her spilled hot chocolate. Her stomach was churning. Who had spoken to Michael Drake on the phone? The kidnapper who'd dragged Rachel out of the car and hit Megan in the face? The kidnapper with the scratchy voice who'd marched Megan into the woods and tied her to a tree?

At least they knew Rachel was still alive.

"This is ridiculous," Josh said. "We finally get some information and they run off and hide."

Trevor's expression was as rigid as his folded arms, but his tone was soothing. "Take it easy. Trust them, all right? They'll be back soon."

But long after the hot chocolate had grown cold and the marshmallows in Josh's cup had congealed into a sticky clump that he kept poking at with his spoon, Michael and Sandra still hadn't returned.

"What do you think they're doing?" Megan couldn't endure the silence any longer.

"Praying, I imagine," Trevor said heavily. "Praying."

"So why couldn't they include us? Don't they think we care?" Josh pushed back from the table so angrily that his chair tipped and slammed against the floor.

"Josh," Trevor said.

"Just shut up. *You* may be happy sitting here like a lump of ice, but I want to know what's going on." He stalked out of the kitchen.

Trevor followed him. A moment later, Josh's angry "Leave me alone!" came from the hallway.

Megan stood, awkward and alone and feeling acutely like an outsider. She'd better go to her room and keep out of the way for the rest of the evening, but first she'd clean up the kitchen. It felt good, if only in a miniscule way, to do this small task to help the Drakes.

She righted the chair Josh had knocked over and started clearing the mugs from the table.

Trevor returned to the kitchen. "You don't have to clean up. I'll take care of it."

"I don't mind." Megan turned on the faucet and rinsed marshmallow residue out of one of the mugs. "Please let me help. It's driving me crazy not to be able to do anything."

"I know how you feel." Misery was raw in Trevor's voice. He sat down and braced his elbows against the table, his head bowed. There were scratches along the back of his neck that Megan hadn't noticed before. Had the kidnappers dragged him across the ground after they'd knocked him out?

"Useless," he muttered. "Completely useless."

Megan hadn't intended to say anything, but Trevor's anguish—the first open pain she'd witnessed from him—brought her guilt to the surface. "If only I'd been quicker with my phone last night, I could have called for help. Or if I'd noticed the kidnappers coming out of the woods an instant sooner—"

Trevor lifted his head. "Don't do this. If you play the what-if game, you'll tear yourself up."

"The way you're tearing yourself up?" Megan guessed.

"Yeah." Trevor rested his forehead against his interlaced fingers. "Something like that."

* * *

Josh slammed his bedroom door so violently that his bulletin board fell off the wall and knocked over two basketball trophies. Spitting out a word his mother would have grounded him for, he picked up the fallen board and jammed it on the hook. The picture of Rachel tacked in the corner of the board made him growl with frustration. It had started out as a picture of Rachel sitting in a lawn chair at a family picnic, but after passing through the Photoshop-savvy hands of

Rachel's friend Larissa Mullins, it had ended up a picture of Rachel as a medieval queen. She was wearing a red velvet dress and a jeweled crown and was sitting on a throne. A cartoon bubble next to her mouth carried the caption, "Off with his head!" When Josh had laughed at the picture, Rachel had given it to him to add to the photo collection on his bulletin board.

Now the picture of Rachel's smiling face made him want to put his fist through the wall.

He knew he'd hurt Trevor, but he was too angry to care. Calm old Trev was content to sit there until the Millennium, if that's how long it took his parents to tell them what was going on. And Kristen O'Connor—

Kristen. Yeah, she looks all sick and scared, but who wouldn't after getting knocked around by a couple of kidnappers?

Did she really care that much about Rachel? A couple of weeks ago, Trevor had talked about Kristen when Josh and he were hiking. He'd admitted he was worried—that Kristen seemed like a manipulator, but that she was so charming and beautiful that Rachel didn't notice her flaws. Why had Trevor downplayed his concerns when talking to their parents last night? Trust Trev to make a big deal about how his suspicions weren't "fair" and how he might have misjudged Kristen. Mr. Parley P. Perfect wouldn't dare go out on a limb and say what he really thought.

Kristen *was* pretty, but she made Josh squirm. Like that time she and Rachel had dropped by the basketball court while Josh and his friend Phil were practicing their jump shots. When Rachel got distracted by a phone call, Kristen had joined in the practice. She wasn't a bad shot, but she'd made a few comments to Josh that were innocent on the surface but had a double meaning. Josh was so embarrassed that he'd missed almost every shot. She'd watched him bumble around the court with a mocking little smile on her face, and Josh could tell she was pleased that she'd flustered him.

So why did Kristen have to be here now, butting in on what should be a time for family?

If Kristen was using Rachel, maybe she'd had something to do with Rachel's kidnapping. Had Trevor and his parents thought of that? Maybe her getting tied up by the kidnappers was a ploy to make her look innocent, when really she'd get a cut of the ransom as soon as Rachel was released. Kristen could have been the one who told the kidnappers Rachel's schedule and the route she always took home from the church.

Determination hardened inside Josh. He had to do something or he'd go crazy. Kristen was downstairs in the kitchen with Trevor. His parents were in their room. No one would notice if he sneaked into the guest room and searched through Kristen's stuff. He didn't know what he expected to find, but anything weird might be evidence that Kristen wasn't someone the Drakes should trust.

Josh tiptoed out of his bedroom and headed toward the guest rooms.

The door to Kristen's room was ajar. With sweat-sticky fingers, Josh eased the door open and crept inside.

It was too dark to see what he was doing, and he hadn't thought to bring a flashlight. He'd just turn on the overhead light. If he heard Kristen coming, he could dart out onto the balcony and hide there until Kristen went into the bathroom.

Josh pawed through Kristen's overnight bag. Clothes, makeup, hair junk. A mystery novel and a paperback copy of *The Brothers Karamazov.* People actually read Dostoe-what's-his-name after they finished AP English?

He closed the overnight bag and unzipped the side pocket. It contained only a crumpled napkin from Dunkin' Donuts.

Her purse. Shooting a look at the door, Josh crouched on the floor next to the bed and opened Kristen's purse. Wallet—credit cards, driver's license, library card. Thirty-two bucks in cash and a handful of change. Comb. Lipstick. Tissues. An envelope filled with photographs. Hopeful, Josh flipped through the pictures. Kristen and some blond guy on a ferry with the Statue of Liberty in the background. Kristen next to a red, double-decker tourist bus.

This was a waste of time. Josh shoved the travel pictures into the envelope and unzipped one of the inner pockets on the purse. It contained some folded pieces of paper. Maybe *this* would be interesting. The first paper was a picture of a wedding announcement, printed on a plain sheet of computer paper. Weird. Who would take a picture of a wedding announcement and print out a copy? Why not just take the announcement itself if you needed the info on it? Maybe Kristen had lost the announcement and a friend had scanned and e-mailed this to her. Lawrence Zuckerman and Tara McCaffrey, getting married at the Cherry Blossom Mansion in Fairfax, Virginia, reception to follow. Thrillsville. Rachel would love this. She gobbled up every detail of weddings.

Zuckerman. Wasn't that the farmer from *Charlotte's Web*? When his brother Evan was here with his kids in the summer, little Jayden had watched the old cartoon version of *Charlotte's Web* so many times that Josh spent weeks with those songs rattling around in his head.

Beneath the picture of the announcement was written "Accord, blue" and what looked like a license plate number. *Huh?* Maybe Kristen was looking to buy a used car and had jotted down the info on this page.

The rest of the pages were maps printed off the Internet. The first gave directions from the Doubletree Hotel in Philadelphia to the Hampton Inn in Fairfax, Virginia. The second gave directions from the Hampton Inn to the Cherry Blossom Mansion. Maybe Kristen had stayed in a hotel in Philadelphia on her way to Virginia for Farmer Zuckerman's reception . . . Who cared anyway? Josh wanted information that might link Kristen to the kidnappers, not the details of some out-of-state wedding.

Josh refolded the papers and put them back in the inner pocket. Three more pockets to try. Why did girls have so many little compartments in their purses?

The first compartment was empty; the second had only a ballpoint pen. Josh stuck his fingers into the third pocket and pulled out a flannel bag with something hard and rectangular inside. He loosened the drawstring at the top of the bag and removed a hinged double-picture frame, the kind you'd set on your desk at work.

One of the frames contained a picture of a balding, middle-aged man with his arm around a young-looking Kristen. Both of them were wearing T-shirts, shorts, and hiking boots. Kristen and her dad?

The picture in the other frame was of two girls, maybe eight or nine years old, sitting on a bale of hay and grinning at the camera. They were wearing matching sweaters. One girl had long red-gold hair fluttering around her face, and the other girl had her hair in a ponytail, but other than that, the girls were identical. They sure looked like Kristen. Twin nieces, maybe? Josh slipped the picture out of the frame to see if anything was written on the back.

"Kristen and Megan." And a date from fifteen years ago.

These weren't her nieces. Kristen was an identical twin. Rachel had never mentioned that.

Weird that Kristen would keep these pictures in her purse. Why weren't they in her apartment on a desk or bookshelf? That frame didn't look valuable. The gold paint had worn away in spots to show cheap metal underneath. Why had Kristen wrapped it in flannel like it was some kind of treasure?

It was odd, but Josh couldn't think why it mattered or how it could have anything to do with Rachel. He put the picture frame into the drawstring bag and returned it to Kristen's purse. This had been a dumb idea, anyway. What had he expected to find? A rough draft of the note the kidnappers had taped to Trevor's shirt?

Josh put Kristen's purse back on the dresser, switched off the lights, and slipped out of the room. Back in his own room, he sat staring moodily at the picture of Rachel the Queen, wondering why that picture of Kristen and her sister was still tugging at his thoughts.

Chapter 15

The adrenaline that had carried Trevor through a sleepless night and torturous day had ebbed, and he was so exhausted that it was a struggle to keep his thoughts organized and his eyes focused. He wouldn't last much longer before fatigue overpowered fear and he fell asleep in the middle of discussing the kidnappers' demands.

"We've got to get the police in on this, or the FBI." Josh was sitting on the edge of the hearth, his fists balled on top of his bent knees. "They can plant cameras and bugs and a homing beacon in the bag with the money—"

"It's not worth the risk, honey." On the couch, Sandra leaned a little closer to Michael so their shoulders were touching. "They warned us if—"

"So we just give them the money and let them sail off to the Bahamas? That's how it works?"

"They've got Rachel," Sandra said. "We can't risk angering them. We have no idea who they are, where they are, or even how many of them are involved."

Trevor finished a yawn before adding, "We also don't know if they're amateurs or pros."

"Pros?" Josh looked at Trevor. "A professional kidnapping organization? Where do you find *those*? In the Yellow Pages under Thugs-for-Hire?"

"I mean like a terrorist group wanting to use our money to fund their cause."

"A terrorist group," Josh muttered. "In small-town Massachusetts."

"Our family is known beyond small-town Massachusetts." Michael put his arm around Sandra. "We can't rule out any possibilities yet."

"We'll never rule out *any* possibilities at the rate we're going," Josh said. "By the time we start looking for the kidnappers, they'll be out of the country. They almost killed Trevor, and now we're trusting them so much that we're willing to hand them two million bucks and close our eyes while they run away—and take their word for it that they'll give Rachel back?"

"We have to cooperate. It's our best hope." The grayish shadows under Sandra's eyes made her look ill. Trevor wanted to suggest that she go lie down, but knew she'd just throw the words back at him.

"Josh, I think they made it clear they didn't want to kill any of us," Trevor said. "Even when Kristen tried to stop them from taking Rachel, they didn't shoot her or even seriously hurt her."

"Yeah, okay, they didn't murder Kristen. Give 'em a medal. But how do you know things went down like she said? Maybe she was just trying to make herself look good by telling you she tried to help Rachel."

"That's enough, Joshua," Michael said. "This decision is up to your mother and me. At this point, we're not willing to risk the kidnappers' anger by bringing in the police. The money is just money—let them have it. Once Rachel is safe, we'll set the law on their trail. They won't get far."

A painful silence settled on the room. It was strange, Trevor thought blearily, how a room that usually seemed warm and welcoming with its comfortable leather furniture, brick fireplace, and multitude of bookshelves now seemed cold and dim.

Josh rested his forehead on his knees. "You're going to bring the police in anyway when you try to take two million dollars out of the bank."

"We'll get the money from a few different sources," Michael said.

"That's a lot of ATM visits," Josh mumbled.

"Don't worry about the money. I started the process this morning—even though we hadn't heard from the kidnappers—so things are already underway. Trevor, how are you holding up?"

"I'm fine. Tired. But fine."

"The ransom drop will be somewhere in Boston," Michael said. "That's all they told me. And they specified that you be the one to do the drop. I protested, but they insisted. Are you willing—"

A fragment of relief punctured Trevor's exhaustion. "I'm willing." He was glad the kidnappers hadn't demanded that his father or mother make the drop. Sandra maneuvering through Boston traffic when she was distracted and sick with worry about Rachel was an accident in the making. And his father—Michael didn't like to drive anywhere, anytime, and if anything would be enough to bring his old phobia to high pitch, it would be driving when his daughter's life was on the line.

"The drop will be on Friday," Michael said. "You're to leave for Boston at ten in the morning. They'll call you on your cell phone with instructions."

"So we don't even know where the drop is going to be?" Josh lifted his head off his knees. "How can we blunder into their trap like that? We'd better at least put a homing bug in—"

"We're not taking any chances!" Sandra shrieked. "Get that through your head!"

Josh stared at her, his mouth slack. Jerkily, he lowered his head back to his knees.

"I'm sorry," Sandra said shakily. "Josh . . . I'm sorry, sweetie. I didn't mean to yell at you. I just . . . please stop pushing this. We're not going to risk Rachel's life on a miniscule chance that we might be able to track her kidnappers. They'll probably get rid of the bag and put the money in their own container as soon as possible. And they probably won't even take the money to where they're hiding Rachel. It's not worth doing something that might anger them, especially since once they have the money, we have—" She stopped. She didn't need to finish the sentence; Trevor knew what she was thinking.

Once they have the money, we have no bargaining power. We have nothing that they want, no way to influence them.

"I'm sorry, Josh," Sandra said again. She was crying.

Josh didn't lift his head.

"Trevor." Michael looked at him. "Don't take any risks while you're doing the ransom drop. Just leave the money where they say and come home. Don't play hero."

Hero. Some hero he'd been so far, lying insensible while Rachel was kidnapped and Kristen was dragged into the woods.

The thought of Rachel in the hands of her attackers created a mass of red-hot anger in Trevor's chest. That scum would be near him, watching him, grabbing at the Drakes' money. And if he didn't want to risk harming Rachel, he'd have to turn away and let them escape.

A painful thought came to mind: Rachel at the pumpkin-painting project, joking about Nephi. *"Don't count on such quick forgiveness if you leave me in the desert to get devoured by wild beasts."*

The irony was that Rachel could and would forgive him for anything, including his failure to protect her from the kidnappers. Sweet, humble Rachel couldn't stay angry at anyone.

But if anything happened to Rachel because of his fury at the kidnappers and his determination that they wouldn't escape—

Rachel could forgive him, but he couldn't forgive himself.

"Trevor." Michael's voice was sharp. "Are you listening to me? Just do whatever they say and don't take chances. We'll let God and the law deal with them. Is that clear?"

"Yes, sir." Trevor loosened his clenched fists and settled back in his chair. "It's clear."

* * *

It wasn't until she awakened in the Drakes' guest room at five o'clock in the morning that Megan realized she was in trouble. She'd neglected to tell Evelyn she no longer had her cell phone. If Evelyn had needed to get in touch with her yesterday evening, she'd have tried Kristen's apartment first, then her cell. With no answer at either number, Evelyn would have been fretful, then frightened. She even might have tried to contact Rachel in an effort to locate Kristen.

Megan pushed back the blankets and dragged her sore body out of bed. If Kristen found out she'd messed up again, she'd be livid. And what if Evelyn had become so worried that she'd called the police to tell them Kristen was missing and to ask if there had been any accidents? Megan shrank from the thought of how the Drakes would react if they found out she had drawn police attention.

She picked up the phone on the nightstand and dialed the number to check Kristen's voice mail.

There were no messages, but Megan was only partially relieved. She could picture Evelyn calling repeatedly but disdaining to record a message. It would be just like her to feel that talking to a voice mail system was beneath her dignity.

She'd better head straight to Britteridge. Evelyn would still be asleep—Megan hoped—but the instant she awakened, Megan would be there with tea and profuse apologies.

The Drakes would all be in bed now. She'd have to leave them a note. She'd take a taxi to Britteridge and, once she'd calmed Evelyn down, she'd drive Kristen's car back here and offer another set of apologies for running out on the Drakes—after which she needed to return to her apartment and finish moving her things to Evelyn's house. Kristen's contract expired tonight, and Kristen had warned her that the manager wouldn't cut her any slack.

Megan showered and dressed in ten minutes flat, whisked a comb through her wet hair, and tiptoed out of the guest bedroom. She'd leave a note in the kitchen.

As she neared the kitchen, she saw to her dismay that the lights were on. She was going to have to explain in person why she was leaving.

Michael Drake was sitting at the kitchen table with a copy of the Mormon scriptures open in front of him. He gave her a look of mild surprise.

"You're up early, Kristen."

Megan smiled uncomfortably, sure that every word she spoke to the founder of Britteridge College would showcase her incompetence. Hoping she didn't look as flushed and flustered as she felt, she explained the situation.

"Would you like to call your aunt from here?" Michael's voice was matter-of-fact, and Megan was relieved that he didn't seem to be condemning her carelessness.

"I don't want to risk disturbing her," Megan said. "I'd rather go to her house and be there when she wakes up, so she doesn't have to worry any longer than necessary."

Michael nodded and closed his scriptures. "I'll have Jay—my driver—take you there immediately."

"You don't need to do that," Megan protested, mortified at the thought of Michael rousing his chauffeur at this predawn hour to drive her to Evelyn's. "I'll call a taxi."

Michael rose to his feet. "Please don't. You'd make me feel like the world's worst host."

"It's so early—I don't want to disturb—"

Michael smiled. "Kristen, I don't enjoy driving, so I pay Jay a great deal of money to be available at a moment's notice to drive me—or my guests—wherever I choose. Let him earn his salary. You've been more than kind, staying with us these past two nights and cooperating with our decision to keep silent on the situation despite being a victim too. The least we can do is assist you in taking care of your responsibilities at home."

Michael's gracious response made it easier for Megan to get her next words out. "I should stay in Britteridge now. I have to finish moving out of my apartment today, and my aunt expects me to stay at her house starting tonight. She'll be upset if my plans change. Her health is—" Remembering Kristen's warning that Evelyn didn't want people to learn of her terminal condition, Megan finished vaguely, "Her health is poor."

Michael studied her. His gaze was penetrating but kind, and Megan sensed none of the condemnation she'd initially felt from Trevor.

"I'll be—very careful not to start any rumors." Megan didn't want to leave Michael with even the smallest doubts about her intentions, if she could help it. "I'd never do anything to put Rachel at risk."

Michael nodded and removed his reading glasses. He was still studying her, and she had the sense that those gentle brown eyes were scrutinizing her soul. "Absolutely you should stay with your aunt. Your responsibility is to your family. Go pack your things. I'll speak to Jay—"

"Michael, I'll take her."

Megan jumped and turned toward Sandra's voice. She'd been so focused on Michael that she hadn't realized Sandra had come into the kitchen. Sandra's curly brown hair—so much like Rachel's—was damp from the shower. She was wearing glasses instead of her regular contacts, and she was dressed in faded jeans and a Britteridge College sweatshirt. Somehow it made Megan more comfortable around Sandra to see her dressed so casually.

"Dear, let Jay drive her," Michael said. "You should rest."

"If I could rest, I'd be resting. It will be a relief to get out of the house for a while. I have strained muscles from jumping every time the phone rings. Kristen, have some breakfast before we go. Can I fix you some pancakes?"

"Oh no, please don't bother. And you don't need to drive me. You have enough to worry about."

"The last thing I want to do right now is sit here and worry. I need a diversion." Sandra opened the stainless-steel fridge and took out a jug of milk and a carton of eggs. "Do you like pecans?"

"Yes, but—please don't go to any trouble for—"

"Pecan pancakes it is. Go pack your suitcase, and by the time you're finished, I'll have breakfast on the table. Did I hear you say you're moving out of your apartment today?"

"Yes." Megan gave up her protests. She didn't want to upset Sandra by arguing with her.

"How are you transporting your belongings to your aunt's?" Michael asked.

"I've already stored most of my things in her basement. I just have a couple of boxes to take over there today."

"I imagine you need to clean your apartment before you move out." Sandra cracked an egg into a mixing bowl. "Rachel said your manager is a cheapskate who'll hold back your whole deposit for a spot of mold on the grout."

"He *is* picky," Megan said, thinking how petty and irrelevant this whole conversation must seem to the Drakes. "I'll do the cleaning once I take care of my aunt."

"I'll help you," Sandra offered. "I'm good with a scrub brush. In fact, I'll get started on the cleaning while you're at your aunt's."

Megan was appalled. "Mrs. Drake, you can't possibly—"

"Kristen, I need to get out of the house. Michael is going to be gone a good part of the day taking care of the . . . money issue, and I need something useful to do. Something that involves moving around, not sitting here and sewing those absurd hoopskirts. I need to help someone. Help me by letting me help you, would you please?"

Did Sandra Drake genuinely want to help her or was she just reluctant to let Megan out of her sight? "I . . . don't want to be a bother . . ."

Michael Drake laughed softly. "If you're wise, you'll let Sandra do what she wants. I learned that a long time ago."

* * *

When Megan arrived at Evelyn's house, Evelyn's bedroom light was on, and Megan's anxiety peaked. Something must be wrong for Evelyn to be up at six in the morning. But from the warmth and amazement in Evelyn's greeting—"Oh my dear, you must be a bit psychic to know I was having a bad time and needed you here early. I thought of calling, but didn't want to wake you"—it was obvious Evelyn's insomnia had nothing to do with Megan's carelessness. Megan told her about the "lost" cell phone, and Evelyn clucked understandingly as Megan promised to replace the phone as soon as possible. She'd have to check with Kristen to see what she wanted Megan to do about the phone. She hadn't talked to Kristen since the kidnapping. There hadn't been a time when she wasn't either at Evelyn's or the Drakes'.

Megan spent the next two hours working to ease Evelyn's discomfort. She made tea, which Evelyn refused to drink, rubbed her legs, rubbed her back, read the newspaper aloud, brought her extra pillows as she rested in her recliner, brought her blankets when she complained of cold, opened the window when she complained of heat, and worried all the while about Sandra Drake at Kristen's apartment, doing the work that Megan should have been doing. She hoped Sandra had changed her mind about the cleaning and returned to Andover.

Evelyn refused to let Megan contact Aurora Capra—the home nurse—or her doctor. There was nothing anyone could do; she was simply very weak and nauseated this morning, but what could you expect with her health failing like this?

At 8 AM, Evelyn ordered Megan to help her back to bed for a morning nap and told her to go finish moving so she could be there when Evelyn reawakened. Gratefully, Megan departed.

At her apartment, she found Sandra Drake wiping out kitchen cupboards.

"I'm sorry it took me so long." Megan hastily shrugged off her jacket. "My aunt was awake when I got there and was feeling rotten. It took me a while to get her settled."

"No need to apologize. I'm here to help you, and the more you let me do, the better I'll feel." Sandra's smile was pleasant, but she looked almost as pale as Evelyn, and her eyes were bloodshot. "I've finished the bathroom, bedroom, windows, light fixtures, and closets, and I've made good progress on the kitchen. Your apartment is already so clean that the work is easy."

"You've been so kind to me. I can't thank you enough." Megan picked up a cleaning rag, wondering what Kristen would make of wealthy Sandra Drake sitting on her counter and wiping spilled sugar out of her cupboard. "But please, you should go home and rest now. Let me finish up."

"I don't need more rest. You, however, ought to be taking it easy. I'll bet it hurts every time you move."

"I'm all right." Megan bypassed the fact that at the moment she felt she'd give up half her cut of Evelyn's money for the chance to soak her aching body in a hot tub.

"We'll finish up together. I haven't done anything with the fridge yet, if you want to start there." Sandra slid off the counter and went to rinse her rag in the sink filled with soapy water. "How did you meet Rachel, by the way? She never told me."

"I asked her for quarters." Thank goodness Kristen had told her this story in surprising detail. "I'd taken my laundry to the laundry room and realized I had a grand total of two quarters. On the way back to my apartment, I ran into Rachel. I asked if she could give me change for a couple of dollars. She invited me in while she hunted through her change jar. We got chatting and just hit it off."

"Are you in school?"

I wish. "Not right now. I moved here to help my aunt."

"Your aunt is lucky to have you. Where were you living before?"

"New York." Megan disliked this line of questioning but knew she'd better not be too reticent, or Sandra's doubts about her character would burgeon. "I was working there, but it was a lousy job, not one I was sorry to leave."

"Have you and your aunt always been close?"

How was she supposed to answer *that* question? Not with the truth. She could imagine how the story of Kristen's hunting up Evelyn and coming to woo her into making Kristen her heir would shock Sandra.

"Unfortunately, I didn't get to know her when I was a child," Megan said, realizing she'd let the silence stretch on for so long that Sandra must be wondering what the problem was. "She's actually my mother's aunt, my great-aunt. I never knew any of my extended family on that side. My mother . . . kept to herself. She didn't even speak to her own mother."

"I'm sorry. It must be a sweet experience for you to be with your aunt now."

"It is." Megan emptied the fridge of its remaining contents: three cans of Diet Coke, a tub of butter, a bottle of ketchup, and a container of Chinese takeout. She hoped Sandra wouldn't ask what had led to her reunion with Evelyn. She didn't want to repeat Kristen's lies about her fascination with researching her family. With every lie Megan told, she felt worse. She'd condemned Luke Wagner as a liar and had thrown him out of her life, but how was she any better? She was lying to the Drakes; she was lying to Evelyn. And for what?

Money.

So try telling Sandra who you really are and why you're here. See how well that goes over.

Megan dipped her cleaning rag into the soapy water and scrubbed vigorously at a sticky spot on the top shelf of the fridge. Whether Sandra Drake thought she was Kristen, Megan, or the Easter Bunny, it didn't matter. What mattered was that Evelyn was getting the care she needed and in turn Megan would get the money she needed. It was a fair trade. She wasn't hurting anyone.

"Has your aunt lived in Britteridge all her life?" Sandra asked.

"Just for a few years. She moved here when she remarried. But her husband—her second husband—passed away last summer."

"I'm sorry. She must be so grateful for your kindness."

Megan smiled dismissively and concentrated on wiping the walls of the fridge. *Kindness. Watching the clock until she dies so I can get my hands on her money.*

To Megan's relief, Sandra didn't pursue the subject of Evelyn. She finished wiping out the cupboards and went to dust and vacuum the living room while Megan finished in the kitchen. Megan worked as fast as she could, wanting the work done so Sandra would feel free to leave.

The sound of the doorbell ringing made Megan groan inwardly. She couldn't think of anyone she wanted to talk to right now, but she'd better answer the door. It might be the apartment manager.

It was Trevor. He looked dressed for work in a burnt-orange Oxford shirt, striped tie, and brown wool trousers. "I thought I'd stop in and see how the move is coming. And I thought you two might need a snack by now." He held up a paper bag. "Danish? I've got apple, cheese, or cherry."

Sandra rose from where she'd been wiping the living room baseboards. "You're sweet, Trevor, but I couldn't. You'll have to eat it yourself."

"That was my backup plan." Trevor stepped into the apartment and Megan shut the door. "Kristen, how about you?"

"I'll take cherry." After Sandra Drake's pecan pancakes, Megan wasn't remotely hungry, but she didn't want Trevor to feel he'd wasted his time. "Just let me finish mopping."

Trevor set the bag on the table and pointed at the two boxes sitting on the counter. "Are those all that's left? I'll take them to your car."

"I'll take them. They aren't heavy."

"I'm here. I might as well be useful. Mom, Dr. Gail called this morning and had a conniption when she heard you were out *doing* good instead of *having* good done to you."

Sandra mixed a laugh and a sigh. "Dear Gail. Has it occurred to her that I haven't had major surgery? I can clean a few baseboards."

Trevor and Sandra wore identical expressions, Megan thought. Pleasant on the surface, but when Megan looked closely, she saw eyes clouded with pain and smiles that didn't reach past the forced curve of lips.

"Mrs. Drake, please let me finish up," Megan said. "Dr. Ludlum is right. You ought to go home."

Sandra lifted her glasses and rubbed her eyes. "Perhaps I should," she said tiredly. "I'm way behind on those hoopskirts."

"No you're not," Trevor said. "What do you think Gail is doing right now? Sitting at your sewing machine."

"Her patients and office staff are going to hate me for taking her away from them." Sandra smiled, but the amusement rapidly faded from her face. "And I hope she realizes that if she leaves me nothing to do, I'm going to lose my mind."

Trevor walked over to his mother and embraced her. "Mom, it's going to be fine. Just hang in there a little longer and Rachel will be home this weekend."

Megan looked down at the floor she was mopping, wishing there were something she could do to help the Drakes. All she'd managed so far was to give them additional worries.

Sandra wiped her eyes and stepped back from Trevor. "You'd better get to work."

"No hurry. What's Dad going to do? Fire me?"

Sandra squeezed his arm. "Don't get cocky."

"I'll call you later to check in. Take it easy on yourself, all right?"

"I will. Where did I put my keys?"

"Right here." Megan picked them up off the counter. Sandra came to take them and, to Megan's surprise, drew her in for a hug.

"You'll never know grateful I am for how kind you've been to us this week," Sandra murmured in Megan's ear. "You went through an awful experience, but you've never complained or even asked for anything. Rachel thinks the world of you, and now I see why."

Tears filled Megan's eyes. Instinctively, she clung to Sandra.

Sandra rubbed the back of Megan's neck. "We'll let you know as soon as we have news. And if you need anything, you'll call us, won't you?"

Megan nodded, her face buried in Sandra's shoulder.

"Sweetheart, you're trembling." Sandra stroked her hair. "Rest for a few minutes and let Trevor finish the mopping and the baseboards. I don't think you realize how worn out you are. You take care of everyone except yourself."

Megan's knees were weak as she pulled back from Sandra and made a futile effort to wipe away the tears before Trevor noticed them. Sandra left, closing the door noiselessly behind her as if afraid the bang of the door would shatter all their nerves.

Trevor unbuttoned his cuffs and rolled up his sleeves. Megan would have snatched the mop before he could take it and insisted he leave for work, but her throat was so choked that if she tried to talk, she knew she'd be bawling.

Without a word, she left him to the mopping and fled to the bedroom. Since Kristen's apartment had come furnished, the bed was still there. Megan collapsed on the bare mattress cover and wept, not sure if she were crying for Rachel, for Sandra, or for the longing that had stirred inside when she'd felt the warmth and compassion of Sandra Drake's motherly embrace.

Chapter 16

Megan tried patting cold water around her eyes but soon gave up the effort as useless. No matter what she did, it wasn't going to hide the fact that she'd been crying, especially since the concealing makeup she'd been using on her scrapes and bruises was out of reach in one of the boxes Trevor had already taken to the car.

"Kristen?" Trevor called from the living room.

"Coming." Megan pushed her fingers through her disheveled hair and turned away from the mirror in disgust. Kristen wouldn't look this bad if she'd skidded down a mountain face-first.

The kitchen floor gleamed, and the cleaning supplies were neatly grouped near the front door.

"All finished," Trevor said. "I'll take the cleaning stuff to your car while you check out."

"The vacuum stays with the apartment." Megan's voice came out slightly hoarse. "Thank you for finishing up. Your family is way too nice to me."

Trevor picked up the mop and the bucket crammed with bottles of window cleaner and bathroom cleaner. Megan slid the apartment key off Kristen's key ring and handed the rest of the keys to Trevor so he could unlock the car.

She'd intended to call Kristen before she left the apartment this morning to tell her what had happened to Rachel and ask her what to do about the missing cell phone, but now the thought of talking to Kristen brought a wave of fatigue. She'd call her later.

Megan was relieved to find the manager away from his desk. His young secretary cheerfully accepted Megan's key and asked for a forwarding address so she could mail the deposit.

Megan spotted Trevor standing near Kristen's car. She started toward him and got intercepted by a blond whirlwind with an art portfolio flapping from one hand.

"Kristen!" Larissa Mullins screeched to a halt, straw-blond hair dancing in the wind. "Where have you guys *been*? I stopped by to see if Rachel was home, but she isn't. I tried to call her about ten times, but she's not answering her phone. We were supposed to go costume shopping last night, remember? You stood me up!"

Megan took a step backward, trying to catch her mental balance. Costume shopping. They'd talked about it at Rachel's religion class.

"Oh my gosh, I'm so sorry," Megan said as Trevor walked over to join them. "We completely forgot."

"I guess so! I thought you'd been abducted by aliens or something."

Megan was careful not to look at Trevor, but she could imagine how the joking words must sting.

"What *happened* to you?" Larissa waved a paint-stained hand toward Megan's face.

Megan feigned a sheepish smile. "Would you believe I tripped on the stairs?"

"You poor thing! That's just the kind of stunt I'd pull. You're lucky you didn't break your neck! These stairs are a death trap and—" She turned to Trevor. "Trev! You've got a bonk on the head too. Another set of rogue stairs?"

"I'll give you some advice," Trevor said. "Always close your kitchen cupboards before you stand up underneath them."

Larissa winced. "You dope. You two are quite the cute little pair today. So where's Rachel? I suppose she broke her nose doing the limbo and has gone into hiding until it heals?"

"I think she would have preferred that," Trevor said. "Actually, she picked up a hideous case of the stomach flu. She's been hiding out at our parents' house."

"The poor girl! No wonder she forgot to call and cancel on the costume thing. She was probably too busy wishing she were dead. Look, I've got to run to class, but if you see Rachel, tell her get well soon and to call me when she can break away from the toilet for a few minutes."

"If you think I'm getting close enough to her to deliver that message, you're nuts," Trevor said.

Laughing, Larissa hurried away.

"I'm sorry," Megan said miserably when Larissa was out of earshot. "You asked me if Rachel had anything scheduled, and I said no. I forgot we'd made that shopping date with Larissa. I can't believe I—"

Trevor touched her shoulder. "I forgot too. Rachel told me about it when we were in the car, remember?" He smiled wryly. "These past couple of days I'm lucky if I can remember my own name."

"We should have come up with a coordinated explanation for why we're both hurt," Megan said. "A car accident, maybe. That could have explained Rachel's absence too."

Trevor shook his head. "A story like that is too interesting. Larissa would have pumped us for details and told all her friends. Let's stick with boring excuses like stairs and the stomach flu."

"I'd better hurry over to my aunt's." Megan took the keys from Trevor's hand. "She was feeling rotten this morning."

"She looked pretty chipper when I saw her at Market Basket."

Megan was startled. "When did you see her at the store?"

"This morning when I stopped by to get the—what's the matter?"

"Nothing." Megan tried to smile. "I'm just surprised. She was so ill when I . . . are you *sure* it was her? Did you talk to her?"

Trevor raised his eyebrows. "No, we didn't speak. She looked like she was in a hurry. I don't think she saw me. But I'm sure it was her. Does she drive a maroon Caddy?"

Megan pictured the car in Evelyn's garage. "Yes." But Kristen had said Evelyn was too ill and on too much medication to drive anymore.

"Are you all right?" Trevor asked.

Megan fiddled with Kristen's keys. "I'm just surprised. I wish she'd called me instead of going herself."

"She was probably glad for the chance to get out of the house. She looked about a hundred times better than she did when we were there yesterday. Maybe she's on the mend." Trevor studied Megan, his sand-colored brows drawn together. "I've upset you. I'm sorry."

"Never mind me. I'm not thinking straight. I'm a mother hen, worried she'll do too much." Megan opened her car door and slid inside. "Thanks again for all your help."

"Hang on." Trevor drew a business card and a pen from his pocket. He wrote something on the card and handed it to her. "That's my cell phone number. If you need anything, day or night—or just need to talk—call me."

Surprised, Megan took the card and tucked it in her purse. "Thank you," she whispered.

* * *

"The ginger tea this time, dear." Evelyn's tremulous voice came from the TV room. "I still feel so weak."

"I'll have it for you in a minute." Megan snatched the appropriate box off the shelf.

She tried not to scrutinize Evelyn too openly as she delivered the tea, but she assessed the elderly woman from beneath her eyelashes. Evelyn's face was pale and her eyes bleary, as if she were having trouble focusing. The television room was dim, as always, with the curtains drawn and the heat cranked to a stifling temperature.

Evelyn reached for the tea. "Thank you, darling."

"Would you like anything else?"

"The tea is fine."

Megan steeled herself. "It's so hot in here." She patted Evelyn's hand. "You feel too warm, and the tea will only make that worse. Can I bring you something cool? I noticed some ice cream in the freezer."

"Ice cream? My goodness, no."

"I'm sorry. I thought perhaps you were craving it, since you went out this morning to get it."

Evelyn gave a wheezy laugh. "Oh no, dear. I haven't been out. It must be Aurora's. She stopped by before you got here."

"A friend mentioned that he saw you at the grocery store." Megan busily straightened the blanket draped over Evelyn's lap. "I felt terrible that you'd gone out on your own instead of letting me run your errand for you."

Evelyn gave her a confused look. "No, dear, I've been here all morning. You know I can't drive anymore. My medication makes me woozy." She yawned. "I think I'll have a little nap right here."

Megan moistened her lips. "Aunt Evelyn, where do you keep Aurora's phone number?"

Evelyn's mouth puckered in annoyance. "Why do you need to talk to that silly nurse? I've had enough of her poking at me. Stop nagging and let me nap."

"I'm sorry," Megan said quickly. "Do you want me to help you to your room?"

"No, no. I'm too tired to walk upstairs. The recliner is fine."

"Call me if you need anything else."

Evelyn nodded sleepily.

Back in the kitchen, Megan stood uncertainly, eyeing the freezer. That ice cream hadn't been there yesterday; Megan had fetched ice for a glass of water for Trevor, and she was sure no Ben and Jerry's had been in residence.

Why would Aurora bring ice cream? It *was* possible that Aurora had stopped at the grocery store on her way to see Evelyn and had put her ice cream in Evelyn's freezer so it wouldn't melt while she cared for Evelyn—but that seemed odd and unprofessional. Megan removed the carton of Chocolate Fudge Brownie and opened it. A small serving had been scooped out.

Aurora definitely wouldn't have eaten ice cream while tending to Evelyn.

Megan spent a few minutes tidying up the kitchen before tiptoeing into the family room to check on Evelyn.

Evelyn was asleep in her recliner, her mouth hanging open and her soft snores mixing with the television noise.

Had she lied about the trip to the store because she was afraid of the consequences of driving when she shouldn't have? Or was it possible she didn't remember what she'd done? Kristen had said Evelyn's mind was foggy these days. It *was* possible that she was having spells of amnesia.

If she was driving in an impaired condition, she was a danger on the roads. Megan couldn't ignore that. What if Evelyn went out again?

She'd better consult with Aurora, whether or not Evelyn wanted Megan to talk to her. As Evelyn's nurse, Aurora would know her mental state and could advise Megan on dealing with her.

She didn't want Evelyn to overhear her talking to Aurora. She'd go for a walk and call her from a pay phone or some business courtesy phone.

Megan opened the cupboard where Evelyn kept phone books. She checked Evelyn's leather-bound address book, but Aurora's number wasn't listed there. Megan checked the phone book, but there was no Aurora Capra or A. Capra in the White Pages. Annoyed, Megan realized she didn't even know the name of the nursing service that employed Aurora, or even if she worked for a nursing service. She might run her own business or work part-time taking on clients recommended by a few doctors.

Megan checked to make sure Evelyn was still sleeping, then headed into the office, where Evelyn had a desktop computer. Kristen had said that Evelyn rarely used the computer, but that she'd coaxed their great-aunt into paying for Internet service.

Megan booted up the computer. A round of googling turned up nothing. There was no Aurora Capra listed anywhere in Massachusetts or New Hampshire.

Frustrated, Megan leaned back in her chair and rubbed her forehead, futilely attempting to relieve a tension headache. She knew she had Aurora's name right; she'd memorized it off Kristen's list along with Aurora's picture—a fiftyish woman with short, dark hair and retro rhinestone glasses.

Could Kristen have misspelled the name? Megan tried running searches on possible spelling variations, but nothing turned up. She didn't want to start calling every Capra family within a hundred-mile radius to see if she could hunt Aurora down. She needed to talk to Kristen about this—and about Rachel. No more stalling. She'd call and ask Kristen to meet her somewhere.

Megan stood up. This house was driving her crazy. The closed blinds, the heat, the sickening scent of roses. Evelyn's pale eyes, so bleary one instant, so sharp the next. Megan needed to clear her head, and a walk to a phone would be a welcome way to do it. But before she left, she'd make sure Evelyn would not slip out again for another drive.

A few minutes later, she was walking briskly down Evelyn's driveway, but despite a fresh, damp wind that foreshadowed rain, she still couldn't shake the sense that she was smothering.

* * *

At the thump of the front door closing, Evelyn opened her eyes, threw off the afghan draped over her, and picked up the note she'd heard Megan set on the lamp table.

> *Aunt Evelyn,*
> *I went on a walk. I'll be back by three.*
> *Love, Kristen*

Evelyn hurried into the computer room. Within a few moments, she was checking the history of the Internet searches Megan had made.

So Megan was looking for the mythical Aurora Capra. No doubt she wanted to consult her about Evelyn's deteriorating mental state.

Who had seen her at Market Basket? She should have paid more attention to her surroundings. Perhaps she shouldn't have indulged in the ice cream, but tension mingled with anticipation had tickled her sweet tooth. Evelyn rarely indulged in such decadent treats, but when she wanted a bit of chocolate and cream, she wanted it *now,* and she certainly deserved it, since for the next few weeks she'd have to pretend to be content with meals so small and bland they wouldn't satisfy an infant. She had to slip out for decent food when she had the chance. And no harm done. Megan would chalk up her odd behavior to her illness.

Evelyn trotted into the kitchen to investigate the other noise she'd heard—the jingle of keys on her key rack. She examined her key ring, and her skin tingled with warmth.

Megan had taken Evelyn's car keys off the ring. She was worried Evelyn was driving when illness and medication had rendered her unfit.

It had been a long time—perhaps a lifetime—since Evelyn had felt the youthful urge to sing with joy, but she felt it now. Megan was trying to keep her safe.

Evelyn had spare keys, of course, but that wasn't the point. Megan cared.

Unlike Pamela. If Pamela had cared, none of this would have happened.

Just a few more days. Evelyn hung the key ring on the rack. A few more days and she'd have what was owed to her.

One life from Pamela O'Connor.

One life from Michael Drake.

Chapter 17

"Trev."

Truck keys in hand, Trevor turned to see Josh standing in the doorway to the garage. His fists were shoved in his pockets, and he was staring down at his unlaced sneakers.

"Yeah?" Trevor asked guardedly. Josh had spent all of breakfast—which none of them had eaten—haranguing the family for being fools to cooperate with the kidnappers. If he had his way, an entire SWAT team in disguise would be accompanying Trevor to the ransom drop.

"I . . . uh . . . I just wanted to say be careful." Josh shifted his weight from foot to foot. "Don't get hurt, okay?"

Trevor softened. "I'll be fine."

Josh gave an awkward nod of farewell and headed into the house.

As Trevor drove toward I-93, he repeatedly found himself gripping the steering wheel so hard that his fingers hurt. He understood Josh's frustration. To buckle to the demands of the monsters who had taken Rachel—

The ringing of his phone made him jerk as if he'd been jabbed with a live electrical wire.

He answered it. "This is Trevor Drake."

It was a male voice, not as harsh or cold as Trevor had expected it to be. "You're going to make a detour before you hit Boston. Stop at the Target store on Commerce Way in Woburn. Do you know where that is?"

"I'll find it."

"Buy two suitcases large enough to hold the money. Take the sales tags off the new bags and stick them in the bed of your truck along with the bags holding the cash. Got it?"

"Yes. What do I do after—"

The caller hung up. Trevor gritted his teeth. So he'd get his instructions piecemeal. Keeping one eye on the road, he entered his new destination into the navigation system.

He didn't like the idea of leaving two million dollars in his truck protected only by a camper shell, but he couldn't drag the money along with him while he went suitcase shopping. He'd just hope his truck didn't catch the eye of a thief. This would be a bad time to get robbed.

Inside the store, Trevor experienced a prickle of adrenaline every time another customer glanced at him. Any of them could be Rachel's kidnapper.

In the luggage section, Trevor hastily selected two large suitcases. A plump, middle-aged man ambled into the aisle just as Trevor was leaving. Trevor fought the urge to grab the stranger, slam him against the shelves, and yell, "Where's Rachel?"

He had the same crazed urge when he passed a woman in a business suit and stiletto heels, and a Target employee straightening a display of glass pumpkins and Halloween placemats. He knew he was on the verge of insanity when a glance from a man old enough to have come over on the Mayflower made his muscles twitch and his anger surge.

"Going on a trip?" the clerk asked as Trevor handed her his credit card.

Trevor nodded brusquely, imagining the clerk delivering her report to the kidnappers.

He exited Target, carrying the suitcases, and hurried to the truck. He unlocked the rear window of the camping shell and lifted it.

The truck bed was empty.

The money—*he'd lost the money*—

Trevor drew a deep breath, steadying himself. A piece of white notepaper was taped to the bed of the truck. He ripped it free.

> *So far so good. Now that you've made the drop, you get to relax and enjoy your day. Time for some sightseeing. Start off in Harvard Square. Go to the Crimson Corner on the*

> *corner of Brattle and John F. Kennedy Streets. Buy a Harvard sweatshirt. Use your Visa.*

Trevor resisted the temptation to wad the note into a ball. What kind of game were the kidnappers playing?

> *Next stop is the Museum of Science. In the gift shop, buy three red stuffed monkeys. Use your Visa.*
>
> *Your third destination is the gift shop on the corner of Province and School Streets. Buy ten Boston key chains and ten fridge magnets. Use your Visa.*

Trevor lowered the tailgate, tossed the useless suitcases inside, and settled in the cab of the truck to finish reading.

> *Having fun yet? Your next stop is Faneuil Hall. Buy four boxes of saltwater taffy. Use your Visa. Next is the Old North Church. Stop at the gift shop and buy a couple of Christmas ornaments. Now head out to the New England Aquarium—*

His blood pressure rising with every word, Trevor waded through the rest of his required destinations. He'd be lucky to finish this to-do list before the gift shops closed.

> *Don't make any calls. Turn your phone off. When you've finished your assignment, go home and pat yourself on the back. You'll get a call telling you where to pick up Rachel, safe and sound. But if you blow it now, all you'll get back of Rachel are her bones—when some kid stumbles across them in the forest twenty years from now.*

Trevor threw the note on the passenger seat and started the engine. The kidnappers wanted to eat up his time on a treasure hunt so he couldn't return home and report on the drop until they'd had plenty of time to stash the money. He supposed he should be grateful they hadn't knocked him out and tied him up this time.

Did they really have access that would allow them to monitor his Visa transactions to verify that he'd done what they'd ordered, or was that a bluff? Would they have accomplices following him around Cambridge and Boston?

Target had security cameras in their parking lot. They'd have a record of the kidnappers picking up the ransom. The thought gave Trevor a flicker of hope, but it was only a few degrees warmer than despair. The kidnappers wouldn't be stupid enough to show their faces undisguised. The car they'd driven had probably been stolen, and chances were they'd already abandoned it for a different vehicle.

How had they gotten into his truck? There were no signs that the lock on the back window had been forced, but it wasn't a very good lock. A skillful thief could have gotten past it.

Resigned, Trevor started the engine. Time to head to Harvard Square. It would be idiotic to defy the kidnappers now.

They had the money. They had Rachel. The last thing Trevor wanted to do was give them an excuse to shoot her rather than go through the risks involved in releasing her.

* * *

"Baaaah," Kristen bleated, lowering the binoculars. "Brother Sheep is headed inside the museum. That's two stops down and *lots* more to go."

Alex grunted acknowledgment, his eyes focused on the tangle of Boston traffic.

Kristen picked up the cell phone they'd used to contact Trevor. "Can I call him now and tell him he also needs to walk the Freedom Trail—on his knees, while singing Yankee Doodle?"

Alex smiled with one corner of his mouth, but his shoulders were tense. "You can't call him. You told him to turn his phone off."

"I'll have some tourist pass him a note. Ooh, how about a scavenger hunt? We'll give him a list of fifty items he needs to collect from other tourists. If he doesn't turn in the completed list by sundown, then Rachel dies. Imagine him trying to explain to his mom that Rachel is toast because he couldn't find a state quarter from Louisiana."

Alex added the other corner of his mouth to his smile. "You're getting hyper."

Kristen grinned, thinking of the suitcases stashed in the trunk of Alex's car. "We did it, Alex!"

"Don't gloat yet. It's not over."

"Come on. Nothing's going to go wrong now."

"In that case, can we quit spying on Drake? It's impossible to keep tabs on him in this traffic, and chances are he's going to leave his truck at the museum and hop on the T anyway. We can't follow him onto the subway."

"Sure, fine, break off the surveillance. Enough's enough. He'll do what we told him." Excitement bubbled through Kristen at the thought of what came next. They'd check into the hotel, using yet another of Alex's phony identities, and spend some time making sure all was kosher with the ransom and separating out Evelyn's and Megan's cuts.

Kristen had expected to resent wasting a chunk of cash on Megan, but now that she had the money, she didn't mind sharing a little. Megan had been a great, if ignorant, help, and she deserved a reward. Besides, Evelyn was only willing to keep up the dying-auntie routine for the few weeks necessary to keep Megan in place while the police investigation was at its height. Then she would tell Megan she no longer wanted live-in help, and that she was planning to move to an assisted-care facility for the last few months of her life. *But here's a cash bonus, dear, as thanks for all your hard work, and of course you're my heir.* Kristen smirked as she pictured Evelyn delivering her lines. Megan would leave Britteridge happy and clueless. Given a year or so, she'd catch on to the fact that Evelyn wasn't dying anytime soon, but that didn't worry Kristen. A hundred grand was more than enough to keep Megan from making trouble—no matter what she began to suspect.

Kristen glanced at her watch—plenty of time before she had to head back to Britteridge. Evelyn had specified that Kristen should babysit Rachel tonight and that Alex should stay in the hotel so no hotel worker would wonder why they'd checked in with a bunch of luggage but hadn't used the room.

Kristen didn't mind being assigned guard duty, especially since Evelyn had told her not to return to Britteridge until after dark. She'd have lots of time with Alex this afternoon, and then tonight at the house, she could spend some private time reveling in her triumph, counting and recounting stacks of cash. Heck, she could spread it on the floor and roll around in it if she wanted, or throw it like confetti and dance as money rained down on her head. Stuck in the hotel, Alex would have to be more discreet, and Kristen didn't feel like being discreet tonight. She felt like jumping up and down and cheering.

She could see now why Alex preferred to make his living on the wrong side of the law. Why bother working your tail off when bales of cash were easily available to anyone with the brains and the guts to take a few risks? *See, Dad? Alex and I just made more in a couple of weeks than you made in twenty years of working yourself into a heart attack. Who's the successful one now?*

She twirled the cell phone by the antenna. "Are you *sure* I can't call Trevor and tell him to do the Yankee Doodle thing?"

"I wouldn't push your luck, Kris. If he ever figures out who was behind this, Brother Sheep is going to tear you limb from limb."

"He won't find out. And even if he did, he'd probably thank us for giving Rachel a good scare. Her chatter must get on his nerves. But what do you bet the Bubble-head Princess won't be quite so bubbly for a while?"

* * *

"Could you go check again, dear? Just one more time? I'm sure they'll forget to do the underside of the railing."

"I'll go check." Megan tried not to sound impatient. This was at least the fourth time Evelyn had asked her to check on the painters, who were working on the deck.

Megan walked out the front door and circled around to the back of the house, but instead of talking to the painters—who were already painting the railing, underside and all—she turned back and meandered to the mailbox.

The sky was a spectacular blue, the leaves were neon-bright, and Megan wished she could go for a walk and unwind in the beauty of autumn.

Evelyn had been demanding, impatient, and owlishly alert all day. After ordering Megan to sweep the spotless porch, hose down the pristine driveway, rearrange all the flower pots on the front porch and then return them to their original positions, go twice to the grocery store and once to the pharmacy, check out a long list of books at the library and take the gleaming Cadillac for a wash and wax, she'd spent the rest of the afternoon ordering Megan to pester the painters. Megan couldn't understand why Evelyn wanted the deck redone anyway. The old paint was in almost perfect condition, and the new paint she'd chosen was nearly the same shade of gray.

Megan glanced again at the bright sky. It was only four o'clock. If Evelyn maintained this level of fretful energy until bedtime, Megan would go crazy.

What were the Drakes doing right now? Had they handed over the ransom money?

Was Rachel all right?

"Hey, Krissy!"

Megan looked over to see a sturdy man with bifocals and a white buzz cut heading toward her. He was carrying something wrapped in a kitchen towel.

"Hi, Mr. Welby," she greeted Evelyn's neighbor.

"You okay, girlie? You been standing there staring into space for a while."

Feeling foolish, Megan closed the empty mailbox. "Just enjoying the weather."

"Yeah, nice day. Here's some bread for you." He held out the towel-wrapped loaf. "Deb's been baking today, and she wanted Evie to have some. Evie loves Deb's whole wheat bread."

"Thank you." Megan accepted the bread. The towel was warm, and the aroma of freshly baked bread made Megan want to inhale deeply. "I know Aunt Evelyn will appreciate it."

"How's she doing? I haven't talked to her lately."

Megan wished she could answer candidly. Evelyn's neighbors obviously cared about her. How would they feel when they learned Megan had concealed the terrible news of Evelyn's cancer? "She's been under the weather. I'll tell her you were asking about her."

"Anything you need, you let me know. Leaky faucet, problems with your furnace, whatever. Ain't nothing I can't fix."

"How are *you* feeling?" Megan asked, remembering he'd recently had surgery.

"I'm healthy as a horse. This new surgery they do, it's amazing. Just a few little cuts. Tell Evie I can do her lawn next week like normal. I would have done it this week, but Deb wouldn't let me. It was nice of your friend to pinch-hit for me. Saw him out there taking care of things."

"He was happy to help. Thank you again for the bread," she added, hoping to head off questions about Trevor Drake.

"It's a pleasure. Do you bake, Krissy? Deb tells me a lot of kids these days don't even know how to turn on an oven."

"I'm afraid I've never cooked much." Cooking was one task Pamela enjoyed, so the kitchen had been her domain.

"That's a shame." Welby shook his head. "Especially with you living with Evie now. She'd appreciate it if you could cook a decent meal. Why not come over sometime and let Deb give you some tutoring? She knows all kinds of tips, like how to make your chicken real moist. She'd love to help."

"That's kind of her," Megan said noncommittally. She wouldn't mind cooking lessons from Debbie Welby. Anything that gave Megan an excuse to take a break from Evelyn was welcome. But it seemed tactless to tell Evelyn she was learning to become a better cook when Evelyn could hardly eat anything these days.

Except contraband ice cream?

"Hey, I hope you're keeping Evie's doors locked." Welby changed the subject. "Deb read about some burglaries over near the animal hospital, and she wants me to get a new lock for the sliding door. Deb's always careful. Carries that pepper spray stuff all the time. Even keeps a canister in her car. She buys it from some self-defense expert. If you're interested, she could get the product list for you. Crime is getting bad these days. Even a nice town like Britteridge isn't safe from—"

A rapping noise interrupted him. Evelyn was standing at the kitchen window, gesturing for Megan to come inside.

"Excuse me," Megan said. "I'd better see what she needs."

"Good to chat with you. Go enjoy that bread." With a wave of farewell, Welby trotted toward his house.

Megan repressed a sigh as she started up the sidewalk. If only she'd had a chance to talk to Aurora, maybe she'd have a better idea of how to care for Evelyn without going crazy in the process. But she still didn't know how to contact the nurse; Kristen hadn't answered her phone yesterday, and she hadn't yet returned Megan's message.

"You should be resting," Megan told Evelyn. "Do you need something? Would you like something to eat?" She unwrapped the loaf of bread to show Evelyn. "Mrs. Welby baked this for you. Should I cut you a slice?"

"Maybe later," Evelyn said. "I'm not hungry now. But I *am* feeling a bit stronger today. I'm afraid I've run you ragged."

"I'm happy to do whatever you need." Megan almost managed to sound like she meant it.

"You're so sweet, darling. But you must be tired. Here, sit down. I've made you some lemonade. The day is quite warm for October, isn't it?

"You shouldn't be making anything for me," Megan said in surprise. "I'm here to help you."

"It makes me feel better to be up and doing. Please, sit down and drink it. You deserve a break."

"Well—thank you so much." Megan sat at the table and reached for the filled glass. Powdered lemonade made with lukewarm water. Megan didn't want to finish it, but with Evelyn standing there with a tender look in her eyes, Megan didn't dare leave so much as a swallow in the glass.

"Thank you." Megan carried the empty glass to the dishwasher. "That was very thoughtful."

"Why don't you go lie down for a few minutes, dear? You've been hard at work all day. And there's a teensy project I wanted you to do for me this evening, so now might be a good time to sneak a nap."

Megan swallowed a groan. "I think I will lie down. Call if you need me."

"I will."

Megan hurried out of the kitchen before Evelyn could change her mind. In her room, she sank onto the bed and debated among the new library books stacked on her nightstand. Deciding she needed something light and funny to lift her mood, she selected a P. G. Wodehouse novel.

She didn't intend to nap, but she hadn't even finished the first chapter before she started to feel overwhelmingly sleepy. Giving in, she set the book aside and closed her eyes. She'd be lucky to grab a power nap before Evelyn was after her to scrub the bathroom tile with a toothbrush, or whatever the "teensy project" was.

Chapter 18

Evelyn waited until the sun was low in the sky before she opened Megan's bedroom door. Megan lay limp on the bed, the comforter pulled halfway over her legs as though she'd fallen asleep before she'd had a chance to arrange herself comfortably.

Evelyn gave one sharp clap. Megan didn't stir.

Evelyn walked to the bed and ran her hand over Megan's silky hair. Strawberry blond. Judith's hair had been dark—dark and smooth like onyx.

In the shadowy room, the fragile, white lines of Megan's neck drew Evelyn's gaze. It would be so easy to do it now, slip a rope around that slim neck and pull it tight—

Not yet.

Not until she was done with the Drake girl.

Megan would sleep soundly for at least another four hours. She would never know Evelyn had been gone.

Evelyn shed her housecoat and slippers, dressed quickly, and headed out to her car.

She enjoyed the drive to the house on Britteridge Pond. Salmon-pink clouds streaked the western sky, as vivid as the colors on the trees. For twenty-six years, Evelyn had hated autumn, but now, at last, she could enjoy the change in the seasons.

Evelyn turned on the radio and smiled at the lyrical sounds of Schubert's *Unfinished Symphony.* Interesting that Megan had tuned the radio to a station that played classical music when she'd taken the car to be washed. Judith had loved classical music too. Brahms had been her favorite.

Troy's handsome, white clapboard house was set on the top of a tree-covered slope that led down to the pond. Stairs zigzagged down the hill to the private dock where Troy had kept his boat. Evelyn had squelched her laughter when Kristen insisted on taking the motorboat out of storage and tying it up at the dock "just in case." Kristen was no doubt envisioning herself as James Bond, leaping into the boat and roaring away while police officers stood on the dock and cursed in frustration.

Evelyn had to park in the driveway, as she'd given the garage door opener to Kristen, but she wasn't worried about being seen. It was unlikely that anyone would drive past on this isolated road, and even if someone saw her car, Evelyn had every right to be at Troy's house. She and William had taken care of the house for several years. She'd always thought it silly of Troy not to sell, but Troy loved the house and was determined to return to Britteridge someday. How delightfully appropriate that Evelyn should be able to use the house to compensate herself for all the favors William and she had done for Troy.

Her fingers shook a little as she unlocked the door. Was she nervous? No. Exhilarated.

The sight of soda cans and an empty pizza box on the living room coffee table made her cluck her tongue. Kristen was so sloppy. Pamela hadn't taught her very well.

Evelyn walked up the stairs to where a closed door with a dead bolt marked Rachel's prison. She twisted the dead bolt, swung the door open, and turned on the lights.

Rachel lay on the bed in a drugged sleep. A steel shackle was clamped around her right ankle, and a cable led from the shackle to a metal plate on the floor. Her clothes were crumpled and her hair a tangled mess of brown curls, sorely in need of a wash. Evelyn shook her head sadly. How would it have hurt Kristen to leave Rachel a change of clothes, some shampoo, and a comb? There was no need to be barbaric about this.

Evelyn sat on the bed next to Rachel and examined the blindfold covering her eyes. It resembled one of those masks flight attendants gave passengers on long flights, but this mask had been glued to Rachel's face so she couldn't remove it.

Not without a little help, anyway.

Evelyn fingered the fabric blindfold and gave it a couple of tugs. It was only glued around the edges.

Evelyn opened her purse and retrieved embroidery scissors and fingernail clippers. She opened the attached nail file on the clippers and set them aside.

Pinching the fabric of the blindfold to hold it away from Rachel's eyes, she opened the embroidery scissors and punctured the fabric with a tiny, careful thrust of one blade.

Holding the scissors so the blades were parallel to Rachel's face, she made a careful snip. Meticulously, she made a second cut, ensuring that the blade didn't graze Rachel's eyelids. It would rather be missing the point to damage Rachel's eyes.

When the slit in the fabric was long enough for her to insert her fingers, Evelyn set the scissors aside and tugged and ripped until the blindfold tore. She worked her way around the perimeter of the blindfold, using the scissors when the fabric got stubborn. When she finished, only a glued ring of fabric remained, circling Rachel's exposed eyes like a raccoon mask.

Pleased with her work, Evelyn tucked the scissors in her purse. She took the fingernail clippers and set them on the floor near the side of the bed, where Rachel could easily have dropped them.

Evelyn sat for a moment, stroking the soft skin on the back of Rachel's hand. Happy Rachel, twenty-one years old. Just as Judith had been.

Neither Pamela O'Connor nor Michael Drake had spent so much as a millisecond in prison. But Kristen would. And murder would carry a much stiffer sentence than kidnapping.

Evelyn didn't doubt that it *would* be Kristen who did the deed. Evelyn was superb at reading people, and that shady Alex Hurst didn't have the guts to act in cold blood. Evelyn could envision him committing murder in the heat of the moment, but not as a planned act. He'd be more likely to run and hope his plethora of phony identities could protect him. But Kristen—self-obsessed, practical Kristen—couldn't tolerate leaving a witness behind and spending her life as a fugitive.

The thought of Kristen in a bare concrete cell brought a girlish giggle from Evelyn's lips. Kristen was so proud, just like Pamela. How humiliating arrest and imprisonment would be for her! And how mortifying for Pamela to have the world know the sordid story of her daughter's crimes.

Evelyn strolled downstairs to the living room. Under the couch, she hid a tiny, voice-activated recorder. She taped a second recorder on the underside of the kitchen table. Kristen and Alex would be sure to discuss their plans before they did anything about Rachel.

Feeling thoroughly cheerful, Evelyn returned to Rachel's cell. She opened her purse and took out the plastic baggie containing a pre-filled syringe.

Evelyn removed the needle guard and stabbed the needle into Rachel's shoulder. Rachel would be wide awake when Kristen returned to the cabin tonight.

Wide awake and ready to get a full view of Kristen's lovely, arrogant face.

* * *

Josh sat near the wall of the exercise room, watching Trevor bench-press his own weight. Trevor always liked to hit the weights when he was under stress, and from the sweat dripping off his face, this session had been a doozy. No music was playing, which was another sign that Trevor was agitated. Trevor always listened to music when he worked out, country stuff that gagged Josh, so if he was too distracted for that, he was *really* bothered.

No wonder. Josh would have lost it completely if he'd had to trot around Boston doing stupid tourist things, knowing the kidnappers were watching and laughing at him. From the way Trevor was hitting the weights tonight, it was obvious he was working off the anger he hadn't been able to aim at Rachel's kidnappers.

Josh eyed his brother's bulging muscles and wished the kidnappers were here now. Trevor could take one and Josh the other. Before the kidnappers knew what was happening, Josh would lunge at them, his motions like lightning, his fists like rocks. There would be a crash, a crack of bone, a pitiful yelp from the cowering—

"You okay, Josh?"

Josh blinked. Trevor was wiping sweat off his neck with a towel and looking intently at him.

"Yeah, I'm all right." Josh realized how dumb his fantasy scenario was. Guns and Tasers didn't make for a fair fight. "I wish we could *do* something. I can't stand just waiting. They've got the money. Where's Rachel?"

"It'll take a little time. Right now they're probably counting the money and checking for any clues that we tried to track them or mark the cash. Once they're satisfied that we held up our end of the deal, I'm sure we'll get instructions for where to pick up Rachel."

"No, you're not," Josh said.

"Not what?"

"Not sure. You don't know that they'll release Rachel like they said."

Trevor looked down and rotated both wrists as if inspecting the scrapes and bruises that marred his arms. The bandage on Trevor's left forearm was freshly soaked with red, and a trickle of blood had run along his arm during the workout.

"Do you have any idea who the kidnappers could be?" Josh asked. "Any idea at all? Even some crazy, weird idea you're sure couldn't be true?"

Trevor wiped the blood off his arm. "I have no idea who would do this to our family. Don't you think I would have told Mom and Dad if I did?"

"Not necessarily. Not if you thought you were being paranoid and you didn't want to make Mom and Dad suspect some innocent person. Come on. You can't tell me there isn't a single name that's crossed your mind."

"I don't think there's a single name that *hasn't* crossed my mind, including my home teachers and Sister Jefferson's ninety-seven-year-old mother-in-law. This afternoon I was jumping every time someone looked at me. I was ready to club perfect strangers." Trevor draped the towel around his neck and sat on the bench next to Josh. "But *you* have someone in mind. Who is it? Get it off your chest."

Josh slouched against the mirrored wall. "It's nothing. No one. Okay, it's Kristen. I know it's not fair, but she bugs me. And you don't like her either. You told me that, so don't go all polite now."

"It's funny," Trevor said. "You're right—I didn't like Kristen, and I didn't trust her either, though never in my wildest paranoia did I think she'd do something like this. But now . . . I don't know, Josh. I'm thinking I misjudged her. Either she's the most brilliant actress on the planet, or she really cares about Rachel. And she's been—"

"Yeah, I know, she's been all kind and helpful. But doesn't *that* strike you as weird? That all of a sudden she's so nice? Maybe she's trying to snow us because she's involved in this. She could have been the one to give the kidnappers the information on Rachel's schedule and the route she takes home from the church."

"The fact that Rachel has institute on Tuesday nights isn't a secret. And Josh, you didn't see Kristen the night Rachel was taken. She was in bad shape. I can't believe she'd have done that to herself. Spending hours tied to a tree in the cold—"

"Some people would be willing to go through a lot for a couple million bucks. And being with Rachel when Rachel was kidnapped and having the kidnappers kick her around—great alibi, right? Who's going to believe she had anything to do with the kidnapping when she was a victim too?"

Trevor dabbed more blood off his arm as it escaped from under the saturated bandage. "I . . . don't know. Yes, it's possible. But I just can't believe it. I don't think anyone is that good of an actress."

"Listen, I was wondering . . . do you think we ought to investigate her? Maybe hire someone to look into her past? Like Dad's friend, Dr. Barclay, the one who does background checks for him?" Josh shifted uncomfortably and avoided Trevor's gaze. "I know it's a long shot, but what can it hurt? If Kristen is innocent, she'll never even know we suspected her."

Trevor was silent. Each second he went without speaking made Josh feel like he was shrinking, until only a tiny, shriveled lump of stupidity remained sitting next to Trevor on the bench. Trevor didn't even suspect Kristen. Why would he pay someone to pry into her life?

"Have you tried researching her yourself?" Trevor asked.

"Yeah. I tried to check her out on the Internet, but there are a lot of Kristen O'Connors, and I don't know how to dig up the right information. We need a pro."

"Let me think about it."

Meaning no, Josh thought. Meaning Trevor thought he was nuts.

"Hopefully, Rachel will be home before an investigator could do anything anyway," Trevor said. "Then the police can throw everything they've got into finding the kidnappers."

"Yeah," Josh said. "Sure. When Rachel gets home."

* * *

Kristen turned up the volume on the rental car's stereo and let Ella Fitzgerald's velvety rendition of *Summertime* conjure the warmth of sunshine on her hair and the grittiness of white sand beneath her bare feet. She'd always wanted to visit some luxurious tropical resort, and now it wasn't just a dream.

After years of scrounging up money to make minimum payments on credit card balances, after years of working imbecile jobs where anyone with enough brain function to make a blip on an EEG was overqualified, after years of squeaking by while spoiled airheads like Rachel breezed along with a different color Porsche to match each pair of shoes—at last Kristen had enough cash to enjoy life.

And it had been so *easy*. She could kiss Evelyn for seeking her out and presenting the idea of kidnapping Rachel Drake. No one had been hurt, unless you counted a couple of bumps and scrapes. No one was going to prison. Rachel could go home and share wide-eyed tales of her captivity with her friends. Knowing Rachel, she'd babble about it nonstop for months. This was undoubtedly the most exciting thing that had ever happened in Rachel's pampered-princess Mormon life.

Kristen pulled into the garage of the darkened house and closed the garage door. From the trunk of her car, she heaved out the suitcase that contained her share of the ransom. She loved how heavy it was, so heavy that it was awkward for her to handle it. No way would she have considered leaving her money with Alex at the hotel. Alex was hot and fun and clever, but Kristen didn't trust him with a suitcase of her money any more than she'd trust that she could throw a slab of beef to a hungry lion and he'd take a sniff and turn politely away.

With the suitcase bumping along the ground behind her, Kristen strolled into the cabin. Everything was quiet. Rachel would probably be asleep for a while longer, but Kristen would look in on her just in case. Evelyn had made a big deal about how important it was to verify that all was status quo with their prisoner each time they arrived at or left the house. After Kristen had checked on Rachel, she'd relax with a glass of champagne and a suitcase full of cash.

Kristen thunked the suitcase on the living room rug and unzipped it for a peek inside. *Beautiful cash!*

She all but danced up the stairs to Rachel's cell. When Rachel woke up, Kristen would tell her everything was set and she'd be home in time for Sunday school.

That reminded Kristen—she needed to return Megan's message. Megan probably wanted to cry on her shoulder about the kidnapping. Kristen knew through Gail Ludlum that Megan was acting just as Kristen had anticipated—soft and sweet and scared, worried to death about Rachel and eagerly doing anything the Drakes asked of her. Perfect.

Kristen unlocked the bolt on Rachel's door and swung it open. In the illumination from the hallway, she saw that Rachel's bed was empty. A shiver of adrenaline brought her senses on alert.

Kristen flipped the light switch and spotted Rachel. She was sitting on the floor on the other side of the bed, near the spot where the shackle was bolted to the floor. Her head was bowed, her back to the door.

"Awake?" Kristen said in her bad-guy voice.

Rachel rose and turned toward Kristen.

Kristen gasped. The blindfold glued to Rachel's face had been ripped partially away, leaving only a rim of fabric stuck to her skin. Ringed by torn fabric, two brown eyes stared at Kristen.

Kristen leapt backward and slammed the door.

But she knew it was too late.

Chapter 19

"I don't like the look of that. I think it needs stitches." Sandra handed Trevor a clean washcloth to replace the paper towel he'd been using to put pressure on his arm. "You should have had Gail fix it for you the night it happened instead of waiting around like this."

"I thought a butterfly bandage would hold it." Trevor pressed the washcloth against his aching forearm. "It's not that big. I just put too much strain on it while I was working out. It'll stop bleeding in—"

"Don't be such a baby." Sandra's lips were pale, but she managed a teasing smile. "I'm sure Gail can numb it for you before she stitches it up."

"Or you could ask for general anesthesia," Josh suggested from his perch on the kitchen counter.

"You two are a riot," Trevor said. "Fine, I'll see what the doctor orders, but I don't want to bother her tonight. It's late."

"For heaven's sake, it's only eight o'clock, and you can't let that cut go untreated any longer. You're going to end up with an infection or a nasty scar. I'll call Gail to make sure she's home." Sandra reached for the phone on the counter, hesitated, and nearly drew her hand back. She swallowed hard and picked up the receiver. Trevor knew she didn't like making calls for fear of missing word of Rachel, even though call-waiting would let her know if anyone else was on the line.

"All right, you're set," she said, hanging up a few minutes later. "The doctor is in, and apparently she has fresh cinnamon rolls, so Josh, if you'd like to go with Trevor . . ."

"I'm there." Josh slid off the counter. Trevor was glad to see Josh looking a little more like himself.

"I'm going to hate the phone for the rest of my life," Josh remarked as Trevor drove toward Gail Ludlum's house in Britteridge. "Every time it rings, I feel like my guts just got thrown in the disposal."

Trevor grimaced. "Nice imagery. But I know what you mean."

"You think they might release her in the middle of the night?" Josh turned so he was facing the passenger window. "So they don't have to worry so much that someone will see them?"

"Maybe. I hope so. That's one call I wouldn't mind getting at 3 AM."

"Yeah." Josh's voice got low and mumbly. "Listen . . . Trev . . . I kind of feel like a moron about Kristen. I don't know why I can't get her out of my mind, but you're right. It's crazy to think she'd hurt herself like that. I hope you didn't . . . you know . . . say anything to Mom or Dad about—"

"I didn't say anything. And don't worry about it. The fact is, we *don't* know much about Kristen, so it's far from crazy to suspect her." Trevor promptly regretted his words. He was going to get Josh's imagination going full-throttle again.

When they arrived, Gail Ludlum yanked her front door open before Trevor's hand got anywhere near the doorbell. Her plump cheeks were flushed, and her frizzy blond curls stuck out in every direction. "Please tell me you've had news in the last twenty minutes."

"I'm sorry," Trevor said. "Nothing yet."

Gail groaned. "The waiting! Why can't they just—I'm sorry, boys, please come in."

The air in Gail's house was redolent with the scent of cinnamon rolls. "I just got the last batch out of the oven. Come in the kitchen and I'll have a look at your arm."

"Sorry to bother you tonight."

"Don't be. Distractions are welcome. I've been chewing my nails off trying to keep from calling Sandra every ten seconds. Why do you think I'm baking? I'm trying to occupy myself." Gail hustled into the kitchen ahead of them. "Have a seat at the table. Josh, grab some milk out of the fridge."

While Josh devoured a warm cinnamon roll dripping white glaze, Gail examined Trevor's arm.

"Not too bad, but I wish you'd shown this to me the other night. It could use a couple of stitches. I'm going to run you over to my office. Josh, you're welcome to accompany us, or you can stay here and babysit the cinnamon rolls and the Red Sox. You know where to find the TV."

Josh's mouth was too full to respond. Gail laughed and tugged off her flour-spotted apron. "Trev, help yourself to a roll while I go comb my hair and wash the flour off my face. If I don't, I'm sure to run into a bunch of people I know."

Trevor downed two cinnamon rolls and watched Josh wander restlessly around the kitchen, a glass of milk in one hand and a cinnamon roll in the other. Josh paused next to Gail's fridge and aimed his cinnamon roll at the numerous wedding announcements hanging there.

"Rach would love that, huh? The Wall of Love."

Trevor nodded, thinking painfully of how much Josh loved to tease Rachel about her obsession with anything wedding-related. Rachel's protests that this was business—she had to stay on top of current wedding trends—only provoked more teasing from Josh about ulterior motives and which guys had caught Rachel's eye. Both Josh and Rachel loved the sparring.

"Hey, I didn't know Sarah Ritter was engaged," Josh said.

"Yeah, she met him at BYU. He's from out west somewhere. Colorado, I think."

"Wyoming," Josh corrected, checking the announcement. "He shouldn't part his hair in the middle. It makes him look like a geek." He pointed at another picture. "Check this guy out. Dracula reincarnated. If you *can* reincarnate a vampire."

Trevor refrained from telling Josh that insulting the looks of Gail Ludlum's friends wasn't the most tactful thing to do when she might reenter the room at any moment.

"Lawrence Paul Zuckerman." Josh peered at the announcement. "The name suits—hey, that's weird. Zuckerman."

Trevor buckled to the impulse to reprimand Josh. "You want to quit picking on people's faces and names?"

"I didn't mean the name was weird—okay, it's weird. I just meant it's the same wedding that—" Josh stopped abruptly.

"The same wedding that what?"

There was an awkward silence. "Nothing." Josh stepped away from the fridge, cramming the rest of his cinnamon roll in his mouth.

Curious, Trevor scrutinized his brother. Josh's face was red.

"Spill it," Trevor said. "What's so weird?"

"Nothing," Josh mumbled, but under Trevor's gaze, he went redder and shrugged. "I just . . . heard . . . that Kristen O'Connor went to that wedding too."

Trevor was puzzled, not so much by the coincidence but by the embarrassment on Josh's face. "Did Rachel tell you that?"

"Uh . . . I can't really remember."

Yet somehow he'd paid close enough attention to remember Zuckerman's name? "You can't remember?"

"Okay, yeah, she told me. What does it matter? It's just a stupid wedding."

"Fine, it doesn't matter. The only reason I thought it *did* is because you look like you just got caught robbing Fort Knox. What's up with that?"

"Nothing's up with it," Josh said angrily. "I just thought it was a big coincidence that Kristen and Dr. Ludlum both knew some people getting married in Virginia when Kristen's from New York and Dr. Ludlum is local. Just forget it. It doesn't—"

"Who told you that, Josh?" Gail Ludlum's voice made both Josh and Trevor start. Trevor turned to see Gail standing in the doorway, clutching her purse to her chest. If he'd thought Josh's expression was odd, it was nothing compared to the look on Gail's face. She was ashen, her eyes dark and bulging.

"Rach—Rachel mentioned that Kristen was going, and then I—the announcement there—" Josh pointed to the fridge. "Sorry, I—didn't mean to—"

Gail drew a deep breath, her shoulders rising and falling. "Small world," she said, and Trevor had the impression she was struggling to sound casual. "I don't remember seeing Kristen there, but it was a crowd. I'll have to ask her how she knows Larry or Tara. Let's go, Trev, before that arm gets infected and Superman ends up on antibiotics."

* * *

"How's the arm?" It was the first thing Josh had said in the ten minutes they'd been en route to their house. Repeatedly, he'd drawn a deep breath like he wanted to speak, and then slouched in his seat and remained silent. Trevor suspected he knew what Josh was working up his courage to say. Forthright to the point of abrasiveness, Josh hated lies.

"The arm is fine," Trevor said. "Two stitches and a lecture on not waiting to seek medical treatment. How was the game?" Josh had been sitting in front of the television when Gail and Trevor had returned to the house.

"I—don't know. I wasn't really paying attention."

"A first for a rabid Red Sox fan."

"Trev . . . uh . . . this is going to sound stupid, but . . ." Josh's voice trailed off.

"But you lied to me about Rachel telling you Kristen was going to that wedding?" Out of the corner of his eye, Trevor saw surprise and relief on Josh's face.

"Yeah. Was it that obvious?"

"It was obvious. Sorry. You wouldn't have looked so rattled if it were just Rachel's usual wedding talk. Any particular reason why you lied?"

"Because I feel like a jerk," Josh confessed. "The night we got the ransom call, I went into Kristen's room while she was in the kitchen with you, and I looked through her stuff."

"You searched her suitcase?"

"Yeah, and her purse. I was trying to help Rachel, and I—you know I was worried about Kristen being involved with—" Josh shifted in his seat and tugged restlessly at his seat belt. "I didn't find anything, but there was a piece of paper in Kristen's purse—hidden in one of the inside pockets—that had a picture of the wedding announcement for that Zuckerman guy."

"A picture?"

"Yeah, just printed on a plain sheet of paper. And there were some maps printed off the Internet showing the way to the wedding. I remembered the guy's name because it reminded me of *Charlotte's Web*—you know, 'Zuckerman's famous pig.' Jayden watched it about five hundred times last summer. So when I saw the invitation at Dr. Ludlum's, it surprised me."

"Apparently it surprised Dr. Ludlum too."

"Yeah . . . she looked wicked freaked."

Freaked. Strangely enough she had looked terrified, which made no sense at all, and she'd been oddly quiet the whole time she was working on his arm. What could there be about common friends with Kristen O'Connor that would make her react with fear?

The whole situation was strange. The wedding had been the first weekend in October. He remembered Gail discussing her plans with Sandra at the Labor Day picnic. Kristen *had* been gone the same weekend as Gail, but she'd told Rachel she was going to New York to see her boyfriend. Had she gone to Virginia as well? If she'd been at the wedding, why wouldn't she have mentioned it, especially knowing how much Rachel enjoyed discussing anything related to white lace and diamonds?

Trevor tried to think it didn't matter, but from the look on Gail's face, it clearly did matter, somehow. Whether or not it was any of Trevor's business was another question entirely. He knew it wasn't fair or rational, but two thoughts popped into his head and wouldn't leave: Kristen might have lied about where she'd gone less than two weeks before Rachel was kidnapped. And Gail Ludlum was afraid of something that, on some level, had to do with Kristen O'Connor.

"Do you think Dr. Ludlum will say something to Mom?" Josh asked. "Like that I was snooping?"

"No. Why would she?" Trevor tried to rid himself of what was rapidly becoming rank paranoia. He was worse than Josh. "She doesn't know you snuck a look in Kristen's purse, and it's not nosy to look at a wedding announcement on someone's fridge. I wouldn't worry about it."

"You sound weird," Josh said. "This is bugging you, isn't it?"

Weird was the word for it all right. He was weird to the point of insanity to even let ideas like this rise to the surface. Hadn't he told Josh earlier this evening that he'd misjudged Kristen? Why was he now so eager to suspect her of—

Of what?

"Was there anything else written on those papers?" Trevor tried to make the question sound offhand. "Notes or anything?"

"No . . . wait, yeah. Something about a car. It said something like 'blue Accord' and had a license plate number."

Trevor's chest muscles seemed to tighten, compressing his lungs. Blue Accord. Gail Ludlum drove a blue Honda Accord. "Do you by any chance remember the license number?"

"Sure, Trev. It's all stored in my photographic memory along with every word of *War and Peace*."

"Funny."

"It started with a 4. That's all I remember. No, wait. 48. Or maybe 46. Now *you're* the one who's hiding stuff. What's up?"

"I don't know." Trevor's heartbeat pulsed in his ears like a mallet against a bass drum. The Labor Day picnic. Kristen had *been* there when Gail and Sandra had discussed the wedding. Trevor could picture her sitting with Rachel across the picnic table. Gail had mentioned that Bryce's old roommate, Larry Zuckerman, was getting married and she was driving to Virginia to attend the wedding. There had been some good-natured joking about how much Gail hated flying. Sandra had asked the date of the trip. Rachel had asked Gail to take mental notes on what she did and didn't like about the wedding and reception.

And Kristen had listened and smiled and said nothing. It was inconceivable that she wouldn't have remarked on the coincidence that she was attending the same wedding.

Trevor swung the truck around and headed back toward Britteridge.

"Are you going to talk to Dr. Ludlum?" Josh asked.

"No." Trevor didn't want to admit his fears, but it was useless to try to keep Josh in the dark. "I want a look at her license plate."

"You want to know if that was Dr. L.'s plate number Kristen wrote down?"

"She drives a blue Accord."

"Oh yeah. I knew that. But why would Kristen—"

"I don't know, Josh." If someone wanted an inside source of information on the Drakes, there would be no one better to approach than Gail Ludlum. She and Sandra knew everything about each other's lives. And Gail had been around plenty since Rachel was taken. She knew every move the Drakes had made. It would be invaluable to the kidnappers to have an informant who could tell them instantly if the Drakes were trying to trick them, trap them, or involve the police.

But Trevor couldn't fathom Gail ever betraying Sandra.

Ever *wanting* to betray Sandra.

Was it possible that Gail was vulnerable to pressure? What if someone threatened to harm her or her family? Could someone blackmail her? She was a doctor—could she have made a mistake at work that she was frantic to keep secret? He still couldn't fathom Gail colluding with kidnappers, but he knew he hadn't imagined the look of terror on her face when Josh had mentioned Kristen O'Connor's presence at that wedding.

What if Kristen O'Connor *was* involved in the kidnapping—and she'd ensnared Gail Ludlum in her scheming? Had Kristen taken the opportunity of the Virginia trip to approach Gail far away from home?

But what of the way the kidnappers had treated Kristen?

Josh's words: *"Some people would be willing to go through a lot for a couple million bucks."*

How desperate was Kristen for money?

* * *

"You *idiot*!" Alex hissed. He'd obviously been in a rage on the entire drive up from Boston. His face was crimson, and there were circles of sweat under his arms. "How could you let this happen?"

"You were the one who told me she couldn't remove the blindfold," Kristen lashed back in a whisper.

"She couldn't have torn it off with her fingernails. I thought you searched her to make sure she didn't have anything she could use to—"

"I *did* search her." It was difficult to keep her voice to a whisper when Kristen wanted to scream, but she didn't want their conversation to travel upstairs to Rachel's cell. "I swear, she didn't have so much as a toothpick."

"So how did she tear it? That's thick cloth."

"Maybe she found something in the room. A splinter of wood or a paper clip. But how could she be so stupid? We warned her if the blindfold came off that we'd kill her."

"She panicked." Beads of sweat glistened on Alex's upper lip. "She was hoping she could break out of here if she could just see to do it. But why was she awake anyway? I thought you doped her so she'd sleep the whole time you were gone. You screwed up all the way around, Kris."

"I gave her the dose Ludlum said to give her." Kristen gripped the back of a chair, fighting the urge to punch Alex in the face. "Maybe she's developed a tolerance to it."

"After just a few days?"

"I don't *know* what happened, all right?"

"You'd better go search Rachel and that room millimeter by millimeter to see what she used to tear up that blindfold."

Kristen wheeled around and went to fill a glass with cold water. Her throat was so dry that her whisper was starting to sound like paper ripping.

"Do it now, Kris," Alex said. "We've got to find out what she's hiding."

"I'm not going in there alone," Kristen said roughly, hoping Alex couldn't tell how much she didn't want to go in there at all. "How am I supposed to search her while I'm holding a gun on her so she doesn't strangle me?"

"Fine. I'll hold the gun." Alex went to the coat closet and removed the ski masks they'd worn during the kidnapping. "Want your mask now that it won't do any good?" He flung it at her.

Kristen swore at him and let the mask fall to the floor.

Alex started to put on his mask. Kristen laughed rudely. "Give it up. If she knows who I am, it will take the police about thirty seconds to figure out who you are."

Alex tugged the mask on anyway.

Rachel was huddled on the bed with her knees pulled up to her chest. The remains of the blindfold around her eyes gave her a cartoonish look.

"You little fool," Kristen said. "We warned you to leave that blindfold alone."

"*What?*" It was more a sob than a word. "I didn't touch it. You people are the ones who ripped it up."

"What are you talking about?"

"I don't know anything that's going on here. Someone knocked me out. When I woke up, the blindfold was like this. What are *you* doing here, Kristen? You're—part of this?"

Kristen's face was hot and her palms were wet, but she pretended to ignore the pain in Rachel's voice. "What do you mean the mask was like that when you woke up?"

"She's lying," Alex snapped. "Quit wasting time. Get searching."

"I'm not lying!" Rachel shrieked. "I didn't do this. Your other partner must have done it."

Kristen approached the bed. "What other partner is that?"

"What do you mean what partner? Whoever else was at the car."

Kristen didn't clarify that *she'd* been the other kidnapper at the car. A gleam of metal near the bed caught her eye. She bent and picked up the object. Fingernail clippers, with the sharp point of a nail file left open.

She held the clippers up so Alex could see them. He grunted.

"I didn't do this," Rachel cried. "Talk to your partner."

Alex crossed the room to stand directly in front of Rachel. He aimed the gun at her forehead. "If you say one more word, I'll blow your brains out—if you have any."

Rachel gulped hard and closed her mouth.

Kristen checked every drawer, crack, and corner in the bedroom and bathroom, and finished off with a search of the trembling Rachel. She didn't find anything except for the nail clippers, but they were enough.

Back in the kitchen, Alex snatched a beer from the fridge and slumped into a kitchen chair. "Nail clippers. Nice. How'd you miss that?"

"I didn't miss it. She didn't have those clippers when we brought her here. I'm sure of that. Besides, no woman carries nail clippers around in her pocket, especially not Rachel Drake. I'll bet she's never groomed her own nails in her life."

"So they just appeared in the room, eh? Poof!"

Kristen's fingers twitched with the desire to slap him. "You know who screwed up, Alex? You. Those clippers must have been left in her cell—in the rooms *you* got ready for her. They were probably in the back corner of a bathroom drawer. This wasn't my mistake. It was yours."

Alex looked taken aback. Kristen smiled grimly. It was a victory, but a meaningless one. No matter whose mistake it was, the problem was the same.

"So what now?" Alex asked.

"I don't know." Kristen's heartbeat sped up. "If we send her home to tell Mommy and Daddy what she saw, we've had it."

"Let's get out of here. We'll go across the country. L.A. or San Francisco—"

Kristen snorted. "With Michael Drake pushing the cops around, how long do you think we'd last as fugitives? A week? Every cop in the nation will be looking for us—and every private citizen too. What do you think will happen to us if Drake offers a million bucks for our capture? Even the best phony ID in the world—"

"Shut up."

Kristen's throat was dry again. She grabbed Alex's beer and took a swig. She'd have liked to think she could be cool and efficient in this kind of situation, but this was kicking things up to a whole new level. She'd never intended to hurt Rachel Drake. It was one thing to take her and lock her up for a few days, but the thought of facing Rachel and—

But this was Rachel's fault. They'd warned her to leave the blindfold alone. Why should Kristen and Alex have to pay for Rachel's stupidity?

It's Rachel's fault, Kristen repeated to herself. "If we get caught, we'll be doing—what? Fifteen or twenty years for kidnapping? With Michael Drake's influence, we might get locked up for life."

Alex glowered at her. "This whole kidnapping scheme was your idea, genius. So what are you going to do now?"

"It wasn't my idea. It was Evelyn's." Kristen flopped into a chair. Her spine felt like Jell-o. "It was a good idea. And it worked. Rachel's the one who blew it."

"Tell that to the police," Alex said acidly. "Maybe they'll lock her up instead of you."

Prison. Spending a couple of decades in a smelly little cell, getting ordered around by guards. Her best years wasted while her smooth skin turned rough and pasty and her hair grayed and the muscles of her face started to sag. She might be grandma-aged by the time she saw freedom again. An ugly, penniless ex-con with no future and no friends. No matter where she went, she'd be a freak show, the criminal who kidnapped Rachel Drake and tried to use her identical twin as an alibi.

Ice spread through Kristen's chest. "I won't go to prison. No matter what, I won't go to prison."

"So what are you going to do?"

"Whatever it takes." Her skin was clammy, and a slight, buzzing dizziness hovered over her thoughts, but the coldness inside her stiffened her spine. She sat up straight and glared at Alex. "Are you going to help me, or would you rather run like a fool and play hide-and-seek with the cops?"

Alex crushed the empty beer can in his hand. Pallor had rendered his tan a sickly yellow, but his voice was hard. "I'm not planning on prison either."

"Good." Kristen hid her relief. She'd been worried for a moment that Alex wouldn't have the guts to help with what needed to be done, but obviously his shock was fading and he was starting to think again.

"The first thing I need to do is talk to Megan," Kristen said. "According to Doc Ludlum, she's been doing great, but I need to make sure that when the heat is *really* on she won't melt. I'll call her and set up a time to meet."

Uneasiness flickered in Alex's eyes. "Relying on her sounds risky. Since you two look so much alike, why can't we just get out of here and let Megan take the rap? Rachel won't know if she saw you or Megan tonight. Let her blame Megan."

"Alex! How can you be such an idiot? Sure, the police will arrest Megan—and then once she tells her story and Ludlum verifies it, they'll be hunting for us. Our best shot is to get Megan to stick to the story we want her to tell. Then the police will never suspect us—as long as they don't get a chance to talk to Rachel. Please tell me you're smart enough to see that."

"I see it," Alex said angrily. "But you're the one who keeps telling me that Megan's a wimp. Does she have the guts for this?"

"She can handle it," Kristen said. "All I need to do is pull the right strings."

Chapter 20

"How cocky can you get?" Gail Ludlum burrowed closer to the pay phone at the Circle K and curved her hand around her mouth to further shield her words from anyone who might pass by. She should have waited to find a more isolated phone, but she was frantic to talk to Kristen. "Things weren't dangerous enough? You had to add some extra spice?"

"I never said anything to Rachel about the wedding." Kristen's voice was like nails in Gail's eardrum.

"Josh said Rachel told him."

"Josh was lying."

"So he just happened to dream up the fact that you were at that wedding?"

"I don't know how he found out!" For the first time, the fear in Kristen's voice overshadowed the arrogance. Gail felt worse. If Kristen was panicking, things *were* falling apart.

"*Think*," Gail ordered. "How could he have known? Did you ditch your disguise too soon? Could someone have seen you there?"

"I didn't screw up."

"Retrace your actions. You learned about the wedding when I was talking to Sandra and Rachel at the Labor Day picnic. You got the specifics from the wedding announcement on my fridge when you and Rachel came over to—"

"Quit blubbering." Kristen sounded relieved. "I think I know how Josh connected me to the wedding, and if you don't panic, it won't be a big deal. I had some maps and a copy of the wedding announcement in my purse. I must have forgotten to throw them away. Josh probably went snooping and saw them."

"Why would Josh—"

"He's a teenage boy. Who knows? He's probably obsessed with me and wanted to caress my lip gloss."

"You stuck-up little—"

"Josh isn't going to talk about it to anyone, because he won't want to admit he was snooping, and why would he care about a wedding anyway? You're turning a molehill into Mt. Everest."

"How could you be so stupid? Leaving those maps in your purse—"

"I thought I threw that stuff away, okay? I had a pile of notes and info that I shredded and put in the trash at the hotel in Virginia. I thought the maps and the announcement were in that pile."

"And you didn't think to check your purse before you handed it over to Megan?"

"I did check it. But I didn't notice the maps, because there's an inner pocket that I'd never used before. It's a new purse. I remember now, that pocket's where I stuck them while I was waiting for you at the wedding reception."

"What am I supposed to say if the Drakes ask me about the wedding?"

"Just act all surprised. 'Oh, was Kristen there? I didn't know.' But I'm telling you, they won't ask. Josh won't bring it up again. You're the only person who thinks this matters. They don't suspect you of anything, and they certainly don't suspect me. Even if we were at the same wedding, it's meaningless. Don't get jittery. You're almost finished."

* * *

As soon as Evelyn retired to her room for a Saturday morning nap, Megan crept into the garage to check the mileage on the Cadillac. The odometer had been at 14, 832 when she'd brought the car home after getting it washed yesterday. At the time, her impulse to note the mileage had felt silly, but she'd worried about Evelyn having a backup set of keys. Most people did have more than one set of car keys after all. And Megan had been asleep for most of yesterday afternoon and evening, so she had no idea what Evelyn had been up to.

It wasn't surprising that she'd sunk into deep slumber when she'd intended only a brief nap. She hadn't slept well since Rachel's kidnapping, and apparently her brain had decided enough was enough and had knocked her out cold.

Apparently. Megan was embarrassed at the thoughts that kept creeping into her head, thoughts that passed beyond paranoid and into ridiculous. Yes, the lemonade had tasted a little funny, but Evelyn had probably kept a half-used container of drink mix on her shelf for the past ten years. Yes, Megan had slept for over six hours when the longest she ever napped was around forty-five minutes, but she'd been physically and emotionally exhausted.

Megan shook her head, willing her suspicions away. If Kristen had any idea what she was thinking, her sister would be on the floor laughing hysterically. *"You think she drugged you so she could slip out and—what? Go bowling?"*

Megan inserted the key into the Cadillac's ignition and turned it to illuminate the odometer.

14, 840.2.

There were eight more miles on the car than there had been when Megan parked it here yesterday.

Grimly, Megan switched the key off. Forget trying to contact the nurse, Aurora. She needed to talk to Evelyn's doctor.

The house was quiet. Hoping Evelyn was soundly asleep upstairs, Megan took the cordless phone into the backyard and dialed Kristen's number.

"Hey." Kristen answered on the first ring. "I was just going to call you. What happened to my cell phone, anyway? You shouldn't be calling me from Evelyn's phone."

"I—lost it," Megan said. "It's a long story. But I'm in the backyard. Evelyn's asleep."

"Why don't we get together?" Kristen sounded strangely friendly. Megan had expected to get berated for the lost phone. "Let's meet at the mall again."

"Fine."

"I'll be parked outside JCPenney, as far from the doors as possible without looking conspicuous. White Saturn, in case you forgot. Eleven o'clock sound okay?"

"Fine."

"See you—"

"Kris, wait. What's the name of Evelyn's doctor?"

"Her doctor? Why?"

"I'm worried about her. She's acting funny."

"*Hello*, babe. She's dying. How do you expect her to act?"

"No, I mean—never mind. Just give me his name. Or her name."

"Don't you remember it? It was in the info I gave you."

"No, it wasn't. I'm sure it wasn't. What is it?"

"Uh . . . lemme think. Doctor . . . doctor . . . oh, it'll come to me. We'll talk about it when we meet. Bye." Kristen hung up.

Megan went inside and took Evelyn's address book out of the cupboard. Someone as meticulous as Evelyn would have written her doctor's name in her book.

Megan started in the A's. In the G's she found an entry that looked promising—"Gallagher, Edward, M.D." and an office address in Britteridge.

It was Saturday morning, which meant the office was probably closed, but some offices did have Saturday hours. It was worth a try, and she still had time before she needed to meet Kristen.

Megan punched in Dr. Gallagher's number and was relieved when a receptionist answered in a thick Boston accent. "Drs. Gallagher, Boswell, and Mitchelson."

"Hi, my name is Kristen O'Connor." Megan headed toward the backyard. She didn't want to risk Evelyn's overhearing this conversation. "I'm Evelyn Seaver's niece. She's a patient of Dr. Gallagher's."

"Oh yes, Mrs. Seaver. She's a sweetie pie. Brought us a gorgeous white poinsettia for Christmas last year. What can I do for you?"

Megan moistened her lips. "I'm concerned about her and wanted to talk to Dr. Gallagher. She's been acting . . . strangely. Given her condition, I know it isn't surprising, but—"

"Her condition?"

"Her—illness," Megan said awkwardly.

"I'm sorry to hear she's been ill. Would you like me to set up an appointment for her?"

"I—I think I'll talk to the doctor first," Megan stammered.

"Sure thing. Now, let's see . . . Dr. Gallagher is between patients, so he might have a minute. Can you hold?"

"That's fine. Thank you."

"I hope your aunt is feeling better soon." There was a click. A synthesized version of something that might once have been Beethoven filled Megan's ear.

Mired in confusion, she gripped the phone and waited.

* * *

"You talked to her doctor?" Kristen looked annoyed, and Megan's annoyance burgeoned in response.

"You think it's stupid to seek medical advice for a medical problem? Who do you call when *you're* sick? The psychic hotline?"

"Don't get so defensive." Kristen's voice was unexpectedly soft. "I'm not criticizing you. If Evelyn's acting wacky, you were smart to call the doc."

"So what's the real story?" Megan asked.

"What story?"

"Her doctor didn't seem to know anything about Evelyn's having cancer."

Kristen removed her sunglasses. Her clear blue eyes scrutinized Megan. "You know he couldn't give you any information out of her file. That's confidential, and Evelyn would sue the pants off any doctor who violated confidentiality."

"I know that. He didn't actually *say* anything about Evelyn's condition. But I told him Evelyn was acting strangely these days—she seemed to be forgetting things, and she was driving on the sly, and I was worried her condition was deteriorating. He said if I was worried about her memory and her ability to drive that I should bring her in and he'd check her vision and so on. He didn't say anything about the heavy-duty narcotics she's been taking for pain or about the fact that she's 'not so clear in the head,' as you phrased it. From the way he talked, it seemed he didn't know anything about her being ill. *He* asked *me* what was wrong with her, and I was so flustered I just said I wasn't sure."

Kristen chewed the earpiece of her sunglasses. "That's totally weird."

"It's more than weird. First I try to contact her home nurse, and I can't even *find* any 'Aurora Capra.' Then I talk to Evelyn's doctor, and he doesn't seem to know anything about a terminal illness. What's going on here? Are you conning me or is Evelyn? Is this some sort of scheme to get me to come play slave to—"

"Whoa, babe, don't jump to conclusions." Kristen spoke casually, but her face looked hard and pale, and Megan wondered why she was pretending not to be upset when she clearly was.

"First off, you said yourself that he never gave you specific information about Evelyn's health," Kristen said. "Maybe he was trying to sound optimistic, and you misinterpreted that to mean he thought Evelyn was healthy. And it's possible he was looking at the wrong file altogether, because when I talked to—hey, wait a minute. You said 'he'?"

"What?"

"Her doctor. It's a guy?"

"Yes."

Kristen gave a tight little laugh. "All right, now I get it. I've talked to Evelyn's doctor, and it's a woman. Evelyn must have switched doctors."

"Without telling her first doctor?" Megan asked dubiously. "They'd need to transfer her records."

"You know how private and proper Evelyn is. When she started to suspect she was ill, she probably sneaked off to some doctor who didn't know her rather than show her face at her longtime doctor's office and let them know that perfect Evelyn Seaver was doomed. She probably wouldn't even give her new M.D. her old doc's name. She's strange that way. You know she won't even tell anyone she has cancer."

Megan wasn't sure what to make of this. True, Evelyn was very proud and very private. *But . . .* "I want to talk to this new doctor. Or to Evelyn's home nurse."

"I'm sorry about the nurse. I must have written the name down wrong. I'm sure it's 'Aurora.' How many women have you heard of named after Sleeping Beauty? But I could have messed up the last name."

Megan sighed. "Well, if she stops by the house every few days, I should meet her soon. What about the new doctor? I want a name, Kris."

"*That's* not a problem. If you'd just waited to talk to me instead of jumping the gun and calling the old doctor, I could have saved you from feeling like a doofus. I do remember the name. I knew it would come to me. I've met her several times. Gail Ludlum. She's a friend of Rachel Drake's mother."

Megan gasped. "Gail Ludlum is Evelyn's doctor?"

"I take it you've met her?"

"Yes, I . . . *she's* the one who told you Evelyn's diagnosis?"

"Evelyn had already told me the diagnosis. Dr. Ludlum told me what to expect, how things would probably progress, to call her if the pain meds needed upping, that kind of thing. You should have known this, smarty-pants. I'm sure I included Ludlum on the list of people you were supposed to recognize."

"You included her. But all you said was that she was Rachel's mother's best friend and that you'd met her at the Labor Day picnic. You didn't say anything about her being Evelyn's doctor."

Kristen furrowed her brow. "Are you sure?"

"I'm positive."

"Oops. Sorry." Kristen started laughing, but it sounded to Megan like she was forcing mirth she didn't feel. "Oh wow, you must have had a heart attack when you talked to her old doctor and he thought Evelyn wasn't even sick. I'd kill someone with my bare hands if they tricked me into working for that picky old crone with no hope of any money for another fifteen years."

Megan was relieved at the thought of being able to talk to Gail Ludlum about Evelyn, but then—"I've seen Dr. Ludlum several times and she's never said anything to indicate that she's Evelyn's doctor."

Kristen rolled her eyes. "Duh. Ludlum's probably afraid to mention Evelyn's name. Evelyn didn't even want me to talk to Ludlum, but I charmed her into it. No way was I going to take Evelyn's word for it that she was terminal."

"You were suspicious too?"

"I'm not stupid, Megan. Some old lady says, 'I'm dying, live with me for a couple of months and I'll leave you all my cash when I go,' and you'd better believe I'm going to check to make sure she's telling the truth. That's why I talked to her doctor. That's why I made sure I saw the new will. Happy yet?"

Megan toyed with the handle of her purse. This whole conversation had a chilly tone that unnerved her. They were circling Evelyn like vultures.

I don't like this. I don't like any of it. It's wrong and I want out.

Why couldn't she say that to Kristen, right now?

"I can't believe you could overlook something as critical as telling me Gail Ludlum is Evelyn's doctor," Megan said. "Do you *want* me to blow your plans?"

"I'm really sorry. I don't know how I could have missed that. There were just so many names to remember. I usually dealt with Aurora, see, so that's the name I remembered to put down. It was inexcusable, I know. But Ludlum's easygoing. She won't get suspicious. So how'd you manage to lose my cell phone? Sheesh, it's going to cost a hunk of cash to replace that thing. Lucky for you that Evelyn will pay for it. And it's not a good idea for me to call you at Evelyn's number, so you'd better hurry up and get a new phone."

"I know." Megan avoided Kristen's gaze. She should plunge into telling Kristen what had happened to the phone, but instead she said, "You didn't give me your cell phone account info."

Kristen smacked herself on the forehead. "You're right. My bills are in one of those plastic storage bins from my apartment. I assume you put them in Evelyn's basement."

"I did," Megan said, absently watching a girl in a denim miniskirt amble toward the doors of JCPenney. "Do you want the same model of phone?"

"I don't care." Kristen leaned toward Megan. "Meggie . . . the makeup doesn't work, you know." She touched the bruise on Megan's cheek. "Is Evelyn slapping you around? Is that why you're looking so miserable?"

Megan didn't answer. Now that they were face-to-face, she was second-guessing her decision to tell Kristen about the kidnapping. She wasn't worried that Kristen would tell anyone; Kristen wouldn't risk attracting any attention that might collapse her scheme to win Evelyn's money. But Megan didn't know if she could endure telling Kristen of her own treatment at the hands of the kidnappers and seeing Kristen react with indifference. She thought of the pain and fury both Trevor and Joshua Drake had shown at the thought of someone hurting their sister. Would Kristen care that Megan had been hurt and could have been killed?

"Megan! What are you hiding? Talk to me."

Tersely, without meeting Kristen's gaze, Megan told her about the kidnapping.

"I can't believe it." Kristen sounded horrified. "What hideous luck for you to be with her when it happened. I can't even imagine how scared you must have been."

"I'm fine." Megan felt better at the anxiety in Kristen's voice. "Rachel's the one to worry about."

"She'll come out of it all right. You know her parents will cough up the cash. But what about you? Sheesh, babe, do you need therapy or something? Having someone stick a gun in your face must rattle the old psyche."

Megan cast a cautious look at Kristen. Her eyes were wide and worried.

"I'm all right," Megan said with more conviction. "But my nightmares are a lot more interesting than they used to be."

Kristen laughed and swatted her on the shoulder. "I've got to hand it to you. You've got grit. I'd be a gibbering wreck for weeks after something like that. Good grief, no wonder you're having trouble taking care of Evelyn. Someone ought to be taking care of you. Why didn't you call me as soon as this happened?"

Megan smiled shakily. Beneath all the competitiveness and the insults, Kristen *did* care.

"You ought to call Dr. Ludlum," Kristen said. "She can help you with Evelyn, and she can help you with *you*. Like I said, you don't look so good. I wish I could come to Evelyn's and take over for you, but considering—" She waved a hand toward Megan's bruised face. "Somehow I think Evelyn would notice if I showed up in your place."

"I'm all right. I'll call Dr. Ludlum."

"Good girl. Wow, that's such awful news about Rachel. I hope everything—" Kristen clutched Megan's arm, her fingers pressing painfully against the scrapes concealed by Megan's shirt. "I just thought of something."

"What?"

"Once Rachel is home, the Drakes will go to the police. The police will question everybody involved."

"So?"

"They'll question you."

"I—yes, of course they will."

"Megan, listen to me." Kristen's nails dug into Megan's arm. "Whatever you do, don't blow your identity."

The full impact of what was going to happen hit Megan. "Kris . . . wait. This is a police investigation. How can I—"

"*Listen to me.*" Kristen leaned closer, her gaze scorching Megan. "The police don't care what your name is. They just want to know if you can give them any information to help them catch the kidnappers."

"I know that. But—"

"*Megan.* If you tell them who you are, not only will that kill any chance of us inheriting Evelyn's money, but it will make us suspects in what happened to Rachel."

"*What?* That's ridiculous."

"How can you be so naive? Don't you know how bad it would look if you admitted we've been tricking the Drakes and everyone else? If you admitted we played switcheroo in hopes of getting money? Do you want to be the focus of a criminal investigation?"

Megan shuddered, remembering Trevor's distrust. It wouldn't take much for the Drakes to start thinking she'd had something to do with the kidnapping.

"You don't want to get tangled up in this, believe me," Kristen said. "The Drakes are going to be in a frenzy wanting to blame someone, and the cops are going to be in a frenzy wanting to keep Michael Drake happy. If you admit what we did, that makes both of us look shady. You understand?"

Megan nodded, queasily conjuring a picture of herself being handcuffed and shoved into a police car while Trevor Drake looked on.

"Even if they can't pin anything on us, we'll be notorious the rest of our lives," Kristen said. "The Drakes are big shots, and anything to do with them is big news. We'll end up as a freak show, the interchangeable twins who tried to scam a sick old lady out of her dough.

Front page of the *Boston Globe* for weeks, front page of the tabloids for eternity. Is that what you want?"

Tension seized the muscles in Megan's neck as she imagined what the Drakes would think of her if they knew how petty and greedy she was.

"*Megan.* Swear to me you won't lose your nerve. We'll lose everything. It'll ruin our lives. And what if the kidnappers—I feel terrible saying this right out, but it's not like we're not all thinking it—what if the kidnappers *don't* return Rachel? Can you imagine how livid the Drakes would be? They'd be ready to hang anyone they could get their hands on. Don't offer us as victims. Promise me, Megan."

"All right," Megan whispered, her thoughts echoing with the clang of a cell door slamming shut. "You're right. It would just be a mess."

"Good girl." Kristen smiled, her hand still bruising Megan's arm. "Hang in there. It'll all be worth it in the end."

Chapter 21

"Haven't I done enough for you?" Gail Ludlum clamped the phone between her ear and shoulder and buttoned her flapping raincoat. The morning had started out sunny, but now clouds clogged the sky, the wind had picked up, and rain was imminent. "Why isn't this over? You have the money. *Where is she?*"

"Don't get flustered, Doc," Kristen said. "Obviously this would be a bad time for Megan to blow things. And this is your easiest job yet. Megan will believe anything you say, as long as you put it in medicalese. But make it good. I don't want her calling Evelyn's doctor again. And tell Megan that the home nurse, Aurora, called you and said she was going out of town for a couple of weeks, and you told Aurora not to worry about getting a sub, because Evelyn doesn't need much nursing care right now. Got it?"

"Yes." Hatred roiled in Gail's stomach. "But has it occurred to you that someone in Evelyn's alleged condition wouldn't just be under the care of a family doctor like me? An oncologist would—"

"If Megan asks about that, tell her you referred Evelyn to a specialist, but when he told her she was terminal, she came scrambling back to you because she thinks you're mighty special. Sheesh, Doc, just make something up. Megan will buy it. The story doesn't have to last forever. In a few weeks, Evelyn will send Megan packing."

"Fine, whatever. Now *where is Rachel?* You said—"

"I said this weekend. It's still the weekend. Don't be so antsy."

Gail gritted her teeth and waited in silence until a customer walked inside the gas station and the door swung shut behind him. When no one was in earshot, she hissed, "Listen to me, you scaly witch. If you hurt one hair on her head, I swear I will cut your throat."

"Hoo, Doc! That's an ugly threat for a loving mama like you."

"You've got twenty-four hours to get her home, or I'm going to the police." Gail fought the tears that blurred her vision. "And I don't care what—hello?"

Kristen had hung up.

Gail swiped her hand across her eyes and hurried to her car. Fine, she'd give Megan an earful of doctor-speak, if that was what Kristen wanted. It would be a good excuse to meet with Megan and sneak the wretched wedding announcement and maps out of her purse. Kristen might think those papers were no big deal, but Gail wanted them destroyed, and she wanted to do it personally. She'd never sleep a peaceful night knowing there was solid evidence out there that linked her to Kristen O'Connor.

* * *

Rain dampened her black wig as Kristen hurried toward the doors of Barnes and Noble. She needed time to think; she was tired of driving around, and the atmosphere at bookstores always relaxed her. She ordered a cup of coffee, sat down in the café, and opened a magazine she'd plucked off the shelf at random.

Gail Ludlum was going to be a problem. She'd go far to protect Bryce, but Kristen's intuition told her Gail had limits—and Rachel's death would exceed those limits. Gail had only cooperated this far because she'd believed Kristen's insistence that they weren't going to hurt Rachel.

When Rachel didn't come home, would Gail remain quiet? Or would she go to the police, no matter what it meant for her and Bryce?

Kristen bent lower over her magazine and stared sightlessly at the rows of words. Gail loved Sandra Drake. Gail would blame herself for Rachel's death. Whether or not she went directly to the police, one thing was certain—she'd crack. Her guilt would come spilling out. And Gail's guilt would lead inevitably to Kristen.

Gail Ludlum was dangerous.

Kristen drew a deep breath, inhaling the soothing odor of new books and magazines. As soon as Gail reported that she'd talked to Megan about Evelyn, then—

Then what?

Kristen felt strange. Off balance. This wasn't what she'd planned at all.

But she couldn't lose her nerve now. It was either push onward or quit and resign herself to twenty years in prison.

It wasn't, Kristen thought, a very difficult decision to make.

* * *

Megan expected Evelyn to be annoyed at how long she'd been gone, but Evelyn was placidly watching TV when Megan walked into the house. She greeted Megan with, "Did you have a good time, dear?" and seemed pleased with the slipper socks Megan had bought for her—Megan's excuse for going to the mall. Evelyn requested some applesauce; Megan brought it, and Evelyn returned her attention to the television.

With Evelyn occupied, it was a good time for Megan to do some preparation for her talk with Dr. Ludlum. She planned to call Dr. Ludlum on Monday, as soon as Evelyn dozed off for her morning nap.

Evelyn would assuredly keep excellent records of medical bills, insurance payments, and so on. If Megan could get an overview of what tests had been performed and treatments given, she'd feel much better prepared to talk with Gail Ludlum.

She didn't dare ask Evelyn about the records. Evelyn would forbid her to look at them. But Megan was responsible for caring for Evelyn now, Evelyn was not in her right mind, and the more Megan knew, the more she could help her.

As quietly as possible, she slipped into Evelyn's office and headed for the oak cabinet nestled in one corner. She didn't know the name of Evelyn's insurance company, or under what heading Evelyn would file medical information, so she didn't know how much progress she'd make before Evelyn lost interest in the television.

Megan looked for files labeled "Health," "Medical," or "Insurance," but found nothing. She skimmed the rows of file folders, each labeled in Evelyn's neat handwriting, and sighed. This could take awhile. She'd start in the A's and look for relevant topics.

She thumbed past a few tabs and stopped in surprise. On the tab of a crimson hanging file was written *Ashby, Pamela (O'Connor).*

Mom.

Kristen had said that Evelyn and their mother had a falling out years ago, before Kristen and Megan were even born. Why would Evelyn keep a file with Pamela's name on it?

Megan glanced at the door she'd left ajar so she could hear if Evelyn called. All was quiet except for the sound of applause on *Wheel of Fortune.*

Megan drew the file out and opened it on the desk. The top item was a snapshot of Kristen lounging in a chair next to a swimming pool. Kristen wasn't looking at the camera; she was talking to someone next to her. On the back of the photo was written: *Kristen Marie O'Connor* along with the address of an apartment in New York and a date from this past summer.

The next picture in the file startled Megan. It was a picture of Megan at Trina's Barbecue, dressed in her gingham uniform, a tray of ribs and fries balanced on her shoulder. She flipped the picture over. *Megan Nicole O'Connor*. A date from the same month Kristen's photo had been taken. And her address in Morris Glen.

Kristen had said Evelyn knew nothing about their family.

Kristen had said Evelyn didn't even know Megan existed.

Her heart racing, Megan flipped to the next page in the file, a paper labeled "Pamela's Address" with a list of what must be every place Pamela had lived since adulthood.

Next came a set of newspaper articles held together with a binder clip. Each article was preserved between sheets of clear contact paper.

The first article was her father's obituary.

Megan removed the clip from the stack and turned to the next article. It was the article that had run in the small *Morris Glen Chronicle* when she'd graduated from high school. It featured a picture of Megan and the headline "Valedictorian Headed to Cornell."

The whisper of Evelyn's slipper socks against the hardwood floor of the hallway made Megan jump. She dropped the articles into the open folder and lifted it so hastily that several articles slid out onto the desk. A newspaper photo caught her eye. Evelyn's daughter. The headline read *Bicyclist Killed on Bridge.* Snippets of other headlines registered in her mind as she shoved the articles back into the folder: *Driver Not Charged in Fatal Accident—Mother of Slain Bicyclist Files Suit—*

"Kristen, dear?" Evelyn called.

Megan swooped the file into the drawer, slid it shut, and hurried to the door to meet Evelyn.

"I was just checking my e-mail," Megan said. "Are you all right? Do you need something?"

"I'd like you to run to the mall again, just a quick little trip. These socks are a wonder. This is the first time my toes have been warm in as long as I can remember. I'd like a pair for each day of the week. Would you mind, dear?"

"I'd be happy to get them for you. Do you need anything before I leave?"

"No, I'm doing fine. I think I'll lie down for a bit." Evelyn shuffled toward the stairs.

Taking Kristen's purse and keys, Megan headed out to her car, her mind a whirlpool of confusion. Why did Evelyn keep a file on Pamela? Had Evelyn lied to Kristen about her knowledge of their family? Or had Kristen lied to Megan?

Why?

And why would Evelyn keep articles about her daughter's tragic death in a file labeled with Pamela's name?

* * *

"Such a nosy girl," Evelyn murmured. And a silly one, to assume Evelyn was so deaf she wouldn't hear the hiss and click of the filing cabinet drawer rolling shut. Evelyn had always had superb hearing.

Why had Megan been poking around in the filing cabinet? Likely she was looking for medical information. Kristen had called Evelyn before Megan got home to warn her that Megan had talked to Dr. Gallagher and Kristen had claimed Gail Ludlum was her doctor now.

Had Megan found anything of interest? She hadn't had much time in here. Evelyn rolled the top drawer open and drew out the file on Megan and Kristen's mother, the first file she was concerned about Megan seeing.

The contents were in disarray. Megan had obviously gone through them and hadn't had time to put them back together properly. How much had she learned?

No matter how much or how little she'd had time to read, she'd learned that Evelyn was well aware of her existence. That was a direct contradiction to what Kristen had told her.

But it didn't matter particularly. Tonight, Evelyn would finish things.

Kristen would be here in fifteen minutes. When she'd called this morning, she'd demanded a meeting. Evelyn suspected she wanted reassurance on the matter of silencing Rachel—under the guise of informing Evelyn of her plans, of course. Kristen would never admit she was seeking support, but she was doubtless still shaken by everything that had happened.

Not to worry. Evelyn would give her all the support she needed. She'd support her all the way to life in prison.

Evelyn returned the newspaper articles to their proper order and replaced the binder clip, smiling at the thought of Michael Drake awaiting Rachel's return, jumping every time the phone rang or a door opened. Waiting, like Evelyn had waited for Judith to come home that night.

Until two police officers had arrived on her doorstep.

Michael would finally comprehend the pain his carelessness had caused her. As for Pamela, she thought Megan was in Phoenix. Kristen, pretending to be Megan, had been e-mailing Pamela to tell her about the mythical new job.

Pamela wasn't worried yet. But soon the e-mails would stop. Pamela would wait desperately for word from Megan.

Until the police found Megan's body.

Evelyn wished she could be there to witness Pamela's pain. One daughter in prison. The other dead.

Justice.

With her work finished, Evelyn would leave Britteridge and head south. The little house in Florida was waiting—the lovely cottage she'd rented in cash under a false name, paying for a year in advance and offering the owner a nice bonus if he rented to her without running any kind of credit or background check. She'd told him she was planning an escape from an abusive husband and couldn't risk creating a trail he could follow. The sight of stacks of cash had made the landlord all too eager to accept her story.

The police would never find her in Florida. If she dyed her hair brown and exchanged her flower-print dresses for slacks and T-shirts, she would look completely different.

Not that it mattered if the police did find her. Once Judith was avenged, it didn't matter what happened.

* * *

"You'll have to start eating ten thousand calories a day to maintain your weight if you keep exercising like this," Josh observed.

Trevor didn't slacken his pace on the treadmill. "Look who's talking," he said, looking Josh over. Josh's hair and T-shirt were soaked in sweat, and he carried a basketball under his arm. "How long have you been out there burning up the court?"

"I'm not sure. What day is it?"

"One that never ends."

Josh bounced the basketball once and tucked it back under his arm. "I'm trying to keep from going crazy."

"Same." And Trevor was trying to keep himself from running to Kristen O'Connor and asking her point-blank if she'd had anything to do with Rachel's disappearance—and when Rachel would be home.

Josh pushed his sweaty hair off his forehead. "Have you said anything to Mom and Dad about the—"

"I told you I wasn't going to do that yet."

"I thought you might have changed your mind."

Trevor said nothing. Since confirming that the license plate on Gail Ludlum's car matched what Josh remembered from the paper in Kristen's purse, Trevor had spent all of Saturday embroiled in a raging debate with himself. Should he confide his suspicions to his parents or keep his mouth shut? He didn't have any evidence of wrongdoing on anyone's part, and to accuse his mother's dearest friend of being involved in Rachel's kidnapping would be such a slap in the face to Sandra that Trevor couldn't bring himself to say anything yet. It wouldn't do any good to lob accusations when his parents were still forbidding police involvement.

Besides, the whole idea that Gail and Kristen might be linked to the kidnapping was ludicrous. There *had* to be an innocent explanation for the way Gail had reacted when Josh mentioned Kristen and the wedding.

"This is crazy." Josh echoed Trevor's thoughts. "How can Dr. L. be involved?"

"We don't know that she is. We don't have proof of anything. We just have an unexplained oddity." Trevor increased the speed on the treadmill. "And if you're here to blast me for not taking action, nobody's stopping *you* from telling Mom and Dad what we discussed last night."

"Yeah, I can't wait to tell Mom we think her best friend is a kidnapper."

"We have no idea what's happening here. But if you think you've got it figured out, go ahead and—"

"What's up with you?" Josh gave Trevor a curious look. "I never said you were wrong to keep your mouth shut."

"Okay. Fine. So for once I'm not wrong."

"Wow, you're defensive tonight."

"Sorry." He ought to keep his mouth shut now instead of taking out his frustration on Josh.

"Yeah, you should be sorry. Just because I've been ripping everyone apart all week doesn't mean I'm going to do it now. Give me a break." Josh smiled fleetingly and Trevor realized he was trying to apologize. "You mad at me?" Josh asked.

"No." Trevor's breath came fast and his leg muscles burned. "I'm angry at myself for being so useless. I'm angry because I can't figure out what to do. I'm angry because I'm thinking in circles."

"You? Since when have *you* ever not known what to do?"

Panting, Trevor stepped off the treadmill. "Most of the time I fake it, Josh. Surprised?"

"You fake it good."

"Yeah, sure." Trevor opened his water bottle and gulped.

Josh slouched onto the bench. He looked exhausted, Trevor thought. A limp collection of drooping, bony limbs and sweaty clothing.

"One good thing," Josh said. "If Dr. L. *is* involved, you can bet she'll make sure Rachel is safe. No way would she let anyone hurt her."

"True."

"This is going to sound weird," Josh said. "But something keeps bugging me. Something else I saw in Kristen's purse."

Adrenaline sent needle-sharp prickles over Trevor's skin. "What did you see?"

"I just keep thinking, you know, about what you said earlier about misjudging Kristen. How you didn't like her before, but now she's been so nice and thoughtful and really seems to care about Rachel and all that stuff. And how the kidnappers knocked her around and how it was crazy to think she was in on it, considering what she went through. And I thought, you're right—Kristen *has* been different. And . . . this is going to sound crazy . . ."

"Spit it out."

"I saw a picture in Kristen's purse. A couple of pictures. She had them in one of those hinged frames, all wrapped up in this little bag like they were some kind of treasure. One of the pictures was of Kristen and her sister. They were just kids, but you could tell it was Kristen. Besides, their names were written on the back."

"So?"

"Trev, Kristen and her sister look exactly alike. She must be an identical twin."

This time the adrenaline was an explosion inside of Trevor. "You're suggesting the girl we think is Kristen is actually her sister?"

"It's weird. But it's possible."

Trevor's throat was dry. "What are Mom and Dad doing right now?"

"They're in their room. Mom was crying a lot, and Dad made her go lie down."

"Come with me." Trevor headed for the door. "We need to do some research."

* * *

When she returned from the mall for the second time, Megan went through the motions of caring for Evelyn, but she was so anxious to get another look at the file labeled with her mother's name that it was difficult to concentrate. The instant Evelyn went into the bathroom to take a shower, Megan sped into the office and opened the top drawer.

The file was gone.

Megan checked the entire drawer, hoping that in her haste she'd misfiled it.

No file.

Megan closed the drawer, her heart drumming against her ribs. Evelyn had taken the file. She must have heard Megan hunting around in the filing cabinet and had removed the file, either because she knew Megan had looked at it, or because she was afraid Megan *would* look at it. If Evelyn opened the file and saw the haphazard arrangement of the contents, she'd know Megan had seen at least some of the information there. What else had been in that file?

Why would Evelyn lie to Kristen about her knowledge of Kristen's family?

Megan had the sense that she was walking through a house filled with optical illusions—rooms that appeared to be one shape but were really another, pictures that could be interpreted as two different images depending on how you looked at them, mirrors that distorted everything they reflected.

The phone rang. Megan was surprised to find that her knees were shaky as she hurried to answer it. "Hello, this is Kristen."

"Hi, hon. It's Gail Ludlum. How are things?"

Megan nearly burst out with the response that Dr. Ludlum must be a mind reader; Megan had been desperate to talk to someone who could explain Evelyn's mental state, but just in time, she realized Dr. Ludlum might be calling as a spokesman for the Drakes.

"Is Rachel—" Megan began eagerly, but Gail cut her off.

"No, doll, no word yet. I'm sorry. I'm sure it'll be soon. I'm calling to check on *you*. How are you holding up?"

"I'm—I'm doing—" The word *fine* caught in her throat, too big a lie to emerge. *I don't know what's going on,* Megan wanted to say. *I don't know who to believe anymore.*

"Kristen?"

Megan swallowed. "I'm worried about my aunt. She's been . . . strange. She's just—I don't know how to explain it—" The rush of water through pipes died. Soon Evelyn would emerge from the bathroom.

"Maybe I could set up an appointment to come talk to you," Megan said hurriedly. "I don't want my aunt to overhear this."

"Why don't you come over tonight?"

"I couldn't take up your Saturday evening. It can wait until—"

"Hon, I'm not doing anything except waiting for news of Rachel, and you know how *that* feels. Come distract me, all right? You'll feel better to get your questions answered. Erratic behavior on your aunt's part is to be expected at this point, but the question is whether it's getting past the point that you can handle it at home."

"No . . . no . . . she's fine most of the time."

"Truly, there's not a lot we can do for her except keep her comfortable, and you're doing a superb job of that. I'm so sorry. I know this is hard on you. And as you probably know, her home nurse is going to be out of town for a couple of weeks. Aurora asked me if she should arrange for a sub, and I said no, Evelyn doesn't like strangers, and she'll be all right with you to care for her. But if you need help, I'll get someone to come in."

"I'll be all right," Megan said.

"You don't sound very sure. Grab a pencil. I'll give you directions to my house. Get your aunt settled and then come see me. Okay?"

"All right." Megan took the pencil from the notepad near the phone. She wrote the directions, thanked Gail Ludlum, and hung up.

Apprehension tingled her nerves as she stood listening to Evelyn's whispery footsteps approaching the kitchen.

Chapter 22

"I'm sure that was difficult for you." Trevor tried to speak politely, but after five minutes of conversation with Kristen and Megan O'Connor's mother, his good manners were already cracking. "Mrs. O'Connor, if you could tell me—"

"No warning at all. I thought she was at work like usual, and then I get a call—she's *gone,* took a suitcase and moved out, and she's on her way to *Phoenix* of all places. Do you know what that sun will do to her fair skin? She'll fry is what she'll do, and I try to feel sorry for her, but she brought this on herself. I've cared for her, loved her—"

Trevor gritted his teeth and stared fixedly at the computer screen displaying Megan O'Connor's address and phone number in Morris Glen, Pennsylvania. Next to Trevor, listening on the speakerphone, Josh pretended to bang his head against the desk.

"—not like her at all. I think she's mentally ill, I really do. If you're a friend of hers, Mr.—I beg your pardon, what was your name again?"

"Trevor Drake," Trevor said, and forged onward before Pamela O'Connor could cut in. "Can you tell me the date Megan left? How long has she been gone?"

"Of course I can tell you the date. Do you think I'd forget the day my daughter abandoned me? She hasn't even *called.* She sends e-mails saying how busy she is and how she doesn't have a phone yet, but her new job is wonderful and she's so sorry she had to leave, but she hopes I'll understand, as if I *could* understand the impulse to abandon people who love you. This kind of selfish behavior isn't like Megan at all, but I should have known she'd do something crazy. She's suffering from a broken heart. She's told you about Luke, I imagine."

"Uh—"

"I tried to tell her she was making a mistake to get so upset over his silly flings. Such a handsome and successful man, and he adored Megan. If she could have just put the past behind her, she could have married him and settled in a beautiful home right here in Morris Glen. I know it's what she wants, deep in her heart. Megan loves it here. She's never wanted to leave. You know what I think, Mr.—?"

"Drake," Trevor said wearily.

"Mr. Drake. I think her sister must be influencing her. Kristen's always been unbelievably selfish. Her father died the summer after she finished high school, but she left anyway, marched off to college like she didn't care what happened to *me,* newly widowed, consumed with grief. If it hadn't been for Megan, I don't know what I would have done. But now Megan's done the same thing to me, turned and left without a word. Haven't I had enough grief in my life?"

Josh put his hands over his ears. Trevor fought the temptation to do the same.

"This is Kristen's doing—it has her fingerprints all over it. I'll bet she's the one who lured Megan to Phoenix. Megan would never have come up with such a dreadful idea on her own."

"You think Kristen—"

"She wouldn't give Megan the time of day while they were teenagers, but Megan worshipped the ground Kris walked on—Kris was so popular, you know, tons of friends, though why they liked her so much I can't imagine—and I just *knew* Kris would get Megan into trouble someday—"

"When did Megan leave?" Trevor boomed.

Pamela O'Connor didn't seem fazed by his rudeness. "Two weeks ago. October 3rd."

A shiver shot down Trevor's spine. That was the weekend Kristen had been out of town—in New York or Virginia or on Jupiter, for all Trevor knew.

"I'll remember that day forever, like the date of my own death," Pamela said.

Trevor and Josh exchanged a look. "*The date of her own death?*" Josh mouthed.

"Mrs. O'Connor, I'm sorry for everything that's happened to you," Trevor said. "If I'm able to get in contact with Megan, I'll tell her you miss her and that she should call home."

"That's good of you." Pamela's voice became throaty, almost flirtatious. "Are you a good friend of Megan's, Mr. Drake? She's never mentioned you."

"We—haven't known each other long. Mrs. O'Connor, this will sound strange, but do Megan and Kristen ever fool people by switching places with each other?"

"Oh, well not for a long time, but they did occasionally play games on their friends as children. And Kristen bribed Megan into taking her place a couple of times when there was something she didn't want to do, like the time she was supposed to do that presentation on—oh, I can't remember who, some president or other—and she didn't want to prepare, so she paid Megan to do it for her. How Kristen ended up so lazy is beyond me. Megan's always been such a hard worker. The teacher didn't notice the swap at first, but it wasn't very bright of the girls, really, because Megan had given the same report in her own class, and teachers talk about these things—"

It took Trevor another ten minutes before he could disengage from the conversation. Even then, he only managed it by giving a swift "thank you, good-bye" and hanging up before Pamela could say anything else.

"No wonder Megan bailed out without telling her," Josh muttered. "I'd have run away in kindergarten."

Trevor nodded. It was Kristen who evoked his sharpest sympathy. Were those the kinds of negative comparisons she'd had to endure from her mother all her life?

"So Kristen leaves Britteridge and Megan leaves Morris Glen on the same week. A few days later, 'Kristen'—" Trevor mimed quote marks around the name—"is back in town. A week and a half later, Rachel disappears. I think you nailed it, Josh. No wonder Kristen seems different. She *isn't* Kristen."

Josh nodded. "So we're all convinced Kristen couldn't have had anything to do with the kidnapping because she was with Rachel at the time, she got hurt too, and she was here with us for a couple of days after the kidnapping. Megan is the alibi for Kristen."

"The wedding," Trevor said. "Those maps that were in Kristen's purse. Do you happen to remember the starting point for the trip to Virginia?"

"Some hotel in Philadelphia."

"Okay, that follows. Kristen went to Pennsylvania to fetch her sister. Then she went from there to meet with Gail Ludlum at the wedding and—"

"And threaten her into helping somehow," Josh finished. "Time to talk to Mom and Dad?"

Reluctantly, Trevor nodded.

* * *

Gail Ludlum threw butter and sugar in the bowl and switched on the mixer. Her hands trembled and her vision blurred with tears, but she couldn't stop working. If she held still even for an instant, the pain would seize her and tear her apart.

This whole devil-inspired scheme was collapsing. She'd heard the fear in Megan's voice, the below-the-surface tremors of questions she didn't dare ask. What had Evelyn Seaver done to frighten her? Gail had had no direct dealings with Evelyn, but knowing Evelyn was a woman who'd conceal evidence of her husband's murder and cold-bloodedly use that evidence as a tool in a kidnapping scheme—Gail shuddered at the thought of Megan O'Connor in Evelyn's web. What if Megan started to suspect what was happening? What would Evelyn and Kristen do then?

And what if the Drakes started to suspect the truth?

Kristen was still armored in arrogance, sure her alibi would keep the Drakes and the police from even glancing in her direction. But if the police *did* take a look, they'd immediately reduce Kristen's alibi to scraps. And if Kristen went down, Gail and Bryce would follow.

Gail *had* to get those papers back from Megan before Megan noticed them. Maybe Kristen was right and the maps and wedding announcement weren't enough to make anyone suspicious, but there were enough loose threads fluttering around the edges of this sordid scheme without Gail's leaving evidence in Megan's possession. Megan was already uneasy about Evelyn, and her misplaced eagerness to believe the best about Kristen would carry her only so far.

Gail added vanilla to the bowl and cracked four eggs so clumsily that she had to pick out a dozen pieces of shell from the brownie batter. When would Rachel be home? What was Kristen waiting for?

What if Rachel *didn't* come home?

She couldn't think like that. Kristen wouldn't hurt Rachel. She knew Gail wouldn't let that go, not for anything. Not even—

Not even for Bryce.

The tears came faster, making it difficult for Gail to see the markings on the measuring cups. Bryce was a good kid with a generous heart. He hadn't meant to hurt anyone. Of course Gail had protected him from Kristen's blackmail. What mother wouldn't protect her child?

The agony in Sandra Drake's eyes flashed into Gail's thoughts.

Even if her role in the kidnapping never came to light, this would never be over for Gail. She'd know her treachery every time she walked through the Drakes' door and saw all those innocent, cheerful faces, all of them thinking she was jolly Dr. Ludlum with her jokes and her famous apricot crumb cake.

The peal of the doorbell made Gail spill flour down her apron. She hadn't expected Megan for another hour or more. She splashed cold water on her swollen eyes and went to answer the door.

A young woman with long, black hair stood on the porch. She held a canvas tote bag and an umbrella, and for a moment Gail thought she was selling something until she smiled and said, "You alone, Doc?"

"What are you—" Realizing the porch wasn't a good place for this conversation, Gail jerked Kristen into the house and clapped the door shut.

"You'd better be here to tell me Rachel is home safe," Gail hissed.

"I am." Kristen pulled away and propped her wet umbrella in the corner. "We just gave the Drakes instructions for where to find her. By the time she wakes up, she'll be safe in her own bed. Isn't that a happy ending?"

Gail wanted to be relieved, but she'd believe it when she heard it from the Drakes.

"I'm here to make sure you understand what you're supposed to do and say the next few weeks when the cops are crawling all over this," Kristen said. "Wouldn't want to make a mistake and end up in prison, would you?"

Gail nearly told Kristen that she'd better clear out before Megan arrived or she'd have a lot of explaining to do to her sister, but she changed her mind. When she'd called Kristen to tell her she'd spoken to Megan and pretended to be Evelyn's doctor, she hadn't mentioned that Megan was coming over tonight. She wasn't sure why she'd held back.

Maybe because she wasn't sure exactly what she wanted to say to Megan.

"What's cooking?" Kristen pointed at Gail's apron. "I'm starving."

"Anything I'd feed you would be laced with cyanide."

Kristen smiled. "Let's go into the kitchen anyway and sit at the table. I've got some notes and stuff to show you, and I need room to spread them out."

"This had better be the last time you contact me." Gail turned and started toward the kitchen. "Because next time I see your cute little neck, I'll—"

Kristen's footsteps were too close behind her.

Alarmed, Gail whirled around.

Something metallic flashed in Kristen's hand, swinging down toward Gail's skull.

* * *

Megan rang the bell a third time and added a vigorous knock. Why wasn't Gail Ludlum answering the door? Her car was in the driveway and the lights were on inside, but Megan had been standing here for five minutes. Perhaps Dr. Ludlum was in the shower. Megan was probably earlier than she had expected. Megan had intended to wait until Evelyn was in bed, but when Evelyn had returned to the kitchen, there was something odd in her manner that, combined with the missing file on Pamela, gave Megan the creeps. Evelyn had kept staring at Megan and smiling, her pale eyes as bright as sun reflecting on water. Megan had offered an excuse about needing to meet a friend and had left Evelyn watching television.

Megan returned to her car and waited fifteen minutes, listening to the rain pound on the roof of the car. Then she returned to the porch and rang the bell again.

No answer.

A gust of wind brought the rain under the porch overhang. Megan pulled up her hood. Was something wrong with Dr. Ludlum? Maybe Megan was being paranoid. But with kidnappers running around, and Gail Ludlum being a friend of the Drakes—

Her anxiety for Gail rising, Megan reached for the doorknob. She swung the door open and leaned into the entryway.

"Dr. Ludlum?" she called. "It's Kristen O'Connor."

No answer.

"Dr. Ludlum?" Megan stepped inside and closed the door. As awkward as she felt barging into Gail's house, she couldn't just go home and spend the rest of the night worrying.

"Dr. Ludlum?" Maybe Gail had taken the dog for a walk. Did she have a dog? She seemed like a person who would own a big, friendly dog. But what a night to go on a walk.

Megan glanced uncomfortably into the living room, scanning the charming hodgepodge of furniture, the colorful stained glass of the floor lamps, the quirky player piano. It was one thing to stick her nose in the front door, but to start searching the house? Maybe she should—

Maybe she should quit being a coward and see if something was really wrong. Gail could have slipped and broken her ankle stepping out of the bathtub or tumbled off a step stool and cracked her hip. And Megan was sure Gail wouldn't be offended by her friendly intrusion.

"Dr. Ludlum?" Megan started down the hall toward the back of the house.

Megan saw her almost instantly. Gail Ludlum was sprawled at the end of the hallway, not moving. With a cry, Megan raced toward her.

She skidded to a halt, the toes of her shoes inches away from a spreading pool of red.

* * *

"You're jumping to a great many conclusions, boys." Michael Drake kept a protective arm around Sandra's shoulders.

"We're not jumping to any conclusions at all." Trevor kept his gaze on his father. He didn't dare look at his mother. "I'm just telling you what we've learned, so when Rachel is home and we go to the police—"

His mother's voice was icy. "I refuse to let the police bother Gail. She couldn't possibly have had anything to do with this. Have you lost your mind? Gail Ludlum has been like an aunt to you. You were good friends with Bryce for years, until his problem—"

Trevor jerked forward in his seat. Bryce. Was he Gail's weak point? She'd done a lot of covering up for him in high school and during his attempt at college. What if he'd done something worthy of blackmail? It was a lot easier to imagine Gail buckling to threats if they were aimed not at Gail herself but at her only child.

"What?" Sandra said harshly. "What are you thinking?"

At a warning look from his father, Trevor sank back in his chair and said nothing.

"You need to get some rest, Trevor," Sandra said. "Exhaustion is the only explanation for the way you're—"

The ringing of Trevor's cell phone cut off Sandra's words. Praying fervently that this would be good news of Rachel, Trevor opened the phone. The display read *Ludlum, Gail.*

"It's Gail," he said to his parents.

Sandra stiffened. "Don't you *dare* say anything about your insane theory—"

"Mom, you know I wouldn't." Trevor opened the phone. "Hello?"

A stuttering, sobbing breath filled his ear. "This is—it's Kristen."

"Kristen, what's wrong? *Rachel*—"

"*No*. I'm sorry, I didn't mean to make you think . . . I'm at—I'm at Gail Ludlum's. I had—I had an appointment with her—"

Kristen's—Megan's?—sobbing was making it difficult for Trevor to understand her words. "Take it easy. Just tell me what happened."

"Dr. Ludlum is . . . dead."

"What?"

"Someone—they—she's lying in the hallway. There's blood—they hit her in the head—"

"Listen to me." Over the sickness rising in his chest, Trevor forced himself to speak calmly. "You need to call 911."

"I—I did." She drew a jerky breath and spoke in a lower voice, obviously struggling to regain control of herself. "The police are coming."

His parents and Josh were all on their feet, staring at Trevor with uncomprehending fear. Trevor wished desperately there were some way to avoid giving his mother this news.

"Kristen, listen to me," he said. "Don't touch anything."

"I know. I haven't. Just the phone, but I had to—she's lying in the hall—"

"Go outside. Get in your car, but don't leave. Wait for the police. I'll be there in a few minutes."

"I can't just *leave* her—"

Trevor closed his eyes, willing himself to stay calm. "Are you certain she's—gone?"

"Yes, I'm sure!" Her voice rose to a shriek.

"Kristen, go outside. I'll be there as soon as I can."

"I'll stay with her. I don't want to leave her alone."

"Kristen, *get out of there*. Get in your car and lock the doors. Whoever did this might still be around. Do you understand me?"

"Yes—I—all right—"

"I'll be there soon. Just hang on."

"Trevor?" Sandra whispered as Trevor jammed his phone into his pocket.

He looked at the agony of fear in his mother's face and said softly, "Gail Ludlum is dead."

* * *

Megan huddled into a corner of the couch and tried not to hear or see anything that was happening down the hall. She breathed slowly, concentrating on the need to keep herself from crying. She had to stay calm, in control.

The uniformed officers who had responded to the call had asked her some questions and told her to wait here. She assumed someone was coming to question her in more detail, or maybe to take her to the police department and talk to her there.

Flashing red-and-blue lights pulsed through the lace curtains at the living room windows. Clammy with perspiration, Megan stared at the lights.

She hadn't even had to wait until Rachel came home to start lying to the police. She'd started tonight, telling the responding officers that she was Kristen.

She'd lied. In an official police investigation, she'd lied. Like she'd been lying all along, to Rachel, to Trevor, to Sandra, to Evelyn.

She could still feel Kristen's fingers gouging her arm. *"Swear to me you won't lose your nerve. We'll lose everything. It'll ruin our lives. We'll be a freak show. The Drakes will be in a frenzy wanting to blame someone for Rachel. Don't offer us as victims."*

Megan twisted and pulled at Kristen's statements in her mind, but she couldn't break them. Kristen was right. If Megan admitted who she was, the police and the Drakes might assume a host of terrible things. At the least, Kristen and she would end up publicly humiliated and maybe prosecuted for fraud.

Abruptly, she thought of Abinadi, the man she'd read about while trying to distract herself the morning after Rachel had been taken. If he'd been willing to lie, he could have walked away. Instead, he'd proclaimed the truth and he'd died.

Why was she thinking of that now? Abinadi was a prophet, teaching God's words. Megan was a nobody, giving a phony name when it didn't matter anyway.

So lie to the police. Who cares? They just want to know what you know about Dr. Ludlum's death. They don't care what your name is.

It doesn't matter.

It doesn't matter.

It does matter.

What she and Kristen were doing was wrong. She'd known it from the beginning, and now, sitting in Gail Ludlum's living room with police officers swarming through the house, the discomfort she'd felt when Kristen first proposed this scheme sharpened until it pierced her with physical pain.

"We aren't hurting anyone."

Weren't they? At the least, she was hurting herself.

But if she blew this, Kristen would hate her forever.

But what was really going on? Either Evelyn had lied to her or Kristen had lied to her, or both.

With a mingling of relief and fear, she heard Trevor Drake's voice talking to the officer at the door. She wasn't sure why in her panic she had called Trevor. Maybe with the shock of finding Dr. Gail Ludlum she'd needed someone—anyone—to lean on, and she'd had Trevor's card in her purse. And she knew the Drakes would want to know about Gail immediately.

What would it feel like to look Trevor in the face and admit who she was and why she was here in Britteridge? In trying to gain Kristen's respect, what had she sacrificed?

Just her integrity?

A man in a business suit entered the room. He was tall and lean with wiry, black hair. *Abraham Lincoln, minus the beard.* "Miss O'Connor. I'm Detective Powell."

Megan rose to her feet. Powell had kind, dark eyes with friendly crinkles at the corners, but she was sure those eyes missed nothing—especially not the guilty flush in her cheeks and the wild throbbing of the pulse in her throat.

"Swear to me you won't lose your nerve. We'll lose everything."

The officer at the door escorted Trevor into the room and introduced him to Powell. Trevor looked sick, his eyes dull with pain and his jaw set.

"Are you all right?" he asked Megan, but she sensed a layer of hardness beneath the words. Apparently Powell noticed it too. He gave Trevor a speculative look before his gaze shifted to Megan, settling on her bruised cheek.

"Dr. Ludlum has a son living in Georgia," Trevor said. "If it's all right, my family would like to contact him personally with this news."

"Thank you, Mr. Drake," Powell said. "If you would go with Officer Klein, I'll speak to you soon."

Klein and Trevor exited the room. Megan wondered where they were going and hoped Gail's body was covered. She didn't want Trevor to see his family's friend like this.

"Does it . . . look like a robbery?" Megan asked.

"We're still determining what happened, Miss O'Connor. Please sit down."

Megan sank back to the couch, glad for the excuse to get off her feet before she started wobbling.

"Do you need some water?" Powell asked.

Megan shook her head, then wished she'd accepted; her tongue was parched, a strip of rough canvas. Her face had gone from burning hot to tingling cold. *"Swear you won't lose your nerve."*

Powell sat next to her and opened a notebook.

Chapter 23

Trevor parked his truck in Evelyn's driveway. "I'll make sure you get your car tomorrow morning." He spoke quietly, his cool voice deflecting Megan's effort to read his emotions.

"I'm so—sorry about Dr. Ludlum." Megan stumbled over the words. "This must be terrible for your family, especially now."

Trevor looked at her steadily. Was it just her own guilt that made her read hostility into his silence?

"I didn't say anything to Detective Powell about the—situation with Rachel," Megan said. "I know your parents don't dare involve the police until Rachel is home. He asked about this—" she touched her bruised cheek, "—but I said it had nothing to do with Dr. Ludlum and I didn't want to talk about it. I know it made him curious, but he didn't press me."

Trevor nodded acknowledgment.

The truth—all of it—rose inside Megan on a gargantuan wave of regret. It seemed almost ridiculous to discuss it right now, but she didn't want Trevor to hear it from Detective Powell or anyone else.

"Trevor . . ." She'd thought she'd calmed down, but now she was shaking again, convulsive trembling that left her shoulders hunched and her stomach muscles in knots. Before she could lose her nerve, she flung the words out.

"I'm not Kristen. Kristen is my sister, my twin. My name is Megan."

Trevor's eyebrows went up. The pounding of Megan's heart, the drumming of rain on the truck—every noise seemed painfully loud as she waited for Trevor's response.

"Go on," he said simply.

Wishing her voice would stop shaking, Megan gave him the same explanation she'd given Detective Powell, conscious with every word of how Kristen was going to despise her.

"Kristen invited me here to help her take care of Aunt Evelyn. Evelyn is terminally ill. Kristen didn't want to care for her solo, but she felt Evelyn would be upset by a change in caregiver, so she wanted me to tell Evelyn—and everyone else—that I was her."

"Where is Kristen now?"

"I'm not sure. Last weekend she was at a hotel in Wakefield, but she said she was moving somewhere else. The plan was for her to stick around for a few weeks until I was comfortable. Then she'd head to Paris with her boyfriend."

"Did you tell this to Detective Powell?"

"Yes. I haven't been comfortable with what we're doing, but Kristen was so sure it was the best way to handle Evelyn . . . but tonight . . . a murder investigation—" Megan tilted her head so it rested against the cold glass of the passenger window, her trembling finally ceasing under a numbing wave of exhaustion. "I'm sorry. I was wrong to lie, and I feel like an idiot."

Trevor was silent, his big hands tight around the steering wheel. Megan bit the inside of her lip to keep herself from filling the silence with a landslide of apologies and pleas to know what he was thinking.

"That was generous of you to drop everything in your life—including your identity—and move here to care for your aunt," he said at last.

Megan assumed he was being sarcastic. She hadn't exactly earned the remark as a compliment. "There's money involved, if that's the missing piece you're looking for. An inheritance. Evelyn has willed her money to Kristen, on condition that Kristen cares for her until she dies. Kristen didn't want to risk upsetting Evelyn by throwing a sister in her face . . ."

But how had Evelyn ended up with Megan's picture in her file? Certainly Pamela hadn't sent it to her, nor had Pamela sent her the picture of Kristen. Pamela had never visited Kristen in New York, let alone taken a picture of her there.

Megan stared at Evelyn's tidy, white-shingled house with its jewel-blue shutters framing darkened windows. The thought of going inside made Megan's skin crawl. Something was wrong there.

Everything was wrong there.

"Money isn't the missing piece I'm looking for," Trevor said. "It was obvious money was involved. I'm trying to figure out your motive in telling Powell—and me—who you are, but then leaving out the rest of the truth. Why were you really at Gail Ludlum's tonight?"

Megan was startled. "I told you before—I was there to consult her about Aunt Evelyn. I know it was an unusual time for a medical consultation, but she insisted I come over."

"That claim is going to fall apart in about ten minutes' worth of police work. Don't you know the police will check everything you told them? How long do you think it will take them to figure out Gail Ludlum wasn't even your aunt's doctor?"

"She *was*."

"On the morning after Rachel was taken, when Gail offered to go care for Evelyn, you said something like, 'I don't think my aunt would be comfortable with a stranger.'"

"At that point I didn't know she *was* Evelyn's doctor. Kristen had forgotten to tell me. Sometimes she's careless, and she had so much information to give me—"

"And somehow Gail forgot as well? She didn't say anything to us about being your aunt's doctor."

"My aunt is very private. She didn't want anyone to know she was ill and that she'd changed doctors—" Doubt and confusion rose again in Megan, but she damped the feelings with one soothing fact. She'd talked to Gail Ludlum earlier this evening, and Gail had confirmed everything Kristen had told her.

"Did you kill Gail?" Trevor asked.

Horror-struck, Megan stared at Trevor. Images of Gail's smiling face filled her mind, overlaid with images of Gail's bloodied body.

"How can you—how can you possibly think—"

"Because you're still lying to me. If you're coming clean about your identity scam, why aren't you telling the rest of the truth? Like what you were doing at Gail's tonight. Where Kristen is. Where Rachel is."

"Where *Rachel—*" It was just as Kristen had warned her. People would take their identity switch as evidence that they were involved in Rachel's kidnapping. And now in Gail Ludlum's murder.

"Gail was involved too, wasn't she?" Trevor's voice was a steady contrast to the maelstrom of fear inside Megan. "On the same weekend Kristen went to Pennsylvania to pick you up, she went to Virginia and met Gail where no one would see them. I imagine she threatened or blackmailed Gail into helping her. But Gail was cracking, wasn't she? She couldn't endure betraying my mother. You were afraid she'd go to the police. You panicked."

Megan rested her head on her knees and closed her eyes, drawing deep breaths to combat waves of nausea.

"I didn't kill Dr. Ludlum," she whispered. The way Trevor talked about Kristen's coming to pick her up—he'd already known about the switch. How had he figured it out? Had he suspected her of being involved in Rachel's kidnapping all along?

Trevor gripped Megan's shoulder and pulled her upright. "Is Rachel still alive?"

"*Please*—I swear we had nothing to do with—"

"Megan." Trevor's voice was still quiet, but the suppressed fury and anguish behind the way he spoke her name cut through Megan like a knife. "Is Rachel alive?"

"We had nothing to do with the kidnapping. I told you why I took Kristen's place. It was nothing to do with Rachel. It was nothing to do with Dr. Ludlum—"

The way Gail had greeted her when she came to help on the night of the kidnapping leapt into Megan's mind. *"Hi, doll. Remember me? We met at the picnic."*

That was the same information Kristen had given her originally about Gail: she was Sandra Drake's friend, and Kristen had met her at the Drakes' picnic.

It was one thing for Gail to refrain from talking to the Drakes about Evelyn's condition. But it was ridiculous to imagine that she would play "remember me" with Megan, like their only connection was having attended the same picnic.

None of this made sense. If Gail weren't treating Evelyn, why would she have lied to Megan about it tonight?

Because Kristen wanted to shut down Megan's efforts to talk to a doctor about Evelyn, and she knew she could get Gail Ludlum to say whatever she wanted?

Evelyn. Evelyn who'd kept a file on Pamela Ashby O'Connor and her daughters. Who'd known very well that Megan existed, contrary to Kristen's claims. Who'd slipped out of the house when Megan was away and had shown up at the grocery store looking spry as she purchased ice cream she'd later told Megan she was too sick to eat. Who'd offered Megan a glass of lemonade that had knocked her unconscious for over six hours while Evelyn went out doing who knows what. Who had a home nurse who didn't exist and a doctor who—who—

Maybe Evelyn and Kristen—

No. Trevor was crazy. He wanted to blame someone, so he was blaming Kristen and Megan. But Kristen would *never*—

Gail Ludlum, her wild, curly hair matted with blood.

A rush of dizziness made Megan feel she was both falling and floating. None of this was real. Rachel's kidnapping, Gail Ludlum's death, Trevor Drake's accusations. Even Kristen's coming for her in Morris Glen. Something had happened to her that night when she'd been hurrying to Trina's Barbecue in the rain, late for work. She'd slipped on the sidewalk. She'd hit her head or been hit by a car. She was in a coma, in a hospital in Philadelphia—

"Megan." Trevor's hand tightened on her shoulder. "When did you last talk to Kristen?"

"This afternoon. I met her at the North Shore Mall—" Megan pressed her knuckles against her lips. Trevor's words filled her mind. *"Gail was cracking, wasn't she? She couldn't endure betraying my mother. You were afraid she'd go to the police."*

"But it was a robbery," she cried; there *had* to be another explanation for what had happened to Gail. "The police thought it looked like a robbery."

Trevor released her shoulder. "Anyone can dump a few drawers and grab a few valuables to make a crime scene look like a robbery."

"But Kristen couldn't have had any kind of hold over—"

"Maybe she threatened to kill Rachel unless Gail cooperated. Or maybe Kristen blackmailed her. Gail's son is a recovering drug addict.

Maybe he did something Gail desperately wanted to keep quiet, and Kristen found out about it."

"You're jumping to conclusions. You're misinterpreting—"

"No, I think I'm finally getting it. Kristen brought you here with some cockamamie story about an inheritance and paraded you around Britteridge as her alibi while she was taking care of other business. Like kidnapping Rachel. And collecting the ransom. And—"

"*No!* Kristen wants money, but she'd never hurt anyone to get it. She'd never—she wouldn't—"

But from the beginning, Kristen had talked about Rachel Drake's money.

She'd been almost pathological about Megan's concealing her identity.

She'd insisted Megan cozy up to Rachel and her friends.

And she'd lost her temper when Megan had initially balked at going to the religion class held on the night Rachel was kidnapped. It had never made sense to Megan why her attending that class had mattered so much to Kristen. *"She parades you around Britteridge as her alibi."*

"No," Megan whispered. "She couldn't have gone to Virginia the same weekend she came to pick me up. She didn't have time. She was in New York with—"

In New York. What proof did Megan have of that? The pictures? Those could have been taken earlier.

"Check the inside pockets in your purse," Trevor said. "Kristen's purse, I mean. There's a copy of a wedding announcement giving the address where Kristen met Gail in Virginia, along with maps showing the way—unless Kristen already took them back. And written on one of the papers is a description of Gail's car and her license plate number."

Megan clutched the purse. "That's impossible."

"Josh was suspicious of you, so he went snooping. He saw the papers. Check the purse."

She wouldn't look. She couldn't look. Trevor was wrong. Kristen would never do this.

"Megan. Don't let her hurt Rachel."

Megan swung her door open and jumped clumsily out of the truck, nearly falling.

"Megan."

Megan didn't look back. She stumbled into Evelyn's house and locked the door lest Trevor decide to pursue her.

He didn't get out of the truck.

Megan could hardly make her fingers work as she unzipped Kristen's purse and fumbled around the inner pockets.

She found several folded pieces of paper. A copy of a wedding announcement. A map showing the way from the Doubletree Hotel—where Kristen and she had stayed in Philadelphia—to the Hampton Inn in Fairfax, Virginia. Another map showing the way from the Virginia hotel to the location for the wedding reception. A license plate and the description of Gail Ludlum's car, penned in Kristen's handwriting.

Megan shoved the pages into the purse and zipped it shut. Feeling like her legs had turned to lead, she walked into Evelyn's study, picked up the phone, and called Kristen.

* * *

Praying all the way, Trevor drove to his condo in Britteridge. Should he go back to Evelyn's, kick the door down, and try to force Megan to talk to him? She was so frightened and defensive already that strong-arm tactics would more likely shut her up than get her talking.

The instant he entered his condo, he called his father and reported on what had happened.

"So she admitted to the switch, but not to any involvement in the kidnapping or in what happened to Gail?" Michael asked.

"That's right." Trevor shucked off his rain-wet coat and tossed it on the kitchen counter. "She got panicky when I suggested she was here as Kristen's alibi. She kept insisting Kristen would never do anything like this."

"Do you think she panicked because she knows you've got their scheme nailed, or because she didn't know the real reason she was here and she's terrified that you're right about her sister?"

Trevor hesitated. "My gut feeling? The latter. It's far-fetched to think she wouldn't have been in on this from the beginning. But from the way she reacted—and the way she's been acting all along—I think she *didn't* know, at least not all of it. If she were involved in the kidnapping, why would she have been foolish enough to tell Detective Powell who she was? And why would she have called the police from Gail's in the first place? She's planted herself smack in the middle of a murder investigation."

"I've got Anita Barclay looking into the O'Connors, Evelyn Seaver, and Gail and Bryce Ludlum."

"Good." Trevor pictured the petite, soft-spoken statistics professor from Britteridge College who had an almost uncanny ability to gather information on anyone or anything. Dr. Barclay could get more from an Internet search than most people could get from an inch-thick police report.

"What do you want me to do?" Trevor asked.

"Stay in Britteridge. Megan O'Connor trusts you, at least on some level, or she wouldn't have called you from Gail's. Give her a short while to calm down, then go talk to her. See if you can convince her to give you any information she has that could help us find Rachel—anything she knows about Kristen's whereabouts, how she gets in touch with Kristen, who else is in the area with her, and so on."

Trevor swallowed hard, his throat constricting as he prepared to say what he dreaded. "Dad, I hope I didn't blow it by pushing Megan so hard. The last thing we want is for the kidnappers to panic."

"Don't second-guess yourself. I trust your instincts. I also don't think Megan wants Rachel to get hurt."

"I agree with that. But we need to call the police immediately. Is Mom willing—"

"Your mother still adamantly insists that we give the kidnappers time to fulfill their promise of returning Rachel this weekend."

"But considering what happened to Gail—"

"She insists it was a robbery and unrelated to Rachel. She keeps talking about how Gail sometimes forgot to lock her door. At the moment, she can't cope with the possibility that Gail was involved in the kidnapping."

"Dad, she's in denial. We can't—"

"I know. I promised her only that I would wait to see what Anita comes up with in the next hour. We can't wait longer than that. I'll call you as soon as I know anything."

* * *

"What is wrong with you? You've lost your marbles."

"I don't think I have, Kris." Megan made no effort to stanch the tears pouring down her face. "From the moment you contacted me, you were talking about the Drakes. And you made such a point of how I needed to go to that religion class the night Rachel was kidnapped. You wanted me with her, didn't you? For your alibi. That was *you* in the forest, wasn't it?"

"You're nuts. Completely nuts."

"The ransom pickup was on Friday, wasn't it? Evelyn had me all over Britteridge that day, making sure everyone in town saw me. That way there would be plenty of witnesses to confirm that you couldn't have been anywhere near the ransom drop. You and Evelyn hatched this together. She's not sick. There's no inheritance. This was all about Rachel Drake."

"So now Evelyn's part of the conspiracy?"

"You told me she had no idea I existed. She's got a whole file on us, including a picture of me taken just a few months ago."

"Ooh, that's proof all right. Call the cops."

"Have Rachel back here within an hour and I'll keep your filthy secrets. No one else knows about this." Megan had avoided mentioning her confession to Detective Powell, or Trevor's involvement. She didn't want Kristen to panic. "Take your pile of money and go. Just bring Rachel home. Or I'm calling the police."

"You need a straitjacket and a padded cell, babe."

"Bring her home. You've got one hour. You can't be holding her too far away with how you've been able to come back to town. Bring her home."

Kristen was silent for so long that Megan feared she'd hung up. "Are you still there?"

"I'm here. You know, Meggie, there's something you might want to consider. *If* any of your crazy accusations are true and you take them to the police, the police will assume you're as guilty as I am. No cop in the world—and no jury—would ever believe you're so colossally stupid that you came into this blind."

Megan gripped the phone, fighting panic. Kristen was right, but that wasn't something she could think about right now. "If you bring her back, I won't go to the police."

"Well, see, we have a small problem."

"What do you mean?"

"Princess Bubble-Brain was a bad girl and didn't follow instructions. She knows a few things we don't want her to discuss with the cops."

Megan found herself as breathless and racked with pain as if Kristen had punched her in the stomach. "Kris, *no*."

"I don't have any choice. And neither do you. I'm not a fool, unlike some people I could name."

"People like—Gail Ludlum?"

There was a pause. "What do you know about Ludlum?"

"I found her body." Megan choked the words out.

"You found—what were *you* doing there?" Kristen's voice was razor-sharp. "Why weren't you with Evelyn?"

"I went to consult her about Evelyn's health."

There was a longer pause this time. When Kristen finally spoke, her voice was velvety. "Awful experience for you, babe. But it'll become a lot worse of an experience if they pin the murder on you."

Trevor Drake's accusation echoed in Megan's memory. "Why would they?"

"Well, there's the evidence. You were on the scene. And your fingerprints are on the murder weapon."

"*What?*"

"You hung a picture for Evelyn a few days ago, didn't you?"

The lighthouse painting. The hammer she'd used to pound nail after nail into the wall. The hammer. The murderer had used—

She was going to be sick. Megan gripped the back of the chair with both hands and gulped in air. "You—you killed Dr. Ludlum—it was *you*—"

"You'll go down for murder. In fact, you may find you're the mastermind behind all this before long."

"You're a monster."

"No, I'm just practical—something *you* never mastered. You'll go down for Rachel too, by the way. The rest of us, we were just along for the ride. We'll all testify against you. You won't stand a chance."

"The police will never believe—"

"Your word against ours. And the evidence will be on our side. So what do you want to do? Tell the police and fry for two murders and a kidnapping? Or keep your mouth shut?"

"Don't hurt Rachel. Please don't hurt her."

"It'll all be over tonight. Forget about her and save your own idiot neck."

"*Kris*—"

The lights went out. The cordless phone went dead. Trembling, Megan dropped the phone onto the desk.

Clenching her teeth to keep herself from screaming, Megan felt her way across the office and into the hallway. *It's just a power outage from the storm. Power outage . . .*

Who besides Evelyn was helping Kristen? Probably Alex, the boyfriend who was supposedly taking her to Paris. He must have been the other kidnapper at Rachel's car.

"Do you want to fry for two murders and a kidnapping? Keep your mouth shut and save your own idiot neck."

Kristen would do a superb job of pinning the blame on her. And Kristen was right—no jury would believe she'd come to Britteridge because she thought she could inherit money from a long-lost aunt. At the very least, she'd be convicted as Kristen's accomplice in the kidnapping.

And as Gail Ludlum's murderer.

But no matter what happened to her, it would be better than living with the knowledge that she'd crawled into a corner and hid while Rachel was murdered.

Kristen thought that threats would be enough to keep Megan quiet. Megan the coward, the shadow. She'd never had the guts to stand up and defy Kristen.

Forget it, Kris. This time you're wrong.

Rachel was still alive. Maybe there was time. She'd run to the Welbys' house next door and see if they had a cell phone so she could call the police. If they didn't, she'd drive to a gas station or somewhere else that had power—

Her car. She didn't have her car. She'd left it at Gail Ludlum's. She'd have to take Evelyn's Cadillac. The keys were in her purse—where had she left her purse?

The office. Megan started to turn back and banged her shoulder against the wall of the hallway, knocking a picture to the floor. She couldn't see a thing.

Evelyn kept a flashlight in the kitchen cupboard near the phone. Megan groped her way into the kitchen. It was lighter there and she could see her way to the cupboard. She opened the cupboard and reached inside for the flashlight that hung in a bracket on the inside of the door.

Her fingers touched an empty bracket. Where was the flashlight? Had Evelyn taken it upstairs to bed, anticipating that the storm might—

The power. Megan looked at the dim glow that fell across the kitchen sink and floor—illumination from the streetlight. Lights glowed in the windows of the house across from Evelyn's. Was the power only out here? It must be a problem with the circuit breaker.

She didn't have time for this. She had to get to the Welbys' and call the police.

Megan walked out of the kitchen, straining to see in the darkness of the hallway. A shuffle of movement behind her made her whirl around. Faintly, she saw the white of Evelyn's hair and the paleness of her dress.

"Aunt Evelyn! You scared me to death! Something's wrong with the power."

"Yes, it's off, dear. I turned it off." Evelyn clicked a flashlight on and shone the beam on Megan. She brought her other hand forward and something hard and cold touched Megan's stomach.

The barrel of a gun.

"Let's sit down and have some refreshment, shall we?"

Chapter 24

"So dark," Evelyn said happily as she nudged Megan into the kitchen. "Yes, it's very dark tonight, with the clouds covering the moon."

Evelyn must have overheard her accusing Kristen, and now she was making sure Megan couldn't go to the police. "Aunt Evelyn—"

"Look in the cupboard by the phone. There's a candle there and some matches."

Evelyn shone the flashlight into the cupboard so Megan could see to retrieve a candle in a glass jar and the box of matches.

"Cinnamon apple." Evelyn touched the label on the candle. "Every autumn, Judith and I picked apples. She loved the taste of apples fresh from the tree."

Megan opened the box of matches.

"Trim the wick first, dear. You've got to trim the wick or your flame will be too high and you'll get carbon on the jar. The scissors are there in the cupboard."

This is ludicrous! Megan wanted to scream. But the pressure of the gun against her ribs kept her from arguing. She found the scissors and cut the wick of the candle.

"Judith adored your mother," Evelyn said. "We lived just a few miles from Pamela's family while the girls were growing up. Pamela was a year older than Judith, and Judith thought she was the sun and stars. Set the candle on the table and light it."

Megan dropped the first three matches she tried to light. Finally, she got the wick lit.

"Sit down, sweetheart."

Not knowing what else to do, Megan sat down. Her thoughts were a snarl of panic. If she didn't call the police *now,* Rachel would have no chance at all.

"Aunt Evelyn, Kristen is going to—she's going to kill Rachel Drake. You can't let that happen. You don't want Rachel to die. I know it's not what you planned."

"Oh, my dear, it *is* what I planned." Evelyn opened the fridge. "Kristen didn't know it, of course, not at first. She wasn't *quite* ready for it. But she's learning fast, isn't she? Whatever it takes to preserve her own interests. How very like Pamela she is."

Megan gripped the edge of the heavy wooden table and wondered how quickly Evelyn would pull the trigger if Megan started screaming like a lunatic.

"Fresh apple cider." Evelyn took a filled glass from the fridge. "The taste of October! Judith would drink it by the gallon in season, but she'd never touch apple juice. Too processed, she said. Something that belonged in a baby's bottle." Evelyn set the glass on the table in front of Megan.

Megan looked at the drink and her stomach squeezed into a ball. "I'm sorry about Judith. You must miss her horribly."

"You can call her Judy. Everyone did, except me. Did you read about the accident? I know you were poking around in Pamela's file."

"I didn't have time to read the articles." It would be ridiculous to deny that she'd seen the file.

Evelyn clicked the flashlight off so only the small, yellow flame of the candle lit the room. She sat across from Megan and waved the gun toward Megan's glass. "Drink up."

Megan lifted the glass and took a miniscule sip. "How long ago did she die?"

"Twenty-six years. Twenty-six years this month."

Megan's heart was beating so fast she felt dizzy. "I'm sorry."

"Did your mother ever talk about her?"

"No, she didn't."

"I didn't think so. Pamela acted like she'd had nothing to do with what happened. She wanted to forget it all. Never *once* did she admit to me how wrong she'd been to let Judith bicycle home that night."

"She—my mother was with Judith—with Judy—the night she died?"

"Pamela had taken her out to dinner to celebrate her birthday. Judith drank some wine at dinner and more wine over at Pamela's afterward. Judith had very little experience with alcohol. A very innocent girl, and she had no idea how dreadfully it would affect her judgment. But Pamela knew better. And Pamela still let her go home. If Pamela had only called me or kept Judith overnight . . ."

"I—I'm so sorry."

"I did confront her, of course, before the funeral. She told me Judith was an adult and responsible for herself and that nobody had forced that wine down her throat. I wanted to murder her right there. For a moment, I truly thought I would. But if I'd gone to prison, Edward would have had no one." In the candlelight, Evelyn's pale eyes had the iridescent glint of opals. "That's the only thing that stopped me."

"Edward?" Megan asked cautiously.

"My first husband. Judith's father. Such a different man from William. William was rather a trial, I'm afraid. Do you know, Pamela never even told me she was sorry for my loss. I don't think she cared much at all, even after all her years with Judith."

"I'm sure that's not true. She probably felt so terrible that she didn't know what to say."

Evelyn gave a dry laugh. "Oh, I suppose she missed Judith's friendship on a superficial level, but the only person Pamela genuinely cared about was herself. She had no idea how it hurt to lose a child. My only child. She destroyed my life and went on with hers. She married your father. She had you and Kristen. And Judith's broken body was rotting in the ground. Drink, dear."

Megan looked at the caramel-brown liquid. "It's drugged, isn't it?"

"Yes, it is. You'll be asleep. You won't feel a thing. I don't want you to suffer. They say Judith didn't suffer, and I'm a very fair person."

"You're going to—kill me?" Megan felt she was speaking lines from a movie. "Because of my mother's . . . role . . . in Judith's death?"

"She owes me a daughter." Evelyn reached across the table with her free hand and stroked Megan's hair. "You're such a pretty girl. Pretty and sweet. Like Judith. Your mother will miss you."

Megan shuddered at Evelyn's touch. Evelyn had braced her gun arm on the table, and the weapon was pointed directly at Megan, the barrel steady.

"I was going to take Kristen, since she's the elder twin." Evelyn's cold fingers caressed Megan's cheek. "But that wouldn't have been the same for Pamela. Such a strained relationship between Kristen and her. But you . . . oh yes, she'll mourn you."

Evelyn reached beneath the table. Megan heard a rustle as she drew something from the pocket of her skirt.

"This was Judith's." She passed a small cloisonné jewelry box across the table to Megan. "Open it."

Megan lifted the lid on the decorated box. Inside was a gold pendant shaped like half of a heart. She turned the pendant in the direction of the candle so she could read the word engraved on it.

Best.

"Your mother had the other half, the 'Friends' piece. I'm sure she's thrown it away. Why would she keep it? She's spent the last two decades pretending Judith never existed. Put the necklace on. I want you to wear it tonight. I want you to be wearing it when they find you. I want your mother to see it and remember."

Megan's throat was so parched that the drugged apple cider on the table almost looked tempting. She fumbled with the clasp of the necklace.

"You're shaking," Evelyn said. "I *am* sorry, dear. I know you're frightened. But it will be over soon."

"You're crazy," Megan whispered.

Evelyn didn't seem bothered. "The world is so accustomed to injustice that anyone who demands justice is called crazy. I wouldn't expect you to think differently."

With the necklace finally fastened, Megan rotated it so the pendant dangled over the soft collar of the turtleneck sweater Kristen had given her.

"Very nice," Evelyn approved. "Adjust your scarf—it's a little uneven . . . yes, that's it. The necklace is very pretty with your blue sweater and that lovely silk scarf."

"What does Rachel Drake have to do with this?" Megan forced herself to lower her hands instead of ripping the necklace off. "Why did you get involved in her kidnapping?"

"I *planned* her kidnapping. For all Kristen's cockiness, she doesn't have the capacity to manage something like this on her own. A bright girl, but lazy, and not good with details."

"But why—"

"Michael Drake owes me a daughter as well."

"I don't understand."

"The car, dear. He was driving the car that hit Judith. He wasn't even cited. Not so much as a ticket. Witnesses said Judith had swerved directly in front of him and there was no way he could have avoided hitting her, but that's nonsense. He should have noticed the way she was weaving as she rode along. He should have known she might make an unexpected move. If he'd been alert, he could have slowed down such that he could have stopped before he hit her. But no, he murdered my only child and walked away free."

Evelyn's expression became remote. "I tried to let it lie, Megan. I truly did, and as long as Edward was alive . . . but when I lost him too, I realized I could no longer deny justice. And this year, Michael Drake's only daughter turned twenty-one. It was time."

"Aunt Evelyn—"

"I could have killed Rachel directly, of course, but this way is better. It will send Kristen to prison for life—the sentence your mother should have served. And the ransom money will be useful in helping me start a new life. I finally *can* start a new life. People say time heals sorrow, but that isn't true. It's justice that heals sorrow. Tonight the scales will balance. You have two minutes to finish that drink. I'm trying to spare you pain, but if you don't cooperate, I'll still do what's necessary."

Megan's mind hurtled through her options, but every action she could take would have the same ending—herself sprawled on Evelyn's kitchen floor with a bullet in her chest.

Rachel. Someone had to help Rachel. If Megan fought Evelyn, if she screamed in an effort to attract the attention of neighbors, was there any way she could delay her own death long enough to summon help for Rachel? But she didn't even know where Rachel was.

Megan picked up the glass and took a tiny swallow. "You're going to have trouble moving me once I'm unconscious. Wouldn't it be easier for us to go where you plan to leave me?"

"That's a nice thought, dear. But I can handle things just fine. I'm in good shape, you know. Far better shape than many young people. And I have a plastic tarp in the garage. Once you're asleep, I'll bring it in. The tarp will make it easy to slide you across the floor. You're a skinny gal, anyway. Drink."

Megan held the glass near her lips, but she was afraid to take another swallow lest her senses begin to dull. "Where is Rachel now?"

"In my nephew's house, the house I tend for him. Unless Kristen has already killed her. You're stalling, Megan. One more minute. I'd rather not shoot you. My aim is not *that* good, and I fear it would take me several tries to achieve a fatal wound. So painful for you and so very messy for me."

Megan looked at her full glass and imagined the crack of multiple gunshots echoing through the neighborhood. Someone would surely call the police. It would be too late for Megan, but maybe they would catch Evelyn and figure out her connection to Rachel's kidnapping—

They'd never find Rachel in time.

Help us. Megan wanted to pray, but no words came beyond one desperate plea. *Please help us.*

"Can you turn the power back on?" Megan asked, her fingers chilled from the glass she held. "I don't want to die in the dark." It was a pointless request, but she couldn't think of any other way to delay.

"No, dear. It was dark for Judith. Not rainy like tonight, but a very cloudy, dark night." She raised the gun. "Thirty seconds."

Megan slung the contents of the glass into Evelyn's face and threw herself to the side.

Evelyn cried out and the blast of a gunshot left Megan's ears ringing. Megan threw herself flat on the floor. She snaked under the table, found Evelyn's legs, and yanked. Evelyn slid down in her chair, and her chin thudded against the table. Megan shoved Evelyn's chair, knocking it out from under her. Evelyn landed hard on the floor, her head striking the wood with a noisy thunk.

In the flickering light of the candle, Megan saw the gun near Evelyn's limp hand. She snatched the gun and stumbled to her feet. Evelyn moaned.

The candle was teetering at the edge of the table. Megan shoved it toward the middle. She jammed the gun into the back waistband of her slacks and snatched the scarf from around her neck. With frantic speed, she tied Evelyn's hands together and knotted the scarf around the leg of the table.

She had to call the police, but the cordless phone wouldn't work with the power off. Where was the circuit breaker? The basement or the garage? She grabbed the flashlight that had fallen to the floor and raced for the basement.

There was the breaker box—padlocked shut with a combination lock.

Megan sprinted up the stairs. *My nephew's house.* The letter from Troy Seaver in Germany. The house Evelyn and her husband tended for him while he was overseas. *With Evelyn's organized recordkeeping—*

Megan rushed into the study and wrenched the bottom file drawer open. Within seconds she'd found a file labeled *Seaver, Troy.* She flipped through the file and tossed aside a dozen letters before finding what she sought: a paper filled with instructions and information about a house on Britteridge Pond Road.

She had to stop Kristen. Megan snatched her purse off the desk. Clutching the file, she sprinted toward the garage, where Evelyn's Cadillac was parked.

The *door.* The automatic garage-door opener wouldn't work without power, and Megan didn't know how to manually release it. With a cry of frustration, she raced through the garage and out the side door toward the Welbys' house.

Howard Welby was already standing on his porch when Megan rushed across the grass, the slick soles of the ankle boots she'd taken from Kristen's closet causing her to skid and nearly fall.

"Krissy! I heard a noise that sounded like a gunshot—"

"I can't explain it all now. I need your phone. Please, *I need your phone.* No—I need your car."

"My *car*? Hey, kid, that's a little—"

Megan thrust the folder at him. "Call the police. *Now.* Tell them Rachel is at 109 Britteridge Pond Road. It's in the folder here. Tell them to get there *now.* The kidnappers are planning to kill her tonight."

Welby wobbled on his feet. "Rachel—wait, who's that? What's going on?"

The police wouldn't understand, Megan realized. They didn't even know Rachel Drake had been kidnapped. And she didn't have time to explain. Megan reached into her purse and yanked out the business card Trevor had given her. "Call Trevor Drake and tell him what I told you. Here's his number."

"What's going *on*?" Welby took the card. "Would you just—"

"Not now. Your car, *please*."

"You're talking crazy, girlie, but I guess if Evelyn trusts you—" Welby was slowly drawing the keys out of his pocket. Megan swiped them and sprinted toward the Chevy parked in the driveway.

"Call Trevor Drake and call the police," she hollered back at Welby. "And tell the police to come to Evelyn's. She's tied up inside. She planned Rachel's kidnapping. And she tried to kill me."

"*Wait*—" Welby yelled, but Megan slammed the door and sped away.

Chapter 25

Howard Welby gaped at his empty driveway. When Kristen had turned to run to the car, he could have sworn that just above her belt he'd seen the handle of a gun. Had Kristen fired that shot he'd heard? Welby looked at the folder she'd thrust into his hands. The tab read *Seaver, Troy.* Who was that? Some relative of Willie's?

Sweet old Evelyn responsible for kidnapping and attempted murder? That was a load of fertilizer. Kristen was crazy. She must be taking drugs, smoking that stuff that made people paranoid and violent. And just yesterday Deb had been saying what a nice girl Kristen was to be so devoted to her aunt.

He'd never see Deb's little Chevy again, at least not in one piece. In this rain, Kristen would have it wrapped around a tree before long. But what had she done to Evelyn? She couldn't have—no matter how out of her mind she was, she wouldn't—

His heart thumping wildly, Welby started across the yard. All the lights were off at Evelyn's. Bad sign. He swung the front door open and called out, "Evie? You okay?"

Wind rattled the trees, and rain slammed against the house, deafening Welby to any response Evelyn could have made. He stepped inside and shut the door behind him. "Evelyn?"

No answer. Where were the blasted lights? Welby fumbled along the wall until he found a switch, but when he flipped it, nothing happened. Power was out. Welby hadn't heard of any other outages in the neighborhood. Had Kristen switched off the breaker before she . . . did whatever she did to Evelyn?

A sick feeling in his gut, Welby bolted back to his own house to get a flashlight.

Deb was watching television in the family room. Welby almost called to her to come with him, but stopped himself. He didn't want Deb to see anything that would upset her. Welby took the flashlight and raced back to Evelyn's.

"Evie?" Shining the light ahead of him, Welby moved cautiously through the house. To his relief, he heard a moan from the direction of the kitchen.

He found Evelyn lying on the kitchen floor with her hands tied to the table leg. Her expression was dazed, and a big, red bruise marked her chin. Her hair and the front of her dress were wet.

"Evie!" Welby knelt next to her. "Can you talk to me? Do you know who I am?"

"Oh . . . oh, Howard. My head . . ."

"What happened?" Welby propped the flashlight against the table leg, then pulled out his pocketknife and sawed at the silky piece of fabric that bound Evelyn. "Your niece has gone nuts. She went tearing out of here, shrieking something about a kidnapping and how you were a murderer and how I needed to call the police. She grabbed my keys and drove off in Deb's car before I could stop her."

"Oh no . . . oh, Howard, I'm sorry."

Welby finished severing the scarf. He helped Evelyn sit up and rubbed at the red dents in her wrists to restore circulation. "Your niece takin' drugs, Evie?"

"I'm . . . afraid so. She . . . promised me she was quitting, but tonight I . . . found evidence of—that she wasn't keeping her word. When I confronted her, she accused me of all kinds of things, and when I told her she had to move out, she went . . . she went insane. She knocked me down and tied me up."

"She was hollering something about a girl named Rachel who's being held at some house by the pond and how she's going to die tonight."

Evelyn groaned. "Oh dear. Not Rachel again."

"Who's Rachel?"

Evelyn leaned against Welby's shoulder. "Rachel is . . . was . . . a friend of hers in high school. She was—" Evelyn moaned and patted her cheeks. "I'm so sticky. She threw apple cider on me."

"Rachel," Welby prompted, still troubled by the anguished way Kristen had shouted her name.

"Oh, it was a terrible tragedy. She went on a date one night with a boy she barely knew, and she never came home. A few months later they found her body in a lake near her house. Kristen never got over it." Evelyn winced and reached for the back of her skull.

Welby probed through Evelyn's silvery hair and felt a lump. "You've got a huge goose egg. We better get you to the emergency room. And we better call the cops and have them pick up your crazy niece before she hurts someone else."

"No!" Evelyn clutched his sleeve. "Howard, no. I don't want her to go to prison. She's family. She's such a darling girl most of the time. These horrible drugs, they turn people into demons. I want to get her into a treatment program."

"She could have killed you."

"Oh no, she'd never—"

"I heard a gunshot."

"That was me. I was trying to scare her, so I shot William's gun at—oh dear, I probably hit the cupboards or the wall. There will be a terrible hole. I suppose I panicked."

"No wonder, with her going nuts like that. But Kristen has the gun now. I saw it."

"Oh dear . . . but she won't use it. If you could just help me to the couch and get some ice for my head . . . why is it so dark in here?" Evelyn looked confusedly at the red candle burning on the table.

"Your power's off." Welby helped her to her feet, feeling the fragility of her limbs as she clung to him. "Kristen must have done it."

"What a silly thing to do. She did that once before when she was . . . high. She was ranting something about the light hurting her eyes. Could you switch it back on for me? If there's a lock on it, the combination is 24-38-1."

"24-38-1," Welby echoed, settling Evelyn onto the couch. "You lie down here, and I'll be right back."

With the power restored, Welby went to the kitchen to fetch Evelyn an ice pack.

"Thank you so much," she said. "You're a sweetheart to help me out."

Welby shifted his weight from foot to foot, watching Evelyn apply the ice pack to her head. "We really should call the cops," he said. "I know you don't want to see your niece do time, but she's dangerous. She's got your gun. Besides—she stole Deb's car."

"You'll get your car back. In fact, I think I know where Kristen is headed. She has some friends in Danvers, and when she gets like this, she often runs to them. If you'll bring me the phone, I'll call them and warn them she's coming."

"Better warn them to be waiting with clubs and chains."

"They know how to handle her. And she won't hurt them." Evelyn smiled ruefully. "She always takes her anger out on me."

"That girl belongs behind bars. I tell you, she sure had me fooled. She seemed like such a nice kid."

"Bring me the phone, would you please?"

Welby fetched the phone from the kitchen. "Once you talk to her friends, I'm taking you to the hospital. You might have a concussion."

"Just a headache, I think, but I'll rest for a while. Thank you for understanding why I don't want to bring the police into this. I promise, you'll get Deborah's car back, and if there's so much as a scratch on it, I'll pay to repair it."

Welby grunted. "I'm not so worried about that as about what she's going to do to some other poor soul in traffic."

"Well, there's not much the police could do about it now. No doubt she's nearly to her destination, so they wouldn't catch up with her before she arrived. I'll make sure her friends don't let her drive home."

"You sure of that?"

"Very sure. Would you run home and ask Deborah if I can borrow her heating pad? Mine is broken, and I have such an ache in my back."

"Sure. I'll be right back. But I still think you should go to the—"

"You're a dear, Howard, but I'm all right. Just fetch me the heating pad."

* * *

"What is it?" Alex snapped.

Kristen closed her phone. "Evelyn. Bad news. Megan's lost it."

"What do you mean *lost it*? I thought you took care of her."

"I thought I did, all right? But she confronted Evelyn and said if we didn't let Rachel Drake go—" Kristen embellished the story, adding an element she knew would anger Alex more—"*and* give Megan a million dollars, she's going to the police."

Alex picked up a pottery vase filled with wheat stalks and hurled it across the room. It struck the wall and shattered.

"*That* was intelligent," Kristen said. "Anything else you want to smash before we come up with a real solution?"

"A real solution? Like what? Your flaky sister is ready to call the cops on us even if it means she ends up in the slammer too. What's Rachel Drake to her anyway?"

"Megan's always had one of those soggy, do-good consciences. She feels bad for Rachel and thinks this stunt will save her."

Alex gripped his hair as though ripping it from his scalp would vent some of his anger. "Not such a do-good conscience that she doesn't want to grab more than her share of the money."

"Yeah, I know. If she really cared about Rachel, she would have gone to the police already instead of coming here to beat us over the head with her demands. She just wants to show me up. She's always wanted to outshine me in something and thinks she can finally do it."

"Wait. She's coming here?"

"Yeah. She got the location out of Evelyn. Evelyn said she's flipped—attacked Evelyn and kicked her around until she talked. Evelyn sounded pretty shaken."

"Your wimpy sister beat up an old lady?"

"I'm telling you, she's flipped. Evelyn said she has a gun and she's coming here. She thinks she'll be able to take Rachel and a suitcase of cash away with her."

Alex paced around the kitchen, randomly picking things up and setting them down. "So what do we do?"

Kristen couldn't figure out the emotions churning inside her. Anger? Fear? Regret?

Megan was her sister, her twin. But beneath that thought, an idea tickled her consciousness.

This could work out perfectly if they could make Megan's death look like an accident. Knock her out, put her in her car, run it off the road into the pond. The police would find her in Kristen's car with Kristen's ID in her purse. They wouldn't question her identity.

And Kristen could assume Megan's identity and go somewhere far from the heat of the police investigation that would erupt as soon as Rachel didn't come home.

So Megan was her sister. What had that ever meant? A fertilized egg had split in half and two people had developed where there should have been one. Megan was a freak of nature, a genetic joke. And now she was a danger. It wasn't Kristen's fault that Megan was a fool. Kristen had given her the chance to keep her mouth shut and collect a fair cut of the money. Megan was the one who had blown it.

"It's pouring rain tonight," Kristen said. "A careless driver could skid right off the road."

"Huh?"

"Megan's not a very confident driver."

"That so?" Alex caught on. "We'd better get ready for her. You said she has a gun."

"I'm not worried about *that*. She'd never shoot me. Give me ten minutes and I'll talk that gun out of her hand, no problem."

* * *

Rain lashed the car, forcing Megan to slow to a crawl as she drove toward Britteridge Pond Road. She hoped it was only the din of the rain that kept her from hearing sirens behind her. She'd expected the police to be tailing her by now. Howard Welby must have called them the instant she drove away.

The road curved, and Megan slowed further. The delay made her want to hammer her fists against the steering wheel, but if she skidded into a ditch, she'd be no help to Rachel at all.

Evelyn was insane, her mind distorted with the bitterness and grief she'd harbored for two decades. Did Kristen have any idea *why* Evelyn had orchestrated the kidnapping? Not that Kristen would care what Evelyn's motives were, so long as her plans involved money for Kristen.

She tried to kill me. White-haired, prim, fussy, supposedly sickly Evelyn, planning to—what? Probably strangle or smother her once she was unconscious and drag her to her grave on a plastic tarp. Megan shuddered at the memory of Evelyn's eyes in the candlelight.

Her hand went to her throat, where Judith's pendant hung. She wanted to remove it, but couldn't while she was driving. She wrapped her fingers around the necklace and nearly yanked it to break the chain, but at the last instant, she dropped her hand, unwilling to tear apart this memento of Judith.

Megan leaned forward, squinting through the rain. If she remembered the map of Britteridge correctly, the road that circled the pond was coming up. She whispered a prayer that something would delay Kristen and Alex's killing Rachel. Would the rain delay them? That depended on what they were planning to do. The rain might be a hindrance or it might provide helpful camouflage as they hid her body or dumped it in the pond.

Megan glanced behind her, hoping for flashing lights. Nothing. She gripped the steering wheel harder, wishing fervently that she'd replaced Kristen's cell phone.

The sign for Britteridge Pond Road was small, and Megan didn't see it until she had almost missed it. She slammed on the brakes. The car skidded.

Regaining control, Megan turned onto the road. For over a mile, all she passed were trees, but finally she spotted the end of a driveway and a mailbox. She pressed on the brake and strained to read the numbers painted on the mailbox: 109. This was it.

Megan accelerated past the driveway, pulled over, and parked on the shoulder of the road. She didn't want her headlights and the hum of her engine to forewarn Kristen and Alex. Turning in her seat, she shot one last desperate look along the empty road behind her.

The police should have caught up to her by now. What if Howard Welby hadn't called them?

Why wouldn't he have called? He wouldn't stand silent when a woman's life was in danger.

What if he hadn't believed her? Megan tried to think back on what she'd told him, but she remembered the panic more than the words.

She'd probably sounded crazy. But if Welby thought she was crazy, he'd still have called the police, if only to send them after

Megan and his car. And he would have told them Megan's crackpot story about someone being held prisoner on Britteridge Pond Road.

She couldn't wait any longer. A one-minute delay might mean the difference between life and death for Rachel. She'd have to face Kristen on her own.

Megan opened the glove box and reached for the gun she'd stashed there.

Chapter 26

Within seconds, Megan was drenched. She ran toward the house, blinking water out of her eyes, lighting her way with Evelyn's flashlight.

The beam of the flashlight caught the white bulk of a house at the end of the curving driveway. No lights were on inside or outside the house.

Tears mingled with the rain on Megan's face. This place looked deserted. If they'd kept Rachel here, she wasn't here now. Maybe they'd taken her somewhere else to kill her.

Or to bury her.

Megan shivered. She should have given the police a description of Kristen's rental car. She'd go call the police from inside this house, even if she had to smash a window to break in. And it was possible Kristen did still have Rachel here. Lights might be visible from the back of the house, or the windows might be covered to keep passers-by from realizing the house was occupied.

Megan hurried forward, clutching the gun. The thought of actually shooting someone made her knees feel as soft as whipped cream.

"Don't let it come to that," Megan whispered. "Please let Kristen and Alex be reasonable."

Megan halted and stared. In the light of the flashlight, she saw a figure sitting on the porch steps, barely out of the rain. Black hair, a tan raincoat. Kristen had been wearing that coat and wig this afternoon at the mall.

Kristen was sitting with her elbows on her knees and her face in her hands. With her face hidden, she apparently hadn't noticed the beam of Megan's flashlight and, over the drumming of the rain, she obviously hadn't heard Megan's footsteps.

Megan edged closer. Panic and hope thrashed inside her. Was Kristen out here looking so dejected because she'd finished with Rachel and was finally feeling a twinge of regret? Or because she'd changed her mind and couldn't go through with it?

Megan stopped near the bottom of the stairs and drew a deep breath of rain-washed air. "Kristen."

Kristen's head jerked up.

"*Megan?*" Kristen lifted a hand to shield her eyes from the flashlight. Megan didn't lower the beam. She liked being able to see Kristen when Kristen couldn't see her.

"Raise your hands," Megan said. "I've got a gun."

"Where did you get a—whoa, take it easy." Kristen raised both hands. "I'm not armed."

"Is Rachel dead?" Megan made the words cold, but she knew Kristen would hear her terror.

Kristen groaned. "No, no, she's alive. I swear, I haven't hurt her. How in the world did you find us?"

"Evelyn."

"Evelyn *told* you?"

"She tried to kill me. And since she planned on my being dead before I could talk to anyone, she figured it didn't matter what she told me."

"Evelyn *what*? Why would she—"

"Long story." Keeping a wary eye on Kristen, Megan stepped past her so she was standing on the porch with Kristen a step below her. "Bring Rachel to me. *Now*. I'll take her home. And you and Alex can start running. I assume Alex is in on this."

Kristen made a noise that sounded amazingly like a whimper. "It's not that easy. Can I please put my hands down? I won't try anything."

Megan tucked the flashlight in her pants' pocket, went to Kristen, and did a one-handed search for weapons, keeping the barrel of the gun pointed at Kristen's chest while she worked.

"This is ridiculous." Kristen's voice quavered. "Can't you just put that gun away? You know I wouldn't hurt you."

Megan gave a harsh laugh that scraped the lining of her throat. "You tied me to a tree and left me there half the night. That *was* you, wasn't it?"

"Listen, I didn't think—Megan, I honestly didn't think it would take Trevor that long to wake up and break free. I figured you'd only be stuck a little while. I know it doesn't mean much now, but I'm sorry."

"Thanks for the apology." Megan returned to her place at the top of the stairs. "Too bad you can't apologize to Gail Ludlum."

Kristen pressed the heels of her hands to her eyes. "I didn't kill Dr. Ludlum."

"But you said—"

"I never said I did it." Kristen sniffled. "I was trying to scare you into thinking we'd framed you. I was terrified you'd go to the police. But do you honestly think I could sneak into the house of some nice middle-aged lady and . . . and . . ." Kristen swiped at her eyes. "This is such a mess. I never thought it would—I just wanted some money. That was all. And the Drakes would never miss it, they have so much. But now—"

"Bring Rachel to me. Don't make things worse."

"You don't *understand*." Kristen gave her a wild look. "I don't *want* to kill her. Ever since I got off the phone with you, I've been arguing with Alex, trying to convince him that we should let her go and run while we have time. He's got a lot of fake IDs, so we could hide out somewhere. But he's determined not to leave any witnesses behind, so he said as soon as it's late enough that we won't meet other cars on the road . . . I'm such an *idiot.*" Kristen bonked her head on her knees. "I thought I loved him. But now, I'm scared of him. After what he did to Dr. Ludlum, I'm afraid if I don't go along with him . . . and he even took my gun. He doesn't trust me with it anymore. What am I supposed to do?"

Megan swallowed. She'd never heard cocky Kristen sound so frightened and she didn't know how to take it. "Come with me. We'll take Rachel. The police can protect you from Alex."

"Yeah, protect me in a prison cell."

"It's better than being dead."

"This is such a mess. But now that you're here . . ." Kristen's eyes widened. "Maybe we could . . . but it would be so dangerous . . ."

Megan shifted her grip on the gun. Her hand was cramping, and her soaked clothing left her shivering. "You can't let Rachel die. Let's go in now, through the back door. We'll catch Alex by surprise—"

"Sheesh, babe, this isn't a movie. Things aren't that easy in real life. Have you ever even fired a gun?"

"Not a handgun," Megan admitted, "but—"

"Meggie, listen to me. Alex knows guns. He's had a permit for years and he's spent a lot of time on a firing range. You're a nice kid who doesn't want to hurt anyone. Do you really think you could aim that thing at him and pull the trigger?"

"If I had to." Megan wished she didn't feel so queasy at the thought.

"Even if you have the guts to pull the trigger, you'll hit a window or the wall while Alex comes over and murders us. I'm not trying to be cruel. I'm just saying you'll get one chance with Alex, and if you miss, he'll blow your head off. At least let *me* carry the gun. I know how to handle it. Alex has taken me shooting a bunch of times. And I'm not afraid to kill him, if it comes to that."

"You said you loved him."

"I said I *thought* I did. I didn't know what he was really like. Could you love someone who bashed a lady's head in?"

"If we sneak inside—"

"We can't sneak in. The back door is locked and I don't have a key. The only way in is through the front door. We'll have to face him directly." Kristen rose to her feet. "When we go inside, Alex is going to size us up. If he thinks he can get away with it, he'll go for his gun. He knows me. He knows I'll kill him if I have to, so I don't think he'll try anything stupid. But you—don't take this wrong, but he thinks you're a piece of Silly Putty. If you're the one aiming a gun at him, this will end in a firefight, and he's got a lot better aim than you do."

"In the dark, how is he going to know—"

"The lights are on. We covered the windows so light wouldn't be visible outside. And with your face all bruised like that, there's no way he'll mistake you for me. Please, Megan. I want to help Rachel, but I don't want to get killed trying. Let me take the gun and let's go in before Alex gets tired of his beer and comes to see if I'm still sulking out here."

Feeling the warm beginnings of relief, Megan pictured it: Kristen holding the gun, the two of them bursting through the door, shoulder to shoulder, to rescue Rachel. Kristen was right—if Megan aimed a gun at Alex, he'd be sure to read her inexperience and react accordingly.

Kristen looked up at her with pleading eyes, clear blue in the flashlight.

"You think I'm a monster, but I'm not." Kristen's lips quivered. "I just . . . got in too deep."

As Megan's gaze locked with Kristen's, knowledge Megan had pushed beneath the surface for years rose into plain sight. It wasn't relief she was feeling, Megan realized. It was a false echo of hope, the feeling she always got when the real Kristen seemed to merge with the sister who lived in Megan's imagination, and Megan got to pretend, just for an instant, that Kristen cared about someone besides Kristen.

It had never been anything but a fantasy. And now, looking into Kristen's eyes, it was hard to comprehend that she had ever believed it.

"It doesn't work anymore, Kris. You think I'm an idiot, and maybe I am, but I'm not stupid enough to believe you'd risk your life to help Rachel or anyone else. Take that belt off your raincoat and hand it to me. Then stick your arms through the railing behind you."

"You're going to tie me up while you go in there and get killed? Megan, don't be a fool for once."

"Give me the belt."

"Give it up, babe." Kristen dropped the faux-pleading expression and smiled at her. "You wouldn't shoot me no matter what I did."

"Try me." Megan made her voice stony and saw Kristen's smile fade. "You're right. I wouldn't kill you. But I won't let you follow me. I think at this range even I could manage to incapacitate you."

Kristen grimaced and started tugging the belt loose. "Fine, go in there alone if you want. Get yourself killed. What do I care?"

"Hurry." Through the noise of the rain hammering on the porch roof, Megan couldn't hear if any cars were approaching, but in the darkness, she should have easily been able to see lights.

Welby hadn't called the police. They weren't coming. She'd have to get Rachel out of here on her own.

An arm went around her throat and jerked her backward, constricting so rapidly that Megan didn't have time to scream. The barrel of a gun pressed against her temple.

Chapter 27

"Howard, we should get her to the hospital," Debbie Welby whispered as she hurried into the kitchen, carrying the washcloth she'd used to clean apple cider off Evelyn's face and neck. "She might be hurt worse than—"

The doorbell rang.

"I'll get it." Welby jogged toward the front door, not wanting the visitor to disturb Evelyn. He hoped fervently he wouldn't see a police officer standing on the porch, come to report that Kristen O'Connor had died in a traffic accident—or had killed someone else.

It wasn't a police officer. It was a tall, well-groomed young man with broad shoulders that made Welby think of his own glory days of high school wrestling. This was Kristen's friend, the one who had mowed Evelyn's lawn the other day. Even with the umbrella he held, he was still getting wet from the water splashing up from the uncovered porch. Welby's first instinct was to invite him inside, but he hesitated, thinking of Evelyn.

"What can I do for you, son?" Welby asked.

"I need to speak to Kristen O'Connor."

"Kristen's . . . not here."

The man's face tightened with dismay. "My name is Trevor Drake. I'm a friend of Kristen's, and it's vital that I speak to her immediately. Do you have any idea where she went?"

"Drake?" Welby stuck his hand in his pocket and touched the business card Kristen had given him. This was the guy she'd ordered Welby to call. What did he have to do with Kristen's drug-crazed fantasies?

"Forgive me, sir," Drake said, "but who are you?" Beneath his courtesy, the tension was plain. A closer look at his face made Welby wonder when Drake had last gotten a good night's sleep. Not this week, anyway.

"Name's Welby, Howard Welby. I'm Evelyn's neighbor."

"Where is Mrs. Seaver? Is she home?"

"She's not feeling well right now."

"Do you have *any* idea where Kristen went? This is urgent."

"I don't—" Welby shot a guilty glance inside the house, imagining delicate Evelyn lying on the couch. No matter how angry she'd be at his revealing Kristen's problems to the first person who came to the door, he couldn't in good conscience let Trevor Drake go without warning him about Kristen. Drake might be in danger.

Welby stepped onto the porch and closed the screen door behind him. Drake moved back to allow Welby room and shifted his umbrella, trying to protect both of them from the rain.

"Young man, if you're a friend of Kristen's, you might know she's got a problem with drugs," Welby said.

"A problem with—no, I didn't know that."

"She was on a crazy trip tonight. Attacked her aunt, went tearing over to my house raving about a kidnapping and someone being murdered—"

Drake took a sudden step toward him, and it seemed to Welby that Drake had instantly added six inches to his already considerable stature. "*What did she say?*"

Welby wished he'd stayed behind the screen door. "She was nuts, Mr. Drake, yelling about some girl named Rachel and how Evelyn was a kidnapper and a murderer, and I needed to call the police and tell them where Rachel was—"

"What did she say? *Where is Rachel?*"

Welby couldn't help shrinking back. The knob from the screen door knocked him in the spine. "Take it easy, son. Evelyn said Rachel was a friend of Kristen's from high school who—"

"Never mind all that. *Did she say where Rachel is*?"

Despite the cold and rain, sweat broke out on Welby's skin. This kid might look like a decent guy, but he was as crazy as Kristen. "You ought to calm down and listen to me. Kristen's dangerous, and she might be after you. She has a gun, and she was yelling your name, something about how you could explain—"

"Where is Rachel? If Kristen said anything at all—"

Welby gave up trying to understand what was happening. "She gave me a folder that had information about a house up by Britteridge Pond. Said Rachel was there, but Evelyn told me—you should see what Krissy did to Evelyn. You wouldn't believe it. Knocked her down, tied her up—"

"Where is the folder? What's the address?"

Welby had the feeling Drake was exerting superhuman self-control to keep from grabbing him and slamming him against the house.

"I left the folder at my place, but I can go get it right now," Welby said rapidly. One blow from this kid's powerful fist would have Deb planning a funeral. "I came over here to help Evelyn—"

"Get the folder! Get it *now*!"

"All right, settle down. Come with me." He hurried down the steps with Trevor Drake following closely behind. Rain pelted Welby in the face, and by the time he reached his front door he had to remove his glasses and blot them on the hem of his shirt before he could see again.

Where had he left the folder? The hall table?

Not there. He must have left it on the washing machine when he'd gone into the utility room to get a flashlight.

Welby hurried into the utility room, hoping the folder was there. He had the feeling Trevor Drake wouldn't tolerate any more delays.

What a crazy night.

* * *

Trevor's phone rang as he stood in the doorway to Howard Welby's utility room. He yanked the phone out of his pocket.

It was his father. "Trevor, where are you?" Michael's usually mild voice sounded like the bark of a drill sergeant.

"I'm in the home of Evelyn Seaver's next-door neighbor. He has some information—"

"Listen to me. Anita Barclay just called. Evelyn Seaver is Barbara Newton, the mother of Judith Newton."

Judith Newton. The name sounded distantly familiar, but Trevor couldn't place it. "Judith—?"

"The girl on the bicycle," Michael said, and even through the urgency in his voice, Trevor heard the echo of pain. "The one I—"

"Got it," Trevor interrupted. Barbara Newton was the mother of the girl who had died in the auto–bicycle accident that had scarred his father with guilt and given him a lifelong fear of driving.

"Evelyn is her middle name. Seaver was her second husband. I haven't heard from her for nearly twenty years. She sent me a lot of angry mail for a few years following the accident, letters that stopped just short of threats. She blamed me for Judith's death."

"Dad—"

"Judith Newton was twenty-one when she died."

Fear struck so savagely that for a moment, Trevor couldn't breathe. "Rachel is twenty-one."

"Judith died twenty-six years ago this week. I've already called the police. They're on their way to Evelyn Seaver's. You said you're at her neighbor's?"

"Yes. Hold on, he just handed me—" Trevor flipped the folder open and saw the address typed at the top of what looked like a maintenance log. "Dad, I think I know where Rachel is. 109 Britteridge Pond Road. Call the police and tell them to get there *immediately*. I'm going there now."

Not waiting to hear if his father objected to that plan, Trevor raced out of the house, yelling back over his shoulder, "Don't let Evelyn Seaver go anywhere. The police want to talk to her."

* * *

"Drop the gun." It was the voice of the kidnapper who had dragged Rachel out of the car. *Alex.*

Megan let Evelyn's gun fall from her fingers. Kristen picked it up.

"Kris, you're so full of yourself, it's amazing you and your ego can fit in the same room." Alex's voice was loud in Megan's ear. "Talk the gun away from her, huh?"

Kristen shrugged and walked past Megan to open the door. "Get her inside."

"The police are coming," Megan croaked.

"No, they're not," Kristen said. "Evelyn's doofus of a neighbor didn't call them. He thought you were a wacko on drugs."

"How did—" Megan struggled to speak against the pressure of Alex's arm as he dragged her through the doorway.

Kristen reached out and patted Megan's cheek. "Next time, try hitting Evelyn a little harder."

Megan kicked at her. Kristen leapt gracefully out of range.

"Calm down, babe." She closed the door. "You brought this on yourself."

Alex dragged Megan into the living room and shoved her onto the couch. His face reminded Megan of a mannequin's—perfectly handsome, perfectly tan, perfectly blank.

"If you have any sense, you'll run now," Megan rasped, rubbing her throat. "Even if Howard Welby didn't call the police, the Drakes will. Trevor's got it all figured out. He knows you were involved in Rachel's kidnapping. He knows you were involved in Dr. Ludlum's death. And I told the detective at Dr. Ludlum's that I wasn't you—that we'd switched places."

Kristen rolled her eyes. "Even *you* couldn't be dumb enough to tell the truth to a cop. And even if Trevor does suspect me—which I doubt—he'll never be able to prove a thing."

"You've already lost, Kris. Give it up."

"Give it up," Kristen mimicked in a squeaky voice. "The cops have the place surrounded." She tossed a roll of duct tape to Alex. "Tie her up."

"Get me some scissors or a knife. This cheap stuff never tears right." Alex shoved his gun in his coat pocket and peeled the edge of the tape loose. Kristen fetched a knife and set it on the lamp table near Alex.

Megan eyed the steel blade. "What are you going to do to me?"

"Nothing." Kristen moved to the other side of the living room and stood aiming Evelyn's gun at Megan. "We just need to keep you out of the way for a while."

"You're lying."

"Shut up." Alex reached for Megan's hands.

"I'm going to be sick." Megan wrapped her arms around her stomach and drew deep, gasping breaths. "Please, I'm going to throw up."

Alex recoiled. Megan hunched forward, her hands dangling limply to the floor.

"Tie her up and gag her," Kristen said. "She's not going to puke. She's faking."

Alex bent over her.

"Watch *out*—" Kristen's warning came too late. Megan yanked the canister of Debbie Welby's pepper spray out of her ankle boot and blasted the chemical into Alex's face.

Alex screamed and staggered, clawing at his eyes. Megan grabbed the lamp off the table and slammed it against the side of his head. The lamp shattered. Alex crumpled to the floor and lay still.

The crack of a bullet made Megan throw herself to the floor. A second bullet tore through the couch, a few inches above her head.

"Not bad, Meggie." Kristen's voice was deadly soft. "But what are you going to do about me?"

Chapter 28

Evelyn regretted that she had to be outright rude to Deborah Welby before she could convince the pushy woman that she was strong enough go into her bedroom by herself to change her wet, sticky dress. She appreciated Deborah's concern, but she needed to be alone now, and she couldn't waste any more time lounging on the couch and listening to Deborah fuss about calling a doctor.

From the instant Howard Welby had returned from dealing with the visitor at the door, Evelyn knew she'd have to rethink her plans. Welby had had an uncharacteristically guarded look on his face, and he'd refused to discuss the visitor, muttering only that it was some boyfriend of Kristen's and he'd sent the kid away.

Howard Welby was a poor liar, easy for Evelyn to read. She'd gotten a description of the visitor from Deborah, who'd seen him out the window. Trevor Drake. What had Drake said to Welby to make him so cagey? No doubt he'd said something that Welby was now knitting together with what Megan had told him. Soon Welby would call the police, if he hadn't already.

Evelyn sighed. Her head and jaw ached abominably. She peeled off her soiled dress and slip and dropped them into the wicker hamper. She donned a blue, floral-print dress and navy shoes and attempted to arrange her damp hair with a comb. It was no use. She'd need a shower to get rid of the cider, and there was no time for that. She abandoned the comb and walked to the window.

She'd known it was a long shot to think she could pull things back together after Megan ran, and now, as she watched the first of the police cars come around the corner, she knew she'd lost.

Calmly, Evelyn walked to her dresser and reached into the back of the top drawer. From beneath her handkerchiefs she withdrew a small, plastic bottle wrapped in brown paper. She removed the paper, folded it, and dropped it in the waste can.

The doorbell rang. It pleased Evelyn that the police would ring the doorbell with decorum, not come crashing in like in those silly action movies William had enjoyed.

She smiled sadly. Even in her disappointment, she couldn't help but be proud of the strength and spirit Megan had shown.

It was almost—*almost*—as though Judith had triumphed.

Sitting on the edge of the bed with her back straight and her ankles neatly crossed, Evelyn unscrewed the lid on the bottle.

* * *

Her eyes watering and her skin stinging from the pepper spray, Megan rolled onto her side so she could look at Kristen. "It's over. Don't you get that? The Drakes know you're the kidnapper. Killing Rachel won't help you."

Kristen lowered the barrel of the gun a fraction and fired. Megan gasped at a sudden, burning pressure in her shoulder. Instinctively, she reached for her rain-soaked sleeve and felt the warmth of blood.

"Get Alex's keys out of his jeans' pocket," Kristen said. "One good arm ought to be enough for that. And if you so much as touch his gun, I'll blow your genius brains out. Just get his keys."

Megan slid closer to Alex and retrieved the ring of keys.

"Get up," Kristen said. "Go upstairs. Go down the hallway to the last door. Unlock the dead bolt. Go inside. Use the small, silver key to unlock Rachel's chain."

"I'm not going to help you hurt Rachel." Megan sat up. Tentatively, she tried to lift her arm to see if it still worked. It moved, but clumsily, and the pain left her gasping.

"I don't want Rachel dead." Kristen's gaze was glacial. "I want her protection. If anyone follows me or tries to stop me, I'll kill her. If they leave me alone, she'll be fine."

A hostage. "Take me instead."

Kristen gave a rude laugh. "What good would *you* be as a hostage? No one cares if you live or die. Get up. Do what I told you, or I'll kill you and Rachel both. I'll do it, Megan. You know I will."

Megan stumbled to her feet. The blood that had saturated her sleeve was now trickling along the back of her hand.

"Hurry," Kristen said impassively, aiming the gun at Megan's legs. "Or you'll be dragging yourself along on one elbow."

Megan walked up the stairs and along the hall to Rachel's cell.

Rachel was standing near a bed, her eyes ringed by the shredded remnants of what looked like a sleep mask. A steel shackle encircled her right ankle, and a cable led from the shackle to a metal plate on the floor.

Rachel looked from Megan to Kristen and back again, her mouth opening in surprise.

"Unlock her," Kristen said.

Megan moved to Rachel's side and knelt to unlock the shackle.

"Twins?" Rachel asked.

"More like one actual human being and one genetic joke," Kristen said. "Megan, when you've got her free, snap the shackle around your own ankle."

Megan tried to insert the key in the lock, but her hands shook so much that she kept missing the opening. She didn't try to steady herself; she needed those extra seconds. She glanced up at Rachel. Rachel was staring down at her, terror and confusion in her face.

"She shot you?" Rachel whispered, looking at the blood now dripping from Megan's hand in large, crimson droplets. "Why?"

"I'm not part of this. I was never part of this. And I got in her way."

"Save the boo-hooing," Kristen said, but there was a distracted look on her face, and she was looking at the cardboard-covered window. "You've got five seconds to finish or I pull the trigger."

Megan inserted the key in the lock. Kristen walked to the window and bent back a corner of the cardboard.

With Kristen's attention diverted, Megan looked up at Rachel and mouthed the words, "*Don't go with her.*" She saw the panicky question in Rachel's eyes—"*What do I do?*"

"*Faint.*" Megan gave the word the barest breath of sound so Kristen wouldn't hear it. "*Pretend to faint.*" She rolled her eyes back and tilted her head to illustrate, while clanking the shackle on the wood floor to distract Kristen.

Kristen stepped away from the window, and when Megan looked at her, hope brought a surge of energy that made her forget the blood streaming down her arm. Kristen had gone pale and at last, through the gusts of wind and rain, Megan heard what had caught Kristen's attention.

The faint wail of sirens.

"I—my head is—I feel like—" Rachel spoke in a gasping whimper worthy of an Academy Award. "I need to sit down."

"Get over here." Kristen sprang toward Rachel, her free hand outstretched to snag the hostage she thought could provide her shield. Her fingers clamped around Rachel's arm.

Rachel's head lolled to the side and she crumpled, dragging Kristen's hand down with her. Grasping the steel cable, Megan swung it like a whip, flipping the heavy shackle upward.

The shackle caught Kristen on the side of the face. She reeled, losing her grip on Rachel as she struggled to keep her balance. She squeezed the trigger of the gun. Rachel screamed.

Megan tackled Kristen. With her elbow jammed against Kristen's throat, she grabbed Kristen's wrist and slammed her hand against the floor. The gun fell from Kristen's fingers. Megan and Kristen both reached for it, and the combined force of their grabbing hands sent it skittering across the hardwood floor and under the bed. Out of the corner of her eye, Megan saw Rachel crawling toward the gun, dragging her left leg behind her. The thigh of her jeans had bloomed dark red.

The sirens were growing louder. Kristen smashed her fist into Megan's face, catching her just below the eye, and threw Megan off her. Dazed, Megan grabbed for Kristen's leg, but her injured arm moved too sluggishly and she missed, her hand thudding uselessly to the floor. Rachel was groping under the bed for the gun.

Megan expected Kristen to try to beat Rachel to the weapon, but Kristen headed for the doorway.

Megan staggered to her feet and followed Kristen down the stairs. In the living room, Kristen paused momentarily by Alex's prone body, but apparently realizing Megan was too close to allow her time to snatch his gun, she turned and raced for the door.

"You're . . . not getting . . . away," Megan panted. "Not after what you . . . did to Rachel. And Dr. Ludlum."

"Watch me." Kristen plunged out the front door.

Megan sped after her, determination obliterating pain.

* * *

The house on Britteridge Pond Road was dark, except where the front door gaped open, exposing a lighted interior. Trevor stomped the brake and his truck fishtailed to a stop. Police cars pulled in behind and around him, their flashing lights tinting the wet landscape an eerie red and blue.

Trevor leapt out of his truck. He wanted to go tearing into the house to search for Rachel, but if he got in the way of the police, he'd only hamper—

In the open doorway of the house, a familiar figure stood, clinging to the doorframe. *Rachel.*

In an instant, Trevor was up the steps. He swooped Rachel into his arms and carried her away from the house.

"Are you all right?" He threw open the door of his truck and set Rachel on the seat. She was holding two guns. The torn remnants of a blindfold encircled her eyes, and the left leg of her jeans was red with blood. A huge smile of relief lit her face.

"*Trev.*" Rachel dropped the guns and threw her arms around his neck, a strangling embrace broken only when a police officer pulled Trevor back so he could tend to Rachel.

"One of the kidnappers is on the floor in the living room. He's unconscious," Rachel spoke rapidly to the police officer. "I don't think anyone else is in the house. Kristen O'Connor—I think she ran outside." Rachel shook her head and blinked like she was trying to clear her thoughts. "I heard the front door open, and she's gone. Her sister was chasing her—"

"Chasing her?" the officer asked.

"Her sister—I didn't even know she *had* a twin—was trying to help me. She was hurt. Kristen had shot her. But she fought Kristen and knocked her gun away and Kristen ran and the sister—Megan?—took off after her."

"Did they drive away?" the officer asked.

"I don't think so. I always heard the garage door going up and down whenever anyone came or left, and this time I didn't hear it, or any engine sounds either."

The officer turned and spoke into his radio. Police officers were entering the house, guns drawn.

With one last glance to reassure himself that Rachel was really there and really alive, Trevor snatched a flashlight out of the glove compartment and left the officer tending to Rachel's wounded leg. Megan was hurt, and she was somewhere nearby.

He joined the officers fanning out around the house, his relief at finding Rachel tempered by thoughts of what would happen to Megan O'Connor if she were left to deal with Kristen alone.

* * *

The rain slapped Megan in the face, and she had to wipe her eyes repeatedly to clear them as she raced after Kristen. Kristen was following a set of wooden stairs that zigzagged down the hill behind the house. She must be heading for Britteridge Pond. Did she have a boat there? Did she think she could make it to the opposite shore and run from there before the police caught up with her?

Megan slipped on the wet steps and grabbed at the railing to keep from tumbling headfirst down the poorly lit stairs.

"Down here on the stairs!" Megan screeched out their location for the twentieth time, knowing the police must be all over the area. This time, her voice was so raw that she knew no one would hear her over the rain.

At the bottom of the stairs, Kristen started along the path that led to the docks. Megan spotted a small motorboat moored there.

Kristen wasn't going to make it, Megan realized. She'd never get the boat freed and the engine started before Megan was on her.

Kristen apparently realized this too; before she reached the boat, she stopped, spun around, and started toward Megan. The feeble illumination from the dock lights reflected off the knife in her hand.

The knife. That was why she'd paused near Alex—to grab the knife she'd set on the table.

"How . . . many chances do I . . . have to give you?" Kristen was gasping for breath, but her steps were steady as she came toward Megan. "You really asked for this one, Meggie."

Megan knew she couldn't outrun Kristen. Already her head was starting to feel fuzzy from the effects of her injuries, and her legs were shaking.

"Down here at the dock!" Megan tried the cry one more time, but all that emerged was a croak.

Holding the knife out in front of her, Kristen charged. Megan flung one desperate glance around her in search of anything she could use as a weapon. There was nothing, unless she could break off a tree branch in the second before Kristen reached her.

Not knowing what else to do, Megan lunged toward Kristen.

Kristen froze in mid-stride, startled to have Megan approaching her instead of fleeing. Then, in a burst of movement, Kristen jumped at Megan, swinging the knife toward her neck.

Megan swung her uninjured arm up as hard as she could. Her forearm caught the flat of the knife blade, knocking it up and away from her.

Kristen took a step backward, dropped her arm lower, and swung the knife again. Pain seared Megan's ribs.

Panting, Kristen struck again, and Megan felt a sickening pressure in her side. She drove her fist into Kristen's face, and Kristen stumbled. Megan slammed the sole of her boot against Kristen's knee, and Kristen fell backward. She landed half on and half off of the dock with her upper body dangling over the water.

Kristen flailed to catch herself. The knife plunked into the water.

Megan's knees buckled and she fell, her palms striking the soaked wood of the dock. The dizziness was overwhelming now, dizziness and coldness that chilled her entire body.

Someone grabbed her from behind. *Alex.* She struggled feebly, but his hands were stone.

"Megan."

Trevor Drake's voice. Trevor was lifting her. The dock was full of shadowy shapes and flashlights. Police officers.

"Rachel's at the house, up the hill," Megan rasped. "She's injured—her leg—"

"I know. We've got her."

Dimly, Megan saw officers hauling Kristen to her feet. Kristen's face was so contorted with fury that it was almost unrecognizable.

"I'm sorry, Kris," Megan whispered, and passed out.

Chapter 29

Megan had been bracing herself for this confrontation ever since she had been lucid enough to worry about it, but the sight of Detective Powell entering her hospital room along with another man in a suit and tie still sent a shock of fear through her body.

It was Monday morning, thirty-six hours since she'd been brought to the hospital—plenty of time for Kristen to make good on her threat to convince the police that not only had Megan been a willing partner in Rachel's kidnapping, but she'd also murdered Gail Ludlum. Powell had probably already found the hammer with Megan's fingerprints on it, along with whatever other evidence Kristen had concocted.

And all Megan had as a defense was her own stupidity.

Megan tried to sit up as Powell approached, but he pointed at her pillow with a long, bony finger.

"Lie back. I had to twist your doctor's arm just to get twenty minutes with you, and if you exhaust yourself, he won't let me near you again until you're strong enough to run a marathon."

Megan sank back against the pillow, regretting her effort to sit up. Every movement tugged at her injuries and augmented the constant aching with burning jolts of pain.

"How are you feeling?" Powell pulled the one chair in the room up to Megan's bed. The other man stood behind him.

"I'm fine." Her voice sounded as scratchy as her throat felt.

Powell smiled. "Let's try that again, this time without the assumption that I'm making meaningless chitchat. How are you feeling?"

Megan's tense muscles relaxed a fraction. Powell looked genuinely concerned about her, much as he'd looked when he'd interviewed her after she found Gail Ludlum's body. But maybe he used that sympathetic demeanor to get criminals to underestimate him.

"I'm sore," she said. "And tired."

"Sore and tired, but extremely lucky." Powell gestured at the blond man standing behind him. "This is Detective Simmons."

Simmons nodded. He looked grouchy compared to Powell, and Megan wondered if she was about to experience the good-cop/bad-cop routine.

"How is Rachel Drake?" Megan asked.

"Rachel is doing very well," Powell said. "Bullet in the thigh, but it was a flesh wound, and the doctor said it will heal without difficulty. She's already gone home." Powell glanced at his watch. "Nineteen minutes left. We've got some questions for you, but if you find yourself too tired to answer them, we'll cut this off and pick it up again when you're stronger. Fair enough?"

Megan nodded hesitantly. She nearly told Powell she didn't want to say anything without a lawyer present, but changed her mind. She wasn't planning to conceal anything or guard her words. After she was arrested and a trial was looming, that was when legal counsel could help her.

But she had to know what they believed about her right now, or she'd go mad. "Kristen told you I was responsible for most of this, didn't she?"

"For most of what, Miss O'Connor?"

"For planning Rachel's kidnapping. For murdering Dr. Ludlum."

"Why would she tell us that?"

Megan's mouth was dry and her raw throat burned. "Because that's what she threatened to do when I finally realized what she was doing and tried to stop her." Megan reached awkwardly for the cup of ice water on her bedside table. Powell picked up the cup and pressed the button to raise the head of the bed so she could drink more easily.

"Thank you," she murmured, taking the cup.

"It may interest you to know that your great-aunt, Evelyn Seaver, kept extensive written records of the planning of Rachel Drake's kidnapping, including her reasons for targeting the Drakes and the way in which she recruited your sister and Alex Hurst. She also audio taped her discussions with Kristen and Hurst, including the discussions where they talked about recruiting you. We're still wading through the stack of records we found in her safe deposit box and in her closet, but there's plenty of interesting material there."

Megan was so astounded that for an instant she thought she was asleep and dreaming. Evelyn had kept records of all of it? And Kristen hadn't known? Would those tapes be admissible as evidence in court?

"What has Evelyn said to the police?" Megan asked.

"I'm afraid we never had the chance to talk to Mrs. Seaver directly," Powell said. "She's dead."

Megan gasped. "Did she—is this from—when I fought with her she hit her head—"

"This was unrelated to your struggle. It appears Mrs. Seaver took her own life."

Megan gripped the bed rail as if sturdy plastic could steady her against shock.

"I'm sorry," Powell said formally.

Megan stared at the IV tubing taped to her arm rather than meet Powell's gaze. She didn't know how she felt about Evelyn's death. "What about Alex Hurst?"

"Hurst is trying hard to save his own skin, so he's talking like crazy. His information contradicts much of what Kristen told us."

Megan looked at Powell. He adjusted his glasses on his nose and smiled slightly. "My point, Miss O'Connor, is don't put too much stock in your sister's threats. Answer my questions honestly and I have no doubt we'll be able to sort truth from lies."

* * *

". . . can't believe you left without a *word.* Just ran away, like some teenage delinquent. Do you have any idea how worried I was? I couldn't sleep. I couldn't eat. I lost three pounds—"

Sitting on the edge of her bed, Megan pressed her sock-covered toes against the hospital's tile floor and willed the painful tightness in her stomach to loosen. "Mom, I know it was wrong of me, and with all my heart, I'm sorry. But we did keep in touch via e-mail—"

"Fake e-mails that Kristen wrote for you."

"I'm sorry. I really didn't want you to worry about—"

Pamela waved the words away. She was wearing a bracelet that Megan hadn't seen before, thin gold links alternating with pink pearls. It matched the pink-and-gold flecks in her new wool jacket. "So you think lies should have comforted me? A job in Phoenix indeed!"

"I don't mean it was right of us to lie. We only meant to let you know I was fine, that I hadn't—"

"Been kidnapped? Like little rich girl Rachel Drake?" Pamela leaned forward in her chair and lowered her voice like she was confiding a secret. "I should have known Kristen would suck you into something terrible. I warned you about her so many times. I don't know what went wrong with her, but she's got a heart of ice. She never cared about me, or about you either. Do you believe me at last, now that she tried to *murder* you?"

Pain tore through Megan's side. She pressed her hand against the bandages beneath her robe. "I don't want to talk about this right now."

"Do you have any idea how bad this has been for me? My ulcer—"

"The doctor said you didn't have ulcers."

"How long do you think the police will want you to stay in town? Are they going to arrest you too? Both my daughters, jailbirds—"

"I'm not being arrested, at least not now. The police just asked that I—"

"So how long will we be here? We can't afford a long stay in a hotel."

"I'm not planning to stay in a hotel. I have—"

"You're not working now, I presume."

"Of course I'm not working," Megan said through gritted teeth. "I was too busy getting shot and stabbed to hold down a steady job."

Pamela's flawless face showed no reaction to this sarcasm. "How are you going to pay your hospital bills, now that you've realized the money from that nasty old creature Barbara—or whatever she called herself—was just a fantasy?"

Megan bristled at Pamela's rude dismissal of Evelyn. "She was a sick woman. And why didn't you ever tell me about Judith?"

"What was there to tell? That was a lifetime ago. I can't believe Barbara was stewing about it all these years. What an obsessive woman. If she'd just moved on, she could have lived a normal life."

Megan wondered how the relief and joy she'd felt when Pamela had walked into her hospital room could have turned so quickly to stress. "She needed help."

"When will you be discharged? Has your doctor told you?"

"Probably tomorrow."

"I'm going to speak to the police person in charge of this. If they aren't arresting you, they can't keep you here in Massachusetts. You need to come home."

"I don't want to push the issue. I don't mind staying in Britteridge for a while."

"Luke Wagner was asking about you. He's very concerned. He misses you."

"That's nice of Luke to worry about me. I'll send him a postcard."

"Megan! Now that you've told a pile of lies, too, darling, I'd think you wouldn't act so stubborn about Luke's mistakes."

Inside, Megan churned with guilt and humiliation, but she kept her voice steady. "I forgive Luke. I wish him the best. But I'm not going to get involved with him again."

"If you don't hurry, you'll lose your chance. I hear he's started seeing Melinda Ellsworth, but if he knew you were interested, he'd drop her in a heartbeat."

"*Mom.* I'm not interested. And I'm not coming home right away. I need some time to . . . to think about what I'm going to do. Where I want to go."

"Where you want to go!" Pamela's pearl earrings swung as she drew her head back in overdramatized astonishment. "How can there be any question? You can't tell me you haven't learned your lesson."

"What lesson is that?"

"You can't manage on your own yet. You leave home for a few weeks, and look what happens. You almost get yourself killed."

"That's an absurd thing to say. This situation was not typical of—"

"If you had any common sense, you'd never have gotten mixed up with Kristen and Barbara. You're too naive. Too trusting. You need to come home before you get in worse trouble. Who knows what con artist will rope you in next?"

With difficulty, Megan hid her anger. "I'm not a complete idiot."

"Besides, you can't afford an extended stay in a hotel. You can't possibly have that much in savings."

"I tried to tell you that I'm not staying in a hotel. A friend called and offered me a place. Her family owns and rents out several houses in the area, and one of the houses has a small, furnished basement apartment. The last tenant cut out on her lease when she got engaged to a guy back home, and the apartment is currently vacant. This friend's family offered to let me stay there as long as I want."

"A friend! You haven't been here long enough to make any trustworthy friends. Who is this girl?"

"Her name is Larissa Mullins. I met her at Rachel Drake's church. She called to see if I needed—"

"What makes you think she isn't trying to cheat you?"

"How can she be cheating me when she's offering me the apartment at less than half the usual rental rate—because I turned down her offer to let me stay there free? It sounds more like I'm cheating her."

"Don't think she's not getting something out of this. Her family is trying to cash in on your fame."

"Fame! Try *infamy*."

"You haven't seen the newspapers, have you?" Pamela beamed. "You're a celebrity. Rachel Drake had a heyday telling the *Boston Globe* how you single-handedly saved her life and stopped Kristen from taking her hostage, even while you were wounded and bleeding—"

"It wasn't that dramatic, for heaven's sake."

"You're headline news, darling. The reporters have a lot of questions for me. I was quoted in the paper this morning, and I have a television interview scheduled for this afternoon. As soon as you're released, the reporters will want to talk to you as well. You do have something nice to wear for interviews, don't you?"

"I'm not talking to the press."

"Why in the world not? Everyone's fascinated by our story. This could prove lucrative, Megan. Talk shows will pay top dollar to get us as guests."

Megan was starting to feel light-headed. She knew she ought to lie down, but her muscles felt locked by tension.

"And never mind that crummy basement apartment," Pamela said. "It sounds like a dive, darling, not a good place for me to take care of you. I'll find us a nice hotel. We'll only need it for a week or so until you're strong enough to travel home—"

Megan wadded the edge of the sheet in her fist. "I'm not coming home right away."

Pamela's lips tightened in irritation. "I want to take care of you, but you're making it difficult. I can't stay here forever, you know. I have responsibilities at home."

Megan drew her legs onto the bed and leaned against her pillow, feeling sick and exhausted. "I know. I'm grateful that you came to help me, and I certainly don't expect you to stay more than a few days."

"But you plan to stay indefinitely?"

"I'm not sure what—"

There was a knock at the door.

"Come in," Megan called with a hopeful glance at the closed door. "Mom, it's the nurse. I should be resting."

Pamela didn't take her eyes off Megan. "You'll leave me on my own while you lounge around Boston and 'think'? That's so selfish I can't believe you'd even consider it."

It wasn't the nurse. It was Trevor Drake. Startled and unsettled, Megan gave him a tentative smile and opened her mouth to greet him, but Pamela's words cut across hers.

"You're acting more like Kristen every day. Maybe you *are* more like her than I realized. After all, you are identical twins. You have the same genes."

Humiliation and fury struck so viciously that Megan had to ride out a wave of pain before she could respond. "I am *not like Kristen.*"

"You always wanted to be. You certainly idolized her. And at least she was quite practical, while you always had trouble with—"

"Mrs. O'Connor." Trevor's voice was a sub-bass rumble.

Pamela sprang to her feet and whirled to face him. "Who are *you*?"

"Trevor Drake. We've spoken before. It's a pleasure to meet you in person."

"Oh—yes, of course. Mr. Drake." Pamela was plainly flustered by the contrast between Trevor's courteous words and his grim tone.

"Your daughter has suffered serious physical and emotional trauma and is under strict doctor's orders to rest," Trevor said. "This would be a good time for you to go get some lunch so Megan can nap."

Pamela lifted her chin. "I've just driven for hours to get here. I'm not going to rush off when I've hardly spoken to my daughter."

Megan gathered her courage. "I *am* tired. I'll be better company later. There's a slip of paper there by the phone. I wrote the address to the apartment where I'll be staying. I'll give you Larissa's cell phone number so you can contact her about picking up the key."

Pamela didn't move. "I do *not* have time to be scrubbing out some grimy basement apartment to get it ready for you. I'm exhausted after the drive, and I have that interview this afternoon. I'll call a hotel for us—"

Trevor picked up the slip of paper and held it out to Pamela. "You'll find the apartment clean, fully furnished, and ready. A group of women were there this morning preparing it."

"Oh? What do *you* have to do with this, Mr. Drake?"

"Nothing. The Mullinses are friends of my family. They told us what was happening." Trevor was still holding out the address. "If you don't want to stay there with Megan, I'm sure we could find someone else to help her."

Pamela snatched the paper. "Don't be ridiculous. I came to take care of my daughter, not to throw her into the hands of strangers."

"It's good of you to come. I know Megan appreciates it. But she needs to rest now, and I'm sure you need some rest as well. You might want to head over to the apartment and grab a nap while you have the chance."

Pamela wavered. "Well—I do need to pick up a few things before my interview. But let me help you get comfortable before I go." She pulled the bedcovers up to Megan's shoulders. "Do you need anything, darling?"

"No, I'm fine. Thank you."

"I'll call you later."

Megan nodded, kissed Pamela on the cheek, and watched with profound relief as she walked out the door, her heels clicking elegantly on the tile.

Megan and Trevor looked at each other in silence.

"Sorry to be so pushy," Trevor said with a wry smile. "But you were in clear violation of doctor's orders."

"She's not usually this bad," Megan said. "She's under a lot of stress, and I'm not making it easier on her."

"*You're* not making it easier on her? What does she expect you to do for her right now?"

"She thought I'd come back to Pennsylvania as soon as I can, but . . . I'm just not sure. It's hard to even think right now, and the idea of going back and trying to pretend nothing ever happened . . . or worse yet, of going along with her schemes to cash in on this . . . She's already salivating over the prospect of talk show appearances." An all-too-familiar stinging in Megan's eyes presaged another bout of tears. She blinked hard. She didn't want to cry in front of Trevor—again.

"You look exhausted." His voice was gentle. "Would you like me to leave?"

"No." Megan managed a shaky smile. "I want you to barricade the door in case she comes back."

Trevor laughed softly. "Megan, look at it this way. In one night you took on and defeated three armed attackers. If you can handle that, I think you can handle telling your mother to take a hike. I know you love her, but loving her doesn't mean letting her run—or ruin—your life. I get the feeling she's good at making you feel you're responsible for her happiness. Am I right?"

Megan nodded—a mistake; the motion tipped the tears out of her eyes like she'd dumped a bucket.

"You know that isn't true, don't you?" Trevor said.

"Intellectually."

Trevor took the box of tissues from the table and set it on the bed next to Megan.

"Thank you." She took a tissue and wiped her eyes. "I'm sorry. I can't seem to make it ten minutes without bawling."

"Then you've got my mother beat. She gave me orders to apologize profusely for the fact that none of us have been here to see you. It took half the SWAT team to keep her away from you once you were out of surgery and out of danger. She wanted to come thank you. But Detective Powell—"

Megan cut the words off with a shake of her head. Shame already filled her heart with a weight as heavy and scorching as molten lead.

She didn't need Trevor to enumerate why Powell hadn't wanted to permit contact between her and the Drakes.

"I'm sorry," she said. The words were so inadequate that even speaking them made the shame hotter. "I can't even begin to tell you how sorry I am. I was such a fool."

Trevor sat in the chair Pamela had vacated. "You condemn yourself because you were slow to realize the sister you loved was using you and lying to you?"

"I should have known something was wrong. From the beginning, everything seemed a little off. But Kristen had an answer for every concern I raised, and no matter how absurd her explanations, I wanted to believe them. So I did. Or at least I told myself I did."

"Rachel didn't do any better at cutting through Kristen's lies, if you'll recall." Trevor pulled a new tissue from the box and handed it to Megan. "Rachel was dazzled by Kristen."

"Rachel just wanted a friend." Megan wadded the tissue into a ball as the tears dripped down her cheeks. "I fell for Kristen's lies because I wanted to believe she'd found a way to get money by manipulating it out of a dying great-aunt. No matter how you look at this, I'm a greedy and dishonest little creep."

"I imagine it was more than the money. You wanted to please Kristen."

Megan touched her bruised forearm where it had deflected the flat of the knife when Kristen attacked her. How much did Trevor know about her relationship with Kristen?

"You made some wrong decisions, and you did some things you regret," Trevor said. "That doesn't make you a creep."

"I played a key role in causing your family a lot of pain."

"You saved Rachel's life, putting your own life in danger. I can't even begin to say how grateful my family is to you." Trevor laid his hand on hers. "Megan, I know this won't help, but I'm so sorry about Kristen."

The tears increased their flow, but Megan didn't bother to wipe them away. It was like trying to blot up Niagara Falls. "I may end up in prison with her. I'm still waiting for them to charge me with fraud."

"I wouldn't want to be the prosecutor trying to make a case against you, seeing as how the woman you were supposedly defrauding arranged the whole charade and manipulated you into her home so she could murder you."

Megan closed her eyes, exhaustion blunting the jagged edges of emotion. Trevor sat in silence, holding her hand as the flow of tears gradually slowed.

"Thank you for coming," she murmured.

"You're very welcome. But I'd better leave now. You need to sleep."

"I'm fine," she said, not wanting to lose either the warmth of Trevor's hand or the comfort of his presence.

"Sure, you're fine. If you were any paler you could be Casper the Friendly Ghost, no costume required."

She smiled. "I think the bruises and black eyes would ruin the effect."

"Casper the Friendly Boxer."

Megan laughed, but stopped as pain flamed in her side. Trevor squeezed her hand and stood up. "We'll see you soon. My entire family would have stormed in here today, but we didn't want to overwhelm you. But be warned—they'll probably be camped out on your doorstep once you're discharged, armed with casseroles and chicken soup."

"Your family is incredible. I didn't think they'd ever be able to forgive me for . . . I don't deserve . . ."

"Hey, we don't do grudges, ma'am." Trevor tipped an imaginary hat, smiled at her and exited, leaving Megan in a glow of wonderment.

Chapter 30

Megan envisioned an extended and painful trial, with Kristen putting every speck of charisma and duplicity she possessed into the goal of raising reasonable doubt in the minds of a jury. But apparently even Kristen could not maintain her arrogance when confronted with the mountain of evidence against her.

She plea bargained. Massachusetts had no death penalty, but faced with the overwhelming probability that a trial would result in life in prison without parole, Kristen bargained for the only thing she could—life in prison with the possibility of parole. Apparently she was willing to surrender a losing fight if it meant the chance of seeing freedom again someday.

Snow fell in thick white flakes, blanketing the ground as Megan hurried away from the courthouse on the last Friday in January. She kept her head down as she brushed past the reporters who thrust microphones in her face and bombarded her with questions. She didn't want to talk to anyone right now.

Not once during the plea had Kristen looked at her. But Megan had watched Kristen, wondering if beneath her sister's smooth face she finally sensed some of the anguish her crimes had inflicted on others. The Drakes. Gail and Bryce Ludlum. Megan.

Megan doubted it. Kristen's pain would be only for herself.

Pamela hadn't attended the plea. A case of the flu had kept her unable to travel, to her dismay—she'd looked forward to more limelight and more media questions about her Cain and Abel daughters. She'd begged Megan to talk to the press in her place—hoping, Megan supposed, for some reflected glory—but Megan refused. With the support and guidance of a counselor, tactfully recommended and paid for by Sandra Drake, Megan was beginning to learn the art of tuning Pamela out. It was a difficult and often painful process, but to her amazement, Pamela was learning as well. After two months of her finest guilt-tripping in an effort to get Megan to move back to Morris Glen, Pamela could now make it through an entire conversation without any references to Megan's "abandoning" her.

Megan brushed the snow off the windshield of the old Dodge she'd bought from Howard Welby. The car was hideous, but thanks to Welby's mechanical skills and insistence on providing free oil changes and maintenance, it was a reliable ride. Welby had sold her the car for almost nothing when she'd let it slip that she was without transportation now that Pamela had claimed Kristen's car. Welby felt so guilty about letting Megan down when she'd asked him to call the police that he was always looking for ways to help her. Megan repeatedly tried to assure him that, in his position, she wouldn't have believed herself either, but Welby was never impressed by that argument.

She drove slowly back to Britteridge. The snowplows were out in force, and sand coated the roads. Traffic inched along, but she didn't mind. She wasn't in a hurry.

Once inside her basement apartment, she went to her dresser and took out the flannel bag containing the hinged picture frame Kristen had given her. She opened the frame and studied the two photographs.

Herself and her father. Herself and Kristen as children.

She set the frame on the dresser and waited for the pain inside her to turn to tears.

The tears didn't come.

Megan slipped the pictures out of the frame and dropped the frame into the trash. The picture of Kristen and herself she tucked in an envelope and slid to the back of her drawer. The picture of her father she laid on the dresser. Next time she was out shopping, she'd pick up a new frame for it.

Seated at the kitchen table, she surveyed the stack of books waiting there. After a moment of debate, she opened her anthology of American literature.

She was nearly finished with her homework when enthusiastic knocking shook the front door, startling her.

"Ho ho ho!" Rachel's cheerful voice came clearly through the thin wood. "Anybody here order a pizza?"

Smiling, Megan went to let Rachel in. "I thought your family was getting together tonight. Are you AWOL?"

"I won't tell if you won't. Actually, the party hasn't started yet. The snow delayed Evan's plane, so we're eating late." Rachel held up three ceramic mugs. "Are these as cute as the dickens or what?"

Megan blinked at the red-eyed snowmen painted on the mugs. "Uh . . . they're darling, Rach."

"Okay, you're right, they're goofy. But something about them just called to me."

"And said, 'I'm a freaky demon snowman—buy me'?"

Rachel laughed and set the mugs on the counter. She produced three packets of hot chocolate mix from her coat pocket. From the other pocket, she took three candy canes.

"Leftovers from Christmas." She set the candy canes next to the mugs and removed a half bag of marshmallows from her purse. "Look at you go, you dedicated girl." She nodded at Megan's open textbook. "You come home from today's stress-fest and *study?*"

Megan smiled sheepishly. "I don't want your Dad to think he made a bad investment."

"Oh Megan, he would have renamed the college after you if you'd have let him. Now shut the books, because it's time to relax. This is a hot chocolate night. Snow equals hot chocolate. That's a basic math fact."

"Your basic math could use some help." Megan indicated the three mugs. "Unless you brought your imaginary friend."

"Trev's here too. He got sidetracked helping your upstairs neighbor clear off her car. His Eagle Scout radar went off when we passed her. He'll be down in a minute." Rachel filled the first mug with water and stuck it in the microwave.

"The missionaries are struggling to keep up with you, you know." Rachel picked up the Book of Mormon Megan had left on the counter where she'd been reading it that morning. "Try not to learn *everything* quite so fast, huh?"

Megan laughed.

"How are you?" Rachel's voice went soft. "Really, how are you?"

Megan sighed and sat down at the table. She'd thought she didn't want to talk about it, but the concern in Rachel's voice made it a relief to open up.

"I'm amazed and relieved that both Kristen and Alex decided to plea bargain," Megan said. "Testifying at a trial would have been—well, it was hard enough just seeing Kristen again. I can't imagine what it would have been like to relive everything while getting grilled by her attorney." Megan fanned the pages of her textbook with a fingertip, wishing she could banish the memory of that rain-drenched dock and Kristen with a knife in her hand. She knew the memory would never leave. "How are *you* holding up?"

Rachel brushed melting snow off her brown curls. "I'm on a roller-coaster. All happy one minute and a bawling wreck the next. But it's been harder on my mom than on me. Besides having nightmares about losing *me*, she's hurting over Dr. Ludlum. Not so much that she betrayed us, but feeling terrible about what Dr. Ludlum suffered. And it's so crazy that it wasn't even Bryce who killed Mr. Seaver after all."

Megan shuddered. Evelyn's records had set that fact straight. She'd been watching for Bryce that night, having lured him to her house with tales of money under the mattress. She'd hidden in the garage while he fought with William. After Bryce fled, she'd killed her injured husband herself, eager to be rid of a man she despised.

It boggled Megan to realize how meticulously and patiently Evelyn had planned her revenge for Judith's death, moving to Britteridge and marrying William, researching the Drakes and the O'Connors, learning of the Ludlums' connection with the Drakes, hiring Bryce to re-landscape and care for her yard, setting him up for blackmail in order to give herself an inside source of information on the Drakes, recruiting Kristen, recruiting Megan. From the voluminous records she'd left behind, it was obvious she had reveled in every detail of her elaborate scheme and gloated in her ability to manipulate the participants.

She hadn't wanted revenge to be simple. She'd wanted revenge to consume her, burying her pain.

The microwave pinged. Rachel removed the mug, ripped open a packet of hot chocolate mix and dumped it in. "Marshmallows or no marshmallows?"

"Marshmallows."

"Candy cane or no candy cane?"

"Candy cane."

"Good choice." Rachel ripped the plastic off the candy cane and tucked it in Megan's mug with a flourish.

"Thank you for stopping by." Megan took the mug from Rachel. "That means a lot to me."

"Trev's idea. He sensed a damsel in distress."

"Eagle Scout radar again?"

"Some other kind of radar too, I think," Rachel said with a wink that made Megan blush. Rachel filled the second mug and put it in the microwave.

There was a rap at the door accompanied by the stomping sound of Trevor knocking snow off his shoes.

"Come in," Megan called.

Trevor swung the door open. "Hi, Megan. I hope you don't mind the intrusion."

"Not at all." Megan hoped the flush in her cheeks either wasn't obvious or could be attributed to the cold.

Rachel mixed the second mug of hot chocolate, added a sprinkling of marshmallows and a candy cane, and presented the mug to Trevor.

"Thanks." Trevor sat opposite Megan, his warm brown eyes searching her face. "Are you doing all right?"

Megan lifted the snowman mug and smiled. "I am now," she said.

About the Author

Stephanie Black now resides in northern California, but five years of New England autumns left her with a soft spot for Massachusetts. She blogs weekly at Six LDS Writers and a Frog (www.sixldswriters.net) and enjoys spending time with her husband, Brian, and their five children. She is the author of *The Believer*.

Stephanie enjoys hearing from readers. You can contact her via e-mail at info@covenant-lds.com, or by mail care of Covenant Communications, P.O. Box 416, American Fork, UT 84003-0416.